Satyriasis
LITEROTICA²

IAN PHILIPS

suspect thoughts press
www.suspectthoughtspress.com

Cover art by Stevee Postman
Author photo by Linda Catalano
Cover design by Shane Luitjens/Torquere Creative
Book design by Greg Wharton/Suspect Thoughts Press

First Edition: October 2003
ISBN 0-9710846-5-3

Library of Congress Cataloging-in-Publication Data

Philips, Ian.
  Satyriasis: literotica 2 / Ian Philips.
    p. cm.
  ISBN 0-9710846-5-3 (pbk.)
  1. Gay men—Fiction. 2. Erotic stories, American. I. Title.
PS3616.H457 S37 2003
813'.6—dc21

2003011654

Suspect Thoughts Press
2215-R Market Street, PMB #544
San Francisco, CA 94114-1612
www.suspectthoughtspress.com

Suspect Thoughts Press is a terrible infant hell-bent to publish challenging, provocative, stimulating, and dangerous books by contemporary authors and poets exploring social, political, queer, and sexual themes.

For Monkey
my hero and my heartthrob

Grateful acknowledgement is made to the following publications and online websites in which these stories originally appeared in slightly different form:

"Just Another Lesbian Potluck": *suspect thoughts: a journal of subversive writing (www.suspectthoughts.com)*, Issues 3-5, 2001-2002. "Love in the Time of Cold Cuts": *The Best of the Best Meat Erotica*, Greg Wharton, ed., Suspect Thoughts Press, 2002. "Nearer My Greg to Thee": *Sex Buddies: Erotic Stories about Sex without Strings*, Paul J. Willis, ed., Alyson Books, 2003. "Overexposed": *View to a Thrill: The World of the Voyeur and the Men Who Like to be Watched*, Paul J. Willis, ed., STARbooks, 2003. "Shameless Self-Promotion": *Velvet Mafia (www.velvetmafia.com)*, Issue 1, 2001. Reprinted in *Best Gay Erotica 2003*, Richard Labonté, ed., Cleis Press, 2002. "The Red Thread": *Kink: True Tales from the Sexual Adventurer*, Paul J. Willis and Ron Jackson, eds., STARbooks, 2003. "Through a Glory Hole Darkly": *Best Gay Erotica 2004*, Richard Labonté, ed., Cleis Press, 2003. "Stripping Towards Gomorrah": *The Gay Read (www.thegayread.com)*, July 2003.

Nothing good or bad gets done alone. We're too social a species for it to be otherwise. That said, this control queen seizes all credit for all evil deeds of grammar wrangling, willful misspelling, fact twisting, fictional character assassination, and every other act of slung mud that sullies the zing of these stories. Now as for the good, the phone book of helpful souls I singled out in *See Dick Deconstruct* still deserve a heaping helping of hosannas. But this time, I want to kiss the ring and/or hemline of a few fellow artists (of many a media) and journalists and reviewers and booksellers and editors and publishers for making the profession of writing so merry for yours truly at a time when we are supposed to be engaged in a low-budget remake of *Valley of the Social Darwinists*:

Charlie Anders, Joe Arcangelini, Bear, Dodie Bellamy, Adrienne Benedicks, Kevin Bentley, Paul Borja, Scott Brassart, Bill Brent, Susie Bright, Poppy Z. Brite, Rebecca Brown, Rachel Kramer Bussel, Fairy Butch, Patrick Califia, Drew Campbell, Anne

Campbell, Justin Chin, M. Christian, Randy Conner, Greg Constante, Suzanne Corson, Dana Cory, Dan Cullinane, Jameson Currier, William Dean, Kate Dominic, Mark Ewert, Jennifer Fink, Fish, Storm Florez, Michael Thomas Ford, Rink Foto, Emery Frank, Jamie Joy Gatto, Ted Gideonse, Jim Gladstone, Anthony Glassman, Daphne Gottlieb, Ron Hanby, Doug Harrison, Patsy Hatt, Trebor Healey, Greg Herren, Thea Hillman, Michael Huxley, Francisco Ibañez-Carrasco, Susannah Indigo, Maxim Jakubowski, Aaron Jason, Matt Kailey, Katastrophe, Kevin Killian, Krandall Kraus, Miriam Kronberg, Garland Richard Kyle, Richard Labonté, Chad Lange, Robert Lawrence, Anthony Ly, Jeff Mann, Paul Marquis, David May, Rebecca McBride, David McConnell, Sean Meriwether, Lisa Montanarelli, Marshall Moore, Patrick Morrison, Alvin Orloff, Miss Betty Pearl, Felice Picano, Linda Poelzl, Martin Pousson, Jim Provenzano, Andy Quan, Carol Queen, Andrew Ramer, Kirk Read, Rick Reed, Wendell Ricketts, Larry-bob Roberts, Thomas Roche, Roxxie Rosen, Dave Salcido, Steven Schwartz, D. Travers Scott, Lori Selke, Simon Sheppard, Jack Slomovits, Mel Smith, Michael V. Smith, Karl Soehnlein, Rob Stephenson, horehound stillpoint, Ron Suresha, Matt Bernstein Sycamore, Tristan Taormino, Robert Taylor, Michelle Tea, Katy Terrega, Tarin Towers, Sage Vivant, Jeff Walsh, Mark Weigle, Jennifer Williams, Rob Williams, Paul Willis, Karl Woelz, Ed Wolf, Mark Wunderlich, and Emanuel Xavier.

And many special thanks to the following psychic wet nurses: the Furies; Auntie Virginia and Old Horny; Chloe, who copyedited each page by grooming on it; my flaming (liberal) mom, Lynne, and my sisters, Gretchen and Heidi (for embracing my son/my brother the pornographer); Gil Kudrin, the hottest curmudgeon/activist around; Kirk Read, my bold, brazen, beautiful soul sister; the chain gang at Damron/Attagirl Press (current: Chane Binderup, Ed Gatta, Gina Gatta, Krandall Kraus, Louise Mock, Erika O'Connor, Kathy Pratt, Mikal Shively; liberated: Kiki Carr, Rebecca Davenport, David Howley); Stevee Postman (www.stevee.com) from his hot and holy artwork; Shane Luitjens (www.torquerecreative.com) for working once more his miracle of the killer cover; and finally, the two men without whom this book would not have happened: Patrick Califia, first among readers, writers, and friends; and Greg Wharton, the great love of my life.

The lust of the goat is the bounty of God.

— William Blake, "The Marriage of Heaven and Hell"

Table of Contents

Doing Pan Proud

Patrick Califia

"Satire is born of the instinct to protest; it is protest become art."
—Ian Jack

"In my first book, people got punished for being pretty. Now everybody suffers."
—Ian Philips

*W*e've barely had time to recover from the tornado *See Dick Deconstruct*, which picked up several sacred cows and nimbly drop-kicked them through the roof of the circus tent that houses postmodern (and not-so-modern) queer identity. A few naughty straight people also received a metaphysical drubbing in that righteous storm. Perhaps because the best defense is a good offense, Ian Philips' first book of literotica for the satirically bent was given a Lambda Literary Award for best erotica in 2001.

As we, the readers and survivors of that humorous holocaust wander through the woods, seeking shelter from the storm, wondering wherever we shall live and work and love now that the trailer park has been deconstructed, what to our wondering eyes should appear but a cascade of brand new stories: *Satyriasis*. Literotica squared! Perhaps we can put some wheels on this and drive it into town, looking for somebody else to tell how very much we hate Ian Philips because he wrote this book, and we did not.

Oops. I think your First Person Narrator has slipped into the Royal We in that last paragraph. And I can't really hate Ian, because I am much too busy laughing (or getting turned on, or both together). You might say this is standup comedy with a vengeance. Only this time, it's not Andrew Dice Clay on stage or somebody else who picks on mothers-in-law, menstruating women, fags, poor white trash, people of color, or any of the other obvious and all-too-usual

9

suspects. The author of *Satyriasis* has pointed the inky-black wand of Maleficent at the people who usually get away from being ridiculed in our society. Because if money buys anything other than a Presidential tax cut or a $1.3 million severance package, it buys insulation from scorn. The powerful expect to be greeted with open arms, legs, and mouths, and are perpetually attended by the sucking sound of fervent ass-kissery. If doves came down to carry their poop away, they wouldn't find many turds on the red carpet. You only wish the poor got to eat cake.

Philips doesn't have much patience with the queer people who emulate the upper echelons, either. Come to think of it, fools of all stripes are not suffered gladly within these pages, but are sent away with a coat of many-colored stripes of their own, funny hats pulled down over their eyes, the stick of jingle bells wedged sideways where even the tongue of every Cabinet member laid end-to-end could not fish it out. Toads will be kissed before toadies are embraced withal. There's no rule that says hetero people can't read this book, but if you get these jokes, you have to wonder how straight arrow you actually are-perhaps we'd better start calling you "gaily forward" instead.

Although the word "satire" is not derived from the satyrs of ancient Greek mythology, the tradition of politically inspired ridicule in Western letters dates back to playwrights of that era, who were expected to compose one "satyr play" for each trio of the grand and chilling tragedies they are more famous for today. Many of the satyr plays were destroyed for political reasons during the early centuries of the Christian era. Only one play survives complete, *The Cyclops* of Euripides, and about 400 lines of Sophocles' *The Ichneutai*. So we can only imagine how caustic the sixty-plus lost plays by Aeschylus, Sophocles, Euripides, Pratinus, Aeschylus, and other masters of the form may have been. We do know that they included a great deal of sexual horseplay at the expense of otherwise revered religious or historical figures. It's a tradition we should revive. Have you sat through too many episodes of *Hercules*, watching that muscular and banal closet case stringing along poor Aeolus? Don't you want to see him get buffeted and harassed by a horde of goat-footed men bearing huge, inflated leather phalluses?

Given the fact that human mores are usually at odds with our covert pleasure-seeking behavior, any malcontent who's lost patience with the status quo has a perfect target in Eros. (And if we turn that dimple-bummed brat's arrows back on himself, nobody deserves it more, after all he's put us through!) It's the disrespectful tone of Catullus, Ovid, and Juvenal that got them bowdlerized by Victorian translators, as much as their sexually frank, mordant comments.

You don't even have to be a rebel to aggravate the censors. Defoe's *Moll Flanders* is hardly an assault on Judeo-Christian values, but for its too-detailed perusal of the heroine's misdeeds, it became a scandal. De Sade fancied himself above the bourgeoisie's notions of morality, but when you read *Justine* back-to-back with *Juliette*, you get an all too rare glimpse of a potential sense of humor in this unbelievably tedious author, for it is the wicked sister who triumphs every time, while her virtuous dumbbell of a sibling never wises up enough to realize it is her purity which makes her a victim. So many French pornographers specialized in reviling the church by doing exposés of the bogus celibacy of the clergy during the late 1800s that it's a genre unto itself. The prostitute Fanny Hill winds up a respectable woman of means; the author of *My Secret Life* questions society's taboos against women's sexuality, homosexuality, and prostitution; and a host of other voices join them in trying to tell all of humanity's dirty secrets, and shine a light on what church and state would like to repress.

For every "Thou Shalt Not," there is a writer screaming, "But I did! I did! And I liked it. Loved it. Can't get enough of it. This is what it feels like and this is where I went and what I wore and these are the people who did it with me. Hoooooeeeeee!"

Patrick Califia

I don't know which real-life writer Robert Caliban was modeled after, but the fictitious narrator in "Shameless Self-Promotion" must be a descendent of one of those Irish bards whose ridicule in verse could turn a man's bones to water or cost a king his throne. Any top who has questioned his or her own motives for plundering an exquisitely self-absorbed bottom will enjoy this morbid romp through the remaindered aisle. Oh, wait-Robert Caliban's books will never be remaindered; he'll buy up any unsold stock and pile the neglected but beloved volumes up into a Tower of Babel upon which to perch his callipyges. The crack of that ass speaks in a hundred confusing but alluring voices to all of us who haplessly and witlessly love beautiful behinds.

"Overexposed" reads like an X-rated episode of the *Twilight Zone*, which I could never watch because (unlike this story) you always knew things would end badly. It celebrates the power of the Gaze. We are not only what we eat, we are what we behold; and the pictures that become our obsessions take on a life of their own.

But what happens to a face queen when the lights go out, and he cannot see the part of a man that is, for him, the key to his attraction? "Through a Glory Hole Darkly" may be one of the most poignant accounts of sex club cocksucking that I've ever read. There was a power failure at this grimy establishment, but the only sizzle that really counts is that which passes between these two men, divided by a wall. This story may also lead you to meditate upon what separates you from the people you desire. Even bare skin constitutes a barrier of sorts, an existential wall which desire pierces only briefly, just enough to allow us to savor intimacy with isolated bits and pieces of one another.

Perhaps my favorite story in this collection is the poignant and finely detailed "Shrimpboat Willie." This is Southern Gothic without the pretentiousness of Carson McCullers or the homophobia of William Faulkner. How can a man be the sum of his parts in a world where only one part really matters? If you read nothing else in this book, you should stay in one evening, paint your toenails, and read it while you're waiting for your pedal shellac to dry. Have toluene, will travel, y'all.

But man (or, in this case, woman) cannot live by seafood alone. Some of us can't live on any sort of fish, flesh, or poultry. That doesn't mean we are not ruled by our craving to consume. "Love in the Time of Cold Cuts" ponders the transubstantiation of vegetable matter into faux-pepperoni, just as a cunt can morph into a shark-toothed mouth, a girl who won't let herself have anything to eat has a bottomless appetite for adulation, and a public shaming can metamorphose into stardom. This story puts the wood back into Hollywood.

The lesbian-merged dentist boyfriends in "The Red Thread" probably have their practice set up in Beverly Hills. Where else could a set of pearly choppers become such a fetish? These are big mean men in uniform that I don't think Jack Fritscher would touch with a ten-foot pole. You won't see this story in *Annals of Orthodontry* or *International Leatherman* magazine. I didn't know whether to laugh until I had to spit up in the little swirly sink, or run screaming from the room with my bib still attached. Take a valium, make an appointment with this story-and don't bother to floss before you show up.

A kinder, gentler tone is set in "Stripping Towards Gomorrah," a fictitious memoir by Queen Anne, who escapes from the troubles of her old age by reminiscing about one of her courtiers and lovers. This man was once a boy beloved by her husband, King James, who has fathered many children upon the queen while still managing to pursue a host of well-spoken and beautiful youths. While it's set in an altogether different era, this story reminded me of the Bloomsbury Group, where marriages between gay or bisexual men and women intellectuals were by no means unhappy or unfruitful. The queen conjured up by Philips has the same eye for a handsome male figure that her husband does, and as he passes his lovers on to her, it becomes a loving and erotically charged bond between them. This is a wise woman who faces the incipient darkness with a candle that has burned at both ends.

In "Cyber Interruptus," I was astonished and pleased to learn that the lesbian yuppie, Heather, in my book *No Mercy*, has a fierce gay hustler brother! People who are glued every spare moment to their favorite nude-live-girl or camera-in-the-fraternity-shower website will probably not appreciate this story. (But do such people read anything other than pull-down menus and pop-up ads?) It's about many things-the stigma placed on sex workers, the erosion of privacy in a post-Internet world, indignation about bad bondage...take your pick. There's plenty of dudgeon to go around.

Unfortunately, the course of true love and good bondage is not necessarily going to run any smoother than a bad date with a poorly screened john. All the good men are taken already, so when illicit love comes calling, you have to lie if you want to get laid. "Nearer My Greg to Thee" is a trenchant piece about what happens when two hearts join together on top of the shards of promises broken to a love that's faded. It's an explication of sorrow and passion, the grief and joy that overtake two men who have to break faith in order to be true to themselves.

The two gay men who have the bravado to attend "Just Another Lesbian Potluck" would probably have been better off staying at home with their separate boyfriends, watching *Trading Spaces* and being in denial about suffering from bed death. In this epic roman à clef, a lesbian performance artist channels the Emperor Nero and arranges a tableau of depravity and destruction from her cracked green recliner. There's a cast of characters more colorful than the guest list for one of Caligula's week-long orgies-a gay FTM with a shady lesbian past, a genetic gay man with a big sausage that swings at the wrong angle, a misbehaving femme who doesn't deserve the sound thrashing that others long to give her, bi-curious straight men, musicians, dueling academics, innocent bystanders. And did I mention the peanut sauce?

Lest you think Philips is a snooty misogynist who can't

stomach dyke slam poets or feminist spoken word events, there's a tale that will earn him the title of a bear basher as well. "While Visions of Plumber's Crack Danced in Their Heads" is a cautionary tale that you might want to read before you plan your very fabulous Christmas Eve party. Well, as soon as you heard there was such a thing as A-Bears, didn't you think they were ripe for ribbing? I've always thought that gay male cruising was motivated at least as much by a need to crush the "undesirable" as it was by the whim to get off with the perfect stranger. The Red and Gray Eminences who snubbed this narrator ought to have remembered the precept, "It's not who you are, it's who you know."

Proponents of S/M often remind us that all the role-playing, dress-up, punishment, restraint, and drama is make-believe. The top assumes power temporarily, consensually, and abandons it when the scene is over. The bottom is the one who is really in control. But because bottoms outnumber tops, we have a specialized niche in the sex industry for beautiful and bent women who collect a fee for pretending to dominate men who often leave their dungeons to wield a depressing amount of wrong-headed power. It's axiomatic among professional dominatrixes that many of their clients are politicians, financiers, religious leaders, and captains of industry. It seems that the more influential a straight man becomes, the more he wants to compensate with an hour or two under a skilled female sadist's pointy high-heeled boots.

But what if one of these women decided to hold her clientele accountable for their sins in the real world? What if she just couldn't stand by and stomach their wickedness any longer, and was willing to pay the ultimate price for grabbing history by the balls? "What the Market Will Bear" is priceless.

If sex workers can talk back, is it possible that the inanimate objects we heedlessly flop upon will someday rebel? Do they, too, have opinions about the deeds they witness? "7 Just 7 True Tales of Lust on a Bed" takes Adam,

Eve, and Steve on some romps that even Pat Robertson hasn't dreamed up or railed against. You'll think twice before you leave a used condom in a rumpled motel bed after you've heard this bitter litany of tricks that were no treat at all.

I think Philips might have been able to get away with claiming that "Heterodoxy" was an unpublished manuscript discovered among the papers of Gertrude Stein. Like Quentin Crisp, Philips takes on the horny gay archetype of the Big Tough Straight Guy and finds it wanting in girth, breadth, and depth.

The book begins and ends where the introduction began and will, I promise, end: with the great god Pan, his attending satyrs, and this particular tribute to him, penned by a smart, articulate, and radical queen of bitchy smut and poetic erotic fiction. In "Satyriasis," Pan kicks up his heels (and wants to keep them in that position). He isn't dead, he's just run out of lube. Why do we always assume that the god of rural fecundity and rut is a glutton for running the fuck? When his divine paramours can't pencil him into their Dayrunners quickly enough, Pan sets out to find a mortal ram. Like most deities, he's a terrible liar, and causes all kinds of trouble when he takes the guise of his chosen one's unrequited love instead of showing up hooves and tail and all. (Hey, it's a time-honored tradition in the personal ads.) But Pan eventually finds someone who is amused and erect in the presence of his furry butt and goat tail. He still has enough energy left to surface briefly in "Just Another Lesbian Potluck," to whip an already out-of-control situation into a frenzy.

In this madcap, pansexual, and polymorphous perverse collection of short stories, everybody has to pay the piper. But if we've paid him, doesn't that mean we can all start to dance now? One of the things I love about Ian Philips as a writer and as a friend is his essential good-heartedness. He keeps faith with the hope that we can be better people and through this spiritual exercise create a better world. He firmly believes in our right to our pleasures, even when we are silly in their pursuit and enjoyment. In fact, as he points out with great glee, sex is inherently silly. But that doesn't mean it isn't also profoundly nourishing and diverting. When we laugh at our enemies because we see through their hatefulness, and when we laugh at ourselves because we can forgive our own shortcomings, we take a few lifetimes off of our karmic sentences upon the Wheel of Death and Rebirth.

Arcadia is a flourishing green realm where ordinary woes no longer exist, where we are free to love as we will because it harms no one. I believe it springs into being any place where we touch the earth with joy. Feet will do, but the Great Mother prefers to embrace and support us more completely, and she does not care if we lie down with man or maiden. Now that you have had your fill of contemplating folly, perhaps you'll be ready to commit some. Great Pan winks and leers, and invites you within. Go now, and see what he has made ready for you.

Patrick Califia (www.patrickcalifia.com) is the Not At All Benign Daemon of Quality Control in Pornography. He believes that when we write about sexuality, we are creating a priceless record of our deviant and devious lives, and throwing our weight against the tottering idol of heterosexist hegemony. Since there is no overtime pay in this business, it's good to have the occasional fan who will put out or spicier masturbation as a perk. Patrick has two books forthcoming, a short story collection (*Hard Men*) from Alyson Publications and a vampire novel (*Mortal Companion*) from Suspect Thoughts Press.

Satyriasis

for horehound stillpoint

Contrary to the 2,000-year-old rumor spread far and wide by a one Mr. Plutarch, Great Pan is far from dead. He is simply tired of topping the usual worshipers — be they female or male. Animal, vegetable, or mineral...

"Yea, verily, thus," Pan yawns as a grove of olive trees pushes and shoves its way up through the buckling dirt. A feat considering we are deep in what's left of the wet green forests that straddle the fictitious line called the California-Oregon border. It is his not-so-subtle hint to us to move this prologue to our story along.

We smile and pluck at our lyre as kindly as we can. Rather than risk divine ire, we will whisper this aside over our strummings: The last 40 years have been a near-timeless orgy of love-ins and Earth Days and Ren Faires and Wiccan circles and over-40 pervert play-parties and the occasional Mardi Gras and lesbian potluck. But nary a good ass-fucking of the god. Whereas once upon a time, his woolly fur flew, for many a year it's barely rustled. Until last May Day among the Faeries.

The faeries? you ask. Pixies and sprites? No, Radical Faeries, we reply. More Puck than Pixie. Late twentieth-century gender essentialists who believe that there is a royal way to the rutting you call gay and name it the third path and themselves the third gender. Usually found with dicks and in skirts. Often living in forests in huts and lean-tos and rambling ramshackle farms...

At this, Great Pan coughs and scratches his thigh. He flicks a flea our way. He is in love and we are jealous and we miss the comforts of our old haunts in Arcadia. It is too wet here. We have embellished when we should have abridged.

So we must confess that only some of the Faeries

believe what we have said they all did. Most notably their Queen Mother, Harry Hay. But she is now with that old goat Socrates and those boys he picks up at the gym in an eternal round of discourse and dinner and dessert in that upscale suburb in the afterlife we once called the Elysian Fields. The remaining earthbound Faeries actually try hard to live well with the land and often live well off the land. Not easy in your day and age, we might add. They don't live in huts or lean-tos or rambling ramshackle farms all year long. Well, not many of them.

It's a nice life, if you like eating beans of all manner and in all shapes cooked by a tousled-haired reed of a man high on hemp and wearing nothing but a pink apron with a sheer ruffled border and pumps.

A second flea. Yes, we are bitter. But wise. We will move on.

O Muse, tell us of the clash of arms and woolly thighs and dicks and mouths and holes more dark and deep that Cerberus' snarling maw, of the love between a God and his boy, a Ganymede even Almighty Zeus might strain to lift Olymposward...

A third flea. We will leave the epic poetry to the dead before we join their shadowy ranks.

It was the first day of the month of May, a day when Faeries and other earth spirits love to make merry. Usually around a big thick pole that they wrap tight with long strong ropy ribbons. Round and round the tight wood they twist till all fall down flushed and red in the head and fuck in the ripe furrows of the freshly and firmly plowed earth. Rich and moist dirt that clumps in hot soft balls of...

Wait...

You, over there. Behind the ferns. Yes, you. The one in the T-shirt that says "I'm Cuckoo for Metafiction's Cocoa-Puffs." Why aren't you sitting with the rest of the listeners? You're distracting us from our rhapsody. What? You're Arthur. Greetings, Arthur. What? The Arthur? What an odd accent you people of Oregon have. It sounds like you said "Ahthor." We believe we've met that god once before.

Very nice. Egyptian fellow. But you look nothing like him. Especially when you're making that rude gesture with your finger. Really now. Come on, Arthur of Oregon, come over and sit with the others.

Ow! That was no flea. That was a rock, you pale imitation of a Theban cur. Fine, fine, fine! We shall give you our back. Next time it's the evil eye. Everyone else, unevil eyes on the lyre.

Except you. Yes, you dear. Hand us that wineskin. Rage has left us parched.

Thank you.

Yes, fine. A fine day it was a year ago. The first of May. May Day. And Pan was in a foul mood like we are now. He hadn't been hit by a rock thrown by an uppity troglodyte in a too-tight T-shirt. No, he was just tired of topping. And he wanted to get fucked.

Great Pan had looked high among the immortals to no avail, not even the teensiest bit of cosmic tail. Dionysos' Bacchantes are very possessive of the god's divine wand. Thor only does hard-core S/M scenes and it has to include his hammer. Loki is a voyeur and spends all his time at the end of the world watching the serpent suck its own tail. Jehovah is a chronic masturbator since he loves no other gods but he. Zeus is once again hobnobbing, literally, among the mortals as a producer of boy-bands. Ganymedes galore to hold his cup and ride his lightning-fast love bolt. And Coyote and Pan are still not speaking from the last time. Coyote had promised to do him and good and ended up detaching his dick — as usual to get a bit of sleep — and wandered off when he awoke, leaving it to fuck the Great God Pan for a solid year straight. He still walks bowlegged from that.

Did you feel that? We think that was a flea. You didn't see Arthur throw a pebble? No? Okay. Onward and upward with the prologue.

And, of course, Ganesha is the greatest lay above or below, but he is so swamped with the prayers of a very troubled and good-luck-hungry planet, especially the plaintive late-night solicitations of lonely writers, that he and Pan now have to book even a fuck-buddy romp a decade in advance.

That date has been set. See, we've carved it here on the back of our lyre. But that still left Pan unfucked.

It was time for the great god to look low among the mortals. And May Day is also known as Beltane. There is no better day in all the High Heathen Holy Days for getting your divine freak on. So he came to the Faeries in the hopes that one of these wild things would want to shag a furry ass. After all, he'd heard that Hermes had been bragging all over Olympos about finding a flock that loved to worship the Horned God, even his hole, some especially the hole. It was like these mortals took for truth every rite in that comic book of horrors, the *Malleus Maleficarum*, said Hermes. Day after day of daisy chains. Night after night of beauties bowing to kiss his asshole. Neo-pagans, they were called. Not all alike. Not able to get along for long. But almost as wild a roll in the hay as the priests of Christianity's middle age and the inquisitors of the Counter Reformation. And the Faeries were the funkiest of all.

Of which we now know he meant hygiene.

Yes, that was indeed a flea. Two, to be exact. Our prologue is done.

Now to tell of the night Max Feybear fucked a god.

When all is said and done — and we'll pluck away to get us there — Max is a nice boy, a good boy. Saul Pinkus is the name on his birth certificate. And he kept it all the years he lived in his parents' properly progressive, intellectually observant Jewish home on the Upper West Side of Manhattan. And for four years of college. And then another year and a half. Until he had a dream in graduate school.

He was attending NYU, if you really must know. It was an amazing dream. A dream in which a god Max hadn't believed in since babyhood told him personally to go west, young man. Leave sociology, the Academy, New York behind and wander among the wild and wily goyim of the West. And perhaps it was the fact that the Lord God

Himself told him. Or the endorphins released by the ropes and cuffs and the hood. He was on a date when the dream came. Dreams don't give a flying succulent fig about when and where they happen. We blame the god of dreams for that. Morpheus has always thought he is as clever a prankster as Hermes. And as cute. But hanging back in the shadows for eternity hasn't done wonders for his love life. So now he really lets mortals and immortals alike have it with the dreams.

But that's not the point. Oh, how we stray in a language whose poetry is obsessed with free verse.

The point is, whether from the stature of the deity or the strength of the chemicals, Saul heeded the dream and came West. Max Feybear was born. And here, in the forests of western Oregon, Max ended up and here Pan ended up, too and in time, with a little help from the great god, Max finally ended up in Pan.

Pretty sketchy, we confess. We've asked Max more about his past, his dream, his years lost wandering in this wilderness. All he says is for us to wait. Someone else is writing his tale. Philip somebody. No, that's not right. Phillip? Philip? Fillip? Phillips. That's it. Ian Phillips. Whoever he may be.

What? We can't hear you, Arthur, because we have our back turned.

Can any of you, kind listeners, tell us what Arthur's shouting?

Oh, Ian Phillips with one "l." Isn't Arthur the eavesdropping know-it-all?!

Ow!!!

Stop that, you faux-Corinthian pillow-biter. Here, take this rock and throw it back at him. We've a story to sing. But wait. Once more, rage leaves us as dry as the nether lips of an old whore. The wineskin.

Thank you.

Of where and why Max Feybear came, we know not much. Enough for a simple quatrain at best. Or a doozy of a couplet. But this we can tell: how he looked and how Pan came to him that May Eve.

The night before May Day.

April 30.

Walpurgisnacht, for any homesick German witches who've joined us here in the wet wilds of western Oregon.

Once again, the wineskin.

Thank you.

Of charms and a Max, I now sing.

Both sets of his grandparents worried, when they saw the blue eyes, blond hair, and the thin nose, in that very order, appear on their baby boy, that a Cossack had gotten in their bloodline during one of the pogroms their own grandparents had fled. And wherever these features came from, they grew all the more pronounced as Max grew into them. All five and a half feet and two hundred and some pounds of him.

Today, the clear paleness of his skin makes the once-cornflower blue in his eyes look like the glowing otherworldly color that follows in the sky after sunset and the thick wave of his dirty blond beard that washes down to his broad chest draws the eye to his slender nose, the only hairless outcropping on his face before the eye continues up and across his bald forehead and lands in more hair, shorter than the beard but even more tousled. And this disarray isn't the result of overuse of hairstyling products. He isn't that kind of faygeleh, as he likes to call his kindred. Nor is it from neglect. He isn't that kind of faygeleh, either. It's simply that, like Max himself, his hair is prolific and very willful.

In fact, it grows thickly about his face and dick and nowhere else. Just little tiny hairs along his solid arms and sturdy legs and a few around his stand-at-attention nipples and his sinkhole of a belly button. But his wide back and his ample butt and almost all of his impressive gut are bare. When we first saw him naked, we could tell by the angle of Pan's dick, for that was all that hadn't shifted its shape, that the god was pleased with his fey bear. But to us, Max looked like a lion shorn like a poodle. Or as Max likes to scold himself, and he rarely talks to himself in any other way, he looks like some creature out of Dr. Seuss with a thyroid problem.

How do we know all that? you ask. Well, it's not like Max doesn't love to talk about himself and his woes. Of course, we can relate. Each of you knows how much we hate this forest. But that's not how we know what Max thinks. Not at all. Like Pan or any other immortal worth the ichor in their veins, we can read the minds of mortals. Trust us, it's usually less interesting than it sounds. Especially after the fourth or fifth millennia.

But mind read, we can. And mind read, Pan did that May Eve when he spied Max, a few long, warm hours before sunset, wandering through the woods.

In less than a second, the Great God Pan sized him up and discovered within the young man a top that few boys were wise enough to bend over for because they saw only a beard or a belly attached to a pair of full but bitter lips. But Pan read on. He also learned of Max's dream, his odyssey, and his mad love for a Faerie named Titania, who unlike Circe, the sorceress queen in Odysseus' own wandering tale, didn't bother to turn Max into a pig. Titania thought Max a pig on first sight. Still, no one else but this boy would do for Max. Who amongst us has not had a doomed obsession or two? Eh? Let them cast the first stone. No one. Not even you, Arthur? Good. And so Pan took that very shape to get the very fucking he'd been so tirelessly seeking.

But why? you ask. Why does Pan need to shapeshift when Hermes gets fucked right and left and up and down and sideways and slantways by tricking everyone into thinking he's Pan?

"Yea, verily, what a fuss," says Pan. "Because I can, kids! I am a god. Zeus gets to do golden showers with Danaë. Or that fly-by snatching of Ganymede. While Poseidon lets Demeter know he's hung like a horse. And no seahorse, mind you. So why not a bit of trickery for little ol' great me to get a good fuck."

Why, yes indeed, o Pan! Nothing like the love-starved man eating out his forbidden fruit. And devour you he did! Hades himself couldn't have licked you cleaner to the bone.

Lean in to hear us. Closer. Actually, Pan never shapeshifts when he tops mortals. He's tried but he's usually rebuffed. The worshipers want the whole horned-god experience. But bottoming, well, that's never been done with a mortal before. Never done well, that is. He's become very sensitive about the tail as a result. Everybody's eager to put the pipes of Pan to their lips, but most mortals, save a sanctimonious US senator or two when they're imagining the happier sex lives of others, find the tail a cunt-drying dick-shriveling turnoff.

So it was to be with Max.

But the first night, Pan searched out the mind of Max's beloved, read it, and became him down to the small mole on his right inner thigh.

There Pan stood in the clearing, posing himself with the perfectionist care of a cinematographer, forcing the slanting late-afternoon sun to light the exact portion of his naked body when he willed it. He toweled his dry body to draw Max's gaze his way. Nothing. He kept changing the color of the towel to catch his eye. He felt a flicker when he made the towel of golden silk. Then he waited. He wanted Max to think he'd come upon Titania after skinny-dipping in the trickle that the Faeries call a stream.

Max stopped on the path to the itsy-bitsy brook. A flash caught his eye. Like sunlight on water but hovering midair.

He stared into the open heart of the grove. Again a flash of light. Pan had thrown down the towel. This time it was the sun reflecting off Titania's eyes. For Pan knew that Titania's eyes are the first thing to catch your attention about the boy. They glint, no matter the time of day, like small, overly polished stones. Common riverbed stones that appear to be precious because of their flashy sheen. It is the only subtle clue of his talent with artifice. For Titania has willed himself to become a diva in the world of opera.

A gay diva. No, wait. We've told the obvious when we meant to tell the truth. An openly gay diva. In fact, the world's greatest countertenor, despite the hindrances that he cannot read music and is lost in the wilds of Oregon. Whether he will or won't, I leave for others to tell. Perhaps this Ian Phillips with one "l" fellow.

You think he will, Arthur?

Good.

Better him than me.

The second thing about Titania to catch your eye is what you most remember about him when you come to dislike him, as many have and will: his regality. Though he is small and lithe, he has the commanding bearing of a prince. Like in a 1930s film. Like Errol Flynn. Or Douglas Fairbanks. Senior or Junior. A beautiful and proud face. Aristocratic. And when he's had a few lines of coke, the jutting jaw and thin lips, made all the more pouty by the tirelessly clipped beard, and the haughtier and haughtier heights of his arching eyebrows take on a queenly tone. He is Titania, after all. Like the true Queen of the Faeries, the un-Radical and immortal ones, that is. Our cousin, Puck, serves at her and King Oberon's court. She let me drink wine from her cupped hands. An exquisite beauty, indeed.

Max's Titania, too. On the beauty part. Yes, I grant you it's a self-conscious choice of name. Behind his back, Titania's name is simply, Her Majesty The Baby. For he is twenty, if a day. But still it shows his wise estimation of his assets and his ambitions among the Faerie folk. And he does have one particular asset that all who enjoy such pleasures would be happy to have spread across their faces or wrapped around their dicks.

This is the third thing about Titania that those who love to look at him never forget. Max had seen it dipped into and arising from countless hot tubs and beds. He dreamed of caressing and kissing and then entering it night after night. Now, lo and behold, it was rising to greet him on the path, for Titania had bent over to arrange his towel.

Max stopped, gulping for air like he'd been punched in the gut. And, well, to be honest, on a cosmic level he had. He was so befuddled by the beautiful bottom before him he didn't know which burned more from his blushing, his forehead or his foreskin.

Titania did not turn. He hadn't noticed Max's approach. Max didn't know whether to turn and come back or stay and cough. What would be polite? What would prolong the view? Then the testosterone boiling in his balls goaded him to speak.

"Any more hair in there and you could grow a tail."

Max watched the skin on Titania's back gather as he cringed.

"I think it's sexy," Max stammered as Titania turned toward him. "Honest. Very animal."

"And what of this beast?" Pan said, mimicking perfectly the imperious tone Titania always took with Max, as he stroked his long, red, upturned dick.

"It can bite me any day."

"Always the droll one, eh, Maxie?"

Max grimaced. He hated that name. Mostly because Titania always followed it with "Pud" and then a pause and "Not!"

But Titania surprised him. "Perhaps you should suck out its venom, Max."

Max, now firmly convinced he was dreaming and in a race to touch Titania before he woke, ran up to the naked boy and dropped to his knees, gripped the stiff dick, and rammed it in his mouth. He closed his eyes and sucked, moaning so enthusiastically that he drowned out the loud daytime drone of bees and wasps and flies and grasshoppers and beetles and even cicadas.

"Max," Titania said quietly, taken aback by the ferociousness of his desperation. "Max. Max!"

The moaning and then Max stopped.

"Arise, Max, and strip before me. All who worship me must be naked."

Max was truly startled. He hadn't awoken and now

Titania, the very Titania who'd always ridiculed Max's dick size to punish him for his all too obvious desire of the Faerie Queen, wanted to see him naked. Wanted to watch him undress.

He stood very slowly and looked into Titania's eyes. He'd never looked at them, at him, this close and for this long. They were a brilliant hazel. Like small, polished pieces of the stone called tiger's-eye. The very eyes of the Great God Pan himself. For earlier we said only Pan's dick retained its true shape. Wrong. All wrong. We blame the wine. And our desire to forget this place and our lingering year in it. His eyes, too, remained Pan's own. And Max looked into them as deeply as he could. There was no mockery in them. Titania was even smiling at him. He nodded his head as an encouragement for Max to get on with the show. So Max stripped down until he was naked, too.

And since we've already described how he looked once before we won't do it again. But we will repeat that great Pan was pleased with what he saw.

For the dick pointing right at him was as solid and as earnest as the man who bore it. And it would fit quite nicely in this little rounded ass he'd fashioned. It was perfect.

In fact, Pan said in Titania's voice just that. "Perfect." In the hopes the man, who had always judged his dick either in the eyes of others or from on high as he perched over his gut to determine its measure and thus his own, would hear the genuine praise of a god and realize the god meant him, all of him.

But Max was too amazed and aroused to be standing dick-to-dick with Titania. He heard nothing but his own blood wildly pulsing. Until Titania stepped even closer to him and took hold of his dick. Max nearly came but fought off the orgasm by straining to hear each syllable Titania spoke.

"Rather than you suck me, I'd like you to fuck me. Are you up for it, my good stud?"

Max whispered his answer: "If I let my dick have any

more blood, my brain will die."

"We can't have that, can we? You are a man with many impressively large organs, Max Feybear. I want to make the most of them all."

Out of the glittering sunlit air appeared a condom and several packets of lube. Titania snatched them before Max fully understood what just happened. He handed them to Max before turning himself and dropping onto the outstretched towel. He leaned forward onto his elbows and turned his head and gave a lecherous smile Great Pan perfected millennia ago.

Once more, Max quickly fell to knees and dropped his head till he was a breath away from the crack between Titania's asscheeks. To the god who had started him on the travels that led him to this very moment, he offered up a silent prayer. Then he inhaled. He smelled all that was ripe and delicious about the earth. The loam carved by the stream. Clumps of black dirt, pushed up by seedlings beneath old trees. Roasted nuts and still-warm fresh-baked bread.

Max sat back and smiled. He didn't know what else to do. Then he tore open the condom and struggled to find which way to roll it down so the lubed side was facing out. Next he attempted to unfurl it over his swelling head. It was a snug fit and his fingers trembled but he did it. Now to twist and twist the tops of the lube off. And finally to lube his dick and Titania's hole. Where the other two lube packets came from, he didn't know but he was grateful for them.

He slid his cockhead inside Titania with a shout. And was nearly whooping by the time he'd pushed himself as far as his dick could go.

Then he fucked him and he fucked him and he fucked him.

Three separate times: three minutes the first time, thirty minutes the second, and three hours the last. Max's well-milked dick shot invisible sperm that third time, but he huffed and puffed to keep pumping into the sweating and growling and laughing Titania, who sat atop him now just as he himself lay atop the softest bed of moss. And with his last grunt of lust, Max passed out from elation as much as exhaustion, long before he could see Pan retake his form or tuck Max into his bed on the bottom bunk in the far bedroom of a rambling ramshackle farmhouse.

Poor Max. He didn't know he'd been paid the highest compliment by being played by a god. And so he was left stunned — as too many of us have been when shunned on the street or in the thicket by a sheet-burningly good one-night stand — after he came up behind Titania, also on his way to a lunch of lentils and more lentils, and goosed him and said sweetly into his ear, "Hey, Fuzzy Butt," only to have Titania turn and say before he slapped Max hard and stormed away: "Listen you bear of a *berdache*, I don't care if you were We'wha herself, or in your case, Wee-Wee. It shan't come to pass. Not now. Not never. So, kind sir, please fuck off and die!"

Everyone, with feeling: Poor Max!

Yea, verily, thus it was no great surprise, to us at least, that Max paid no attention whatsoever when later the divine manifested in front of his own very downcast eyes.

"Greetings, lover," Pan shouted as he leapt from behind a tree and before Max.

Max was unfazed. All he could think of was Titania's withering exit hours before. "Oh, nice costume. The talent show's over in the barn," he said glumly.

"Costume?" Pan laughed.

"Oh. I'm sorry." Max actually looked Pan over from hoof to horn. "Are you one of the witches from San Francisco?"

"I love San Francisco. But I'm not from there. I love witches, too. But I'm no witch. What about you? Are you a good witch or a bad witch?"

"I'm bad to the broom," Max said with a dramatic pout.

Pan laughed even louder, finally startling Max with his snorts and whinnies.

"Yes, you are," said the stranger and stranger creature.

"And you certainly know how to make the most of that broom handle of yours." He placed his hand, surprisingly muscular for the long fingers, over Max's crotch. "Can I have another ride?"

Max gasped at this latest display of West Coast forwardness. "Another? I don't remember the first."

"Allow me to reintroduce myself." Pan shifted into the shape of the beloved Titania, naked and hard and then with a quick turn, bent over and, grabbing his asscheeks, showed Max his hairy hole, and then, staying in the same position, returned to his true godlike form. "I am the Great God Pan."

"Oh fuck," Max shrieked. "No way. No, no way. This only happens in Latin American literature."

Pan now laughed so loud the forest rang with the shrill wail of pipes and the staccato bleats of a flock of singing goats.

Before Max could flee in a panic, the god grabbed him and pulled him, struggling all the way, into a deep kiss. He let go of the mortal only when the calm of exhaustion had overtaken every cell Max's brain still had any remaining communication with and possible command over.

What Max could not or would not remember of their happy rutting, Pan told him between tight hugs and long kisses. And then Great Pan asked him for another go and Max was forced to take a backward glance at the sex life he'd known before now.

If he subtracted all the millions of times he'd jerked himself off, the dried cum of his lovers and tricks would have made a minuscule pillar of salt. Some sinner he was. He looked at it and compared it to others' burning plains of Sodom and Gomorrah. The disparity froze him. Now a god wanted him for a fuck buddy. And to take him to Greece. Of course, with my luck, thought Max, it would be Pan and not Apollo. But he was a god and he wanted him. Who else did? Certainly not Titania.

"Okay," Max said, punctuating his assent with the

stagy huff of resignation. "But on one condition. You give me a year and a day to make up my mind about going with you to Greece. We can meet here every Saturday night until then and I'll fuck your divine brains out."

The forest roared with delight.

Why did Pan agree to such a bargain? you ask. Simple. Max is a great fuck. You do the math. Take every lousy human lay you've ever had and divide that whopper by the fucks that still make your pubic hair quiver. The remainder, in Pan's case, equals Max.

And so for the next six days, Pan roamed the world fucking his worshipers with renewed vigor. The curls along his inner thighs singed. And on the seventh day, he returned to turn the other cheek.

Yes, my dears, we pagans have a few golden rules of our own.

And each week Titania ignored Max. Fucked with every Faerie save Max. And come Saturday night, Max would faithfully slump off into the woods to have his blue balls painted red. The red of cum bombs bursting in woolly hair. But the first condition had given way to a second. They always do. From their first Saturday night together as Pan and man, Max always made the same demand of the god: he may take his true form, except the ass and tail. Especially the tail. His divine hind quarters must always look exactly, down to its very down, like the smooth, small, round and bouncy butt of the sluttiest countertenor in all Faeriedom. That, and no kissing.

No way! you cry foul. What? You thought just because a fat boy knows the searing bite of ridicule's arrows he would see beyond the goatish ass and tail to the welcoming hole of the god within. That a boy who's spent every day looking at his own flesh, willing some to slough off in his sleep, would somehow be unable to count every hair on the ass of another.

And what's more, you thought just because Pan is a god he can't have poor taste?

Zeus the Goose! (Forgive us, Lord of Olympos, it

rhymes better than swan in this barbarian tongue.) What do you people remember of your ancestors' tales?

Hand me that wineskin.

Thank you.

And so we wait now for the high noon of May Day and its mayhem. A year and a day has passed. How you ask is that possible? The earth travels round the sun and this year leapt along for an extra day. Ah ha! you say. Easy for you to exclaim. You listeners experience our interminable year but in a second. We had to sit here each Saturday night while Great Pan returned to this dank — delightful — place to woo a boy with hidden charms. And each Saturday night as we played our gayest tunes for ass-plowing, we prayed that this dithering queen would make the right choice and fall for the right man — or God in our woebegone case — and we could hightail it home.

Home again, home again to Arcady. Hey diddle diddle hee hee hee.

That's ancient Greek for Will he or won't he?

A flea. We shall quit while we still have a head.

Hush. High noon and a mortal approach. Will it be a wavering boy or a resolute man?

Oh my. All bets are off. It's someone we've never seen. Oh my oh my. Our skills are at hymning, not reporting. We can't do hexameter on the spot like this. You there. Arthur. Yes, you. The one in the T-shirt that says "Third Person Omniscient." We see you behind that pine. What's that? Ahthor? Yes, Arthur. We've sung that part already. What, you are a writer? Then where's your stylus and tablet? Under your arm? Won't that melt the clay? A lap top? What nursery rhyme babble is that? Oh, yes, yes, the virtual tablet. Very well, Ahthor. Can you help us out with the reportage? We'll throw in some epic flourishes afterwards.

It would be an honor, Mr. Tumnus.

Listen hear, mortal, he was a faun. Strict teetotalers, the whole prissy lot of them. We're a satyr. Horny and hard-drinking all the way. Silenus, if you must know a name.

An honor, Mr. Silenus. Hey, aren't you the drinking buddy of Dionysos?

That was thousands of years ago. We split up after he decided only he could enjoy the worship of his groupies.

Ah, I see.

Really? How? Were you hiding under a Maenad then?

No, I was just sympathizing.

Well, stop it and get on with the story. That listener over there has stopped touching themself. We shall go and help them. But first, hand us the wineskin.

Thank you. I'll keep this.

All right then, my dear Silenus, let me introduce you and the boys and girls and girlie boys and boyie girls and either/ors and neither/nors to the boy who is approaching. He is the Faerie known as Nux Vomica.

What a name. The Faeries have some of the best.

His means the seed of the strychnine tree. In a pinch, a very small one, it helps digestion.

But this Nux is already very easy to swallow.

And that's not why he chose this name, either.

Nux is a bit of a punk. Or so he'd like to think. And he has to wear his wildness in his name because all who see him see only a gentle-looking beauty. With green doe-eyes, if does had green eyes. But not like a cartoon animal. A real deer. They are large and liquid. A small nose, too. You're not aware of it until it ends. Not with a cutesy-pie upturn. It just ends. And it's small for his wide face. Wide, not round. His chin and jaw are not part of a perfect circle. And there, above the point where chin and jaws collide, are lips you want to kiss as much as fall asleep on. And every one of these features under a crazy mop of dreadlocks, each tip dyed blond, that he keeps under a tan kerchief an old Russian grandmother might wear, leaving his hair to fan out behind him like a mane.

With each step closer, you realize he is tall, with a slender build and large hands that make him seem less slender. You reappraise him and see the sinew in the long

Ian Philips

curves of his chest and arms and legs. He wears a brown
camouflage tank top that makes it almost down to his olive
drawstring pants. When he stands on one hip you can see
the jutting cut of muscles beneath the clear skin there. His
obliques. From each side, they draw your eye toward his
nature trail and beneath the pants, where your gaze waits
for any hint of his dick and balls to surface in the material
as he walks. As he does, you are teased, but not rewarded.
And then, at the end of his pants, you see his long feet in
Birkenstocks.

As I said, he thinks he's a punk. The only punk ever to
wear Birkenstocks until Johnny Rotten lands in a retirement
home.

The Great God Pan sees him, too. He pauses from
polishing his Syrinx with the long hair of one of his fairest
attendants.

"Son, I'd change Syrinx to pipes. People will think I'm
wiping down a hypodermic or a car or some odd piece out
of a computer."

Good idea, my Lord Pan.

The Great God Pan sees him, too. He pauses from
polishing his pipes with the long hair of one of his fairest
attendants. He lets go of the hair and then the tight bundle
of reeds and stands up from his moss-covered throne of
stones. With the maddening farsight of god, he knows that
Max will never come now. Poor Max has chosen to chase a
shadow. Pan hopes that the boy will come to a better end
than sweet Orpheus. The god blinks back a tear. He is
surprised, even slightly embarrassed, that after so many
loves and so many years this loss is able to sting his heart.
He gives a snort. Shakes his head and blinks again. The
tears are clouding his view of the beautiful boy.

The tears are clouding his view of the beautiful boy.

The tears...

Lord Pan, forgive me but the Muse tells me that this is
your cue from the Kosmos to go and enchant Nux. On
today's walk, he's managed to remember his lighter, but
he's forgotten the joint and will be wandering back to Cocks

36

Crow Farm soon. That and Lord Ganesha says if you two hook up to bring him along on your date next month. He's been able to push it up nine years.

"Thank you, Arthur," Pan says with a little tug to the narrator's beard as he walks past him toward Nux, who is standing still in the middle of the path, staring with great intensity at the forest's canopy.

Pan circles the boy. The boy never flinches, never notices. Pan walks around him a third time, slowly assessing and then esteeming, his dick curving like his lips as he leers. Great Pan is very pleased with his prey, caught it would seem in a hemp net of his own smoking. Pan stops before the boy, still straining to look up at the tops of the trees, balancing on his unsteady toes much like his admirer's dick, twitching as it wobbles from one fat ball to the other. The horny god reaches behind Nux's head and pulls the kerchief over his face and away, letting the dreads fall wherever gravity tugs them. He runs his long fingers through them and speaks in a hoarse coo so the boy will feel his breath before he hears the words:

"I see you are part wild beast as well."

Nux falls back to earth. He looks Pan squarely in the eyes. Two eyes just like his. But different. No goatlike slits. It's their colors. Each similar but different from the other. Each alive. The commingling greens and browns and golds and faint grays shift in the brilliance of their hues faster than the presence or absence of sunlight as it falls through the branches overhead could effect. Nux's remain their steady luminous green. The color of new shoots of grass awash in their first rain. He blinks and watches Pan sniff the air about his face until the broad hook of the nose and the longest curls of the beard brush the boy's skin.

"And I smell it, too," says the god.

Nux laughs easily. As if this were an ordinary interchange among the oldest of friends.

"You remind me of someone."

"I do."

"Yes. Someone very beautiful."

The boy grows still, almost tense. The god is uncertain. Either Nux is offended or touched.

"A shepherd boy I loved very much."·

"What was his name?" Nux asks. There is a minute upturn at the edge of his lips. A shy, halting smile. Pan sighs. The boy has been moved by the praise of the god.

"Daphnis."

"That's a funny name for a boy."

"So is Nux."

"How did you know my name?" Nux protests.

"A god knows these things."

"A god?" Nux punctuates this by rolling his eyes. It is a come-on line worthy of a singles bar far from this isolated clearing in an old forest.

"Yes. A god. Ever fuck a god before?"

"No. Well. No. Wait, yeah, some guys who claimed to be gods…"

"But it was like making love to a marble statue. No matter how good the drugs." With the word "drugs," Pan gives Nux a knowing wink.

"Yeah, kinda. Now that you mention it."

"We've all fallen for them, baby." He lowers his head and shakes it slowly. The tight ringlets of hair bounce first against one horn and then the other.

"Hey, wait. I recognize you."

"You do?" Pan says as he looks up.

"Omigod." Nux draws out every syllable.

"Yes."

"You're him. Cernuttios."

"Who?!" The god's question comes out too shrilly, like a child trying to play a flute for the first time.

"The Horned God!"

"Whoa there, studlet," Pan says as he composes himself. He gives the boy's nipple a gentle tweak through his shirt. "You make the old man sound like a box of cereal. His name is Cernunnos. Herne to his hunting buddies. But I am Pan."

"The Pan?"

"Is there any other?"

"I guess so."

Pan bleats in amazement.

"I swear I already met The Pan at a gathering in Tennessee. He looked a bit like you except he was a lot less hairy and no tail and his hooves had little golden wingy tattoos on them. He actually had a lot of gold on him."

There is a wild snort. Pan digs in the wet dirt with one of his hooves. "Dad, you old fucker," he whispers under his hot breath. To Nux, he says, "That was Hermes doing me to get laid…"

"Man, did he. He and Thumper disappeared for the rest of the gathering."

"Yes, all creation knows. But on the thigh of Zeus himself I swear to you I am the real deal. The Great God Pan."

"Cool."

"Cool?"

"Yeah, cool. You're way hotter anyway."

It is the great god's turn to fidget.

"You know," says Nux, "I've heard about you since I was a kid. You're the musician who loves to fuck."

"What musician doesn't."

"I thought you were all horny for chicks, you know. But like you just asked me to fuck you. Are you gay or what?"

"Or what. Is that what the cool kids are calling bisexuals these days?"

Nux grins. He is less stoned than Pan has thought. "Could be. I never thought of it. I'm gay."

Pan smiles. This boy is younger than Titania and new to so many things. He is charmed by how he announces the familiar and obvious to navigate his way through their seduction.

"Bully for you. You wear it well."

"And you?"

"I'm a god."

"A gay one?"

"Orientations are for mortals, sweet boy." Pan tugs at the knot in the drawstrings.

"Like Trix are for kids."

Great Pan brays and pulls the knot free.

"Back to cereal. Someone has the munchies."

"Has anyone told you you look kinda like the leatherguy in The Village People?"

He brays again and lets go of the string. The pants fall. Nux's uncircumcised cock lolls on his heavy balls, like a fat slug in a parka chillin' on a beanbag, which is word-for-word how Nux likes to describe them when hooking up online.

"No one who's lived to tell another."

Nux laughs too and steps out of his pants without ever looking away from Pan. His dick is starting to swell. "I mean it in the good way. You know, you're superhairy and sexy and I bet you'd kick ass in leather."

"This tail and these hooves in leather. You're high, my friend. I'd look like a circus animal."

"Nope. You'd look hot." At this, Nux kicks off one Birkenstock. His dick bobs when he does it. "And I could make you a killer pair of chaps that would make you think different." The other shoe flies away.

"You could?"

"I could." And if Nux didn't want so urgently to rub his face deep in the thick wool about Pan's inner thighs, sniffing all the while he rolls his face and extended tongue closer and closer to Pan's impressive and still-growing godhood, he would spend a minute or two explaining to the god that he works above a leather shop back in San Francisco, cobbling together, along with several other designer-in-training fags like himself and a several more Asian mothers and grandmothers, all manner of S/M-inspired haberdashery. Instead he pulls off his shirt.

"Maybe you should take my measurements."

"Right on. But I'll have to use my hands. No tape." Nux holds up his open palms before Pan. The god's skin slightly burns, darkening from the ruddy browns the sun has dyed it over the thousands of years to the black of a boar's hide, as he tries to stop himself from flinching before the sexy innocent. The boy has no idea he's hitting Pan at point-blank range with a double-whammy of the Old World's evil eye. This one knows nothing about the Old World, and, for once, Pan finds this ignorance exciting. They can be each other's New World. Let the exploration begin, he thinks.

"No problem. Start with the inseam."

Nux drops to his knees in the middle of the path. The cool dirt and grit of broken rock and stone soften under the tufts of dense moss the god invites to grow beneath Nux. It is an hour after noon, if that. The hottest part of the day is to come. But all is cool in the grove. The shadows of branches and leaves high above dance over the boy's face as he looks up at the god.

Great Pan is giving him his wickedest grin as he wags his dick in his face. It slaps against his lips then chin then cheek then nose then...Nux takes it with both hands and deep throats what he can of the mythic prick that fathered the horse-hung Priapus. Pan rests his weight on the back of his muscular legs, thrusting more of his dick into Nux's mouth. The boy's dreads bounce about his head as he sputters and gags, but neither will stop. Neither want to stop.

Until the mortal must breathe.

Nux pulls Pan's dick out of his mouth and leaves it to bob in the air while he gasps, wiping at the edge of his eyes, his mouth, with the back of his hands. He is laughing while he coughs.

"How," the god pants, winded himself, his brown skin red and glistening, "can one so young be so good at so ancient an art?"

"Passion and practice," says Nux as he weaves his fingers into the hair of Pan's thighs.

The boy closes his eyes and inhales and follows the scent until he is nuzzling in the wild-smelling crook where inner thighs and balls come together. He sniffs out burning candles made of musk and ambergris and just-broken ancient oak casks of dark red wines and the underbellies of a thousand little mushrooms and laughing mouths washed in streams of cum and imperfect beards wetted with spunk and wiry-haired cunts soaked in their own juices.

Nux sticks out his tongue and lets it rasp over the hairs to this side and that. He laps upwards, like at fast-melting ice cream, and comes to Pan's balls. They are large, drooping, sagging under their own weight of fat and hair, big like a bull's; the Minotaur has nothing on Pan. The god's throaty bleatings inspire Nux to keep tonguing and sucking them. Until, by accident at first and then intention, his throbbing tongue strays up the underside of Pan's dick. Over lone kinky hairs and long snaking veins and the thick ring of foreskin hooding the swollen head, each cleft and curve of it strained to definition by the glut of burning blood.

The boy opens his eyes and smiles at the narrow pinched eye in the beet-red face. He licks it again and again while he jerks the length of the dick in a fist made of two hands.

"Blow," shouts Silenus from the midst of the growing chorus of huddling nymphs and Faeries and witches and satyrs and druids and dryads and deadheads and, yes it is, Puck. Silenus' beard and lips are stained a faint shade of purple. The empty wineskin is tented over his erection. He is happily caressing a very ample breast with one hand and dandling quite hairy balls with the other. "Blow," he sings, "blow, o blow, you fat pipes of Pan. Blow o blow."

"Blow, o blow," chant those around him until they fall silent, eating whatever flowering fruits they are drawn to: those showy ones, all reddening flesh, or the delicate dark, pink, hidden ones.

Nux swallows the great god in time to the dying song and when there is nothing but a muffled and humming stillness in his ears he pulls away, letting his tongue drag after the skyward-curving dick until he gives it a final lick with just the tip. He stands and wipes his lips, never unlocking eyes with Pan. Nux begins to stroke his own dick and the god's wild eyes are drawn down to it. The slug in the parka has pushed off its hood. And grown to twice its girth since it got off its beanbag. It is one mean, really fat dick.

"You've got me so hot," Nux says, halting his hand at the base of his dick and gripping it till it swells to the very edge of physics' laws.

Pan almost crows as he imagines that inside him. "Really," he whispers, "an old horndog like me." He never once looks up from Nux's dick.

"Yeah. God yeah. I really wanna fuck you. Now."

Pan holds a golden bowl in his hands. "Then you will need this."

"It's empty," the boy strains to observe as he keeps stroking his dick.

"This is ambrosia," Pan says and lifts a tiny dollop on the end of his finger. He holds it out to the boy's lips. To watch them part. The expert tongue licks his finger clean. The lips return to their sensuous embrace. He smiles to hear him moan.

Pan takes the empty finger and dips it in the bowl. "This is honey." He brings it to the boy again who licks it away. The god smiles anew to hear him hum.

"This is sea water." His finger is slick. Pan laughs to see the boy's face pucker as the salt and sweet combine in his mouth.

"This is my own ambrosia. You are a more shortsighted people. You call it pre-cum. So boring a name for such a delight." He rubs two fingers over his dickhead. He nearly howls when Nux sucks them both into his mouth.

"You must mix all of these to fuck the ass of a god," he says while he stirs the bowl with one finger. "But only take a little or you will slip more than you will slide."

Pan hands the bowl to Nux and turns to the nearest tree. It is a tall pine. He whispers something to it and then bends forward to grip its trunk.

There is a wail and a groan or two in the vast pile that was once their onlookers. Pan twists his head back to give Nux a wink. The boy stands holding the bowl. With a quick dip of his horns, the god encourages him to begin.

The boy looks as stiff as his dick.

"What has happened to the beautiful creature so eager to fuck my ass? Well, go on, my Nux. Anoint that fat dick of yours."

Nux drags his fingers once around the bowl. As he does, the god stares at him with a deeply furrowed brow.

"Sweet child, your concern for my well-being is touching. If I were a mortal, I would be scrounging in my pocket or bag right now for a condom while you lubed yourself up. But I am not a mortal. You cannot kill me. You can break my heart. But you cannot kill me." For a moment, he looks truly ancient. He shakes his head and his leer returns. "So finish playing with your dick and fuck my hole."

The boy nods and puts the bowl down. He takes his two slimy fingers and touches the head of his dick. He visibly shudders.

"Feels good?"

Nux nods more enthusiastically.

"Imagine what it will feel like when you're inside me?"

Nux refuses to waste a moment on imagination. He seeks knowledge. He rubs the Olympian lube all over his cock until it shimmers. Pan sighs contentedly and leans into the tree, arching his ass up to welcome a boy and his dick.

As Nux marches the few excited steps toward Pan, he lets his eyes lead him up the hind legs of an enormous goat, but with the matted fur of a sheep in the dead of winter, until the sinew of the animal gives way to the broad curves of muscle and fat in a well-made man, the hair grows thinner as it comes to the cleft between the cheeks, and there above it all is the fat brush of a tail. It flicks enticingly and Nux grabs the Great God Pan's ass with each hand, spreading it to reveal an even more flirtatious hole, winking wildly, against which he places the slick swollen head of his wide dick and pushes.

Pan bellows for joy.

He makes a menagerie of sounds as Nux fucks him: he whinnies for each deep thrust in; he yelps for each long pull out; he grunts whenever there are quick rapid pumps; he brays for every splendid ram that starts outside his hole and ends at the base of his throat; he gives an unearthly squealing snarl for all the side-to-side rockings.

All about the woods the pipes are playing and the earth is rumbling to the pounding of Pan against the pine tree.

Pound, pound, pound.

Somehow the sun is six hours farther to the west than when Nux plunged into Pan. And these six hours have been filled with sex, which is fitting since six in Latin is *sextus*. I don't know why that's important to tell you for no one has been listening to me for any of that time. Everyone is writhing in piles over here or over there and in the middle, Pan hugs a tree while Nux fucks him like the god he is.

The boy's lips are moving frantically. He's trying to shout but I can't hear over the quaking of the earth. Wait, now he's yelling clearly:

"I'm gonna come!"

He grabs hold of Pan's tail and bucks against the god. His dreads flail about his head while he stands on his toes. Every muscle clenches and is thrown into relief and still Nux bangs on as he calls out a prayer more ancient and sacred than the oldest temples on earth.

At last he grows still and collapses atop Pan, wrapping his arms around his broad chest and pushing his dick even deeper inside him.

Now it is the Lord of the Wild's turn to give thanks. For Great Pan has never been so alive.

His cum hits the bark of the tree. The wood hisses and buckles and grows. A big fat cone drops on Nux's head with a declarative thunk. He shouts and slips out of Pan and the god echoes him. Another cone falls on Pan's arching back. Then a third but when this hits his horns it bursts with a slow-motion explosion of white petals. Then another and another. And with each new shot of Pan's cum, the old pine spurts higher and higher, its cones fall from farther and farther, many exploding in midair. The air is soon clotted with the drift of white petals and a pungent tang.

Nux has forgotten the ache in his head and laughs and spins about in the flowery rain until he grows dizzy and collapses with a plop on the petal-strewn moss. All the while Pan keeps coming until the entire forest roars. Satyrs and nymphs and dryads and deadheads and dozens of Faeries encircling Puck all shout at once and pipes shrill and goats sing out what sound like hallelujahs.

The wilds grow quiet when the sun starts to droop behind the tops of the westernmost trees. The air is electric and still, save for a sigh or purr or warbling or two. Until Nux breaks the post-coital calm with a laugh that starts deep in his belly.

"Ohmigod," he says. Each syllable preceded and followed by a laugh.

"Omiboy," answers Pan, still hugging the now enormous tree.

"Omifuckingod that rocked." He brushes petals from his cheeks and forehead. "Can we do it again?" He rolls back and forth across the moss and dirt and flowers, humming what sounds like Handel's "Hallelujah Chorus."

"Now?" Pan coughs. He is still winded from laughing and coming. He turns and looks down at his new beloved, his own eyes squinting from both his smile and the light of the setting sun.

"Hell yeah."

"Ever been to Greece?" Pan says as he pats the tree goodbye and walks toward the boy.

"Nope."

"Want to go to my place and really fuck like crazy?" The great god nudges Nux's butt with the tip of his hoof.

"Cherry. Cherry bomb."

"That's a yes?"

"Fuck yes." Nux laughs anew, grabbing fistfuls of dirt and petals and moss, hurling them above him, letting them rain back over his glimmering body.

"Then away we go, my wild thing," says Pan as he scoops the boy up into his brawny arms.

In the blink of an eye, my eye in fact, they are gone and...

Thanks, Arthur. Watch the hands and legs, hoovesss coming through. Thanks, thanks, thanks. Make way for the second-combing of Homer. Thanks, Arthur. Not blad for a journaliss. I'll take it from here. Wanna wineskin? It's dry as an old widow's dugs, alas. Not bad for sucking but nothing comes out. You, however, look like the kinda man who thucks things hanging lower to the glound. Eh, Ahthor?

But, Mr. Silenus...

No, no. My turnee. For pluckee and singee. Home again, home 'gain to Arcady. Hey diddle diddle hee hee hee.

Tha's ancient Geek for Wait for me!

Just like that, it's over? you says.

Just like this! Click your hoovesss together three times and repeat: There's no place like home; there's no plates lack home; there's no play like ho...

Okay, then...Well, boys and girls and girlie boys and boyie girls and either/ors and neither/nors, the god and the boy and the satyr have split. But The Arthur is still here and I'm the only one left it seems who hasn't come and until I do, my fingers are twitching to tap out a story or two more. Stay if you will, go if you must, I understand. The heat from rutting is starting to cool; this forest is damp; we've sat here a long time. But the rest of you stretch, jog in place, stretch some more. Do a toe-touch. Do a knee-bend; that's it. Now pull up a moss-covered rock or log, take a deep breath, grab a partner or three or just yourself, and listen:

Overexposed

for Sean Meriwether and Jack Slomovits

W. 42nd & 8th Ave.

Words aren't my thing. You'll get that as we go along. It's not like I'm illiterate or won't read. (Translations of classical Japanese haiku or graphic novels when I feel in the mood.) It's just I'd rather see the words of others pass by — like the blur of houses and parking lots and trees seen from a commuter train — than spit them out all by my lonesome. The reason is one of the few uncomplicated things about me: I'm all about the eye. Not just what we can see but how we see what we need to see. Like in framing a shot. With a camera. Not a gun. That's traditional weird. I'm not traditional.

I'm into guys too. Okay, that's more traditional than you'd think. I like to watch guys. Not all guys. Just the hot ones. What makes a guy hot? It's in the eyes. His some. Mine mostly. I get hard for the ones who make my eyes widen a bit as they walk toward me. Dart quickly to the side before they pass. Force my whole head to turn to check out the curve of the back of their heads, the slope of their necks, the breadth of their shoulders, the heft of their asses. Again, very traditional. But that's not what I really wish, really want to see. It's the look on their faces in those singular seconds before they come and that sole magical one when they actually do. That's what I walk the city searching for. That's why I take the pictures through my fingers.

Not so traditional.

W. 22nd & 8th Ave.

Take six months ago. I'm walking to hook up with a

friend for coffee. I spot this guy. I don't really *see* him until I look at the pictures later. And I'll look at them a lot. But I'll get to that. Now, looking back (see how words fail me), I remember him as a tall slight Black man. As for his face, I don't need a memory. I have hard proof of why he makes me hard. He's got a kind of wild 'fro that must've waved with each step, skin the color of coffee (one cream), a thin nose that flares a bit as it points down to his lips that are so beautifully swollen they barely touch. His eyes are closed so I can't tell, can't remember either, what color his eyes are, but I've imagined them from every shade of brown to a piercing green.

Anyway, the first moment his face washes out of the crowd, when he doesn't catch my eye but seizes it, I shove my hand in my pocket and squeeze. Not my dick. That always comes later. No, I grab for my digital camera and hold it as tight as I can. I press my fingers into the warming metal and rub my middle finger over the lens. Again and again. Then I head home. I know I'm blowing off my friend. But I'm no good for coffee. I'm too distracted. I have to go home and download. I can't wait. If I do, the image fades. Or doesn't even show up. I've "taken" hundreds of photos before this one and done a few controlled "experiments" that've left me convinced of this. And as blue as my aching balls.

I get inside my walk-up walk-in closet that only in New York can be called a studio and still get the rent they're asking for it. I turn and slam the locks shut. All the while I'm kicking off my shoes, fishing the camera out of my pocket before my pants fall to the floor, tossing it from hand to hand as I shuck my jacket and sweater and T-shirt, stepping on the end of my sock with my other foot and wriggling free. I hear my feet slapping against the floor as I walk the few steps, literally, over my futon to my desk — my boner pointing through the fly of my boxers, pointing the way. As I plug in the camera, I slip off my shorts and put them over the cold plastic of my chair. Mouse in one hand and dick in the other, I download.

A couple of clicks and there he is. In some of the most intimate seconds of his life, a whole string of them which I double-click to enlarge until I find the one. Each is a head shot. Of the man who has seized my eye today. The lighting and framing just right. Illuminating, if you want to get arty or religious about it. As if done in a studio, not the street where I've just seen him. I don't know how I am able to do this — to capture the face of a man at his most private — or why this happens to me. Maybe where there's a will there's a way. I don't know. I just make the most of my good fortune and watch. Stroke my dick and watch his face. Stroke and imagine what has gotten him to the point that he has to make this totally pure expression: a beautiful frown that makes the hairs on my balls stand on end.

I find the one. It's him at the second he comes. The perfect moment. The perfect face. I mirror him and I become aware my hand is sticky and a shudder is fanning out over my shoulders. I sit back, close my eyes, and run a finger over the tip of my wet dick.

God, he's hot.

For the rest of the day and into the night, I imagine him. The color of his eyes, which, like I said, I can never know because they are always closed — almost — always rolling back. The slow jumping of the muscles in his chest and his forearms as he pumps or jerks or fondles or strokes, underhand or overhand or on the side or with both hands, his dick, which is sometimes fat and cut or long and veiny or curved and uncut, the skin so black it's nearly purple or a swirl of earth tones giving way to the pink or the hard red of the head of his dick. Until each and every one of these different, beautiful dicks shoots, cum splattering his ribbed or soft, small gut and his muscular or narrow, lean thighs with the heavy sound of paint hitting a drop cloth.

God, he's hot.

8th Street–NYU (subway entrance)

A month (and forty or fifty men) later, I run into The

One. He's coming out of the subway as I'm at the top of the stairs about to go down.

He's not super hot. What's super hot? A guy who knows he's foxy. Humpy. Well, that's what the old farts who were my age in the last century used to say. You know, like the guys in a really good porno that you rewind and fast forward over and over to watch. All hard — cut, ripped. Nothing soft but their asses and lips, maybe. No, he's beautiful. A perfect mix of hard and soft. Like the model in a painting or a statue. That's it. Like a model, but more ancient. Too perfect almost to be part of this grimy world.

I can't tell if he's tall at first. Until we climb/descend the stairs closer. I can tell now that he is. Tall, that is. And muscled, some, in his shoulders and arms, as they stretch against his long-sleeved black T-shirt. Maybe from playing guitar, painting huge canvases, bagging groceries. His hands look soft though. (No guitar, no groceries. Probably a writer.) And his face. It's framed by long, dirty-blond hair, parted in the middle, tucked over his ears. His eyes are wide and blue and deceptively gentle. His nose is all straight lines ending in rounded angles like on a classical sculpture. As I said, he's beautiful like an ancient model. His skin is smooth, a hint of blush, like he would be apple-cheeked when he gets drunk. And his full pink lips are the softest feature of all. They're almost artificial, plastic in their color and unblemished fullness — like the wax lips you got at Halloween as a kid — but perfectly rounded. In the picture I will take, they are parted, but only a bit, for breath to escape. For moans. And for the cigarette he always keeps at the end of his arm, swinging back and forth, the burning end of a metronome, until it slides its way back into his wet pink hole like a fat beer can of a dick taking an ass that's been fucked by every man in the room in some classic porno.

I'm stumbling down each stair, never breaking eye contact, gripping the railing with one hand and fingering my camera with the other. I feel the image of him flowing from my eyes, through my nerves. I feel the particles break up, pulse out my finger into the camera to develop. I can see myself downloading these pictures in twenty minutes, if I'm lucky, and daring what I've never had the balls to do before. I'm going to put the printout of his perfect face at its most perfect moment on my pillow. Then I'm going to crouch on all fours in front of it. And finger my hole. Get it wet with spit. Stretch it while I pull on my dick and push the finger in deeper.

I imagine the hurt. The burning. I've never been fucked before. Mostly because I've been afraid. Not ready. I've been waiting for the right boy with the right dick to come along. He has. I keep pulling and pushing...

Until this dickhead on the stair behind me shoves me into the wall to get by. I wave him on with one finger and look over. The One is gone.

Thirty-five minutes later (what do I expect at rush hour), I'm in my apartment, sitting naked before him, and he is staring straight back at me. He's even more beautiful when he's angry. Or aroused. I can't tell. I'm so confused how this has happened. No guy has ever looked back at me in a picture before.

I come so many times before I fall asleep — sweating and panting and sticky and happy — that I'm sore for the rest of the week.

E. 11th & Ave. "A"

I keep my favorite pictures on the ceiling over my bed. At first, to cover up the peeling plaster. Now, to help me sleep. To help me dream. Sometimes I like to go a week without taking my camera with me, without coming, without touching my dick except to take it out to piss. Then I lie down and look up and imagine them all in one big circle jerk. I've hit the wall behind my head several times doing just that.

I put a photo of The One in the center of all of them: white boys with freckled faces and red hair who look like they're just off the bus; real blonds from California and fakes from everywhere else; brown boys and Black boys: Puerto Ricans, Cubans, Dominicans, banjee boys and gastas and brothas; Vietnamese, Thai, Chinese, just-arrived and fourth-generation New Yorkers; some a mix of races, a mutt of nations; all of them either bike messengers, suits, dealers, DJs, actors, writers, boys in the band, hookers or the ones who want you to believe you should pay; each with a story I've given them to get me off.

They surround The One. I stare and watch for them to take notice of him. They're in their usual enormous huddle, each one with his hand wrapped around his own hard cock. Then, he's standing in the middle of the circle. They don't swarm him. They must know he's mine. But they do turn and start making out with each other, grabbing this dick or that ass, falling into groups of three or four or fifteen. There's so much fucking and sucking going on in the broken and collapsing circle of bodies around him it looks like when a painter takes his palette and twists his brush around and the colors with them. And finally that leaves him, standing, pulling a hand, then just a finger to his lips, those lips, and sucking it. His back arches and his other hand grips his dick and begins to pull. Almost as if he's lifting his whole slender body by his dick. He takes the wet finger and slides it behind his back and into his butt. It has to be that when he's making such a face. He pushes and pulls. I do the same. Until we come (first him, then me) and I hit my lips and chin and chest. I run my tongue over every inch of skin on my face it can reach. I convince myself that each drop of cum I swallow is his.

8th Street–NYU (subway entrance)

I'm hooked. Okay, I'm fucking obsessed. Mad. I search all over the East Village, NOHO, and LES—the Lower East Side. And The Village and Chelsea and, well, you get the idea. I come here. Same spot. Same time. Same stairs. I never see him.

I see plenty of other guys. Each picture is hotter than

the next. Each one closer to the very second the seed shoots out like a volley from a cannon. Or like the circus acrobat in the tight white satin suit blown out of its mouth and across the gasping crowd to the waiting net. Corny, huh? Like I said, words and I don't work so well together. I get too flowery. Too girly for my own good, my old man used to say. Still would if I ever went back. Whatever. If I had some pictures on me, I'd show you.

Anyway, none of them are him. And then about three months ago, I'm here again. I go down the steps. Nothing. I toss my token and go through the turnstile and wait on the platform. He's nowhere. It's my train and I shove my way to the doors with the rest of the crowd. I stop dead. It's him! On the other side of the doors. I want to jump or wave or shout or something. The doors open. He wades through the oncoming tide of people and when he's an inch from me, he turns and forms those lips into a smile. These are for you, he says, handing me a small brown envelope. I grab it before this suit walks through it and then shoulders and briefcases and backpacks jostle us away from each other. Now we're on opposite sides of the doors again. He waves. I want to cry or blow him a kiss. Something totally over the top. Instead, I smile feebly. I feel like all I've had to eat or drink today has been coffee. I'm shaking. Not enough to notice. (Hell, I could've had a seizure right then and nobody would've noticed.)

Twenty minutes later, I'm fiddling to close the locks on my door while I unbutton and yank all my clothes off. I tear open an end of the envelope and am on my back on my bed with a very wet finger up my ass before I spill whatever is inside all over my chest. It's too big an envelope for just a letter. It has to be photos. It is.

It's me. My face. My perfect face. I've never seen what I look like when I'm coming. My dick now is twitching to stand higher and higher. The next picture is me again, coming. I don't know how I know it's that very instant but I do. I look away from myself and he's there—in the photo—with me. Biting my ear. About to come himself. I close my eyes and press my finger in as far as it can go. I let the hot, sharp pulsing subside and then rock my finger from side to side. And back and forth. I open my eyes again and fumble for the next photo. It's us. Both of our faces twisting toward the blinding flash, eyes clenched, each face an exquisite grimace, as if the bulb — his bulb — is bursting inside me. Our faces are slick with sweat. His long hair is wet and matted to the sides of his face. Like he swam his way inside me. Like he stroked his long, muscled arms and kicked his strong but slender legs through rivers and seas of air to get to me. To get inside me.

I see him. I feel him. And I blow hard. No hands near my dick. Cum flies over my head. And then again onto my chest and the fronts and backs of the photos lying across it. And then one last time onto my stomach.

But the photo I hold in my hand is untouched. Perfect in every way.

And when I finally think to flip it over, there is his name and number.

W. 42nd & 8th Ave.

Did I call him? Of course. Did we fuck? Still are. Made some videos even that put the pictures to shame. He's my boyfriend. But we have an arrangement, BenJ E. and me. I can look at other guys — they can be naked, stroking their dicks, shooting even — just as long as I'm shooting through the lens of a camera. It's kind of old-fashioned — this arrangement and the camera I use now — but it works. No fights. No fears. Best of all, no guilt. And sometimes he watches me watching them watching...us, I guess. My camera lens or me or me and my camera lens or me and my camera lens and BenJ E. All three of us. And I like to work naked. I make BenJ E. strip down too. I want whoever I'm shooting to feel cool with it. And to know how much I love what I'm doing. How much I appreciate them for letting me see them totally exposed. In the raw. Real.

So, what do you say? Can I take your picture? Or do I

Ian Philips

have stick my finger in my pocket and rub?

What the Market Will Bear

for Lori Selke

i serve at the pleasure of the Goddess. my Mistress commands me to write this at Her behest. That is Her word. Behest. She says if i have an MBA from Harvard and a Ph.D. from MIT i should have a vocabulary to show for it. She says right now i have nothing to show but my body. i am naked. Stripped of everything. Even my hair from my neck down. i write in a little girl's diary my Mistress gave me. It's pink and plastic and covered in cartoon drawings of red and green and yellow girls with huge eyes and a green monkey in a turban. She wants me to write down everything She does to me the next three days. i must offer it to Her. If She is pleased, She will let me return.

I am called Lysistrata. Mistress Lysistrata. Few of my clients will get the irony when they hear of what I've done on this Web site. Irony and the power to rule millions rarely go together.

They assumed Mistress Lysistrata is simply my name. I told them it is Greek. I told them I am Greek. They replied, "But you don't look Greek." They imagined Christina Onassis or Zorba. "I wax," I answered and ordered them onto all fours.

I know who I am and I know who Lysistrata was. Both of us sick of the ways of men. Both of us mindful of how to use what is between our legs to control the dangling bits between theirs. I cannot stop a war as she did — or I did not when I had the neck of the emperor of the free world beneath my boot, to be more truthful — but I hope I have stopped one of its newest weapons. (Click here for the cure.)

I give you this post–post-modern (i.e., it has a plot; it has a heavy-handed moral) spin on ancient drama's give-and-take between chorus and actor. It tells not all, but enough.

Our good doctor came to me and I to him by word of mouth. Highly recommended. A force to be reckoned with. A shaper of destiny. And in the end, one of us was.

I'm sure he expected enforced feminization. Put him in panties. Wrap his shriveled pink prick up in a satiny bow. I have only one thing to say to that: bush league.

my Mistress' limo was waiting outside the FDA yesterday. Last minute lobbying before Friday's high noon and the government shuts down. i was in a new suit. It didn't fit. Too big. i've been doing the Atkins diet. my wife's idea. All the fats you can eat and then some. Bacon cheeseburgers — hold the bun — for breakfast. Steaks with butter for dinner. And walk the stairs at work every day. i've lost sixty pounds. my Mistress is tapping me on the shoulder with Her crop. No more lies She says. OK. 57 pounds. i'm used to rounding up. Still a lot. And a good thing too. i've been sitting on my ass for the last 3 years. Plus i wanted to look my best for my reward. A gift from my business partners. Sweet fuckers. They told me about my Mistress once our product began Phase III. 6 months later here i am waiting for the FDA to give us the green light.

Our mystery man may be the guru of virology (Click here for his CV) and a whiz at genetics who can map and resequence DNA, but string together more than a few words and fewer syllables he cannot. No verbal double helixes here. Nor single helixes. Not even a base pair sequence. Nor a rudimentary grasp of spelling and grammar. A weak-wristed, splayed-fingered grip. I've had to edit his entries down to all but their myriad missing-in-action commas and quotes. Barren patches on these pages I have kept as a tribute to the original chaos from which all life has tumbled like clowns out of a dented red toy car. A necessary bit of editorial license and largesse so that only one of us would be [sic] of our lackluster Pepys by his second limp entry.

i was blindfolded for the ride to my Mistress'. Some kinky and pricey-looking leather replica of what old ladies wear over their eyes to fall asleep. The driver put it on me then wrapped duct tape around that. i told him if i lost any more of what little hair i have i was gonna bust his nuts with the tire iron. He just laughed and shoved me onto the floor. It was a long ride — a lot of it was waiting in traffic. Roll. Stop. Roll. Stop. Then we picked up speed. It felt like an hour after we got out of traffic. i really have no awareness of time without a watch. Even with a watch. A final stop. i was dragged out of the car and pulled roughly godknowswhere like some bawling kid through a mall. Up stairs, then a long period of no stairs and then around corners left and right and down stairs and down more stairs and then no stairs and our feet began to echo really loud. i heard a voice. A woman's. It must be my gift i tell myself. Her voice was musical but cold. Like a killer who would stroke your head before blowing it off. Take it off i heard Her say. i flinched.

"Flailed" would be a more apt description. He looked like a string puppet undergoing electroshock. Who knew the brain behind Proteus would be such a live wire? I waited a beat, listening for the telltale trickle. I watched for the stain to appear on the front of his pants like a vision of The Blessed Mother in an oil slick. Nothing. He had not let go of all control. Yet.

i heard the tearing before i felt it. Everything's blurry. i couldn't see. Only feel the burn where the tape ripped my hair out. And smell. A musty smell. Not bitter like jizz but definitely funky. Same genus. It smelled like a workroom under a house. Dirt behind all the cinderblock walls. Wet dirt. And dark like the shadow wavering in front of my eyes. Like an image under the microscope coming into focus. 10x. A blonde in a leather dress holding a riding crop. 100x. A tall woman with brown hair with blonde highlights that falls to Her shoulders. They're bare and lightly tanned. She has large dark eyes and a long thin nose and wide red lips and a jaw and matching cheekbones that could cut glass and breasts like two loaves of golden bread rising up out of Her black leather dress. What a dress too. It pushed up Her breasts and held tight around Her little waist and dropped down like a long skirt. But with no front. It's cut out and She's wearing nothing underneath. Except boots that lace up the front and stop just above Her knee. And that brought my eyes right back up to Her privates. my Mistress is frowning. She says i'm holding back. No man says privates. What would i say if She weren't reading my every word. Pussy. And it looked perfect. Just a bit of hair and all that smooth skin and big lips trying to cover up that dark pink slit.

Cover up, indeed. We'll get to that soon enough. For now, suffice it to say I was less than flattered to read his weakass rhapsody on my nearly priceless beauty. What woman would thrill to hear her breasts compared to bread cooling on the rack? Perhaps the paramour of one Mr. Poppin' Fresh®, The Pillsbury Doughboy™. Certainly our diarist is doughy in the extreme. But he's never giggled no matter how hard I've poked him.

I think he misses carbohydrates more than he knows. Certainly more than his wife.

And as for his mangling of metaphors and viruses, he deserved far worse and got it.

She said something and i looked up. You may look Me in the eyes only when I say you may. And She said this very softly. Like She was singing to Herself. i got goose bumps and focused on Her tattoo. It goes across Her chest — above Her breasts [writing illegible]. She just whacked me hard across my back with Her crop and i dropped my pen and this diary. She commands me to write Her heaving bosom. Right above Her heaving bosom. Now She's laughing. Write! i am a good little monkey. i am a good little monkey. i am a good little monkey. Good. You know how to listen. Now tell the story you stupid shit. The tattoo is the Medusa's head She said more loudly. One look at Her and She turns men to stone. It's working i said. i was getting hard. my Mistress laughed. She told me that i do not know the first thing about hard. But i will after my three days in the tomb. Eyes on the floor, Dr. Dumbass.

It took him a moment to realize what I'd said. Then he looked up — time for the operant conditioning to begin — and I finally saw what I long to see in the eyes of men like him: fear. Fear and lust. A profitable combination.

my Mistress slapped me across the face. Eyes on the floor or I'll knock them onto it. She didn't shout it, just whispered it in my ear. i looked at the tip of Her boot while She told me Her name. Mistress Lysistrata. i nodded. i didn't know what to say. I'm Greek She said. You don't look Greek was all i could think to say. I wax She said louder and more annoyed. On all fours. i got onto my knees after She hit me the second time. The first time i was too shocked. i'd never been hit before. The commands kept coming. From this nanosecond forward, you will speak only when commanded to. And you will do all that I ask or be returned to where We found you.

An empty threat. I would not return him until I'd made a lovely bomb of him.

There came a familiar series of knocks at the door. A Morse code devised between friends. I relaxed and smiled to myself. "Rise and meet my pet groomer," I said to the back of his head.

i got up as quick as i could. Out of the corner of my eye i saw this guy coming into the hall from a room on the right. That was the first moment i realized i'd been standing in a hallway all this time. He's naked. Except for a gold ring in the head of his dick. The first thing i thought was ouch. That and this fag has no body fat. His name is Theo my Mistress said. Short for Theodoros. my Mistress then told me it means gift of god. It fits. He must a model. Or gay.

"Theo, I have another dumb beast. What can you do with it? Perhaps a rinse?"

He smiled. At my Mistress and me. Then he walked over to me with his pierced dick waving back and forth. i didn't look at it. i never looked down once. But i could still see the flash of gold. And then he raised his hands for my neck and i backed up. i didn't know if he was going to kiss me or strangle me. Next thing i felt was my Mistress' crop pressing up hard under my chin.

Gently but firmly, I told our Dr. Demented, more or less, the following: "You will let Theo touch you wherever and however he wants. You will thank me for the privilege of being manhandled by a real man. One flinch, one pout and you're out, naked as the day your mother never should have let you be born." He tensed up as if preparing for the volley from a firing squad. Perhaps he was more farsighted than I imagined. I pressed my crop deeper into his second chin. "Well, I don't hear a thank you," I sweetly hissed. He muttered something. I pressed further. Politeness is so rare in these lawless times. "Thank you, my Mistress," he blurted. I stepped aside to let Theo begin his work. "Leave his socks and shoes on him," I whispered.

The fag didn't speak a word. He just looked me in the eye and smiled as he undid my tie and then removed my jacket and unbuttoned my shirt and pulled off my T-shirt. He didn't do anything queer like lick my tits. He was very professional and i barely felt his fingers on me. Maybe i was numb. Maybe cold. All i really remember was my Mistress smoking while She watched us. i could see Her hands while i stared at Theo's head sinking down below my stomach. It was some really smelly cigarette in a very long cigarette holder. All i could think was Cruella DeVil. Not that my Mistress looks anything like her. It's just i've seen the animated and the live-action 101 Dalmatians nearly 101 times with my daughter. She's four. my daughter. my Mistress says that it will be obvious to anyone smarter than me that She Herself is not four. She also wants me to write that She can live with being compared to Cruella a lot better than having Her heaving bosom equated with a rack of rising bread.

What the Market Will Bear

It was tobacco soaked in ouzo. My own concoction. I've called them Cruella Slims ever since.

i could feel him undoing my buckle and then my zipper. He pulled my pants down and helped me step out of them. i kept waiting for him to take off my shoes and socks before he went for my underwear. He didn't. Then i felt it. His fingers pulling the waistband of my boxers away from my skin and pulling them down. i never felt so cold. i tried to stay as calm as i could. i left the rest of my body behind. i was a head. Just a head. Then my Mistress began to laugh.

I was not laughing, as you might assume, at his dick. If he lost a bit more weight, he'd have a rather average-sized one. No, I laughed at how ridiculous he appeared as he stood beside my Theodoros, naked save for black socks and wingtips and his eyes scrunched together so tightly he looked like he was holding back tears or expelling a reluctant fart. "What lovely dress manacles you're wearing," I complimented.

She took Her crop and pressed it under my balls. i tried not to jump but i didn't expect that. i didn't know what to expect anymore. i prayed She wouldn't take a whack at them. Look what we have here She said. Dr. Lawrence H. Bergson III. The driving engine behind Proteus, that upstart startup. Rival of august Genentech and co-creator with the good folks at Narque Pharmaceuticals of the newest noxious AIDS drug, Elanovital. i watched my dick and balls bounce. Then She pulled the crop away and i could feel my balls fall. Then my heart.

"My balls fall and then my heart." How like a country-western ballad written by a focus group. There is a word for the heartbreak of the heartless: bathetic. It comes from the Greek word for depth: βαφοσ. Bathos. Wasn't he one of the Musketeers? you ask. No, that would be Porthos. Which sounds like pathos and that is what bathos aspires to. But pathos is suffering that wrings tears of blood from the sufferer. Think of Christs Passion, if you are so inclined. (In my case, you can take the girl out of the Greek Orthodox Church but...) Pathos is passion's long-lost forefather. Bathos is when pathos trips on a banana peel and falls Icarus-like into the depths of a bowl of children's cereal where it is forced at toy-gunpoint to wash in the syrupy-sweet milk that is left behind when there is no more sugar-coated grain to eat. Simple water can wash away all traces of this pain.

my Mistress took Her crop and placed it under Theo's dick so his balls swelled. His dick started to balloon too. i still wasn't sure who he did — guys or girls — but i knew where with a dick like that. Pornos. Still he looked a hell of a lot better than any of the guys in the ones i've seen. You like what you see? my Mistress asked. Take a good look. Here's a dick that can actually satisfy a woman unlike your wilted blade of grass. If you're a very good boy, My very bad man, I might let you find out for yourself. That's when little Larry cringed for the both of us.

Little Lar cringed for all three of us. At this point, I had planned to wax Big Lar all over, but I didn't have the time for all the squirming and shrieking — even with his lips locked in a long kiss with some cheap piece of duct tape. So instead, I used Nair. Did you know they make Nair for Men? They have for over a decade. What a triumph of civilization.

my Mistress sounded pissed all of the sudden. She ordered Theo to take me to the showers and wash away as much of the outer beast as he could. He then went and grabbed me by the balls and pulled me into the room he'd come from. i did my best not to jump out of my skin, but i'd never had a naked man take me by the family jewels.

And I'd never seen a duck waddle so fast to water. Or quack so hard when confronted with the delicious aroma of today's cutting-edge depilatory.

i smelled the Nair before i read the bottle and knew what the fuck it was. God that stuff reeked. i don't know how my wife has used it all these years. i'd rather have the razor.

No, my ignorant keeper of the Y chromosome, you would not if you knew all the places it had to go.

Theo wiped it all over me. Over my back and chest. Under my pits. Up my crack. Down my legs. All around my dick and balls. Then my Mistress told him he had 5 minutes to kill. So he went and started to stroke my dick with even more Nair. i closed my eyes. i couldn't watch. i just tried to keep breathing. The stinky cigarette smoke and that fucking Nair were giving me a killer headache. i wanted to puke. No matter what i did i could feel his hand tugging on me. Like he had all the time in the world to get me off.

It was the most deliciously disinterested handjob I've seen. My Theodoros, always the pro. It was perfect. Nothing frightens the hardcore heterosexual male like the thought of another man near his beloved privates. And nothing humiliates him like the thought of the man between his legs growing bored.

Is it hard yet my Mistress said. i opened my eyes and looked down. No thank god. Pity She said. OK. Wash him clean. And Theo let go of my dick and pushed me slowly under the water. i felt his hands all over me. Like they were on me but not trying to touch me. And all i could think was <u>this</u> is my gift as i waited for him to turn off the water and give me a towel. He dried me off himself. i felt like the biggest queer in the world. The biggest queer baby.

"Why don't we look as smooth as our little girl's pussy," I said. All mock enthusiasm. Clapping my hands with brittle glee. "Here," I added as I tossed Theo the chastity belt, "clamp this over his dangling bits. And you, when Theo's done wrapping you in your chrome-and-leather swaddling clothes, it's time to get down on all fours again and lay you away in your manger."

i just stood there and let Theo put the chastity belt on me. i couldn't think what else to do. i was too stunned to run and it hurt less than the Nair or the handjob. He yanked it once and i got onto my knees. my Mistress pushed the end of the crop in my face. Bite down She said. i did as She ordered and was led from the shower room down the hall to the last door on the left. my Mistress snapped Her fingers and told me to heel. i stopped. Let go of the crop you dumb dog She shouted. i did. Then She whacked me hard on the ass but i didn't move. Good boy She said. She whacked me harder. 12 more times. i think it was 12.

It was 13. Lucky 13. The Goddess' favorite number.

i couldn't count because i was trying not to scream or cry. When She stopped She touched me for the first time. She patted me on the head and i shivered. No you didn't do what I think you just did? She said. She was laughing too. Did you shoot with no hands? i shook my head since i didn't dare disobey and speak. Bad puppy my Mistress scolded. She didn't sound mad though. No dinner for you tonight. And straight to bed. She tapped me lightly on my ass with Her crop and said to go. i crawled into my room. It was empty. OK, almost empty. No windows. White walls. One very bright light bulb. No shade. 100 watts. A TV monitor bolted up into the corner. Playing CNBC without the volume. And in the corner across from it was a pile of straw and a chewed-up blanket that smelled like a dog. A very dead dog. His water bowl is still here. Plus no toilet. Just a drain in the center of the floor. my Mistress walked over to the straw and blanket and bent down and dug around in the straw. She came back with the girl's diary and the oversized pink pen with a clear plastic end filled with glitter. i've spent a lot of time since then watching the sparkling metal dots float up and down. Counting them and memorizing their colors. Open this and write She said as She threw the diary at me. Write I serve at the pleasure of the Goddess. And i wrote. Pages and pages. i wrote with Her for what seemed like 30 minutes. Maybe an hour. Until my Mistress left. i'm still writing. i'm too angry? frightened? horny? to do anything else. After what i've seen since She left. The last thing She said to me tonight was Listen up you sonofabitch. Her voice still soft and sugar and spice. Except now it makes my skin prickle like someone's turned the air-conditioning in here even higher. She was tapping Her boot with the crop. Waiting to see if i'd forget Her commands and look Her in the eye. i didn't. i wouldn't. She spoke again. i shivered happily. If you soil yourself on the outside like you have on the inside then to the pound in DC you go. As is. You will hold it till I decide I'm ready for you to part with it. Piss too boy. She closed the door and locked it. i heard Her laugh and then Theo and then the door to the room behind the wall with the TV opened. Then silence. i kept writing. For a long time. Then i heard Her and him and the TV channel flashed and there's sound. It's like i was at the movies. The sound was so loud and all around me. i couldn't get away from it. Even if i closed my eyes. But i couldn't. It was my Mistress on TV and She was naked and straddling Theo's dick.

Every once in a scene, I like to put the crop down and be a true-blooded Greek passive. My asshole bobbing on the fat head of God's gift. I was Aristotle's empty vessel of womanhood gone awry: painfully — he was almost too big — and pleasurably — thank the Goddess he was — awry.

I played with my clit. For myself and for the camera. I'd interrupted Dr. Mangled's regularly scheduling program with the following news flash: outside you can kill millions, here you are impotent.

I rubbed my fingers over my lips. They were slick to the touch. And flushed. My lips and I both. I parted them with one hand to get at my clit with the other. I thrust my hips forward and pushed down on Theodoros. With each sharper and sharper wave of warm pain, I brailled my clit with greater abandon until all my lips were mouthing for the camera. Laughing obscenely at him. I knew he could hear us through the wall. I was nearly singing now.

"You're hung like a fucking bull, my Minotaur. Fuck

me, Theodoros. Fuck me, you fuckin' bull." Until I babbled the word "bull" with every wave of each orgasm. Until Theo shot and shouted what I'd ordered him to say.

"Go bull market."

Saturday. Early evening i think. i'm wet and in love. i can't jerk off and rubbing against this belt hurts so i'll write. OK, first Theo's definitely not gay. He likes fucking my Mistress too much to be gay. But he's too pretty to be part of the real world. Definitely works in pornos. Probably gay for pay.

Even a fool can be prescient. Or a closeted collector of *Jason and the Argonuts 1, 2, 3* and *4.*

i woke up to my Mistress kicking me in the ass. Rise and shine, Cinderfella She said as She kicked me harder and harder. i have no idea what time it is or where i am. i haven't had any coffee. i have a headache and blurred vision and i smell like a dead dog and there is straw stuck to my face and in my asscrack. Get up She ordered. i do. i'm remembering everything about yesterday now. Come here and let me unfasten your pacifier.

Fortunately for me and Little Lar, I'd had a cup of Greek coffee — "1 part coffee grounds and 2 parts sugar" as Theo describes it — and was nimble enough in mind and finger to undo the chastity belt.

Piss my Mistress commanded. Keep your eyes on the floor fool. Preferably focused on the drain. Then out of nowhere She slapped the side of my head. i heard the heavy metal from Her rings bouncing off my skull before i felt the stinging pain. i wanted to scream out. Beg for mercy. Beg for coffee. i almost beg to go home. And if you dare to get hard without My say-so you've lost your golden opportunity to piss this morning. i think of the dead dog i smell everywhere and don't get hard. i piss. It makes a loud sound. Not as it hits the floor but when it goes down the drain.

I made him crawl to the bathroom to shit. I didn't want

to waste the day when the good doctor had so much work to get done. As he crawled back, painfully slow and head hanging down low enough so he can almost suckle his swinging breasts (he has learned he has no toilet paper in his bathroom), I crouched and hit him on the back of his head with a box of Crayons. Sixty-four shades of wax. Sullen and silent like him. Each a miniature effigy of Dr. Bergson that I would like to take to a candle and melt.

"If I were truly cruel," I told him, "I'd order you to spin that straw into gold. You are good at turning things into gold, even death. But I am a much kinder and gentler person than you, Dr. Death. I will give you a simple task and yet reward you for it with gold. Gold more precious than any you hoard away in vaults."

i barely felt the crayons hit my head. All i could think about was my ass. She boxed my ear with the crayons and i listened. my Mistress commanded me to use them to list as many toxic elements and substances as i can remember from my training and my work and diagram their chemical composition. She doesn't put my chastity belt back on. She must be waiting for my shit to dry too. i feel like a fucking baby. Naked. Covered in my own shit. On all fours. i'd cry like a baby too if my Mistress would let me. She doesn't say a word. i watch Her feet in the shiny black boots with long thin heels walk to the door and leave.

I returned after six hours to see how Dr. Bergson's arts-and-crafts project was coming along. I could see faint streaks of color all around me as I put down the two dog dishes I'd carried from the kitchen. One filled with fresh water and one with chunky peanut butter. I was tempted to put a bit of straw in both but decided to wait until I'd really looked at the walls.

It was the usual rogues gallery of toxins. In waxen and washed-out colors, there sprawled one enormous cave painting of rampaging porcupines, their quills skewering letters and numbers alike. But I spied something I did not expect to see. I could only imagine it was an overlooked insight from his unconscious. But still a spark of some conscience. The right hand might know what the left hand does after all. For there, front and center, were two small letters. Unadorned but utter death in their elemental simplicity. Am. Lucky atomic number 95. Americium the beautiful, ringing out the call to arms in smoke detectors like a radioactive bell from sea to shining sea.

my Mistress was very quiet as She looked about my cell. i didn't dare to look Her in the eye. Just a quick glance at Her profile. Re-memorizing every feature. Every efflorescence of Her genes. She taps the top of my head now with Her crop. There's the vocabulary I knew someone with too many useless degrees should possess. But I still haven't forgiven you for the bread/breast analogy [writing illegible]. *She just hit right down the center of the diary and i dropped it. Write She commands. i was watching Her walk slowly along the wall like She was grading an exam. Looking for faulty notation. Or judging a work of art. Then She started laughing. i shivered for real this time. She's either going to toss me out naked with my ass caked in shit or She's going to give me a prize. i watched Her feet waiting for them to turn. Only then would She talk to me. i had no idea what time of day it was or how long i'd been drawing on the walls. But it felt the same amount of time passed before She spoke to me. Crawl to me She said in Her softest and most terrifying voice. i scraped my knees getting to Her as fast as i could. She was on the opposite side of the room. Good doctor She laughed. i was so afraid. i had no idea what She would do with me. Sit up on your knees. Now. i did. What do you see? my Mistress. Good eyes, Einstein. What do you see? She said as She came even closer. i was face-to-face with Her privates. my Mistress is tapping Her foot angrily as i write this now. Be honest She shouts in a whisper. i was face-to-face with Her pussy. What do you see? She asked. The sex of my Mistress. She laughed even louder now. Who the fuck are you? Simone de Beaver. i didn't understand and She laughed even more. Beg Me for your reward, Dr. Bergson. Beg Me to shower you with gold. Do it. Say: Please, Mistress, shower me with gold. Say it now. i did again and again and again.*

I let fly. And after all the baklava and Greek coffee I'd had as I whiled away the afternoon, it was a sweetbitter stream. I was truly mellifluous. But with a bite.

Zeus had come to Danaë once more. But the tables had been happily turned and then overturned. My living chamber pot started when my stream splattered against his lips and across his face. We grew closer — I to give and he to catch my rain of gold.

Sunday. It has to be. i had the worst fucking sleep of my life. The floor was cold and hard and i was colder and harder. i'm writing in this stupid fucking diary to get feeling in my hands again. It's March and She's got the air-conditioning on. If She doesn't let me touch Her today i'm out of here. i'd come licking Her elbow.

It was another Greek who said that wisdom is a drop wrung from suffering. He must learn that he is truly impotent.

There were clips — like a video on MTV back when they showed videos. God i feel old. There's no music though. No sound. i had to make it up in my head. Her song. Her shouts. And all these pasty white bodies beneath Her. Squirming. Sometimes just with Her. Sometimes with Theo and Her. Sometimes a group of them together in this fucked-up kind of chain that starts from Her ass and trails back. And i think i recognize some of the faces from TV. Maybe a senator or news anchor. i swore one of them looked like the President. But most of them i'd never seen before. And all the time i was watching i'm going crazy because i want to jerk off. i want to be under Her. Any part of Her. Her boot. i want to be whipped and kicked and fucked. i'd do anything to be one of those lucky fucks. i'd even do one of them to be near Her. God i'm sick.

It is time for a bit of history for those who have come of age in the last ten years. Those who are old enough may skip ahead to avoid remembering the past. I understand. I would if I could. (Click here for the next Bergson entry.)

Ian Philips

Like Cassandra, my true namesake and the one, true patron saint of every fucked soul who falls continually afoul of irony, I have watched the topless towers of my beloved city fall and it drove me mad. Mad enough to let go of my unfinished dissertation: *The Melian Dialogue: An Overheard Conversation on Democracy's Realpolitik Repeated in a Textual Game of Telephone in the Greatest Literary Hits of Dystopia.* The dissertation I was working overtime on a phone-sex line to keep writing after I'd spent every other cent school, the government, and my parents had given me, let it go like the papers whirling about in the smoke outside that smelled like burning human flesh because it was the smell of burning human flesh. My brother's, in fact. Mad enough to give into the endless requests of a repeat client with friends in high places (the greatest understatement ever oversold to get a grieving girl to fuck the shit out of a man who was impotent because he was omnipotent) and meet for a private session. A session that surprised us both. A session that led to the birth of Mistress Lysistrata. Not quite like Venus, born of the severed genitals of a god and sea foam. Close. I was born out of the shrunken genitals of a Good Ol' Boy from the Grand Old Party. And the billowing gray froth of carnage, collusion, and collision that rolled out from Lower Manhattan on a fall morning. And ferocious enough to channel the Goddess on Her bad-hair days.

But that is not the story I want to tell. Yet. And perhaps never all of it. Instead, I want to let our young sleepers know about a fabricated fairy tale told in the dark to make them feel safe night after night. It is for you that I have added this whole sad story of me and Dr. Bergson, a pornographic preamble of sorts, to his scientific paper to follow. And I don't want you to miss one second of its titillation. And since I know you glossed over The President as the mere ramblings of a man with blue balls, I will gloss The President for you.

And, in doing so, I realize I will have to tell you some more of my story after all. They are intertwined now.

What the Market Will Bear

Once upon a time in a country with the same name as ours, The First Patriot was called The President. But president always reminded certain people of certain elections and The First Patriot is for life: the life of our glorious country; the life of democracy; the life of the free; the life of the righteous; the life of the unborn and the born again. The times demanded it. I imagine they will not stop demanding it in your lifetime either.

It came in a flash that blinded all eyes before they could blink. San Francisco vanished in a hellish puff of smoke. Our President had been liberating the Protectorate of Iran when a country called North Korea fired a missile and San Francisco was no more. And as for North Korea, we exchanged one irradiated peninsula for another.

But this you know, more or less. It's ancient history. Something a Greek, no matter how watered down the wine of her blood may be, is very familiar with.

There was much shock for some and awe for others — others whom I have come to know too well. Those "friends" in high places. There were emergency meetings. There were emergency powers. Emergencies came and went. The power remained. And The President was one day called The First Patriot in a speech by the then Vice President. (You call him The Second. Or as The First Patriot calls him, Shotgun.) "First Patriot" was a strategically placed honorific (Shotgun always knows what he's doing). An inspiring moniker that came and ran wild in the mouths of the media and took the word "president" away with it. That reduction happened almost overnight. Especially if you compare it, as I have night after night, to the ten very long years it took to inflate a man into The Father of Our Homeland.

So yes, that was indeed The First Patriot. I have known him well and often. This does not mean I am Mother of Our Homeland. Poor woman. But I have been its Mistress.

How? you scoff incredulously. A simple matter of economics. You don't charge $10,000 a day for your services and not "stumble" across the faceless ones who run the

American Imperium — especially when you live in one of the states that is a suburb to the American Rome. I could name dozens of them, but it would be like reciting from a phonebook. Just meaningless names to you. (Click here for the candid mug shots from my virtual black book.)

Yes, these noble patriots shun the limelight like General Cincinnatus who returned to his farm after vanquishing the enemy, rejecting the call of the Romans to be their king. Or better still, General Washington. How some clamored to make him King. One King George to replace another. And now, after patiently waiting for two hundred years, the shades of these long-dead monarchists have their wish.

All thanks to the illumined ones (for this is how the faceless ones prefer to be addressed when you are privileged enough to look them in the eye and order them to kneel and lick you in the crotch). I am sure each of them is grateful too. In fact, this whole long story of the Dominant and the doctor is my thank-you to them as well. Read on and you'll see.

As for poor Cincinnatus, immortalized in the name of an American city few are proud of, I feel it is time to let his shade return to the sweet sleep of oblivion. For the illumined ones bring other Romans to mind. This mind, at least. Like the imperial families of old, they crave, in those cavernous spaces created only when doors are closed, all manner of excess and release — from their powers, because of their powers. I like to think that if my patrons read any history they would be flattered by my comparing them to Caligula or Nero, both feared as much for their political cunning as their cruelty, both ruling longer than one would imagine for a tyrant vicious enough to sleep with his sister or murder his mother. I won't do that, however. I think of the illumined ones as latter-day stand-ins for Heliogabalus, the most decadent and depraved of Rome's emperors, a boy who let others deal with politics so he could have more time to dispense cruelty, and a high priest who, after reading the omens from the innards of a sacrificed child, walked on gold dust to his dinners of camels' heels, peacock tongues, and flamingo brains before he retired for the night with the whores and wives and sons of Rome. Or in the case of our rulers, French cuisine served on plates made from the melted treasures of Ur and Sumer and ancient Babylon set on a table of Lucite in which float fragments of clay tablets telling the Epic of Gilgamesh.

Of course, by shunning the limelight, the illumined ones believe they will avoid Heliogabalus' end: chased screaming through the streets of Rome by his own army and his own people till he was skewered in a public toilet and dragged back through the same streets on the end of a hook.

Perhaps.

They are not our emperor, they insist, merely his throne.

All that matters is that for now they live and they allow me to live.

But why me?

Supply and demand. For power, my dear children who think Kissinger is a heavy metal band, truly is the ultimate aphrodisiac. And Mistress Lysistrata supplies it very well.

In time, the illumined ones gave me to the First Patriot in gratitude for all he has done for them. Just as they gave me to Dr. Bergson. And in gratitude for all they have done to the world in my name as a citizen of the New Rome, I will return Dr. Bergson to them, wrapped in a red ribbon.

i think it's still Sunday. Definitely the perfect day to follow the perfect night. For all i fucking know it may be Monday morning. i want to sleep but i hurt too much. i fell asleep in my Mistress' bathroom after i scrubbed it twice with a toothbrush.

Big Lar is rounding up again. He scrubbed the whole bathroom once with a toothbrush and then he scrubbed the floor a second time where he'd soiled it.

After my Mistress kicked me awake again She made me lick the peanut butter from my bowl like a dog. On all fours and with my tongue. It was chunky. The peanut butter. i couldn't have any water until i was done. She would take the bowl from me otherwise She said. So i tried to chew and swallow what i could. Make loud gumming sounds. She said the noise i was making reminded Her of a certain deceased nonagenarian senator who loved to eat Her out. That means he was in his nineties She said with a laugh. i nodded and lapped at the same time trying not to picture one more old corpse touching Her beautiful body.

The senator's tongue was mauve with age and cigar smoke, but it was as skilled at giving pleasure as it was at telling lies.

my Mistress kicked my dish away when She was tired of hearing me eat. She was angrier than yesterday. She and i both knew She'd had a long night. She told me to crawl over to the water dish and drink then rise and piss. Then She ordered me to take off my socks and shoes. Now that you're buck-naked it's time for you to do some chores She said.

I made Death's best friend crawl doggy-style all the way from his cell to my bedroom. It was an ungodly mess, which is actually an odd choice of words considering how many men with god complexes I had in that room the night before. And now it was time for their lapdog to clean it all up.

i had to take all the sheets and towels and carry them to the laundry room down the hall. Into the washing machine and then into the dryer and fold the towels and remake the bed. And in between i had to pick up all the condoms and lube packets off the floor. my Mistress sent Theo in to get all the toys and take them wherever She keeps them. i ignored him even though he said hello and goodbye by slapping my ass. When i was done making the bed he came back with a mop and bucket from my Mistress. He told me to mop the floor, working my way out of the room, and then take the bucket to the laundry room. Yes sir faggot sir i wanted to say. But i didn't. i just fucking mopped. It seemed like i'd been cleaning Her bedroom for several hours now. When i got to the laundry room, there was another bucket with a can of cleanser and a toothbrush and a note from my Mistress to clean every inch of Her bathroom if i wanted any inch of Her love.

I watched him on the cameras and had a good laugh. Then I forgot about him. Business first. It was several hours after I'd seen him start to clean the bathroom before I could remember to return. I was a bit disappointed. I'd expected much less from him. Even the grout was a shade or two of white just below bleached. But I was ever the professional. I stood in the door and coughed. He nearly wet himself. Then I began. "Not bad for a man. This floor's clean enough to eat shit off," I said. I squatted down in front of Dr. Domestic so he could see and smell my pussy. He was bright red and smiling. He expected me to shit. So I slapped him hard.

You fool She said. You do what you are. You shit. i didn't know what to do. Just squat and go She said in Her softest voice yet. i couldn't balance on anything. i squatted and my legs began to shake. i was a little nervous. But that wasn't really it. It was the position. Normally i would have fallen over or gotten up. But She was watching. i shook. i turned red. i shook some more. And i pushed.

There is nothing more refreshingly odd but reaffirming than watching the mighty abase themselves with the lowly everyday acts that bind all of us to these waterskins. Shit or die, even for the nearly almighty.

Shit he did. And die he will do soon enough.

It was gross. And those nuts fucking killed coming out. And the worst was i liked that my Mistress was watching me. i'm so sick.

I thought it would have steamed or stunk of sulfur. The palette of brown hues was both highlighted and dulled by the brilliance of the white tile. All very artistic. If the shit had been embedded with gilded gummi bears I could have passed off the entire bathroom as a Jeff Koons.

i kept praying my Mistress wouldn't make me eat it.

"I'm so glad to see our mutual friends gave you the blood money I asked for," I said as I pulled a wad of bills out of my bread rack. I waved what was left of the three thousand dollars in his face. "You thought a few of these were for my tip." It was the first time I laughed honestly with my Pillmaking Dumb Boy. "A hundred dollars. I make this by the minute, you dick. And now you've gone and crapped all over my once-pristine bathroom. But there's no toilet paper to wipe up your mess. You're fucked, dude. But wait. What's this? I'm holding 1, 2, 3...17 Benjamins. Perfect. You can clean up your filth with your filthy lucre."

She handed me a hundred dollar bill. i tried to get as much shit up with it as i could. It made a huge mess and got all over my fingers. That was stupid She said. Always overreaching. Well, brainiac, unless you're going to analyze its chemical composition, go flush that down the toilet. And don't you dare clog it or you head's going in after.

Seventeen-hundred dollars later, my bathroom floor looked like a pair of new underwear with one nasty racing stripe.

my Mistress left me with another toothbrush and a bucket of water. i was to clean the floor and then clean myself up in the shower. i don't know how long it took. i just remember soaping my crack for like thirty minutes. And wanting to throw a fucking fit when i turned the shower off and saw that none of the towels i'd washed all day ever made it back into the bathroom. There was nothing to dry myself off with. Not even a piece of toilet paper. Not even a spare hundred to wipe my feet with. So i went and sat on the toilet and waited till i was dry enough not to leave

any wet footprints on the carpet in my Mistress' bedroom. i don't
even want to think what She would have done if i'd been stupid
enough to do that. Minutes — hours — days pass and i think i'm
good enough to make a run for it when i hear the door to Her
bedroom open and close. It's my Mistress and Theo. And then,
from the sound of it, it's Theo in my Mistress. They fucked for
hours. And i fell asleep on the floor waiting for them to stop.
Until Theo came in to piss. He was as surprised as i was. And i
have to give him credit for being the bigger man and not pissing
on me when he so could have. He told me to get back to my room
before our Mistress saw me. And i started to go but once i saw
Her asleep i stopped. All i wanted to do was crawl in bed with
Her, sleep at Her feet even. Anything. Just finally touch Her.

I'd heard my bigger man pissing. Actually, I followed
the thunderous echo of the rumbling water in the bathroom
out of my dreams and back into a somewhat deformed
state of wakefulness. (Men love for the world to hear them
piss; see, everybody, I've got one helluva noisemaker.)
Through my half-closed eye, I watched a shape stand in
the doorway. Backlit in blinding white light like in every
version of an alien abduction. Theo'd let himself go to shit
overnight was all I could think. Then a second shadow
stood behind the first and told it to get out of the room
before I woke up. It went. Who the fuck is that? I was asleep
before I could answer.

my Mistress fucked me. She fucked me to death. She's laughing
as She stands behind me and reads this. Mistress Lysistrata
commands me to keep writing. Okay. Okay. i'm writing. See.
Keep reading. What the fuck did You do to me?!

I have washed him clean in the baptismal font of the
Church of the Free Market. This is not the same as
showering him with gold. That is Old World. Dead world.
This is the New World Order. Deader still. I have pushed
his head under the waters, raging and white with the billion
chits of one day's bids, and waited until the unseen hand

of the Almighty Market decided to let him bottom out or rise, rise, rise.

She made me get on all fours in my pile of straw while She sat in a chair behind me. And She fucked me up the ass with Her shoe while She made me watch the TV.

I thought of sitting on Theo's back. Very de Sade. The family that fucks together...

I love Theo too much to do that.

Instead, I got a chair. A cushion covered in silk. A latex glove. A bottle of lube and strapped on a custom-made eight-inch pump in fuck-me-dead-red latex. It's cheap-looking but the boys love shiny objects. Well, as long as they don't end in a point. Which this did. A well-hidden one on the base of the Lucite heel. There, sealing the heel, was a material made of a newfangled polymer that would dissolve using the heat generated by the body itself to release the blood contained inside. The lube and fucking only increased the friction and sped up the process. What would take several hours happened under one. (Thank the Goddess.)

Amazing what you can get when you fuck the right people.

i saw my company logo and then She turned on the sound. All they could talk about was how the FDA wanted more tests on our new drug and that Narque was pulling out.

Someone had been a busy domme the morning before. I'd called my "friends" at Narque and the FDA. I told them that Bergson was being a good boy, but something told me Bergson might overreach if he got too big, too rich too fast—and these boys trust my gut impressions without question. All it took was two betrayals by men they trusted when I told them not to. When I'm not giving pleasure to the illumined ones, I'm observing how the new potential members do under duress. It's paid the bills for a life teaching could never have afforded me.

Narque said the drug worked now and they would not invest more. Then the usual bullshit about the impact on innocent victims and the American consumer. And then i watched 80% of my worth disappear as the stock price dropped each time it crossed the screen. Everyone must have sold their shares in Proteus in four hours. Except me.

Go bull market!

And all i could fucking do was sit there on my hands and knees like a dog with a shoe up my ass and scream — maybe cry. i don't remember now. But my Mistress was laughing so hard She was coming.

I was laughing at myself, believe it or not. Here I was avenging my years of complicity and I was finding myself aroused. Not by the sight of a nondescript man with an unbelievably tacky shoe fucking his ass. In. Out. In. Out. It looked like I was doing one half of the gas-brake cha cha cha while speeding my way through rush hour in Washington. And not by the falling stock prices of Proteus. Nor the screams and cries and blubbery protestations to a god we all know, deep in our heart of hearts, to be stone-deaf. But by the rush of knowing that by fucking over the illumined ones' golden boy I was plucking the ley lines of real power to near perfection. Like a lyre. Sappho herself would have been proud. I had spent so many months composing my New World Order Symphony and now it was playing out so well I could almost hear the future roar of my intended audience.

I felt my chest flush.

Medusa's Blonde Highlights Revenge Tour had begun.

If only I could turn the illumined ones to stone. I knew I wouldn't topple them. No one person could. A billion might. But I would make them bleed. A stinging paper cut to make the lords of earth yelp.

I was wet with pride. I strummed along on my clit as I tapped my toe on Bergson's quaking ass. And I came so hard it felt like there was thin blue flame burning beneath my skin. To keep from falling out of the chair and letting slip my Trojan shoe before it had delivered my raiding party, I laughed. At myself. At Little and Big Lar. At life. At death. At the Goddess herself.

And then She tells me She's infected me. There was blood in the heel of Her shoe. She gave me AIDS.

Once again, we round up. I infected him with the strain of weaponized HIV he had genetically engineered. It travels by blood or by air. The perfect weapon. It thrives on overkill. In fact, it can survive airborne for four hours. In this case, at the end of my now open-heeled shoe. We sat those long hours together in his cell that I had specially retrofitted for just this moment. I infected us both so that he would die from his handiwork. Or not.

Now, I told him, there truly is a race for the cure.

She fucked me to death. i'm going to die. Why did you do this me?! WHY?!

Death and Broadway have many stages. Up to six months before I met our good doctor, I'd been taking in daily matinees of denial and bargaining like those out-of-towners who went to see *Cats* every time they were in New York. Then there came a moment when I was no longer mourning my brother's death or those of my parents (my years of bargaining with the illumined ones made sure that the latter two were peaceful ones). Now I was welcoming my own.

That moment? When a garrulous client who liked to "confess" under "torture" told me about a weapon of mass destruction that would usher in the illumined ones' greatest dream: The United States of Earth. It was the golden egg laid by a project called Semper Vi. A project masterminded by the brightest of the illumined ones but made science fact by one genius. Dr. Lawrence H. Bergson III.

It was at that moment that St. Cassandra came to me and doused me with water and touched me with the Taser she uses for a magic wand and I saw the light. The high-priced leather-padded blindfold slipped from my face. I was like my benefactress in more ways than name and family tragedy alone. I too was no more than a slave for a royal household, the house that conquered my country. But I wasn't going to die like Cassandra: an afterthought, slaughtered while Clytemnestra was Lizzie Borden-ing ol' king Agamemnon.

And Semper Vi?

Proteus was the front. It worked on curing AIDS—slowly for the paying customers and swiftly for those printing the money. Dr. B., my confessing client told me, had already engineered a mutation in HIV that created a form of the virus that progressed only so far and stopped, consumed with chasing its own tail and killing off any of its viral and more virulent kin. It was in the last six months, however, that Bergson truly earned his keep. He'd broken the virus' genetic code even further. He'd engineered it to surpass itself. Far and beyond what old-fashioned evolution had given us with drug-resistant HIV. He'd created an HIV virus that could exist in the open wilds of oxygen long enough to infect any who came in contact with it.

Weaponized HIV.

And why not weaponized Ebola? What's the point in killing your customers overnight? And who's going to drill the oil for less money than your own people? No, infect your enemy and have the drugs ready. How much money can China cough up? Beats selling them just Coke and cigarettes. And imagine how many petrodollars the Iraqis and Iranians we blew to bits could have pumped out. (The lack of treasure in the sands of Syria doomed them in any war plan.) It would have made the original $25,000-a-year price tag on Fuzeon, the bitters in many an AIDS cocktail nowadays, or the proposed sticker price of $40,000 for a year's worth of Elanovital seem as quaint as the 10¢ hamburger.

As the illumined ones say one unto the other: Render unto Caesar what is Caesar's; render unto God — oh, fuck Her.

(I've said the second half of that prayer myself. Not as an adversary like the illumined ones. But as a lonely child. If there is a big-G Goddess, She has a lot to answer for. Then again, it's hard to look after others when you're being gang-raped by the Father, the Son, and the Holy Ghost for two millennia.)

And as the illumined ones say unto us, their little ones, the children they suffer: Whatever the market will bear.

But airborne, you fret. Won't that spread? Like a plague. Like *the* plague. And it is the mother of all plagues.

Of course there would be a vaccine ready if the process were further along. Any child who knows his AB*X-Files* knows this. The illumined ones would already be inoculated against this death. Perhaps they have been against all deaths. Perhaps this is why they like to be called the illumined ones.

Perhaps.

i am going to die. Even if i can stop the virus. Before the deadline my Mistress has given me. One year from today. All the specifics for synthesizing a vaccine or everything She's recorded will be shown to the world. She says that what CNN and Fox won't air, the Web will. They're going to kill me.

Yes, he will die. I will die. You will die. But now he has the luxury to choose the day of his death before our "betters" do.

My expiration date has long come and gone. It is only a matter of minutes before they will have read here that I've turned.

i did it. my Mistress is so happy She kissed me. i don't want to

*leave Her again. i will be killed now. Whoever i was before, he's
already dead.*

What do you know? Our Dr. Death is a genius after
all. Weaponized HIV has a flaw. A brilliant flaw. It can be
killed by Bergson's latest creation. A souped-up
modification of the earlier version of the virus that attacks
all other strains of HIV. I have renamed it Ouroboros, after
the ancient symbol of the snake swallowing its own tail. A
virus even the illumined ones don't possess.

Better still, it can be synthesized. (Click <u>here</u>.)

*i am simply Mistress Lysistrata's mutinying mutator now. Her
mutinator. Her gene gnome. Her dork lord. These are Her pet
names for me. They mean more to me than the money i've lost.
More than the family i've lost. They're safer without me. If i was
smarter or a better person, i would have driven them away on
purpose. i'm dangerous. Any obsessed fuck with a hardon is. i'm
just on the losing side of obsessed fuckers. But i don't give a shit.
i am Hers. i obey. Always. Even now. That's everything.*

I did not think he would do all that he did. The Mother
moves in mysterious ways. Blessed are the lost ones for
they are everywhere. This is the illumined ones' greatest
fear. It will be their Trojan Horse. Irony, thankfully, is the
mother of all bitch goddesses.

✳

If you are reading this now on a printed page, it means
that the plug has been pulled — on my gadfly Web site
(where I am now posting this and a thoroughly dry but
detailed description of how to synthesize Dr. Bergson's
Ouroboros strain of HIV to combat weaponized HIV), my
company, my staff, Dr. Bergson, and myself. We are, I am
no longer of service to the illumined ones.

Don't cry. Death was less painful than life. Thank
heaven for little pills.

And irony of ironies, new school *samizdat* gives way to old. Cache and burn, baby. Bytes and bits into wood pulp, smashed and stretched and smoothed. Cyber-smoke signals congealed into ink. In the beginning as in the end was The Word.

Now you know a secret; pass it on.

For, if history — even the one penned by the victors — teaches us anything, it is this: The dead have the last hollow laugh.

I, Kassandra Angelaki, have never served any man. Ever.

They have served me.

I serve at the pleasure of the Goddess.

Through a Glory Hole Darkly

for David Howley

*I'*m in the dark with a hundred dicks. Outside, it's another January night of sideways-flying rain in San Francisco. Inside, everything smells like mold and sweaty crotches. And now the power's out. Gone in the snap of a cable. It was only a second ago. Maybe a minute. I have no sense of time at night in a room without windows — and now no light, thanks to another fucking tirade from that very cruel (and far from Christlike) child, El Niño. I hate children.

Did I mention I'm on my knees in a freestanding dressing room from a department store your mother, or your grandmother more likely, may have visited as a little girl? There's a flimsy curtain and three walls riddled with elongated holes big enough to fit a dick or two or three through.

Yes, I'm in Blow Buddies on my knees in a blackout.

Heaven, you say. It would be if these queens would stop shouting and hooting to welcome the darkness and drown out the jarring silence now that the bump-and-grind bass, the collective musical heartbeat of this hive of cocksuckers, has been stilled. A voice yells out. From the management. Probably the hot guy without a shirt — shaved head, lean, all sinew and a well-worn sneer — who takes yours after you pull it over your head or unbutton it under his unblinking stare and stands back to take all of you in before he stuffs your shirt and his opinion of you in an sandwich bag suffering from gigantism. Stay and play, boys, or go into the good night, the voice says. A fast-deflating roar of manly tittering answers. Little watery circles of light bounce from ceiling to floor nearby. Feet begin to shuffle. Following the wavering balls. Following the call of their own balls. Navigating by the light of the undimmed word EXIT somewhere not far beyond me and this booth. I hear the door open and close. People coming in from the porch most likely. All I can think is: Shut that fucking door! The heat generated by machine and men won't last more than an hour.

I have one hour to get off before going out and getting hosed down by Mother Nature's brat.

I shift on my knees. I've never had much reason before to pay attention to how hard and cold the lopsided concrete of this floor really is. An hour might have been too generous. Hell, how did I ever manage to crawl all those months as a baby? I sigh and startle myself. Usually the music, the heat, the testosterone is too loud to even hear myself think. I reach out for the glory hole. I know it has to still be in front of me. I grip the bottom of the sanded wood, smooth from the fluids of thousands of dicks and mouths. Do I use this handhold to stand and walk out into the corridor and hope to bump into something large and hard? Or do I stay and wait out the return of the power, of my lust?

Alone with my thoughts, I don't realize I've fallen back on my nervous habit of drumming my fingers. Thank god the absence of light and the draining of heat has aroused the last-gasp survival instincts of the reptilian layer of my brain.

I am tapping out a code older than Morse, than drums or smoke signals even.

A jolting brush of warm both-smooth-and-coarse denim against my fingers answers.

My fingers stop. I stop. I am only my heart, furiously pumping blood on the command of nerves soaked in adrenaline. Who is this man? Tall, short, fat, thin, old, young, white, black, hairy, smooth—who knew my eyes were so either/or? is that the worldview of a true predator?—ugly, hot...? The only thing I'm certain of is: His crotch is the last source of heat in the growing quiet and cool of this room. That and the burning awareness that my dick has drunk more than its fair share of my fuck-or-flee blood.

Through a Glory Hole Darkly

I have been beneath, above, inside, beside hundreds of men. I can't remember the name of but a dozen. I do remember, however, each and every one's dick. I'm a face queen, of sorts. (Granted, my favorite way to take a "head shot" is from my knees.) This man has no head I can see. He and his sex will be the first to be truly anonymous. I have never wanted any man more. For he is just that: man.

I lift my hand from the wood and press my knuckles into the tight, giving, warm (except for the cold of the metal buttons), shuddering swell of his dick as it wraps itself around his balls like a snake, bloated on the fat of its recent kill, coiled around its precious, sleeping, unhatched young. A potent, cautionary, endearing, and odd image. My ancient brain remembers the first swamps, the first forests.

His fingers brush against the skin of my hand that is gently kneading his still-rising dick. We both hiss. I reach back, up, out and grab for his fingers. They are thick and long. The ends of them, for the seconds they are still, are blunt. Rough at the nails. I imagine the hands of a mechanic or a sculptor. Or the faux marines, the faux jocks, the faux straight boys who overpopulate porn. Their hands are often square. (How better to make a fist?) But the skin around his knuckles and on the back of his hand is like hide. Thick. Almost muscular. Each pore feels like an indentation in water-smoothed pumice. It has been tanned by time. This man is their father.

Together our hands wrestle to unbutton his jeans. Together we free what I would never have used such a cliché (and worse, quaint) word to describe until this very moment and only in this very moment: his manhood. In the dark, it is just that. How else will I truly know him tonight? How else — where else — will we touch? How else will I remember him except from handling this literal extension of himself? Swallowing it and taking inside, taking away, whatever bittersweet gift I coax out of him until he can do nothing but give it to me freely.

I touch his manhood and I smell his manhood in the same second. A faint sting grows wildly like a chemical burn. My fingers singe and pulse. There is the electrifying odor of flesh reeking with life, like it has been buttered in musk. My nostrils flare; I quiver. I inhale and give thanks. I exhale and shout out an amen. To the uninitiated it would sound only like a deep, grunting sigh. To those men within earshot, still crouching, still circling, it is a call to worship. It is the hymn of the rejoicing sex pig.

My dick strains to testify. As I wrap my hand tightly around his lengthening cock I am aware oddly of just my own. It's not the hyper-awareness I knew almost nightly as a teen masturbating in the dark under the covers, afraid of being given away to the guard(ian)s passing outside my door by the spastic sound-and-light show of a flashlight and bedsprings. Each stroke surreal. My brain jumping from my whining balls (I swear I could hear them whistling like a teakettle before I came or perhaps that was only the beginning of my tinnitus) to my wheezing breath and then back and then off again, now to the light beneath the door or to the growing footfalls that never reach the top of the stairs.

No, this is simply awareness. I am only my dick as I happily drag my fist up and down his shaft. As I take my other hand and fumble with my own buttons. As I hold his and mine and compare and contrast and confirm. Smooth skin where the hairs have given way before it rolls over a vein and then roughens as it slackens — I am crossing the great divide of my circumcision scar — only to balloon at the head of a raging hard-on.

I press my slowly opening lips against that head. I am so drunk on testosterone I cannot tell at first if it is my head or his head I am dragging my tongue across. All the once-reptilian predator perceives with the thimbleful of blood spared for the higher-evolved subdivisions of the brain shared with the born-again sex-pig penitent is that there is a mouth and a dick — head-on-head action — nothing else. Mouth swells to take head in and I come to: rutting about in his fragrant tangle of stiff hairs. My throat constricts with slow pleasure again and again around the dripping tip of his dick.

I hear him gasp for the both of us.

My mouth and hand now compete to see whether a warm and wet or a hard and hot grip gives the greatest pleasure. The hand around my dick keeps time to each push and each pull above. When his hands dig the rough, square ends of their long fingers into my head, sealing his dick deep in my happily aching mouth, I know we have a winner.

Instead of taking a victory lap and then a final sprint to the finish line with some good old-fashioned all-the-way-out-and-then-all-the-way-in facefucking, he surprises me. He pushes his dick further. Until I'm breathing through his skin. Until he triggers my gag reflex, something I thought I'd lost hundreds of dicks ago, as vestigial as a whale's foot, and I choke. He rocks in place. Just a bit of back and forth. Side to side. I'm tearing. I'm sputtering. I'm drooling. He needs me to let him know that he has the dick of death before he batters the point home. I am happy to oblige. Let the wheel of fortune spin. Let the predator become prey. I am simply where I want to be. Happy in my station. Happy in this moment. Happy.

He pulls away. I pull him back. He gives in and I give way. In fewer and fewer flashes of coherence, I remember I have a dick and have never stopped pumping it with my fist, slick with pre-cum. But awareness of something greater causes these images, these sensations to fade. I am no longer my dick. Or his dick. I am a new sexual organ that is the marriage of his dick and my mouth. The rest of our bodies are the expectant wedding party, ready to celebrate the consummation of this most holy union — the instant when we will shout from deep within: I do.

He does first.

My mouth fills with hot salt water. I swallow and suck. My mouth fills again. It is a brief but welcome tide. I moan and moan and moan but my hymn to the waters of life sounds like the hum of a mouth filled with cock and cum. My mouth vibrates. I vibrate. Until I shoot. I howl my vows to love, honor, and cherish around the still-stiff dick. It sounds like a stream of grunts. It ends only when I have nothing left to spill from either head.

*

How quickly everything grows cold without the compressed light we call heat. His cum and dick. My dick. My knees. My desire. He falls from my mouth and runs his hands over my lips. I hear him buttoning up as he walks away. Now there is only me and the dark. I must leave while I am content. The power's still out. It won't come on until sometime after I have fallen asleep in my clothes atop my nest of sheets and blankets, dreaming of what this man looks like.

Love in the Time of Cold Cuts

for Patsy Halt

*M*idway into the second run-through of her twenty-ninth year and sixty-one days into her Gwyneth-inspired macrobiotic diet, Calliope awoke naked in the deli of the Pavilions on Santa Monica to the magical sound of clapping.

Now our Calliope was not just any muse, mind you. She was the future muse of masturbation for horny boys and men and more women than would care to admit and even the most militant vegetarians in love with their own reddening meat. She was Calliope Tabrasa.

When interviewers would ask, their face a paint-by-numbers portrait of puzzlement, why Calliope Tabrasa — in other, unspoken words, why such the odd first name, such the ethnic last name — she'd reply, the expletive added later as her temper and her infamy grew, "Four fucking words: My parents were hippies." No one ever got a word more out of her. Her parents filled many a tape. But no one really wanted to know why she was named Calliope Tabrasa. They wanted to know why Calliope Tabrasa had done what she'd done to become *the* Calliope Tabrasa.

I will tell you.

It began because he tasted like sausage. Pepperoni, to be more exact. To be as specific as possible: his cum had an aftertaste of pepperoni. Even after binging on a mixed handful of Tic-Tacs and Altoids (they'd collided in the particle accelerator of her purse) immediately after the audition, even after brushing her teeth once she'd reached her apartment, even after brushing them again before bed hours later, she could still taste it. Now she could even smell it. And the burning cheese and the baking bread. She fell asleep dreaming of pizza glowing in the mouth of a fiery furnace.

Ian Philips

This was the eve of her big break in L.A. Tomorrow she would read for the producers. And she was ready to wow them, even if there was a woman in the lot, just as she had the director, a certain Mr. Call Me Taz, Baby, Because I'm A Devil.

Getting this part would be the sweet salve for two solid years of stinging and scarring rejection.

First, she'd lost the role she'd wanted since she first heard whisperings of it while schlepping her way from Off-Off-Broadway to Off-Broadway. It was a lead in the musical based on *The Vagina Monologues* called *Vagina Cantata*. She'd been called back three times before some L.A. bimbette who could read a TelePrompTer and look good while holding any manner of artillery expressed an interest. Special Forces Barbie wanted to spread her wings or so Calliope had heard from a former roommate who'd made the cut. And Calliope could easily imagine those wings plucked and shaved, flapping around the small, hairy dick of the producer.

When she lifted herself off the bathroom floor the morning after she lost the part and while she sat on her hungover knees, watching last night's spewed fury swirl away, she decided the only way to take Broadway was to take El Lay first.

Instead, the City of Angels, that ever-metastasizing concrete gin blossom of on-ramps and off-ramps built over prehistoric tar pits, deflowered her. The seduction was slow; the seizure swift. After one month of auditions and call-backs and two months of read-throughs and rehearsals, her strut upon the stage as Vladimir in a Valley Girl-themed production of *Waiting for Godot* at the Mark Taper Forum ran only a week. Just long enough for the reviewers to yip and bark and tear into her like a pack of coyotes with a kitten.

It seemed that the closest she would get to Hollywood after that would be to crawl atop one of the letters wedged in the dry dirt of those infamous hills and leap to her death. But Calliope valiantly pulled herself once more from the bathroom floor and flushed. She marched through the Valley of Head Shots and Hand Jobs. She walked on here and she stood uncredited in a crowd there. She was anonymous again, but she had her SAG card.

Through it all, she smiled and nodded as men with rampant nose and knuckle hair, with bad rugs and improperly applied concealer, or men with shoe-polish-black or warm-butter-yellow hair and skin as honeyed and taut as a suckling pig on a spit, or the occasional skeletal harpy of undeterminable age and origin told her to dye this, augment that, drop the last name (too Latin, said some; too Slavic said others) and, if she ever wanted the camera to linger a little longer on her exquisite corpse than it had as Dead Cheerleader #7 in *Terminal Slayage*, lose some weight.

Fast.

She smiled and nodded till her cheeks throbbed and her neck burned. She smiled and nodded till she grew sick of being anonymous in a land where everyone acts as if somewhere a camera is watching.

So Calliope took out her credit card. She took herself to the salons of beauty, tanning, and cosmetic dentistry. She took herself to Tae-Bo. She took off the weight. And from the ashes of a 5'6" 120-pound brunette there arose a 5'6" 98-pound blonde with a dazzling grimace she flashed to the next dozen casting directors and producers who promised her instant fame if only she could loose just a few inches — from her frame now, not her waist. Hollywood, it turned out, was more than a dream factory. It was the last magical refuge of the dwarf king.

A third time she pried herself from the cold tile's embrace and flushed her pride away. She vowed to undergo one more round of calls before fleeing back to the sanctity, the sanity of Off-Off-Broadway.

And so, that very next morning she'd entered Taz's office for a private read-through in a tasteful pair of flats. A few pages in and she took off a few more inches as she dropped to her knees and took up fewer inches still.

That very night, as she drifted off to sleep, she chanted the same line out loud while she counted pepperoni slices leaping a breadstick fence: *Tomorrow my luck will change.*

Tomorrow she would land the role she'd been promised today. A recurring role on the runaway teen hit, *Passionville.* Calliope was to be Charity Riordan, the childhood friend of the lead "teen" (over pillow talk under Taz's desk, she'd learned the lead was two years older than Calliope) ingenue, Morgan Lane. Charity was to come spend the final week of summer with Morgan and her tight-knit, crisis-prone family. In a series of jump cuts between Morgan braiding Charity's hair before bed and soft-focus flashbacks, the viewers would discover that Charity was also the free-spirited daughter of a widowed pastor and had fallen in love with a bad boy with a heart of gold, Camden Crowley, the son of the leader of the notorious biker gang that ran drugs in the hills outside Passionville. Charity's father, Pastor Mike, had recently brought the troubled youth to the Lord, and the boy had nearly died a fiery death after torching his own father's meth lab. Camden had said no to drugs, and now his father, Waco, was hell-bent on saying no to Camden's life. Meanwhile, Camden had been torn between fleeing with Charity on his bike for La Cañada or standing his ground against Waco. Either way, Camden wanted to marry Charity. But Charity was bound for an Ivy League school. On an athletic scholarship. She was a basketball or a tennis or an equestrian ace.

As he zipped up, Taz, now the director in Calliope's unfolding drama as well, confided the fucking writers were still screwing around on some of the "minor" details. Regardless, Charity was coming to Passionville. And Charity would be, could only be (!) played by no one else but her. Calliope Tabrasa. The bad Valley girl—Taz had seen *Waiting for Godot* he revealed while buckling his belt— with the mouth of gold.

Tomorrow…

"Is that TV's Charity?" a well-trained voice without a

that had taken a whack to the side of its console.

"Cold," David Michael said.

"Yes, it is," she answered to the empty deli behind the softly humming counter.

"Colder," the disembodied voice replied.

She peered over the counter. No one. Nothing. She turned around and the same was behind her. No one. Nothing but empty aisles of stocked shelves quietly listening to a Muzak rendition of Led Zeppelin's "Whole Lotta Love."

"Ice-cold."

"David, where are you?" she asked with a sharp edge of agitation, honed by the imagined late — or probably now very early — hour, the cold air on her naked skin, and the increasingly irritating voice coming from nowhere.

"Down here."

She turned back around and looked through the counter's glass front. Piles of cold cuts, like oversized poker chips of flesh, stared placidly back at her.

"Warmer."

"Warmer?!" she shouted. "Where the fuck are you?!" she hissed as she looked behind the cold cuts.

"Red-hot!" the voice croaked, no longer sounding like a Hollywood heartthrob but a frog with gas.

Inside the case before her, ramrod straight, stood a sausage. It was thin, long, and very red. And it winked at her. *Actually*, she thought, *it didn't really wink at me because it doesn't have any eyes.*

Well, no wide white irises with a pupil of any possible color. Like on a person or even a cartoon. The sausage looked instead like Freddie The Flute on *H.R. Pufnstuf.* Except this was a real-live stuffed skin flute.

"You're not David Michael Jacobs," was all Calliope could say when she finally got the satellite feed from her brain synced up with her mouth.

"No," answered the tiny talking mask carved into a sausage. "He's a dick batting for the other team. I'm the meat stick of your dreams, babe."

"My dreams?" she hooted. "Hardly."

"For an actress, you don't lie very well."

"What?! Fuck you!!! You're the one dildo I don't have to listen to in this town."

"Dildo," he cackled. "Kinky. I like that. But what a waste of my seasoned talents. And we both know that's not what *you* want."

"What I want is to wake up."

"Like hell, babe. You wanna piece of me bad."

"Salami isn't on my diet."

"Salami. I'm insulted. I'm pepperoni."

Calliope heard her breath catch in her throat.

"Yeah, honey, that's a sound I like to hear a woman make."

"You're such a fucking pig."

"Actually, no. Technically I'm soy. I'm vegan pepperoni."

"Vegan pepperoni. I've never heard of such a fucking thing."

"Hooray for Hollywood, eh, babe?!"

Calliope felt flushed and hungry and so confused.

"Let me handle this, doll," a new voice said.

"Elizabeth? Is that you?" Calliope turned around waiting to see the body that went with her agent's raspy voice.

"No, hon, just using a voice you'd recognize. Down here."

Calliope looked down at her feet and the surrounding patchwork of linoleum tile.

"No, hon, up a bit. Read my lips. Up here. That's my girl!"

"Omigod!" Calliope shrieked as she realized her vagina was talking to her.

"That's goddess, doll. But you can call me Betty."

Calliope nearly fell against the curved glass of the case until the image of her tits stuck to the cold clear surface like a tongue on a frozen pipe pushed her back onto her fallen arches.

"What's happening to me?" she wailed.

"We're going off your diet, darlin'," Betty laughed. "One more sleepless night listening to beans and bok choy rumbling overhead and I was ready to pack my lips and leave. Bring it on, you wannabe sausage!"

"Please don't stick me in the pussy patch!" chided the pepperoni. "Not that. Anything but that!"

"Fuck that, pizza face," Betty hollered. "I'm not horny. I'm hungry. What goes in ain't coming out!"

"What are you going to do? Gum me to death?" The pepperoni ribbitted with laughter.

"Just watch me, hot rod." Betty let out a small *pssst* and whispered, "Hey, doll, brace yourself. I'm taking the girls out for a night on the town."

"You're doing what?" Calliope whispered back.

"I'm baring my teeth, our teeth, sweetie. Don't sweat it. It won't hurt you a bit. But it's gonna kill that overgrown hot dog!"

"Teeth," Calliope shouted.

"Teeth," the pepperoni screamed.

"Let 'er rip, girls," Betty howled.

After everything Calliope had heard about teething from her two sisters with their six children, she expected a terrible white-hot searing as her flesh was torn open. Instead, it felt like she was growing one hard clit and then another around her labia. They were dazzlingly white and fang-shaped and just as sharp. She shuddered as she felt each new one appear.

"Hold your hand out, hon."

"What?" Calliope muttered, happily distracted.

"Just hold your hand out and you'll see."

She did and wrapped her fingers around the chilled slab of imitation meat.

"I look bigger up close, huh?" the pepperoni rumbled like a purring frog. "I'm the real deal. A foot-long."

"You'll be less than average in a minute, soysicle!" Betty growled. "Now cover his mouth with your thumb and bring him to Mama. Wait, wait. Get him warmer with a bit of foreplay."

Calliope pushed the tip of the long pepperoni against Betty's slick and swollen lips. She nearly dropped it as she reeled from the sudden wave that jangled out from deep within her vagina to the ends of all her nerves. The pepperoni, though muffled by Calliope's thumb, shrieked in time with her body's pulsing. She swore she could taste it. The more she rubbed the more distinct the tangy burn of pepper grew. Round and round until she was salivating and Betty, always the freer spirit, was drooling.

"Now," her cunt and its teeth clacked. "Feed me now!"

Calliope shoved the still-chilled tip into Betty's mouth. Betty bit down and Calliope swayed, almost toppled, as the teeth dug into the hard, cold meat. From under her thumb, she could hear the muted, hysterical cries of the pepperoni. The contradicting sensations of the small icy bit of sausage thawing in her warm juices and the confusing, alternating pangs of guilt and omnipotence as the tipless pepperoni sobbed, "I'm melting...melting," against the unique but indifferent whorls of her un-opposable digit thrilled her. The pepperoni's rigid bravado was gone. It softened as it pleaded for its life. It was moist from its own molecular transformation from cold slab to hot link. It lubed itself as it slid in her palm, frantic to get away from her voracious maw.

Through the smacking of her lips and the grinding of her teeth, Betty groaned her one-word command, "More." Calliope fed it to her with relish. As much as Betty could tear off, could cram into her mouth, sloshing, overflowing, with half-chewed chunks of shrieking pseudo-beef and her own spicily scented saliva. With each new chew, Calliope came. She sang — vowels, mostly *os* — as her vagina smacked and hummed and burped and gnashed and swallowed until there was not even a fleck of processed peppercorn left.

The security video would only show Calliope from behind, waving a small dark object and then inserting it between her legs, while the first Pavilions' employee on the scene stood by motionless. Mortified, mesmerized. Minute after minute. Facing Calliope, facing the camera. Eventually, it would be learned that his name was Gregg and he was the reigning All-American hottie at the Pavilions on Santa Monica. Highlights and muscles and a caramel-colored tan made the old-fashioned California way: while hanging ten. (Out of the waves, he hung eight.) A wet dream from the loading dock to checkout. And one of the few heterosexuals. Which isn't relevant to his hotness but is to the queer twist in Calliope's story once the rest of the chorus had taken their places around the leading lady.

First two more boys approached the naked woman talking to a sausage between her legs. One whispered to the other and they cracked up. Neither snapped Calliope or Gregg out of their reveries. The two called the rest of night shift to come and see the fresh tuna steak grilling some sausage in her barbie. And running they came — some nearly sliding into the others as they skidded to a halt. Not because our Calliope was naked. No, because Gregg had unzipped his pants and was stroking his own meat. And when Calliope bucked and shimmied like she was riding some wild and unseen runaway beast, Gregg jerked faster and faster. And as Gregg watched Calliope, the others watched Gregg. And one by one, the trousers dropped and the deli became a smokehouse for all manner of meats.

As for the clapping that awoke Calliope, it did happen. She did awaken naked in the deli of the Pavilions on Santa Monica to the magical sound of clapping. But, truth be told, it was probably for Gregg. His was the shot seen round the world. But you had to look very hard through the grainy gray dots to see his smaller gloopy white dots.

Yes, dots. For every minute, from the moment Calliope strode into view at 3:59 a.m. until the moment the cops — called due to policy and not outrage once the security company's monitor had zipped up at 4:43 a.m. — escorted her offstage at 4:49 a.m. to charge her with shoplifting one stick of Mama Soya's Veggeroni, was caught on camera. The charges were dropped at 10:02 a.m. after several cavity searches had failed to retrieve the missing meatless meat. And while the story of the odd arrest of a struggling actress down on her luck and a possible pepperoni sausage topped that day's 5 o'clock news, the security video had been copied and re-mastered five hours earlier. It was streaming on websites worldwide by 12:01 p.m. and had become an Internet classic, crashing server after server, by 12:59 p.m. Before the 6 o'clock news, prurientgaze.com had logged its millionth hit and Betty had called with her first offer. Betty the Agent that is, not Betty the Beaver as Calliope's cunt was hailed once subtitles and transcripts of Calliope's dialogue were added. By day's end, Gregg was doing gay-for-pay in a video called *Double Bagging* and Calliope was signed to a recurring role on Showtime's *Queer as Folk*.

Calliope played Candace the Fag Hag and Our Lady of the Raging Strap-on. She bedded nearly half the cast on and off-screen. Showtime wasted no time to splurge for a billboard near the Pavilions on Santa Monica that was rumored to have made Angelyne's well-sculpted face fall. The fags of West Hollywood — as best they could, the dears — ate it up. Then Showtime ran a faux product endorsement ad in countless print and television markets. It was Calliope, nearly naked, sculpted and stylized and brushed to perfection, with the very same brand of vegan pepperoni in one hand. Beside her in bold black print: *Got Beef? Get Better.* Beneath her, Showtime's logo and the airtime for *Queer as Folk*. She was booked for the cover of *People*, *Entertainment Weekly*, *Vanity Fair*, *Vegetarian Times*, *The Advocate*, and *Maxim* after the first day the ads appeared.

Before too long (and before one of her new cast mates could kill her for upstaging them), she left. The dream offer had arrived. The one role we were born to play.

And when Calliope and I strode out for the curtain call after the first performance of our year-long sold-out run in *Vagina Cantata*, it was New York finally, after fucking us over so roughly once upon a time, that got down on its knees, as L.A. had the year before, and ate us out.

Turnabout is such fair play.

And nothing leaves you feeling fuller than a Broadway gang-bang of an ovation eight times a week.

Well, after DPP. Double pepperoni penetration. Now that'll really get *this* vagina to sing.

Heterodoxy

for Mattilda

A cock is a cock is a cock. Poor Gertrude Stein. When she wrote a rose is a rose is a rose, she was just trying to shake up the word "rose." Give it a shot. Of speed. Or morphine. Help it get up or get off. A mercy resurrection or killing. It was a supersickfuck then. Several hundred years of being compared over and over to a small grocery list of the usual suspects written in cramped broken handwriting: a heart, a vagina, a virgin, a crone, love. Well, except for the one time Arthur Rimbaud and Paul Verlaine compared it to an asshole. But other than that, that's it. She tried, but it's dead now. A rose isn't even a rose today. And Gertrude Stein. Who's that? When she's remembered, if she's remembered at all, she's that scowling woman in a Picasso painting who lived with Alice B. Toklas, the mother makerbaker of all pot brownies, or she's the big butch with the Caesar haircut in a blockish dress and an ill-fitting fur-trimmed jacket stretched across her linebacker shoulders and sensible (i.e., ugly) shoes at the end of two ankleless legs, or for the two or three artsy-fartsy women's studies majors trying to lay the other women's studies majors who dig the classics (like Sappho or frottage or Gretrude Stein) she's the forever experimental author who no one reads still and who wrote about roses and Oakland. Oakland is a place where there is no there there is a place where there is no there there is a place where there is no there there. Really, as clever and as cagey as she was (and she had to be to get all those egos like Picasso and Hemingway and herself in one room for her salons or to survive as an American Jew in Nazi-occupied France), she was only talking about a childhood home that had been torn down and not our after-the-money's-all-gone days down on dour Jerry Brown's dharma farm. And to make matters worse, here I come wanting to write a cock is a cock is a cock so Gertrude must be spinning counterclockwise in her grave or urn or in that limbo realm where all the experimental authors are banished to float among the commas and semicolons and periods they never used in their own writing. Sorry, Miss Furr, or were you Miss Skeene? Either way, I truly am sorry, but I'm a queer writer and so many of us take our first printed steps mangling your words or Oscar's or Audre's or Walt's or William's, Burroughs, that is — though Shakespeare's sonnets will do quite nicely, too. And a cock really is a cock is a cock. So why then is it a gift from god when a bent cock is made straight? Why is my mouth or my asshole transformed into the holy of holies when it is the dick of a true-blue-honest-to-god man's man that dwelleth within? Why isn't the most wanton cocksucker the alpha and the omega of a man's man? Instead, alpha and omega are parceled off. It is those who give and do not receive who lead the pack. I am sucked off, therefore I am man. And we who suck, and damn well, thank you, shuffle awkwardly behind on our knees. *O* is for omega, and outcast. Bottom dog. Just plain bottom. But methinks, the lord doth protest too much. His loss. Not mine. And yes, I'm aware of the power dynamics. Both old school — power trickles down from on high to all god's chosen representatives and races and sexes and classes on earth and they can oversee the plantation for him — and the French-New-Wave-queer-theory-is-*très*-chic school — Foucault teaches us that power is not holed up in the shiny Fort Knox on the hill, oh, no no, cherie, it's pulled here and there like hardened strings of taffy, from you to me, from object to the interpretation of said object (I object! You object!), until all's a giant sling, which you can call god or capitalism or hellacious hegemony or patriarchy or *pax Americana* and on which those who know how to pluck the strings can fistfuck the rest of us. See. See? I'm ever so aware about power dynamics, Mr. Scowling Leftist Academic, #33 on Lynne Cheney's hit list. And you too, Ms Minority Hyphen American Who's Always Seen as

Ian Philips

Minority, or worse Hyphen, and never American except for the sweeps weeks on TV in May and before the elections in November. The boot may not be on my neck but I'm close enough to smell the leather. And furthermore, I understand why the spin on straight cock by straight men. Gotta keep stroking the built-in billy club—anyone up for a game of whack a hole?—or be shuffled off to the harem with the eunuchs, and worse, the women. And yes, I know why my cocksucking brethren aren't really my brethren at all. We can't even call ourselves by one name, be it queer, be it homosexual, be it cockcrazed, without brawling or bawling. The self-anointed betters among us unnamed ones, we sexual others, are always scrambling up, over, and away from those of us who flagrantly, wantonly, gaily misuse our billy clubs in the hopes they'll get a bigger bite of the penis power pie. Last call for white privilege! The escape pods to the multinational mothership in the sky are about to launch! The oppressed do such an impressive dumb show based on the oppressor's antics. It's nearly lifelike, save for the power to pull it off for audiences everywhere. That takes an empire, an army of billy clubs and their big and tall and pointing righteously heavenward brothers packed with uranium. So this quibbling rant, this quavering cant of mine is about something less fun to stroke, less tangible than power. Less tangible but oh-so-visible. It's a nonrhetorical rhetorical question that goes: Why is a straight cock still morally, philosophically, aesthetically more pleasing to the eye that connects to the mouthdickasshole of the beholder? Okay, forget morally and philosophically—the boys with the billy clubs run those outfits too. Which leaves the arts. Not the state-sponsored ones, i.e., commercials and the bits of TV and film and music wedged between them. The real arts. Like you and me now. We may be on the outer rim of power, but we can still make a hell of a din out here. Act up. Act out. And sound waves, the few free-range ones left, will warble the good word out to the untouchables in the shadows beyond us and to untouchables blazing in the bright light within a very white house. Slowly, mind you. And you must be willing to hear the still small voice before it is drowned in the roar of the jam-all-the-frequencies clear-all-the-channels multimedia whirlwind. But back to this shrill small voice. My voice. Why do we queer and/or gay and/or single-gender loving men-identified men keep the spin on straight cock revolving? You thinks this laddie doth protest too much? I write erotica. You may find that a surprise, after following me so far into this thicket. But I do. Say I strategically inserted a very graphic and purportedly true account of how I seduced, bagged, scored — touchdown! — the straight cock of (your straightest arrow goes here). Say I wrote in truncated, hypermasculine barks about how I came to my drug dealer's apartment/house/crib and found him alone. No posse. No pussy. Nada. Just him and me and a television yelling at itself — and my drugs. And I itemized his body parts for you as I made them out in the watery blue light of the TV. I turn him into a discount warehouse overrun by gangs — everything is in bulk and tagged with tattoos. And I don't quite have all the money I need for my drugs so I bend over and let him work out a payment plan. Layaway never felt so fair. Or I can pay and I kneel before him to take my injection. Or better still, I'm pissing c-notes and I buy me a piece of the rock. Not your cliché? Then howsabout I'm at a party. We're in a frat/a dorm/a squat/a loft and everyone's drunk on Everclear or microbrewed beer or wine coolers or Cristall and there he is. A temporarily clothed centerfold from Abercrombie & Fitch. Let's give him a name, like Ashton Kutcher. I've got Dan Savage's attention now. And he's not the only faggot. There's Ashton sprawled out on the couch, his neck all that's keeping his head from falling behind it. I can't tell if his eyes are completely closed or just almost — you know, where you can see the whites squirming between the nearly clenched lids. And his girlfriend, not Brittany, they broke up, someone else, someone after or before or wholly fictitious, like Demi Moore, is passed out across him or beside him or under a friend. And I crawl/stagger/fly to him as the others drift closer to tomorrow morning's hangover. I push "The Girlfriend" off and unbuckle the belt or just pop the top button of his pants if there's no belt with my woozyboozyfloozywoeisme hands and pull the rest apart or off with my teeth and... Stop me when this cliché gets too hot. Okay, I'll admit they do have their heat. As corny and classist and as racist and risqué as they are. We're all voyeurs — well, hell, I am. It's not the observing or fantasizing I have a problem with. It's that it's so damn hot to so many of the Lost Boys of Never Never Land because he's straight. Why? Because he's the ol' forbidden fruit. But isn't that me? You? And if I wrote either of my stick-figure couples all the way to their big bang, till they were rubbing together like the ends of leafless branches in a storm, would you forgive me all the dick-wilting asides about Gertrude Stein and leatherless powerplay? You might. More importantly, once some market-savvy editors had liposuctioned off the front and the end of this piece, I could get it accepted into one of those best-selling gay anthologies with names like *Straight Shooters* or *Hired Straights* or *Straight to Heaven/Hell/Bed* about sex with guess who, Joe Hetero. And don't even get me started on gay video porn where its highest and hardest stars are openly and fly-your-pride-flag-high gay-for-pay. If you have to be paid to be gay that must mean you're — anything but gay. Which leads robin round again to his question: Why is Joe Hetero's cock better? Even if you're just playacting, your dick is still more prized than that of a flaming sodomite. Or the dread nelly queen. Or the further dreaded fat nelly queen. No, I'm not talking bears. That's masculinity without all the trappings. Or so the *Bear Magazine* slogan went. No, I'm talking about me. A fat nelly queen. But on beyond me is the furthermost dreaded fat old nelly queen. A troll with a personality. Actually, trolls, come to think of it, when they're all glum and goggle-eyed are pretty straight-acting. Put them on a riding lawnmower or in a pew in a polyester suit and could you tell the difference? Is there a difference? How about when you're looking at dick through a hole in the wall? A cock is a cock is a cock? Other than sperm that's more likely to swim its way to an egg, which may give way someday to another mouth in this consume-or-be-consumed world, what else comes out of a straight guy's cock? And if someone is straight-acting, will you be able to taste the lie as he fucks your face or a other hole by any other name? Just a spoonful of assimilation makes the cum slide down in the most delightful way. Is gay shame what drives him or is that only after he's found out? So what's the treat of sucking a straight dick as opposed to a gay dick? I won't even dare to ask about the difference between a gay versus a bisexual versus a transgender versus a queer versus a just plain other dick. Not till I get a straight answer on why straight cock is the blue-chip-worth-the-blue-balls stock on the men-on-men sexual commodities exchange. So tell me: Why must the cock of the walk be straight? Why the notch in the kneepads? Does it shoot manna? Manhood? Milk and honey? The password to the promised land? A Get-Out-of-Gender-Bender-Jail-Free Card? Beer? What? And don't start in about Shiva's lingam. I know there's godhead and there's good head but straight head ain't a guarantee for either. Deities are off-limits. I'm just asking about us groundlings. Pick a mortal, any mortal. Prick us, do we not come? All right not always and not always on cue. But it's more or less the same apparatus on every man (a pony keg for sperm with an easily excitable pump) with more or less the same ups and downs in its sexual response cycle (pointclickandshoot). Perhaps if I'd sucked a straight dick willingly — i.e., other than my father's — I'd feel differently. Aha, you say. There's the rub. Indeed. And whaddyaknow, I am more willfully naïve than I'd like to admit. But I bet you figured that out long before I did. Looks like no one escapes the boot of power dynamics. I am as repulsed by it as others are drawn to it. We all have to make peace with the fields of black-and-blue bruises flowering across our bodies — here a toe kick, there a heel grind — or go further insane. And so, a cock is not always a cock is a cock after all. Power dynamics 1, Ian 0. Sometimes it's just a dick attached to a dick. And usually that dick is wearing a nifty set of steel-toed boots, compliments of the Grand Imperial Wizards of Patriarchs R Us, Inc, a Fortune for the 500 company devoted to helping billionaires everywhere lift themselves up by their own bootstraps. But I, because I am willfully perverse because I don't know what else to do, still hold to the wild-eyed notion that there are a few small nooks where I can decide what boot I will lick and how and who will lick mine. I call my nook a bedroom. Your nook may have a different name. Names aside, and that's quite a feat in itself, I think this small act of will makes a minute but mighty bit of difference in the warp and woof of the cosmos. A minute tear. A mighty rift if we all pull the thread. Certainly this is the spit-slick leather heart of the sexual revolution. Of all paradigm-shifting overlord-toppling revolutions that outlive the bloodshed and cults of personality. This ability to make a true-blue choice between two paths in the woods. Not two brands of the same cereal or politician. No, a real choice between real paths and the freedom to pursue it to the sea or till the next fork in the road. Boot-lickers of the world unite! And as for poor maligned Getrude, I think we can all agree with her that a cock is not always a cock and a boot is not always a boot, but a dick is a dick is dick.

Shrimpboat Willie

for Patrick Califia

*W*illie LeGoullon was a man's man. No truer words ever had been or ever would be said of him. Whose man was debatable and would have been hotly if any of the men and the handful of women in the fleet of shrimpers berthed at Galveston's Pier 19 were the type to discuss such matters aloud and Willie the type to tell the many secrets of his manhood. Instead, when talk turned to Willie, and usually only in lulls between gales of laughter and the final bottles of beer before closing time at the Broken Net, all that was said nowadays was that he was the saddest sonofabitch they'd ever known and 'tweren't fair since he was a helluva shrimper, a good son, and, to the nodding of any head in earshot, a man's man.

The old-timers conjectured his current spate of sullen gruffness came from pining (still) over his daddy, Willie the loyal son who was more the faithful dog lying beside the front door, waiting for the never-to-be-heard-again footfalls of his beloved master. Forty-some-odd years ago Hurricane Carla and Pappy LeGoullon, the Agin' Cajun, had come ashore to remake Galveston in their own image and likeness. Two years ago, Pap's soul had set sail while his body flopped on the deck of his favorite ship, choking like the proverbial fish out of water, as his heart drowned in its own blood. Willie took it hard. All the shrimpers had. Like the rest of them, he'd worked his way up to captain of his own ship by being first a header, tearing the shrimp in two, and then a rigger, tending and mending the nets, on various boats in his daddy's fleet. He was beholden to the man who'd raised him up into manhood and then into captaincy.

The young and ambitious, however, would laugh at the old fools and counter that Willie's tighter- and tighter-lipped fury was no more supernatural than a lotus blossoming in a swamp of souring machismo whose dark source was the overpowering shadow of his older brother, a man who went by the understatement of a nickname Lucky. Lucky LeGoullon was King Crawdaddy now and ran Pappy's company like it was a Fortune 500.

And finally the love-burned, unheard but uncaring of the slight, would snicker into the lip of their bottles the timeless one-word cause for any man's woe: woman.

All three schools of thought were right, but the latter, despite the myopia of their bitterness, was the most insightful — and the most mistaken.

The last few months a bit of gossip had been slopped on every deck of every boat along with the nets of shrimp: Willie LeGoullon had finally found himself a woman. Maybe, at long last, Lucky had stopped siphoning from Willie the famed LeGoullon family good fortune like gas from a busted-up truck. Maybe Willie's spirits would lift as he settled down to the modest life the Good Lord had dealt him: all his limbs, a good ship, a small house, and now a woman.

No one had met her yet. Still there'd even been talk of a wedding — a May bride — at Lucky's mansion in Houston after the season's end, which had come and gone today as each weighed their last catch. Last Friday, Willie had finally relented and shown first Willard, a boy with the build and the personality of an old-time Frigidaire and his rigger, and then the rest of the Broken Net bar a photo. By this Friday, all the pier swore they'd seen pictures of his bride-to-be. Her name was TJ. A pissant of a girl with blonde bangs and downcast doe eyes — as best anyone could tell from the blurred photo or the wide and varied recountings of it. What they hadn't been able to see in the ill-assorted color dots on a weathered piece of paper or hear in the well-soused verbal air-brushings it received was that TJ was that very man Willie did belong to.

What few curves TJ had in that photo were the last bits of baby fat still suckling at his titties or gripping his hips as they rode along on his ass. And tucked away from prying eyes was a dick that when he wasn't huffing fumes and could spare the blood for a hard-on grew long and thin like the fingers of the spinster who played the piano in any town's Sunday School. And cropped out of sight were Willie's pride and joy: TJ's two big toes. As fat and smooth as two upside-down and unripe pears.

＊

"Hey, Willie. Where's your boyfriend?"

"What's that Earl?" Willie replied to the old man passing the table whose red face was nearly scarlet in contrast to the white trim of his beard and receding hair. Another captain trained in the school of Pappy LeGoullon.

"Where's Willard? Off to beauty school yet?"

"It's art school, you useless asshole," Willie said, each syllable sharpening the edge in his voice.

"Taking the breakup bad, huh, son?" chimed in Bob Scuggins, an even older, frailer man who'd been retired back in Pappy's day and now looked like no more than a pair of overalls hung from a coatrack. "Where's that future wife of yours?"

"Yeah, lil' Pap, when's the wedding?" It was Joe, the owner of the Broken Net, weighing in from the peanut gallery at the bar. "I 'spected to get a invite on fancy paper when you weighed in."

"We's running off to New Orleans, Joe."

"TJ and Mrs. Lucky don't get along, huh?" said Earl.

"Yeah, Willie, how's that sainted brother of yours?" added the old coatrack.

"Farting through silk, I 'magine." Willie could hear the sound over the laughter and clanking of bottles, like a backfire heard underwater, muffled by the leather in the warm seat of Lucky's Porsche Boxster S as it sped home along the Gulf Freeway.

"Good to hear."

"Yeah, if you like a man in panties, Earl," Willie spat

out through a lopsided smile.

There was more laughter and bottle-clanking.

"Willie, you and that lil' bitty gal of yours fighting that bad already? You could bust her over your knee. What, she got your dick at home in a drawer?"

A double-headed one, he thought. He could see his baby girly boy scratching at the sheets and crawling like a crab toward the headboard as he pushed it in deeper. He winced at the memory from a happier time. But unless he was planning to have CAUTION FLAMMABLE CONTENTS tattooed on his dick on the way home, he knew tonight would be as most every night had been when he was in port these last two months: he would either find TJ gone, not to return till Willie's money had run out, or TJ at home with a swollen paper bag and an empty can that hadn't been in the house when he left, all littered across the couch or floor and TJ deep in his dark metallic dreams. He couldn't afford this anymore. Not just the heartbreak. Not just the unlanced boil of lust. He literally could not afford to feed and clothe and house TJ. Or himself. His business had gone belly up.

He winced again. It looked like a grimace to hold back tears.

Joe, the long-lived barman, noticed immediately. "Boys, I think Willie's had enough today. It's been a long season. Give it a rest." Nothing clears a space in a room full of men like the presence of one of their own on the verge of crying. Willie and his bottle-strewn table were now the center of a very large circle.

So this really is the worst year of my life.

His mama had recently passed and taken her radiant love for him back to Jesus and whatever money she'd left behind for him was on ice, cooling in Lucky's bank while Lucky's lawyers went over her estate; he'd had to trawl overfished waters, steering clear of the Vietnamese—who had everybody but their grandmothers out working on the water!—and the sea turtles and their righteously wrathful human activists; he'd had to wait out three hurricanes only to learn that Willard was going off to college — to be a painter of all things (then again he'd never seen nimbler fingers, fat sausages sprouted from two honey-glazed hams, unsnare a rope or unhinge a head from a shrimp); his boat needed a new bilge pump and refrigeration unit; and finally, his sweet love had gone back to the worst habits he'd picked up to make do while working the streets of Houston. Worse still, before the next season, before too many more days, he was going to have to go to Lucky, who'd be grinning more than usual at the sight of his brother broke and broken and spitting out for the onlookers — Lucky was never alone — a slew of Cajun French fried up with a Texas twang, an odd, excretory sound that left Willie squeamish, like the impact of chewed tobacco hitting the bottom of a Styrofoam cup. He'd have to crawl to Lucky, tail between his leg, and beg for the privilege of working for his own brother.

Tail, that's what I need, he thought. *Let's see what I get.* He headed home.

✳

As he saw the signs for the turnoff to the Gulf Freeway hurtle to the side and into the red gloom behind his truck, he remembered the night over a year before when he'd taken it and the drive into Houston. He was back from three weeks out on the Gulf and too tired to cruise the dunes. Instead, he sat himself down in a dingy strip bar way out on Westheimer, far from the queens of the Montrose and the nearby castle of his brother in Avondale Place, and let the hustlers cruise him. On the stage, an ex-Marine, down to the crew cut and the *Semper Fi* tattoo, let his dick bob up and down in the heavy waters of the audience's need, the stale tension belied by the camp choice of song, "It's Raining Men." It was encased in a zebra-striped thong, an exotic sausage. In time, a face Willie would want between his legs blocked his view of the entertainment. A short but lithe bleach blond, a gymnast crossbred with a surfer, his teeth as white as the tiny shells he wore thick around his neck.

"Hey," he said, his smile the exclamation point to his greeting. "Whaddya like?"

"To watch," Willie said without blinking.

"This tired ol' shit," he gestured over his shoulder at the next dancer, a frat boy who was cradling his beloved not so little man, wrapped in sequined swaddling clothes, while the sound system blared Cher's "Believe."

"Something fresher."

The boy's smile froze somewhere between beaming and baring his fangs.

"I've gotta friend if you've gotta room."

"I will. Follow me."

"Pull in back a here," said the hustler, whose name Willie'd forgotten even then and now remembered only as Trade.

He pulled his pickup into the parking lot behind Lil' Beau's Peep Show, a more traditional strip joint that seamlessly blended, despite its garish neon sign of a randy sheep looking up the fairy tale shepherdess' skirt, with the rest of the shops crammed into the mini-mall.

Great, Willie groaned in his head, *pussy on a pole*. He turned the ignition off. "Your friend work here?" Willie asked aloud as he shifted in his seat to get a better look at the boy beside him.

"Yeah."

"Well, I've seen enough pussy to know I don't care much for the sight. No offense, a course, to you and your girlfriend."

Trade laughed and looked Willie directly in the eye.

"I think you'll like John Thomas."

"That's an odd name for a girl," he said slowly as he pushed the bill of his cap off his forehead.

"He's an odd girl."

The door stenciled EMERGENCY EXIT swung open
and a little girl walked out. She was taller than Trade but
with none of his lean musculature. Just long lines with an
occasional curve, except for her round face made all the
more soft and circular by the long naturally blonde bangs
that curtained it. She wore a pink halter top held aloft by
two spaghetti straps. Bursting on the front of it, almost like
the depictions of the Sacred Heart his mama had loved so,
were three flying girls with bugging eyes, just slightly
smaller than hers. Her nose was almost as small on her
face as the carat drawn to represent theirs. Her lips,
however, were full, those of a mature woman. As his eyes
descended to the tattered pair of Daisy Duke's she wore,
he noted her hips were the same. She was stranded halfway
between girl and woman. He continued to look her over
as she began her walk to the truck, having turned and seen
Trade waving broadly from its window. She was trying to
saunter over but her large red high tops, fitting for a
basketball center in the '50s, kept tripping her up and she
had to nearly stomp to maintain her balance. *Odd indeed.*

"See what I mean," Trade said with a proprietary
snicker.

"For fuck's sake, boy, she's fourteen."

"He wishes. He's been seventeen for two years."

"He," Willie said slowly to catch his breath. "And
you?"

"Don't worry. We ain't chicken but we're still finger-
licking good, if you know what I mean, Colonel." He leered,
his face a mask of a man twice his age.

And that'd still be younger than me, Willie lamented to
himself.

✳

"Ain't you gonna get naked, Mister?" TJ asked. (His
laughter had filled the cab of the truck when he'd been
introduced as "John Thomas." "Name's TJ, Mr. Willie.
Short for Travis Jones. I don't give a almighty goddamn if

you know my real name." His voice was deeper and fuller than the breathy quiver Willie imagined.)

"No, I'm good, son. I like to watch. Just give me something I won't forget when I'm by my lonesome."

"Suit yourself," said Trade as he shucked off his shoes and jumped on top of the double bed nearest the window. "Y'mind if we smoke before we get started." Each word had been punctuated by a bounce.

"Nope. Smoke if you got 'em, I say. Want one of mine?" He delicately retrieved a near pristine pack of Marlboros from his T-shirt pocket.

"No thanks, Mr. Willie," TJ said as he joined Trade mid-bounce. "He means dope." Trade pushed him and they fell onto the bed laughing crazily like the young boys they were, drunk on hormones and the chance to fuck each other again. Trade scooted against the headboard and pulled a joint out of TJ's back pocket. He lit it and inhaled slowly. With his exhale and a gasping, almost soundless "Wow," he pointed it to TJ. TJ nodded his head to Willie, encouraging Trade to offer it first to their "host."

"Want some?" Trade coughed out.

"Naw, thanks though. Stuff puts me to sleep and I ain't ready for bed yet. Not till you show me something nice to dream about."

"Sure, sure," Trade said as he pulled the joint out of TJ's mouth. The glowing tip almost extended to the skin on Trade's fingers as he sucked on it. He closed his eyes, passed what was left of the joint back to TJ, and kept his eyes shut, lost in thought. *Or just plain lost*, Willie editorialized, suspicion about what was or was not going to go down next finally besting lust.

TJ leaned over Trade to stub out the joint in the ashtray on the bedside stand built into the single massive headboard of the two beds. As he pulled back, Trade grabbed his head. TJ froze, startled and afraid, as if he knew what might come and was trying to hold the predator at bay by playing as dead as he could. Trade lowered his face to TJ's and whispered. TJ nodded and smiled with relief.

"Okay," Trade said as he released TJ's head and threw open his eyes. "It's show time, Mr. Willie." He stood up beside the bed, inches from Willie, who was hunched on the edge of the other double bed. "Pardon us, monsewer," and here he pulled Willie's cap from his head and gave a little flourish with it before bowing, "while we get into our costumes." As he straightened himself, the blood slowly returned to his head and he staggered and began to laugh.

Willie's eyes met TJ's and he smiled. They all laughed now.

Willie turned his head to the large mirror along the wall opposite the foot of the beds to check out which of the hairs he had left atop it might be standing on end. He patted at the few strays and frowned. It was thinning faster than the edible fauna and flora in the Gulf. He looked at the rest of his face. It, he, was weathered. There was no better word for how he looked. The color and texture of his skin fell somewhere between tanned leather and smoked meat. Crisped and creased from almost all of his forty-five years spent shrimping under the Gulf sun, burning down from above and up from below as it glanced off the sometimes mirror-smooth and sometimes choppy and shardlike water. His eyes were clear blue green shallows in the recesses of his craggy face, broken up by the large beak of a nose and bushy eyebrows and thick moustache, frayed and yellowed from nicotine. Like the ends of his fingers — pale yellow at the topmost points, thick and gnarled, permanently stained under the nails with grease — that he ran beneath his nose to comb down the overgrowth of three weeks offshore. Behind his brown head, glistening with sweat despite the air-conditioned coolness of the room, glistening like the skin of a well-basted suckling pig, he watched the appearance of more and more white skin.

"Okay, you can look now," Trade snickered, whatever innocence there'd been in his laugh having finally died out.

Willie turned and TJ laid spread before him: blond, white, and pink. Blond hair thick on his head and thinning till it regathered around his white dick, thin and hard as steeple, save for the pink head, a fleshy blossom like his two nipples and, Willie's eyes traced the length of TJ's body, his…

That was the first time Willie saw TJ's toes. His heart, his skin, his dick, all flailed like they were caught in the tightest mesh net. Then Trade, who had a body that put to shame any of those boys in the *Bel Ami* videos Willie kept running ragged and over which Willie would have congratulated himself with the flinty pride of a customer who'd spent his money well if he hadn't been so blinded by the beauty of TJ's twin sideshow splendors, took the coral pink outcropping of skin and fat and bone and nail and hid it away his mouth. Trade crawled closer to TJ, keeping the boy's toe in his mouth, till his dick was not far from TJ's hole, a flash of a darker coral appearing and disappearing out of the black hair with each of Trade's jostlings of the bed. Trade sat and spread his legs, lifting his own toes to TJ's mouth. TJ ran his tongue over each before swallowing both big toes at once and bobbing on them like they were a dick about to burst. Trade let this go on for only a little bit longer before he took them back and scooted as far away from TJ as he could without rolling off the end of the bed. With that, TJ's toe fell back onto the bed and Willie almost gasped in awe. Trade, ever the showman, paid Willie no mind. Instead, he stretched one of his legs out till his toes were holding up the heavy round ends of TJ's large ball sack. He rested on his elbows and now his big toe was tapping at TJ's hole. With only a breathy grunt from TJ to mark the moment wherein Willie's life forever changed, Trade plunged his toe into TJ like he was just a kid fooling around in his Saturday-night bath and jamming his toe into the wide mouth of the faucet.

"Mercy sakes!" Willie shouted, all of them bouncing with a start on their respective beds. "What the fuck's that?!"

"Get a hold of yourself, Granddad!" Trade volleyed back. "You said you're a shrimper. This here's shrimpboating!!"

Willie paused to take in the newness of the world. "Okay then...I wanna see *his* toe up your ass."

"That'll cost you." Trade waited for Willie to blow up or blurt out, "How much?!"

He didn't. Instead, Willie fished in his back pocket for his wallet. He pulled out a few twenties and put them on the nightstand. "How's a hundred?"

"Good enough to get me to roll over," said Trade.

TJ looked out from under his long blond bangs and heavy-lidded eyes and smiled. Willie was hooked.

Trade took TJ's toe three separate times and pocketed the 300 dollars and left TJ to score some more before he would return in the a.m. to take him away as well. After Trade had left his perch in the window for the waiting cab below and closed the heavy door behind him with the echoing metallic clack of a vacuum being sealed, Willie sat on his bed and sipped at his Coors Light and watched TJ come unwrapped from his sheet as he reached over to the far side of his bed to retrieve a forgotten bag of Grandpa John's Hot & Spicy Kettle Cooked Pork Cracklins. His ass was small, an unblemished white, and as perfectly round as the sigh a child makes when no one is listening. TJ rolled back and tore open the bag. He looked at Willie and stopped to appraise the older man's slightly drunken, unblinking stare.

When TJ had tallied up all that he could see and intuit, he spoke: "C'mon. Take off your clothes. I like you. For real."

"Nah."

"Why not?"

"None of your business."

"Not about business. I want you to fuck me. On the house." He grinned slyly and seductively like the girls who'd always tried to get Willie's brother's attention after mass, after school, after his wedding. "C'mon."

"Nah."

"You don't want to."

"Sure I do but I ain't got much of a dick."

"Sure you do."

"No, son, I don't. I got what the doctors like to call a medical condition. I got a dick that when I get a boner ain't no bigger than your thumb."

"Get out."

"God's truth. Doctors' name for it is micropenis. Horrible-sounding word, I think. I just call it the one shrimp I can't shuck. Gonna be with me till the day I die."

TJ sat up and pushed his bangs away from his face. "I know something about hurt, Mr. Willie. You seen my toes. You seen all of me. Barely got to this night alive, being a fairy in Texas and all, so I sure as shit ain't one to judge you on the size of your dick."

Willie blushed, moved by the old wisdom of a child.

"Can it get hard?"

"Huh?"

"Well, can it?"

"Sure."

"Then you can fuck me. Well, c'mon now."

✳

"Can I live with you?" TJ asked Willie's left nipple hours later, his head resting in the crook of Willie's arm, his body curled beside his like a white shadow to draw heat in the artificial cold of the room

Willie took a breath, held it to keep his heart and his tears at bay. He coughed out a barely audible yes. But there was only silence. From the lengths of TJ's breaths, he could tell he'd fallen asleep before hearing the answer. He already knew what it would be.

✳

Willie could hear the music through the cab of his truck once its engine had gone silent in the driveway. He gave the same strained look he would have if he'd been out on the Gulf with a mountain of thunderheads materializing out of thin, but very humid, air.

He opened the front door to the smell of bitter lemons and wood soap. Tammy Wynette was wailing out the refrain from "I Don't Wanna Play House" — the stereo cranked high enough for the whole neighborhood to hear her plaint, high enough to rattle the floorboards and shake the windows. Willie didn't even notice them violently jerking when he slammed the door.

"For chrissakes, TJ," he hollered to the stereo as he switched it off. He turned and saw him and all he could do was moan and shake his head. He checked TJ's breath and left him to sleep it off. He'd tried to rouse him before and nearly had his jaw busted in and his eyes gouged out. As he reheated his gumbo on the stove, he returned to pick up the bag and the can of Pledge he'd bought to dust the few pieces of furniture of his recently passed mama that Lucky hadn't wanted. He came back another time to just stand and stare at the little broken boy, as innocent in his sleep as he was damned — a fallen angel, his winglost back slumped against the couch, his unhaloed head lolling on the bones and nerves of his slack neck, his armorless chest wet with drool.

"What am I gonna do with you, son?" he sighed.

The bag of skin shifted its guts and bones. An eye peered through the veil of sweaty blond hair. "Mikey, that you, man?"

Mikey, that was Trade's name. "Mikey?" Willie grunted. "That who you wanna see? Mikey?!" His voice was picking up like a squall. "That who you want, you mother-huffing-piece-of-shit? Fine. Fuck you, TJ! Fuck us! Soon as you come to I'll take you back to Lil' Beau's and you can start looking for your sweet Mikey. How 'bout that, TJ?! You want that? Hell, I'll throw in can a spray paint as a wedding present and you two faggots can live happily fuckin' ever after till you both drop dead from snorting shit."

Willie knew he was on the verge of bawling, knew he was on the verge of picking up TJ and smacking him from one end of the couch to the other. But he held it in and raised his voice instead. The uncomprehending eye continued to stare at him.

"Jesus, TJ, why?! Why you doin' this shit to me? All I ever did was take you home like you asked me to. Fed you. Fucked you." He paused to press a hand to his forehead and through his hair. "Whaddya 'spect, LeGoullon, fuckin' a goddamn child?! Jesus H. Child-Fuckin' Christ! Why the fuck am I so goddamned stupid to fall in love with a goddamned paint-sniffin' child...?!" he yelled as he ran back into the kitchen to turn off the pot of burning shrimp stew.

I'd rather my tongue was racin' round in circles 'round your sweet little ass, Willie thought as he watched Jeff Gordon take the lead in a NASCAR race whose name had been blotted from his memory with his seventh can of Coors Light. As he popped the top on his eighth, he spied movement — beyond the rim of his second bowl of half-eaten gumbo — crawling and swaggering and stumbling and crawling once more in from the bedroom.

"Mr. Willie," the sluggish insect cried out in a series of squeaks and croaks.

Willie chugged almost half his beer to drown out the eerie sound. He listened to the fervent pulse of his blood washing up and around his head.

"Mr. Willie," said the voice slowly evolving toward humanity. "Mr. Willie don't be mad. Please don't. Look I painted my toes just for you."

TJ crawled in front of Willie's La-Z-Boy and rolled onto his back, lifting his legs toward him, blocking Jeff's and the rest of the roaring cars. TJ was only wearing shorts, his tightest Daisy Duke's with not much more than a large blossom of denim to cover his ass, his hole blowing him kiss after kiss as TJ tried to angle his toes closer to Willie's own, reclining midair.

"You jackass, TJ. Damn if you weren't so cute I'da thrown you out with the trash long ago." Willie slurred his way through the sentence all the while punching at his remote till he hit MUTE. "Well, son, let's see them toes of yours." He lowered his legs and slapped at the armrest and then his thigh. "Well, put 'em on the glass, boy."

TJ scooted on his back toward Willie like a palsied crab. When his ass bumped against Willie's bare feet, he lifted his legs onto Willie's lap. Willie carefully raised his pride and joys out of his swelling crotch. He turned them toward the light falling from his reading lamp and TJ turned with them, flopping onto his side and beginning to laugh. Willie squinted to focus and appraised the two largest gems. He frowned, like a jeweler who has discovered a single flaw in an otherwise perfect stone. The nail polish was askew. Slopped on. Thick to one side. Like TJ had done them in the dark on rough seas.

"Not good enough," Willie said.

"Huh?"

"Apology not accepted."

"What...? But...I...please, Mr. Willie. I love you." TJ's nostrils flared and his eyes grew inhumanly wide as they took on water.

"TJ...son...I love you, too. But you did these while you was high as a kite. Ain't good enough."

"I'm sorry...I'm sorry. I swear. Sorry, sorry, sorry — "

"Yes, y'are. But you can make it right."

"I can?"

"Yup."

"Get clean?"

"Well, that too. Someday you'll have to keep that promise or die — "

"I don't wanna die," TJ said as he started sob.

"Boy," Willie said as he shook TJ's feet, "y'aint gonna die tonight. Listen." He rattled him like the end of snake's tail, warning him to heed. "Lord, you're a weepy girl tonight. Listen—you fuck me with both of these tonight and I'll 'ccept your apology. You hear me, son?"

TJ nodded his head in time with Willie's shakings.

∗

Willie rapidly thumbed his dick as his ass swallowed TJ's big toe the second time. TJ'd tried to push first one and then the other into Willie. They'd done it before. And Willie was open wide enough once he'd pushed his legs over the arms of his La-Z-Boy and his butt to the edge of the seat and once TJ had shoved his tongue and then his fingers and then his tongue and his fingers together into Willie's drooling, cooing hole. But TJ hadn't been able to fuck him with both his feet pressed into Willie's cheeks. He'd flopped on the carpeted floor. *Like a retarded seal*, Willie fumed silently. After some red-faced scolding from Willie and red-faced tears from TJ, they'd agreed to use only one toe tonight. And now Willie was clamped tight around it.

Willie swore he could feel the well-buffed nail nudge against his prostate as TJ pushed against him.

"Oh yeah. That's it, boy. Harder."

TJ smiled and plunged his toe deeper before trying to retract it from the tidal pull of Willie's asshole. It looked like he'd stepped into a solid but sprawled pile of quaking white flesh, browned and haired at the extremities, and was trying to shake it off.

With each flutter, Willie's lips tingled more. They were going numb—the surest sign in Willie's sexual life that he was about to come. And the numbness in his lips reminded him of calm, the dead calm of the gulf on an August day before the storms come, the dead calm of a particular August day when he was alone with Pappy on a boat.

Now that Lucky was running the business end, Pap liked to go out with his own boat and crew, try to go back to when he was without the stresses of a burgeoning business and a distant wife that he'd driven to the state lines of his heart, and two sons who couldn't be more different, a son that he'd molded in his image and likeness and had now surpassed him, and a son that was nothing like him but had the heart he wished he'd been born with. A son that he now fathers in his final years, ashamed at last for what he'd said when a nurse with a pinched face, like she was holding in a sneeze, handed him his second born and he'd unwrapped his bundle of joy only to spit out, once he remembered he was capable of speech, at his wife lying exhausted in the bed below: "You always wanted a daughter, *hein*? Happy, *pauv' bête*?!" He'd left mother and child to cry. *Too late for mother. And probably too late for child*, he thought as he wiped as his neck with his damp handkerchief and stared at his son, hunkered down next to a wriggling hill of shrimp.

Willie lifted his arms to tear the heads from the shrimp, a feat in the monolithic heat and wet weight of the air; he raised his eyes, a major collaboration of will and muscle, sweat trickling steadily down the back of his neck like blood from a wound to the head. He was too hot to scan the horizon and waited for it to solidify into view. And there, at the peripheries of his sight, it came: a circus parade of ghostly freaks. Hydrocephalic dwarves suspended mid-cartwheel; trumpeting elephants, with exophthalmos, bulging eyes wide as those on the great squid in the Disney version of *20,000 Leagues Under the Sea*, rupturing and drifting asunder from the unending bleat of their trunks; a fat lady whose rolls of white flesh lifted her head higher and higher, her face growing dark with rage as she realized she was beyond any chance for love, all the mythic titans having been driven under the earth millennia ago; rabid hippogriffs and chimeras and a mundane duck or two ran after them all, the foam from their mouths rising in faint haloes. With each twist of the head from another shrimp, he willed his body farther away from the boat, across the sluggish water, a tar made of blueberries, and up into the darkening skies. He wanted them to take him along but they would, as every one had and would in Willie

LeGoullon's life save TJ, pass him by without realizing he was one of their kind.

TJ's foot started to cramp and he kicked Willie from his reverie, kicked against his prostate (his joy buzzer he'd called it ever since TJ showed him where it was), kicked him over into that little death by electrocution that was his orgasm, his body — and TJ's and the chair's too — floundering like a stray fish caught in the deckside heaps of net and shrimp.

Willie hollered with each gush of cum that poured the negligible distance from the head of his dick before pooling around it and in the clump of wily hairs. "Damn," he laughed as he stretched back in the chair, pulling up the footrest and accidentally popping TJ's toe from his ass. "Oh shit," he panted, rolling his head from side to side, savoring the throb of his hole, trying to get the image of a gape-mouthed bass out of his head as he felt it open and close.

"O God Almighty, that was good!" he said as he ran his fingers through his hair and down his chest and belly and toward his dick. Then he stopped. He remembered TJ. He remembered everything and forgave him. But he couldn't say it. It felt too obscene to talk aloud of such things. Instead, he told TJ to hand him his sock. Willie took it without looking away from the boy and wiped it over the small wet hill of his dick. Over and around and pulled it up to his nose as TJ's eyes nearly rolled from his head in order to follow it. The soiled cotton smelled like something murky and warm and ancient, like brine.

"Here, son. Suck on this."

TJ grabbed it from Willie's hand and stuffed it in his mouth. He closed his eyes and almost purred. His nostrils opened and closed in time with Willie's still-sighing hole as he tried to inhale the sock itself. He snorted and nearly choked from the rush of smells, their attendant tastes transmuting the gathering saliva in his mouth into the sacramental wine of his own private church. He bowed his head and sucked. At last, he stood, his dick pointing out his benefactor to whomever might be watching, and crawled onto Willie's belly. Through the tight grip of TJ's fist, his solitary long thin finger of a dick jabbed at Willie's face teasingly, tauntingly, accusingly, Willie's mouth opening and closing, always out of reach for the shiny bait on the end of the line. Till Willie's moustache and mouth were slick from its final convulsive touch.

"Thank you, son," Willie said as he licked around his lips.

In the distance, a triumphant Jeff Gordon waved to the crowds and smiled knowingly at Willie and the girly boy, his panting muffled, as he rose and fell on Willie's heaving gut.

Willie slowly accepted that he was no longer dreaming, his head really did hurt that much, and that he was lying in their bed, alone. He dimly remembered, as if it were a quotidian detail for someone else's life, TJ holding his hand and walking him to the room, tugging him onto the bed, and nudging him under the covers. He called for TJ. No answer, save for the distant barking of a dog chained and forgotten. He plodded to the bathroom to piss. He hollered for TJ and then flushed. He walked from end to end of the too-quiet house. He looked out the front window. The pickup was gone. A first. Probably his wallet along with his keys. He stood in the window and waited, till every bone and muscle in his feet throbbed, till each toe was as swollen and as mournful a shade of blue as a drowned corpse. When he could no longer stare into the diffuse but mocking glare of twilight, he hobbled to his bed to listen for the sound of gravel churning, heavy feet hitting the stairs, tumblers in the lock falling: the return of his man.

Nearer My Areg to Thee

I lie.

We both do.

I, naked, in San Francisco. Waiting for your call.

You, naked, there. In Chicago. Dialing the numbers hurriedly.

I shudder as the phone — as thick and hard as Bakelite, as red as Fiestaware — rings. It is an old phone, loudly rattling its metallic phlegm.

"Hello?"

"Hello," you coo. Your voice is deep and sonorous. My marrow liquefies. My bones melt as if they were sculpted of butter.

What a priceless lubricant the sound of your voice has become. My sweet aural sop. Confirmation that you do exist. Evocation of the very body that — because of only a week's worth of hours together since this year began — I am slowly, unbearably forgetting as days accumulate into months apart.

That, and your daily emails.

I read of your body weeks before you ever sent me a photo, months before I finally stripped away the last barriers between us on the way from my kitchen to the bedroom.

Ours was an epistolary seduction. An incendiary flirtation, kindled by each dry, brittle consonant and oily vowel.

Dangerous Liaisons penned by two middle-aged queer men. One as terse as the other is verbose. One with a fondness for the violence, born both of nature and artifice, that flowers so well in the Midwest. Tornadoes spun of cotton candy and blood. The other dreaming of being made a word in an 18th-century novel or a note in a baroque opera. Consumed by seething festoons of trills, of participial phrases.

One with a husband. One without.

Both now with a paramour.

You and I.

Two professional writers pitching woo through an endless stream of ghostly print in cyber–billets-doux.

Love among the fiber-optic cables.

And now, every Monday, while your husband sits unaware at work, in the hour and a half before I go to sit mindlessly myself at a desk, we telegraph—in a series of gasps and grunts and "oh, god"s—our newest desires for what we shall do, one unto the other, the next time we can swap skin cells and spit and sperm.

"Are you naked?" you ask.

I can hear your well-lubed fist sucking on your dick. It is a loud and constant sound. Like the sea.

"Yes," I say, half-present. I am imagining your porn-star dick.

It is the kind that, as it grows, droops. Hangs heavy from the weight of the blood now widening the middle of your river of flesh, tributaries of veins swirling off, before tapering to the small, swollen pink dam that is your head. Without setting eyes on you, I know it is once again broken, leaking—like our love—immoderately, and will inevitably burst.

"Are you hard?" you ask more breathlessly.

"Yes." And I describe the rigid crook of my cock that has delighted you every time I have thrust it—in word or in deed—into your mouth or hole.

"I wish I had my mouth around your dick right now."

"I do too," I think aloud. "I wish I had your head between my hands so I could pull it down onto my fat cock. Shove it all the way into the back of your mouth."

You moan. You are flushed—with memory and more blood filling your swollen dick.

"Yes," you say when you remember to breathe. "Oh, God, my dick is so hard. I don't know what you've done to me but it's bigger than it's ever been."

I imagine it, red and engorged, twitching. My Sears

Tower, I've called it. And it is a marvel. A wonder of flesh that stands alone and several thousand miles from me.

But the sound of you is here. In this room. The earpiece of the phone is cupped against my ear like your hands. It cradles your absent mouth. But I feel your breath. I feel the lips and tongue and teeth that shape it and push it toward me. It is as if you are beside me, whispering as we spoon.

"What are you doing?" I know but I want to hear you tell me.

"Jerking my dick."

"Good boy. I wish I were there to watch. Let me hear you twist your tit. Go on. Pull it."

"Okay," you purr. And then your mouth buzzes with a swarm of consonants that stream out of your mouth as honey-coated mmms.

Mmm. This is the most frequent call and response in our emails. This is the succinct written testament to the vibrations that hum throughout either of our bodies whenever we communicate. However we communicate.

"Harder," I encourage—I demand. "I wish I could be there to bite it. Chew on it. Remember how I chewed on your whole pec."

Now come the sweet vowels. Long *o*s and short *u*s.

"Take that hand and suck on your finger."

The receiver bangs against your jaw and shoulder as you make way for your hand. There is slurping. There is smacking. There is humming. I am happy.

"Rub it over your hole."

"Oh, yes," you throatily agree.

"Now push it in."

Staccato breaths tap against the mouthpiece.

"How's it feel?"

"It's never the same as yours."

No, I think—sad for us both.

"Stick it in deeper. And wriggle it around like I do."

You oblige, warming quickly to the request, but it is I who am rewarded.

"Anything," you sigh in response to a question I have not asked. "You can have me do anything. What do you want me to do?"

"I want you to crawl through the phone," I say without thinking.

You laugh. Either at my breaking of character or a more private joke between you and your finger.

"What do you want to *hear* me do, babe?" you say.

"I want you to slide that butt plug of yours into *my* hole." I swear I can hear you grin. "And I want you to talk me through it. All of it."

"Yes, Sire."

I smile at your nod to my Jacobean fantasies — games we play when we are finally skin-to-skin.

I listen to you move loudly about your bedroom. At last, you speak, winded more from excitement than exertion. You tell me you how you are sitting on your bed, your knees spread and your ass arched, one hand prying a round cheek from the sleepy embrace of its twin, the other pushing in the tip — you groan enticingly — and then the shaft — you grunt out a long, maddeningly arousing string of "unnh"s — and finally the base.

We both "oh, god" appreciatively. I hear the loud tides of you pulling feverishly on your dick and I stroke mine all the faster and tell you so. You are inspired to get off the bed and stand up, thus wedging the plug into a new and more sweet-burning position.

I have never heard you make such a sound — any man make such a sound — the raw, yet stylized last gasp of one of Michelangelo's dying stone slaves.

I have never wanted you more.

I have never felt farther from you.

"Take it…"

"What?" you say as your mind staggers up your spine from your asshole.

"Take it. Take the plug and fuck your hole with it."

You moan something that sounds like "Okay."

And this is what sends us both over orgasm's edge.

Ian Philips

You: the actual sensations which I tell you, graphically, are the echoes of my phantom limb. Me: your rapid, rabid pants and hissed whispers of "fuck me, fuck me, fuck me."

I shoot. I feel my cum slide out of me in time with my spurting breaths. You explode. Howls. As if your cum had crystallized into diamonds that tear and bleed you as you spill a king's ransom onto your bed.

I press the phone to my ear, smiling. It will ring with the sound of you all day. And my dick will thrum from your imagined touch. And your hole will quaver around the butt plug until I write you later to give you permission to remove it.

We gasp our way back to breathing. When we can speak, we talk over the other. To thank you, to thank me for the pleasure of the last hour's lustful riposte and release. You piss and I stop to listen to the water rumbling in the bowl. You have already begun to move about the house. You can only lie still if I am truly there and holding you.

As you inhale on a cigarette I have yet to hear you light in any of our calls, we chatter about the day before us. The errands to run. The chores to be done. The words to be strung into sentences, into paragraphs, into stories to sell. Like this one.

Then we come, at last, to the true little death.

"Good bye," you say quietly.

"Good bye," I echo.

We hang up.

And, until our next telephonic tryst, we will lie.

Here and there.

Lie in wait.

You and I.

Lie.

And wait.

Shameless Self-Promotion

for Krandall Kraus and Paul Borja

This is a true story. That's important. I'm told you won't read this unless it's a true story.

So let me stress, my earnestly post-ironic reader, that this is a true story. There'll be no eight-inch dicks here. And no virgin assholes to suck them in on the first bloodless thrust.

No. This is a true story. About two writers. Writers of fiction no less. Writers of published and praised lies. Which makes this tale all the more poignant and remarkable since it is true.

Of course, I don't understand why nowadays every story must be true. I've always found this unfair. Because it means only those who have interesting lives are allowed to tell their tales. Rather than those with interesting imaginations. Which, in short, means more about The Beautiful People. And don't they already have enough worlds to rule? Why must they come here?

I'm not beautiful. And neither are you.

Oh, don't protest so. If you were one of The Beautiful, why would you be home on a Saturday night and reading this of all things? Reading at all?

Granted I am as biased as I am bitter, preferring as I do fairy tales. Rides on magic carpets woven out of words to a place where there are no ordinary people. No wasted moments. Nothing is pointless or routine.

So unlike real life.

And actually, truth be told, it's not even true stories that set hearts afire and registers a-ringing; it's true confessionals.

Yet if that were the case, you challenge, why aren't Augustine's flying off the shelf? I agree. He got around. Whored it up. Had a bastard child. He had a life worthy of

Ian Philips

E! *True Stories*, of Springer even, before he found God.

But that was ancient history. Worse, that was BTV. Before television. Today, a confessional must be a visual compendium of backdoor gossip about anyone worthy and/or able to appear miraculously in the downpour of colored dots within that odd-shaped box in your living room. Your favorite celebrities caught off-guard and on tape. Inside this. Behind that. Prurient memoirs for the illiterate.

O tempora. O mores.

And so, being a writer who like so many others of my ilk is addicted, with a mixture of attraction and repulsion, to the sight of my own words in print, I must now tell my tale, all true, so at least one more creation of this honest fabulist will feel the crushing weight of the printing press, the hack of the blade trimming its excesses, the searing sting of the needle threading its spine, the hard slap of the covers gluing themselves to its papery flesh, all before it thuds into the darkness of a cardboard box with the dim hope of seeing the promised light on the shelves of the righteous and the for sale.

Gather 'round, my friends. For I'm about to heave another faggot on the fire. And this is one whom all of us who've ever thumbed a recent literary journal or slouched our way towards Bethlehem through a writers' conference will want to see sputter and crackle and blaze.

His name: Robert Caliban. A monster with words. Especially his own.

"Caliban?" you say. "I've never heard of him." But you have, dear reader. Not by that name, perhaps, but he is real. And he is reading these very words, as are you, but he alone is fuming that I have refused to reveal his identity. And he alone is hard for he knows whom I mean.

My asshole.

And he is.

And his is.

But I get ahead of myself. And it is important when telling the truth to tell it exactly as it happened.

So, my prologue, if you will, is through, and, like a masterful storyteller, I will begin now at the beginning.

I was standing alone in the crowd huddled together at the Gala Reception for *Out, Proud, and in Print*, a national conference for writers and readers who are LGBT and beyond. There we all were in a forgotten banquet hall in a forgotten hotel in San Francisco. And I too seemed to have been forgotten as I stood alone for several minutes, waiting for my friend to return with a glass of wine and some soggy hors d'oeuvres, when Caliban and his cocktail, held out far in front of him like Moses' staff before the Red Sea, parted their way through a tight circle of whispered gossip and snickering.

My Moses, his face flush from the glory of the Lord and several glasses of Absolut, stopped in front of me and did a double take. He grinned as if he'd overheard the answer to all riddles and strode toward me until he was a few inches from my face.

"Whatever you've heard about me, I won't bite."

"Excuse me?"

"I won't bite. Come a little closer."

Closer? Any closer and I'd have to be inside him. But isn't that what we all insanely crave? To have another live inside us so that we won't be so alone? Then again, I already have more than enough voices in my head.

"Well, if you won't bite, why should I?"

He laughed, his drink sloshing from edge to edge of the plastic cup's wide rim. "I didn't say I couldn't. Just that I wouldn't."

Already with the semantics.

"Which one of my books is your favorite?"

I grimaced and scanned the crowd for my friend. He must have been abducted. I thought of storming through the throng of scribblers and word-wantons and doing a stall-to-stall search of all the bathrooms on this floor.

"*I Am the Terrible*," I answered.

"I am," he chuckled before sipping anew from his drink. "I am terrible. Especially in bed. A holy fuckin' terror. You ready for the fright of your life?"

Providentially, my friend returned with our drinks — and the bartender's number, I later learned — and I did not have to answer *that* question.

Instead we listened to Caliban rhapsodize about the wonders of a three-way with him. And once more I regretted my unwavering reliance on the social graces or, more truthfully, faux politeness — a habit my mama had spanked into me as a child.

"None," I had wanted to answer to his first question. "None," I should have answered. For I'd recognized Caliban immediately. Unlike many other authors, he truly resembled his dust jacket photo. And I had had the misfortune of seeing that photo twice: once when I did not know better and had read his debut novel, and once when I did know better but had purchased a collection of his erotic fiction with the earnest hope it would be better than the hardbacked debut and read it charitably for several stories before I skimmed the remaining tales and then lobbed both the book and my estimation of Robert Caliban's talents across the room.

Yes, our Mr. Caliban has, as of today, written several novels, a book of poetry, one play, and several collections of erotica under his own and various assumed names. He'd like me to list them for you here. I won't. Sorry, darling. You do it so admirably at your website. But what he'd most want you to know, other than his URL, is how he looks. That I can do.

Warts and all.

Actually, warts excepted. I didn't find out about those till later, did I, my love?

Imagine that a man of average height, build, age, looks, and — oh, yes — dick stands before you. Naked. And far from ashamed.

But, once again, I have gotten ahead of myself. Since this is a true story, how would I be able to describe his body unless I had seen it with my very own eyes? And how, you kindly remind me, could *that* ever have come to pass? For when I first met Robert Caliban, I was annoyed by his bombast almost to the point of revulsion.

Then again, reader, nothing draws a crowd like revulsion. Whether it be a crashed car or a yet-to-be-derailed ego careening toward some distant wall, some jump in the tracks, it pulls you to turn around and look.

To rubberneck.

And I did.

Not that night at the conference. No, the next day.

I had taken a break from the panels and gone shopping. Book shopping. I could have bought from a vendor table, but I was losing my ability to be either social or graceful and needed a respite. And for me, there is no place more restful than inside a bookstore.

Until he walked in.

I recognized him by that trademark shock of hair. And that voice. Few, having heard it, would ever forget it.

"Why did I have to come to the Castro?" I lamented in a whisper. Of course Caliban would come here first in search of praise and propositions.

I picked up the nearest book at hand—some travel guide with an apple-cheeked Czech boy on the cover with a hungry look (literally) in his eye. I let my vision blur and listened to Caliban who, as if declaiming to a mob, asked, *basso profundo*, the bored youth at the counter which of his books was his favorite.

The answer must not have pleased our horny Sphinx. For he quickly began to beat his hand upon the counter, bellowing, "Don't you know who I am?!"

I looked up, no longer able to pretend I was reading. I was not alone; the eyes of every reader were slithering toward him like filings to a magnet.

I was only a few feet from the eruption and able to notice something as peculiar as it was arousing. There was a swelling bulge in Caliban's pants that he was banging against the wall of the counter in time with the slaps of his hand against its top.

"Excuse me, my sweet, innocent, naïve youth, but I

asked you a question: don't…you know…who…I…am?"

"Robert Caliban, what an honor," the manager exclaimed nervously as he rushed to the relief of his harried clerk from his office in the rear corner of the store. "Please," he added as he picked up a stack of Caliban's newest release, "won't you sign a few of these before you go?"

Caliban stopped mid-slap, mid-bump, and turned, the red-bricked hue of his forehead and cheeks softening to the ruddy glow of a dedicated tippler, and showed us all, with several dime-sized stains on his upper thigh, how happy he was to oblige.

As he signed, I tried to sidle by, but Caliban spoke without looking up. "You know it's impolite to stare and run."

"Hello, Robert," I said in a voice that would have made my mother proud. "I wasn't staring."

"Not at my face."

Now I flushed.

"If you'll wait for me to sign this last book," and with the word "last" the manager sighed loudly, "I'll be happy to leave these good people and allow you a more private viewing."

The manager's face mirrored the revulsion I felt. And I was so very revulsed. But I could not move. And then I was ashamed of my infirmity and all the more revulsed and therefore frozen where I stood until he took me, not by the hand nor the ear nor the nose, but by the belt out of the store.

He yanked me around several homeless youths encamped outside the doorway and through a bickering middle-aged couple in matching flannel shirts, dividing their spoils from the emporium that modestly billed itself as a hardware store, and past the imploring looks of more youths, clipboards pressed to their yet-to-be-gym-sculpted chests like Bibles in paintings of missionaries from a century or two ago, doing outreach on safer sex. Farther and farther up the street until we were deep into the crowd, wading against the current of silent commuters heading home and boisterous tourists heading out.

Up, up, up Castro Street and into the parking lot of the Castro Theater. It was filled with cars, but empty of people. It was too early in the evening for the less brazen.

There he found a gate ajar and tugged me into the alley beside the theater. It was overgrown with the fat steel vines of ascending stairs and stray gray thickets of trash cans. I could hear the rumblings of a movie behind the curtain of bricks. The watery white-gold light of twilight slanted through the crevice at the alley's entrance and stopped a few feet from where Caliban had propped himself against the wall. As vigorously as he'd pounded against the counter and its top, he pushed me down onto my knees.

I hesitated but my revulsion had me. By the balls. I hadn't felt this horny since I'd received my first acceptance in my first anthology. And isn't *horny* just a polite way of saying that I had a very curious cock? It had to know. *I* had to know.

Eagerly and yet gingerly, I unwrapped him. His pants and shorts crouched in a heap at his feet; the buckle of his belt hung out like the tongue of an overheated dog. His shirt ended in the curls and wisps and fronds of his pubes. As for his beast, a prominent fixture in much of his prose, there it hung. And my curiosity, alas, was not sated as I had hoped but piqued.

For I lied — just slightly — earlier.

Caliban has a big dick. Not pornographic. Thank the Fates. Though bigger than most. Certainly bigger than what you'd expect on such a prick.

And the harder it got, the pinker it became. As if the rosy-fingered dawn were flipping me the bird. I was quickly incensed and got lippy. First with the small, but growing, bud of the head. Then, in a series of slow, deep sucks, I inhaled the rest of his cock.

I gripped his ass to balance myself and discovered there was, after all, a pleasant side to Robert Caliban. It was round, ripe, and rising still. Not flattened like those of so many of us other office workers at Inspiration, Inc., forever sitting and taking dictation from the Muses. What do the Muses care for asses? Fortune, however, seems to forever favor them. But that is a different story altogether.

Then again...

To allow my hands to cup and clench and claw his cheeks, I had swallow all of Caliban with each faster thrust. And in this case, the penis was a might like a sword. For the braggart had spoken true. He was a holy terror as he ravaged my mouth. But, fortunately, both he and his dick warned me, through a quickening succession of quivers, when to pull away. For I refused to swallow any more of his bitter ink. Better to be safe than sorry, and I knew I would be ever so sorry tomorrow when I recollected the hour I became another notch in Robert Caliban's laptop case.

So there, in front of my face, twitched the pinkest prick I'd every seen. A color so artificial it could only appear in Easter candy or young girls' bedrooms. And then, enraged that I'd abandoned it in this its most needful of moments, it spat hot and hard across my face. What didn't land on me must have splattered the wall opposite. I almost turned to see if he'd written "Caliban was here." Knowing Robert, it wasn't impossible that he'd trained even his own cum to promote its master and his good works.

As his breath slowed, he spoke in low whispers that I should look in his back pocket. There was something there for me.

A finder's fee? I mused. Perhaps a nondisclosure contract?

It was obvious then how little I knew him.

Instead, I extracted a handkerchief as white as blow.

"A little souvenir to remember me and my dick by. I'm sure the cum will make a nice stain on it. It's silk."

And I thought Tom Wolfe was a dandy.

I unfolded it and stopped. I was aghast. There, woven along one edge, was his web URL.

I looked up in time to watch him sneer, "You never know when the mouth you've just fucked may also write for *The New York Review of Books."*

I covered my shame and my face with the handkerchief and wiped.

While hidden, I tried to gather my wits which were running, screaming, to and fro. Do I quietly get up without a word and walk away, never to look back, never again to look in the face any man, woman, or child with a title in print? Or do I punch him in the gut and run? Or...?

I had to regain my dignity somehow.

I dug my fingers into Caliban's butt.

"Oh ho. You want another go?"

But I wasn't finished. With much grabbing and pinching of my fingers and shuffling and near-tripping of his clothes-bound feet, I turned Caliban toward the wall.

He looked over his shoulder; the ugly leer had been expunged. He was, refreshingly, startled.

"What are you doing?"

"I'd like to show you *my* press kit, Mr. Caliban."

I swallowed a fat and fleshy cheek with my open mouth and bit. He moaned. He yelped. The skin and muscle shook between my teeth. I smiled, as much as one can with an ass in one's mouth. I let my tongue lap the well-baked bun while my hand caressed the other.

And as I did so, I came closer and closer to his crack. I felt its heat. I smelled its ripe aroma. Sweat and the merest whiff of shit. I was intrigued that someone so full of it could smell of it so little.

I dragged my tongue up and down and up the crack, never pressing deeply. Only tracing the surface. Caliban was hissing through his clenched teeth, "Eat me. Eat me...please, eat me."

Please. That was probably the first time he'd used that word in months, if not years. And my mother had raised me, by both hand and hairbrush, to be polite.

So I obliged.

And was I rewarded. For that was the first time I ever laid eyes, and then tongue, on the asshole of Robert Caliban. And it was love at first lick.

Ian Philips

It was delicate and yet textured — like the creases formed when layers of silk are placed one atop the other. And it subtly writhed when I touched it with the tip of my tongue. Caliban, however, lacked the refinements of his own hole. He flinched at the first few wet kisses before abandoning himself altogether, banging his fists on the brick and arching his ass until it swallowed both my nose and mouth.

Though I could not breathe, I was ecstatic. Here, at the end of Robert Caliban's bowels, I had found his one sweet and soft spot. Even the devil himself could be redeemed. But it was not merely a network of nerves, wrapped in succulent flesh. It was a mouth with a set of lips more gentle and more enchanting than any I'd known on a man. And I'd known a nearly biblical roster of men who begat a good kiss.

But what it did when I replaced my tongue with a well-sucked finger bewitched me. It gripped it in its wet and firm embrace and suckled. Suckled with its muscular lips. Firmly pulling me joint by joint deeper into its slick throat.

My dick wished to be curious no more. I released it with my free hand and stroked it. It had the answer it had come for. I yanked my cock urgently. It was ready to make known its opinion of his most eloquent orifice with a hot spew of praise and chest-heaving exaltations.

I shot across and into the clump of Caliban's pants and shorts. After wiping my dick with the handkerchief, I wrapped it around my business card and tossed it down into the impromptu well made of walls of sticky fabric.

"Call me when you're ready for the best star-fucking of your life. And, by the way, I hated your last book. Were you sleeping with your editor or what?"

I stood, a bit shakily, and began to walk away, only to hear him whimper, "Yes."

And with that, I returned to my flat and, I assume, he to his and his mate's.

Yes, he had — still does — a husband. Then again, this is San Francisco. What cocksucker doesn't have a man waiting unawares at home or on the prowl himself with his lover's blessing?

Me.

But I am often the odd man out. And when you trick here, you are more likely than not to be the odd man out. Three's a crowd after you shoot. For them. And for you.

And I wouldn't have wanted to go home with him anyway. For a night or for good.

We were both better off this way. If he accepted my invitation, we could come together and he could brag of his authorial prowess and I could nurse from the newly discovered font of his creativity. Then part merrily and remain merry.

I honestly wanted no more than this since I was between boyfriends and books. Suffering those slow, bone-grinding seconds of emptiness, of expectation. Waiting for the angel to trouble the waters and then drag my lame body and laptop to the pool and be filled. And Caliban had built a tolerable home with a lover who shopped and cooked and cleaned and fucked him every Saturday night and, when asked, dutifully read his work and said, "It's nice, hon," or that he didn't get it but he knew it was good before returning to the kitchen or the embrace of the television or the Internet.

Forgive me, sweetness, for telling tales out of school. But you know he'll never read this. Still, just the thought gets your dick thudding against the snug walls of its cotton cocoon, doesn't it?

Ah yes, dear. Now all the world knows you wear briefs. And quite well. Many the dick-licking man who thinks a pair of briefs is the gilded frame around the penis. But it never hangs just right without the swell of the well-mounded ass. And Caliban is an ass like no other.

Aren't you, Robert?

Obviously, I did finally receive his call, and Caliban his fucking.

It came a week after our "writers' retreat" in the alley.

Just long enough for someone to tend a sweetly

bruised…ego.

His partner was away. Where, I did not learn. Still don't know. It has taken a year of fingering and fucking his hole just to be given his name, though his pictures hang throughout the rooms we've rutted in. But I will spare the innocent here and neither reveal it nor coyly obscure it.

He has endured enough.

He alone lives with Caliban.

That first night, I was given the grand tour. Led through a Victorian warren of antechambers before I was granted admittance into the Holy of Holies: the book-lined office wherein he'd conceived each opus in the ever-burgeoning oeuvre of Robert Caliban.

And there, on a floor strewn with pillows from throughout the flat, he crouched on all fours and commanded me to paddle him with hardbacks. A new one for each swat until there were none. Then, at last, I would be allowed the "privilege" of fucking him. I balked until I imagined what that suckling hole would do to my dick.

So I opened the carton and poorly feigned surprise to discover that the forty copies were of his latest book: *Intimations of Aubergine*. His seven-hundred-page novel in which a couple who are cosmologists watch their deaf-mute child roll in a pile of leaves in the park one fall afternoon. Each imagines the history of the universe through their child's eyes. The wife's sections are written in third-person omniscient with a never-flagging fondness for describing all minutiae, everywhere, down to the microscopic. Actually subatomic. While the husband's sections are written in the second person in a series of memo-like emails beginning with the Big Un-Bang at the end of the universe — "you kick apart the last pile of leaves; pow! pow! pow!" — and working backward. (A friend who teaches assigned it to a particularly precious grad student to read and vivisect in a brief paper as a birthday gift for me.)

Poor Robert. If it weren't for his hole, I'd pity him more than I loathe him. After all, I knew publishers didn't give these books away. He must have been spending all his royalties to buy his own works.

But I gave him his forty whacks. And his virtuoso, voracious hole rewarded me with full-bodied shudders that burned their way under my skin like rivulets of thin, blue flame. I convulsed. I flailed. I came.

And Caliban, oblivious to the torrid love affair exploding behind him, bashed his face into his books as he tried to kiss them and that very same picture on the dust jacket until he'd soaked a pillow or two.

I wished he'd called out his own name. That would have been a nice touch. But far too neat and convenient. And, alas, false.

Instead he remained oddly silent. Perhaps the perfection of that moment. Narcissus able at last to consummate his love. It was I who howled out something about being his total butt slut.

And I was.

And I am.

The problem is that to enjoy the hole I have to suffer the ass that grows around it.

So now we get together only when I can no longer resist the siren song whistling out from between his cheeks. And the rest of our 365 days we write about the other in the hopes that we will end up in print. Together. Only pages apart: calling, cajoling, taunting, teasing, bellowing, cooing, serenading the other.

That did it.

I know he's come by now. How about you?

It is, after all, a true story.

The Red Thread

for Marshall Moore

*W*ould you like to hear a story before you go to bed?

Kenneth and Charles are as white as their names. As white as their teeth. As white as their walls in the dental offices they share. No one but they two know that red is their favorite color. The red of well-aged wines, five-star sauces, sumptuous and flowing velvet. The red of sunsets in the South Pacific and the American Southwest. The red of freshly slapped cheeks and swollen lips and angry-to-the-point-of-spitting dicks. Most of all the red of blood. Blood drawn from their most thrilling, their most favorite game: The Red Thread.

Red, red, red red red.

Kenneth and Charles are two very loved men. By friends and family and peers and clients and acquaintances and play-party comrades and nameless tricks and boys with made-up names who charge by the hour and make love by the minute after minute after minute (always wishing they kept the watch on to check the late-night faucet drip of time) after minute.

Tick tock tick tock. When will the end come?

But Kenneth and Charles were still lonely in all those minutes, in all that time, in all that love and knew it and knew it all the more keenly as they said goodbye to that sour feeling and hello to the sweet relief of the Other when they met and vowed never to be parted again after they'd shared a stall in the bathroom deep beneath the Castro Theater while *Marathon Man* danced in the light on the screen far over their heads on a night in February in a month when all nights are rainy in a city where men meet in bathroom stalls and marry and live happily after ever.

Ding dong come along. Ding dong suck my dong. Ding dong ding dong.

As long as they play games together, that is. As long as they play games together well. As long as they enjoy the games they play together so very well.

Kenneth and Charles play all games together. Play all games together well. Play and, better still, love all games. But Kenneth and Charles play and love one game most of all: The Red Thread.

Red, red, red red red. Just like your underwear. My aren't we grownup?!

Tonight Kenneth and Charles shall play The Red Thread and we shall watch. For Kenneth and Charles cannot see us but we can see them. That is our game. We can see and they cannot for a story told well is one-way mirror in a fun house. They see only themselves but we see them sometimes short and sometimes squat and sometimes tall and sometimes thin. They wiggle and we giggle and we watch all the fun.

Watching and touching is always fun. You touch me here and I touch you there. Don't tell a soul. Our special story. Our special secret. Isn't this fun? Watch and touch. Watch and touch.

Watch. Touch. Fun.

Here are Kenneth and Charles now. They have locked the door to their white office and have said goodbye to one and all save the Other. Let us watch them play The Red Thread, shall we? We will all have fun. Kenneth and Charles and you and me.

Kenneth and Charles have many patients and many chairs for patients to stretch out and open wide and close their eyes. You'll feel a little pinch before you go numb. Tonight Kenneth and Charles choose a white chair that stands alone in the large corner room of their white office where there are many windows. Kenneth goes from window to window and twists at this blind and that until all are shut tighter than a dead man's eye. Charles changes the music from the la la la of the day to the dum dum dum of the night.

That's the lullaby for naughty children. Are you a

naughty boy? I think you might be. I think you're my naughty boy.

From room to room they go turning off the lights. In this little office and that. In this long hallway and that tiny break room. Off go the lights at the receptionist's desk. Off go the lights in the waiting room. Now all the magazines with happy shining faces with dazzling white smiles go to sleep. Now all the files with all the secrets behind those dazzling white smiles — here a cap, there a veneer — go to sleep.

Nighty night. Nighty night. Don't let the sugar-plump fairies bite. Yum, you taste so good.

Soon Kenneth and Charles find themselves standing alone in the black-and-gray shadows around the solitary light that hovers over the chair in the large corner room of their once-white office. The light is tilted so a bright spotlight burns through the head of the chair. It is the backdrop and tonight Charles' mouth will be the stage. Time to change, Kenneth says to Charles. It's time for costumes. It's time for the show to begin. It's time for the red red red curtain to go up on their game.

What's behind your curtain? Lift the blanket, let me see. Lift the blanket, let me in.

Into their offices go Kenneth, go Charles. Each next to the other. Each always next to the other. Out comes Charles, out comes Kenneth.

Here stands Charles in a red jock. And there stands Kenneth is a red dental smock and nothing else. Slap, slap. Kenneth hits Charles. Charles wobbles a bit and Kenneth shouts, It's time for your checkup, boy. You're long overdue. Yes, Dr. Sir, says Charles. My jaws ache, Dr. Sir. I think I grind my teeth. I think I have a toothache. Slap, slap, thud. Kenneth hits Charles' face again before punching him hard and fast in the gut. You fucking sugar fiend, screams Kenneth. You teeth must be rotted. Look at your swollen cheeks. You're doubled over in pain. You need a thorough exam now. Into the chair this instant.

Kenneth takes Charles by his shoulders and shakes

him, shakes him, and shakes him. Until Charles spins
himself around and toward the chair. Whack. Even without
his white shoes, even with just his one white foot, Kenneth
can kick Charles square in the ass. Charles stumbles over
the chair and Kenneth not so kindly helps him roll over.
Charles' flesh squeaks as it's pulled up along the sucking
skin of the chair.

Just like when I kiss you here or here. Suck, suck, suck.
Pop.

Pop goes the buckle of the restraint. Pop once more.
Charles' wrists are snug and safe. The arms of the chair
will hold him tight. For The Red Thread is a fun game and
Kenneth doesn't want Charles to get hurt. Much.

Kenneth spits on his fingers. Where are his gloves?
There are no gloves tonight. Tonight is all fun. Kenneth
takes his fingers and shoves them between Charles' legs.
Until Charles' legs are bent at the knees and each knee is
as high as a church steeple and his ass floats in the air like
an angel. Who's my angel? Out come the fingers. Out comes
the spit. In go the fingers. Up goes the ass. Out comes a
moan from Charles. Kenneth laughs.

See, fun!

Kenneth grabs something from the tray beside the
chair. There are many sharp and shiny things on the table.
This is not shiny and not very sharp. It's a red toothbrush.
Kenneth pushes the end of it with a little rubber thorn at
the tippy tip tip inside Charles to get Charles' mouth wider,
wider, dammit, wider. Oh, look at Charles. *O* is just how
Charles' mouth looks. The letter *O*. Capital *O*. *O* is for ouch.

There are several *O*s hidden all over your body. Can
you show me one?

Kenneth stands back and smiles. What a pretty white
smile he has. He should. He's a dentist. He drops his robe.
What a pretty white body he has. He should. He's a gay
man who believes that love is unconditional for only those
with no more than 13% body fat, no matter the age, no
matter the man. 13. So often unlucky. Unless it's inches, of
course. Which in Kenneth's case it's not. But more than

half isn't bad and Kenneth has never been loved less because of it. And what a pretty red and oh-so-hard seven-and-a-half-inch dick it is. It should be. Kenneth's a sadist and he's just begun.

Watch Kenneth climb. Climb on top of Charles. Climb up Charles till he straddles him just below his well-defined chest. How gyms brings such clarity to the life of gay men.

Do you like to work out? I have something big and heavy for you to lift. You'll need to use both hands. Will you help me? You're such a good friend.

Kenneth turns his head and scans the tray of gleaming ramrod-straight steel blades and curved-and-gnarled steel points and chooses an ordinary pick. One that every dentist has taken to all our mouths. He taps it against the hard sides of Charles' molars and he scrapes it and scrapes it against the impervious enamel of Charles' canines and incisors. Now Kenneth reaches for a drill. He turns it on. Whir, whir, whir. Listen to it shriek.

Kenneth doesn't put the drill to Charles' tooth. Where did it go? Kenneth puts the sharp, shiny point at the end of the pick against Charles' tooth and drags it with a tiny screech to the border where white enamel meets pink gum.

Flinch, bitch, and I'll let it rip through your tit, says Kenneth with a spit-filled hiss into Charles wide but scream-less mouth. Here's the drill! Kenneth lets the whining tool get close enough to Charles' tit, as hard and high as a tooth made of skin, so Charles can feel the vibration, the tiny breath of air from the spinning metal spike.

How you tremble so as you help me touch mine. It's not metal. Just me. I'm shaking too.

Poke, poke, poke goes the pick against Charles' pink pink pink gum.

No blood.

Kenneth is both happy and sad. Happy that Charles' gums are so healthy. Who would go to a dentist with gums bloated and red from gingivitis? Not you. Not me. And sad that there is no blood. Yet.

Off goes the drill and away goes the pick. Kenneth turns to the tray once more. What will he choose? So many tools. So many sharp points. So many shiny points. So many ways for Kenneth to draw those red drops from Charles. Each a distillation of the man he loves. How Kenneth loves Charles and Charles loves Kenneth.

How I love you. Here's a drop of me for you. Men have two kinds of blood. One is secret. It only flows on special times. It's the lifeblood. It connects you to me and me to you.

Yank, yank, yank. That's just how it sounds as Kenneth pulls and pulls and pulls something from the tray. It's a thread that's long and white. White? Where is the red thread? Watch. What goes in white comes out red or this game will be no fun.

Around his one pointing finger Kenneth wraps the thread leaving just a bit to wind about his other pointing finger. Kenneth twists and tugs and a tightrope appears. It's so tight that even if a teeny elephant tried to walk across the thread it wouldn't sag or even bounce. When something's that tight it's taut.

Just like when I touch you here. Stay still. Right here. Ooh, that's what taut feels like. How I love taut. How I love you.

When you floss, you're supposed to make a letter *C*. Wrap the ends of the floss around the tooth so it's inside the deep curve where the letter bows out like the belly of a very fat man. Yes, just like mine. But I'm not the letter *C* even with my nice big curve.

C is for curve. *C* is not for scrape. Though there is a letter *C* snug as a bug inside. Hard and fast asleep between the *S* and *R*. It's a hard *C* in scrape. It sounds like the letter *K*.

Skrape.

And that's what you do with your floss once it sits like a *C* that's fallen over on its side. You scrape up. You scrape down. Scrape into the hollow between tooth and gum where bits of food and gunk are mingling and fucking in the hot tub waters of your saliva. Fuck, fuck, fuck. And soon all the Mr. & Mrs. Food-Gunks have babies and Plaque is the de rigueur baby name for that minute. For every minute. Here a plaque. There a plaque. Everywhere a plaque, plaque. It nurses on your tooth till it wears it down. Rots it through and through. Greedy baby. Greedy fuck. The only way to pry the invisible sucking mouths from your titty teeth is to floss.

Scrape. Scrape. Scrape.

If Kenneth were scraping inside my big mouth or your little mouth, we who floss only when a blue moon waxes and wanes, the thread would be red by the second scrape. Not Charles. He has healthy gums. Not a single cavity. Kenneth must go from tooth to tooth — molar to bicuspid to canine to incisor to canine to bicuspid to molar — over and over again. Down and up Kenneth thrusts the floss. Each time he pulls it out from between the teeth there is a loud and popping thunk. Thunk. Thunk. Thunk thunk thunk. Faster and faster goes Kenneth. The floss is growing ragged at the edges. Soon it will break. Soon Charles will break. Who first? Will it be the floss? Will it be Charles?

Wait! Kenneth sees something. Up it oozes between Charles' two front teeth. A teeny tiny droplet that trickles down from the tender gum and over the ragged floss. It dyes the thread to red.

The thread is red.

Red, red, red red red.

Like to like always say Kenneth and Charles. White to white and red to red. Out comes the red thread. In stays the red tooth. In goes the red head of Kenneth's dick.

I'm partial to dark pink. I know somewhere very pink and very dark on you. Out comes my finger. Your exam is through. In goes my dick. Time to drill. Open wide. You'll feel much better very soon.

Look at Kenneth drill. Watch the chair buck. Watch Charles' eyes roll. Watch Kenneth's butt clench. Following the bouncing buns!

Kenneth can't wait till blood and lifeblood mix.

Kenneth can't wait till he and Charles are one. One inside one makes one.

See Kenneth come. Come, Kenneth, come. And come he does. I can't see it. Neither can you. But, boy, can we hear it! Yipee ai ay! Jesus christ oh god fuck!

Fuck! Fuck! Fuck!

Now it's our turn. Give me your lifeblood, son, and I'll give you mine. We'll be connected — you to me and me to you — always. We'll always be special friends. Big Daddy and his not so itty, not so bitty baby boy. Here we lie together in your king-sized crib. Side by side. You on the outside. Me on the inside. Side by side. Oh, how good it feels to share. Hear how we shout for joy!

Fun! Fun! Fun!

Kenneth isn't done sharing yet. He doesn't even notice what a generous gift Charles wants to share with him. Charles knows and shouts with glee. Look at what a big white puddle the big white boy makes! Kenneth laughs because he has a surprise for Charles and now is the perfect time to give it to him.

Time to rinse and spit, boy, says Kenneth. Charles would say, Yes, Dr. Sir, if his mouth weren't so full with Kenneth's dick and Kenneth's lifeblood. No time for Charles to catch his breath. No time for Charles to swallow. Look, now Charles' mouth is filling with hot and bitter water. See it flow out of his mouth. Wait, Charles is pulling away. Kenneth is watering Charles' face. Charles is rinsed. Now it's time to spit. Charles spits Kenneth's water back on him. But not with a tinkling trickle. Just one loud and wet SPLAT!

Is Kenneth mad? Has Charles been bad? No, see how they laugh. The wetter they get the more they laugh. They are soaked. Their skin shines like a just-mopped floor under the bright light of the 4-in-the-afternoon sun, leaning against the kitchen wall like a drunk, lost and bewildered to find himself in a kitchen and one that has just been mopped. Watch their skin dry over the next hour as they wipe down and disinfect the sticky chair together so it is innocently clean before Mrs. Groesbeck reclines for her 8 a.m. final fitting and cementing of her crown.

Crowns, crowns, crowns. Every one is queen for a day at Kenneth and Charles'.

The game is over. Everybody won. Kenneth and Charles are very tired but very happy as they bid each other goodnight and curl up upon their daybeds in their adjoining offices. In goes Kenneth, in goes Charles. Kenneth and Charles sleep alone the nights they play at the office, the nights they play their favorite game at the office, the nights they play their favorite game The Red Thread at the office. But Kenneth and Charles are never lonely in all those minutes they sleep apart, in all that time, for they are in love and know it and have known it more and more keenly since they said goodbye to that sour feeling of loneliness and hello to the sweet relief of the Other when they met and vowed never to be parted again after they'd shared a stall in the bathroom deep beneath the Castro Theater while *Marathon Man* danced in the light on the screen far over their heads on a night in February in a month when all nights are rainy in a city where men meet in bathroom stalls and marry and live happily after ever.

Ding dong come along. Ding dong suck my dong. Ding dong ding dong.

Goodnight, Kenneth. Goodnight, Charles.

Goodnight, sugar. I love you. Sweet dreams.

Cyber Interruptus

for Kirk Read

"There lives no man who at some period has not been tormented...by an earnest desire to tantalize a listener by circumlocution."
—Edgar Allan Poe, "The Imp of the Perverse"

$\mathcal{I}$'m old-fashioned.

Not much for a bold, declarative statement in these days of extreme sports and fabric softeners, I must confess. Yet, gentle readers, if only this very moment before your widening eyes you could see that most confounded juxtaposition that does exist between these genteel words and the brash and modern garb of the living font of their issuance you would reel — I daresay — from the sight of this unholiest of marriages until you were overcome by the sheer ridiculousness of this deviltry and succumbed — of this I'm certain! — to pissing yourselves handily from your own unbridled laughter. Heaven knows my boyfriends have.

To begin, I have liberally availed myself of all the free will that the deities of literature allot to a first-person narrator and thus been pierced from head to crotch: my left eyebrow, both ears several times, my tongue (natch!), my no-longer-itty-bitty titties, my dick (a classic Prince Albert, originally sprouting as a modest 10 gauge before blossoming into an 8), and my taint (or perineum, for the Graeco-Romans and doctors amongst us). I started this trail of adornments in high school and worked my way down during college.

I got my guiche done last at Mad Medea's[*] as a belated

---

[*] For those whose chief delectation is to unravel subtext's Gordian Knot, the Author recommends a thorough perusal of his sister's exploits in "Mercy" and "No Mercy" in Pat Califia's *No Mercy* (Alyson). What a shameless plug, you scoff, my freshly offended critic. Exactly. Everything we do in San Francisco, from consumption to exhibition, is shameless. Let the mutual admiration between its writers, as rare an event in any city's gathering of paper scribblers and keyboard rattlers as a virgin birth — let alone, a virgin — be no less brazen.

Ian Philips

graduation present to myself several months after I'd
moved to San Francisco a year ago June. She—Mad
Medea's owner, Metamorpheen—usually doesn't do
boys—especially down there. But it was a favor to my sister,
Heather, who used to date Meta's new girlfriend Terry. In
fact, my sister is not only responsible for introducing my
now-dear friend Terry to me, but she is also to blame for
driving each of us into the arms of the other. For Heather
is...how shall I finesse this? To my gentlest readers, I'll
describe her simply as a pill. To you chivalrous butches
out there, holding me gingerly in your strong and broad
and tool-hardened hands, she is a high-impact and high-
maintenance femme. (You shuddered; I felt it.) Then again,
in all fairness, so am I. And to those of you whose
Weltanschauung lacks the insight of a bulldagger who won't
bullshit, I'll be frank: As Meta is fond of saying, my sister
is a cunt with no cash limit.

Rest assured, Meta opined even more that day as she
worked, all of which I enjoyed thoroughly but will keep to
myself. If I've learned anything in my so-far short sojourn
in San Francisco, it is that this very city is the world
headquarters of TMI, which, to the most secluded of you
unrepentant bookworms, stands for "too much
information." For in all my myriad travels, it is only here,
in this minor metropolis, that I have found a people who,
despite their oftentimes vacant and nowadays disgruntled
miens, take so great a delight in speaking with such a
remarkably odd gusto to strangers and recent
acquaintances alike of sub-rosa details that in other
environs are best saved for the diary, the priest, the
therapist, or the grave.

After two years in this Baghdad, or as I'm wont to call
it, Blabmad by the Bay, even *I* am no longer immune to
bouts. Why imagine—I, a true scion of the gelid sperm of
our Puritan forefathers, once a boy who blushed with
shame every time he had a boner, have just told you these
two candid facts, unasked and without abashedness. And
I will go on to confess to you, my newest friends, that if

160

any of you happen to be boys and bespectacled and, perchance, British, I remain, as of this writing, very much single and fond of your cheek — especially astride my face.

This is TMI. It is more than over-caffeinated bonhomie. It is a disclosure of either titillating or terrifying proportions and always irrelevant to the matter immediately at hand. In San Francisco, this is how we say "hello."

Hello.

Now, where was I? Somewhere mid-description, no doubt. I tend, as those learnèd 18th and 19th-century authors I've studied of late, to digress — a lot. Allow me to apologize now for my oft-vexing predilection for this and many other antiquated narrative devices. By journey's end, more than a few of you will wish that Papa Hemingway (that hoary hotty!) had given me a good thrashing with his manly prose and a well-earned enema with his hunting rifle.

And — TMI time again; so soon? — much to the dismay of my ill-wishers, I'd be game for all but the gun.

Alas, I must inquire anew: where were we? Lost, most likely, in the labyrinth of tangential anecdotes. Ah, yes, I've grasped the fallen thread; I have my bearings now! Let us return to the aforementioned cunt.

I hinted earlier that I believe Heather drove Terry, her ex, into Meta's very capable hands. Well, after Terry had introduced me to Meta and I had finished recounting my own tiny tale of sibling perfidy to her, I was unshakably certain that my sister had chauffeured yet another into the arms of Mad Medea herself. Indeed, Meta and I became fast friends that night I lay spread eagle atop her surgical drape.

So, you must now be wondering, to what infernal depth of foul wretchedness could my hardhearted sister have sunk? What manner of damnable deed did she perpetrate against flesh and blood? In order to lay bare the bitch, it's best that I begin afresh.

As I proclaimed in my single-sentence prologue, I'm old-fashioned. I shall now promptly modify that: I'm old-fashioned about certain things. I take after Mom here. My sister, however, is like her daddy and hidebound about all things. And since my arrival in *her* city, she hadn't cottoned — not one ball! — to how I was using my B.A. in English from a university back east that she and Dad and most of the institution's benighted alumni, except for myself and a few other malcontents, considered to be eminently prestigious. For, in short, I wasn't.

Nor shall I in the foreseeable future. Not before this little roué has let the good times roll merrily along for several more years. Then and only then do I intend to return to the old intellectual rag-and-bone shop a refreshed prodigal and earn my doctorate. For I am all too aware that I can keep the snarling hounds of fate at bay only so long when both pack and prey know that this boy has been cursed — at the whim of some diabolical prankster I fear — with a yen to teach literature and the subtle art of its composition. And curses, unlike gossamery blessings which even the weakest zephyr can blow off course, are so weighted with pain that they always fall back to earth.

And upon that predestined day, I shall embrace, passionately, my life of poverty. Until then, I beg of you — only metaphorically now — to get real! This is San Francisco at the onset of the twenty-first century (i.e., the last year of the second millennium for those who might have misguidedly partied "like it's 1999" in 1999); it is no place to be poor and penniless. And pennies are all that a B.A. here — excepting it's preceded by an "M" or stands for Bank of America — would afford you as you poured out yet another grande double lowfat latte for an already overly agitated dot-commer. Unless, that is, you were truly possessed by the brainsick spirit of our times to tinker at a computer more hours than Penelope ever wove at her loom and "achieve" through all your hard labors — and a little pat on the posterior from the invisible white hand of the "free" market's sire, Adam Smith, into a sure-fire IPO — the apotheosis that is the dot-commer; a transmogrification I am, by my very perverse nature, incapable of *ever* undergoing — more on that commercial deficiency to follow below.

What my sister remained unaware of — mainly by refusing to ask me even the simplest of questions like "How are you?" — was that I had never been enticed to the eBay Area by the glint of cyber-gold in "them thar hills." No, I was beckoned to Sodom on the Sea by the picaresque tales of my penultimate boyfriend who'd moved here the year before and, to no one's surprise save maybe his mother's, had risen like a rocket within the ranks of the world's oldest profession. And it was again Mike who, once I too had graduated and found myself suddenly homeless unless — never! — I went home, added the last damning bits of bait to Lechery's lure with his earnest entreaties to come and dwell platonically with him in his city of ill repute.

As it is the writer's quest to reach heights of ever greater precision, let me add, and perhaps elucidate further my sister's indifference towards the obvious with, the following: What Heather lacked was not only an interest in her brother's true welfare but, moreover, a grasp of the relevant facts that would have allowed her to deduce with utmost ease that he would require, after his car rattled into a free parking space ten blocks from his future home, but thirteen days of his ex-boyfriend-cum-rent-boy's constant and not-so-platonic tutelage to acquire a thorough familiarity with all the basic bodily skills the trade demanded so he might go from making $6.75 an hour for thirty-something scalding hours a week as a barista to — ka-ching! — raking in $100 an hour for five or six sometimes steamy hours as a sex worker. And thus, she would happily have been freed from much of her fretting over the mystery as to how that "spoiled little unemployed slacker" could, within a month of unpacking his cruddy little diploma and umpteen boxes of belovèd books, be doing so well.

So well indeed, that it was only then that Heather paid me any real heed and, by doing thusly, grew so suspicious that she was "forced" to perform an intervention. One foggy Sunday last July, I'd foolishly agreed to meet with my viperine kin *alone* for brunch. When I was wedged into the ill-boding corner table, my thigh an inch from an increasingly nervous Great White Male — a breed(er) at one time distinguishable from his homosexual homologue, the Gay White Male, who today is little more than a straight man who has piggy sex with other straight men — at the table next to me, she menacingly leaned in over her eggs Benedict and curried homefries and launched into me.

Was I dealing drugs? No, I said, but sometimes I take them. Was I living off my boyfriend? No, Mike is my ex, I replied. We're just roommates and I pay my way for everything. Then where is the money coming from to pay your $700 share of the rent? Actually, I said, my share is $800 — Mike and I live with two other guys on the quaintest tree-lined street in the Duboce Triangle — and it's none of your business. Her face whitened until she looked more dead than peeved. Is Dad giving you money? I laughed with such boisterous jollity that the startled Great White halted his monologue mid-sentence, put down his fork, and turned to shame, and, perhaps, appraise me. I ignored him and my sister. He returned, in true Great White fashion, to barking, with the dulcet tones of a sea lion at Pier 39, his way through his conversation with an especially malnourished blonde; my sister then followed his lead.

"Well, is he?" she hissed under her breath.

Every family, regardless of whichever tax brackets they find themselves pinched between, has one member who is revered and feared as the all-powerful ATM; the ATM giveth and the ATM taketh away. Now for some, said ATM is that very distant relative Uncle Sam. But, for our family, he is our dear old dad. Heather's restrained belligerence made it obvious that her account had been frozen, and for a long while now. I sympathized with her plight — for I affectionately remained her brother on that drabbest of days — but, being still twenty-two, I was blinded by my own ripening youth and flush with my newfound wealth and hence unconcerned if the ATM ever gave me even another dollar. What I had yet to learn was the celerity with which the money machine's dispenser of fatherly affections could also be jammed with ice.

"No," I answered coolly. "He hasn't given me anything since graduation. And that was just a few thousand to move from one coast to the other."

Just a few. I know I sound reprehensible, but I promise you, if I were truly a trustafarian — that class of capitalist spawn which holds the coveted sinecure of trust fund baby but scrofulously masks their eternal infusion of wealth by slumming through life as some ill-starred bohemian — I'd come clean right away. On the contrary, I was simply born and raised, as it were, to be a bourgeois princeling. In other words, I had the attitude of one who was groomed to inherit but would never rule the kingdom on earth. Today, I'm not even that; I am merely another deposed royal-wannabe in the city of Emperor Norton who must fund each of his gala debaucheries out of his own pocket.

"Don't lie to me," she chided, her body rigid with her own righteousness and jerking at her every word. "Well," she spat. The table shook and her water tipped over. As the cold stream began cascading from the tabletop onto my legs, I delved into my back pocket, retrieved my wallet, and essayed to stand. The impassible table had cornered me against the wall; hunched and wet, I twisted my way into the aisle. Once upright, I threw down a $100 bill onto her barely eaten eggs and potatoes. "You want to know what I do?" I challenged. "I'll tell you. I take it up the ass for cash." Her stiff grimace withered; her mouth fell open like a door jimmied by a crowbar. "That's right, Heather. Your baby brother is a hooker." The room fell deathly silent. Whereupon I looked about, thereby catching my own eye several times in the floor-to-ceiling mirrors along the back wall, and added before storming out, "If any of you Überzombies & Zits want to see more, my photo's in the back of the *Bay Area Reporter*!"

I received two calls after that. One came from the Great White himself, believe it or not, for a simple suck-and-fuck that led to two repeats in the back of his Hooker's green — his poor pun, not mine; I am now convinced he was attempting to inveigle a discount for artists, which I do offer but only if they are starving and/or talented! — Range Rover. The other was from dear old dad. Let me just say, in a rare moment of brevity, that thanks to Heather, my family has not only disowned me, they've disavowed me.

Meta was so moved once I'd finished my story that she threw in three fierce tats for free. The ones on my right arm and chest you can see when I work out. Come on down to G—'s Gym in the Castro and knock yourself out. The one on my ass, to see that, you'll have to pay. Since the ill-fated fatherly phone call, I charge a modest $175 an hour.

And — oh! my dear readers — what callipygian wonders would await you. You would be seduced forthwith by the siren sway of these pendulous orbs as they rocked gracefully to and fro on the ebb and swell of each stride closer to your bedchamber. And when we both had entered your room of dreams and your purse of gold slumbered safely in my palm, I would let drop the denim curtains that had hitherto hindered the fullest force of your gaze so you might follow, unimpeded at last, the downy slope of the golden flesh and feel the substantial heft in these twin knots of curvaceous muscle, pressed together — except when passion's most robust rigors tear them asunder — in the tenderest of embraces.

Yes, I am aware that for some of you, the most rakish of the lot, my hooker ass is pretty much all that you've come here to see in action — or, more accurately, to hear told of in lurid tales that chronicle its assorted poundings. Moreover, you would delight in upbraiding me for recounting this story all wrong; for one must never undertake a stroke piece at a slow pace, unless one is a dissolute, imprisoned 18th-century aristocrat with ample years to misspend in idle and wanton digressions; these are hectic times, after all, and thus demand the quick relief of a line or two of exposition and a page of brief-but-blunt herky-jerky that culminates in a Big O heard 'round the world.

Yes, yes; I've heard that all before. I should have

opened with my buttcheeks spread wide and my asshole flaring. And to you, o prurient ones, may I say, stop being such a client. I promise there'll be a licentious — and flagitious — scene or two if — and please forgive this weak, almost unintentional, pun — you keep plowing inward.

But, if you do reenter my gates, I must caution you to abandon all hope that this fairy's tale will lustily flower into a one-handed read from the diary of sex-machine-for-hire. How well this world could do without one more of those down-and-dirty vignettes, rife with perfervid and meretricious displays of *Sperm und Dong*! No, this shall be instead an honest account of poetic and slightly pornographic justice with a postmodern twist. A morality play for immoralists one and all!

Now let us return our attentions, mine in particular, to the story at hand. As I'd said what must be volumes before, I'm pierced and tattooed from stem to stern. You might make me out in a crowd just from that little tidbit. Then again, this *is* San Francisco. Here I'm just another modern-day Queequeg in a city of Moby Dicks. For those who've started to scan the rest of the paragraph to see if the white whale surfaces, sorry. We'll come to that soon enough. And, if you're finally realizing that you lack the pre-cyber-industrial-revolution attention span necessary to withstand the subtle torments of my masterfully prolonged cocktease, might I suggest a naughty video; go ahead; put me down and pop it in; I won't mind.

And so, it is just you, my one remaining reader, and I; the last philistine has been sent trundling merrily towards the nearest McLackluster Video. Now for you alone, o bosom friend, I shall continue — and at a quicker clip; after all, I have a breath-quickening tale still to tell.

As we last left off, you were searching the crowd for a sexy stud pup; you still are. He stands a tall or small, depending on your perspective, five feet and eleven inches. He weighs a well-muscled 185 pounds. That's 13 stone, give or take a pebble, for my British boyfriends. (I haven't forgotten you, luvs.) Would it also help if I told you that your princox charming had recently bleached his short, bland, brown hair and died it a dusky shade of plum that matches the polish of his well-tended nails? It would if he weren't wearing a black Kangol cap backwards. Yet if, however, in this crowd you were to note such a jaunty hat and beneath it to espy a purplish-tinted patch of hair affixed to the lower lip of a sensuous pout, you'd be close — close enough to peer over his sunglasses and into his ever-changing hazel eyes that run the gamut from gold to green brown — close enough, in fact, for you both to kiss.

Perhaps I should also inform you that he's sporting a small T-shirt from his favorite urban dyke café, Red Dora's Bearded Lady (may she rest in peace). It fittingly enswathes his pecs and rides up just enough to show off an ab or two. Across the wide, white field of his broad chest, two flaming dice-from-hell roll forth. And beneath these, it reads: "Red Dora's Bearded Lady Cafe. Liquor in the front. Poker in the rear." Such delicious concision! Just what I like to do unto others and have done unto me.

To complete this modish picture, our lad wears a beltless pair of blue and black camos — camouflage pants, you bookeater — that accentuate the blue in the lenses of his sunglasses. They're held up only by the strong curves of his recently belauded ass. The pants are then tucked with care into two very well-polished black boots that are bound up with red laces.

I'm sure you could spot this dandy now; as the epigrammatic amongst my hustling kin delight in repeating, beauty begets business. Of course, it would help if I were dressed just so this very moment. Alas, I am not. But I would don this gay apparel if you called my ad and requested it. I'll do pretty much anything once — if asked nicely and paid handsomely.

Now, don't — I beg of you! — go and fall face-first into the slough of despond. All this emphasis on my own dandification wasn't in vain. I've set our story's stage in two ways. First, I've introduced sufficient details to establish both character and voice — enough even to leave the ears of the dimmest reader (now long gone) ringing with irony when I profess for the third and, one hopes, final time that I'm old-fashioned. Secondly, I've limned a verbal portrait of my attire at the exact moment *he* called.

But, first things first. My story shall fail to entertain and edify fully if I were not this very moment to make as clear as crystal—the mineral, not the Turkish delight of queens and guttersnipes alike—my meaning with regards to my proud claim of being old-fashioned about only certain and quite specific things. Obviously not fashion, you jest. Family values then? Right, that's so me: the hooker with a heart of gold waiting for an adoring prince that'll revert first into a horny toad and then into an oft-absent husband. No, that would be too much irony even for me, as most of my clients already have husbands who always happen to be out of town. Or the classic wife who doesn't understand a man's needs. That is to say, she won't deepthroat his dick. And, unlike most of my queer peers who freely converse with any and all pollsters, this maverick does not want a monogamous relationship. Maybe if I believed it could work. But I've yet to see monogamy alive in the gay wild. And that hybrid which is bred in domestic captivity, while good for my business, rarely lives to maturity.

No, it's all this "new-fangled" technology that I detest. Yes, you are correct. Your humble first-person narrator is a Luddite. Truth be told, a neo-Luddite. For it is not *every* machine that I wish to smash into a jillion pieces but merely those which are the tools of my trade: pagers and cell phones. Those, and anything and anyone plugged into a computer.

I'm quite certain you can understand why I find those buzzing and ringing shackles—my two concessions to the twilight hours of twentieth-century American hooking—to be such pains in my pleasing ass. Everywhere you go these days you're forced to eavesdrop on some one-sided conversation between a very self-important person and their piece of plastic. But computers? You've undoubtedly run over to embrace your trusty laptop and make sure your Palm Pilot is sleeping safely in the satchel where you keep your keys and debit card. What, pray tell, is wrong with them? you ask, scanning the horizon for bonfires of burning motherboards.

If you employ one as a glorified typewriter or drawing board, nothing, I say. I can't even read my own handwriting; so I wouldn't be tapping out this verbal thicket and you wouldn't be enjoying the prickly pleasure of stumbling through it if it weren't for one. But no one stops there nowadays, do they?

Let me proffer this example.

Mike, who you will remember is my ex, my roommate, and my mentor in the art of hooking, prefers these days to procure not only cat food online but also so many inches of uncut cock—both delivered, within one day and one half-hour, respectively, to our doorstep. The happy outcome: our cat's and my ex's basic needs are met with an unnatural alacrity. Furthermore, our sex-worker-of-the-future, inspired by how well he is now tended to by his computer, has gone so far even as to remove his ad from the papers and peddle his sizeable wares by means of a well-worded profile in chatrooms far and wide. The result here: his clientele—of steady, satisfied repeats—has doubled in six months.

No harm done, you say? Let me disabuse you. For I would wager you an hour with my ass that it is easier to pluck leeches from Mike's smooth, albeit sinewy, flesh than it is to pry him away from his computer. Why he would rather move about the world as a discombobulated phone signal than as a man of blood and bone! But, I ask you, without blood and bone, what are the pleasures of being a man?

Between nil and null, I daresay—if my ever-metastasizing prolixity were, in some very sardonic act of Divine Will and Divine Will alone, to lapse into remission and I to wax as laconic as that sacred spigot of all monosyllabic grunts: A Real Man.

Sic transit gloria mundi.

O reader, how well do I know of what I speak! — the bloodless and boneless part, not the thing about being tight-assed and taciturn. For, while I myself refuse to walk the cyber-streets, I *have* tried online sex. Several times, in fact. And after each electronic foray, I've found myself more deflated than when I'd embarked. All because I seem forever incapable of suspending my critical little ol' disbelief at that most crucial of moments.

Not at courtship's initiation, mind you, when one might suspicion my distrust to be stiffer than my dick. I've already told you that I've studied a bit of literature. Which is to say, I'm no stranger to verbal flights of fancy. So it would follow, natch, that I can take wing rather easily from *SukPump451* and *4skn4eva* and *BadBloke*'s introductory descriptions of their cyber-doppelgängers. I even remain airborne throughout our frantically typed transgressions until the *coup de grace* is delivered. That's when this hidebound sensualist plummets, faster than Icarus being chased with a blowdryer, earthwards.

Why? Because I am doomed to distrust that the man — the specious notion of gender's fixity, however, I can adhere to here with the unflinching faith of a simpleton — on the other end of the cable is honestly ejaculating. And, for some reason known only to my unconscious, I must "feel" their salvo first in order to fire off my own. But, no matter how many *m*s he puts in "I'M COMING!," the shrill, small voice of reason always intrudes and says if he were in the *true* throws of ecstasy, he'd stop typing. I've tried twice more since that first failure; until I realized, as my last partner, flushed with his incipient orgasm, spilled out line after line of characters across the screen, that I would never hear those magic words — "I'm commm…" — and I logged off mid-stream, vowing never to return to these disappointing realms of ether.

And as for Mike's favorite late-night snack of dick delivered hot to your door — <<want2party?>> — let me warn you away from this farrago of false hopes. You want to bump and grind; he just wants a bump. Suffice it to say that men lie more to themselves about what they want than they do about what they have.

So let us instead, most dear and devoted reader, return to the day whereupon I'd appareled myself in the hippest of urban foppery. Cockily, my outfit and I were taking a post-prandial strut through that gay marketplace known to queers in climes far and wide as the Castro when my business phone squawked from deep within a pocket of my camos. I fished for it; pulled at one and then the other end as it trilled louder; and answered.

"Hello, this is B. J." That sobriquet always gets them going. "Is that your real name?" "No." To you, long-suffering reader, I'll reveal it. It's A. J., an abridgment for the dynastic title Alfred Arthur Jackson Reynolds IV. As I confessed to you before, I was raised a full-fledged lord of the suburbs. But to the almost always mocking voice on the other end, I'm often of a mind to ask if "John" or, in this case, "Brad" is theirs. But I don't. The Sass-Master reserves the most stingingly sweet licks from his tongue for boyfriends and off-duty tricks alone.

To my good fortune, Brad got down to business. He offered me $500 for two hours of my time if I performed a certain list of sexual acts—none I haven't done before and won't attempt again. I agreed; it would be the highest hourly wage I'd ever garnered; and it would afford me that certain leatherbound edition of my beloved Poe: a collection of nearly all my favorite stories, including *Hop-Frog*, accompanied by an assortment of fine engravings to illustrate each tale therein, and lavishly so. In my bibliomaniacal reverie I held the precious treasure open within my trembling hands and began to read the magic book until it vanished at the first sound of Brad's voice as he proceeded to expound, unbidden and at length, on his body and the prodigiousness of its most singular extremity.

"Great," I replied in an attempt to conclude our business, "have it raring and ready to go tonight. So, where do I have to be to see the eighth wonder?"

"It's not eight. It's ten and a half," he answered with the tell-tale tremolo of suppressed offense.

"Of course." It was my turn to repress: the urge to roll my eyes, to laugh wildly, to throw the phone into the street. Now I don't know if I would agree with Ms. Paglia that repression is as necessary for great art as the rack is for artistic confessions. But it really does teach a boy, this one in particular, how to refine his artifice.

"So, when and where, Brad?" I said with all the sugary sweet coyness I could ladle out before slipping into a diabetic coma.

That night I changed into some regulation Folsom Street — that's code here, my sweet bookworm, for "Leather Lovers Lane" — evening wear with one damning deviation: the standard-issue leather biker's jacket beaten down in all the right places; a snug, blindingly white T-shirt; a black belt with silver studs cinching up a pair of worn 501s; followed by a final pair, of shoes — two cherry red Converse sneakers, post-millennial ruby slippers, with the butchest black laces you've ever seen. When I choose to, I can be a very bad boy.

After all, my ad does say "Corn-Fed Farm Boy Gone Bad." And no matter how jaded the age and I might be, I believe there should be some modicum of truth in advertising. And, when *I* advertise, there is: I've eaten corn; I know what a farm is; I have the face of a cherub — granted a cherub fallen far behind that great-plastic-covered-couch-in-the-sky known simply as Grace — and will until I'm well into my fifties; and I'm a perverse imp at heart.

I glanced down at the twitching face of my watch as I listened to the cab floor its way the remaining 100 feet of the street, stopping at the intersection only a second before gunning off into the night. It was 7:55 p.m. I was early — a very bad habit to have in San Francisco where everyone else either runs late or never bothers to show up. As I waited, the rubber sole of my tapping shoe rasping against the concrete, I made a cursory survey of my whereabouts. I heard the scrape of plastic bags and the rustle of discarded newspapers as they gamboled along the sidewalk. A few would scurry away from their siblings and dive under the rows of cars, wedged one against the other, along either bank of what appeared to be a frozen asphalt stream.

Something was odd, I thought: all these cars but only one house. The rest were warehouses that, most likely, employed some of the legions of dot-commers who had possessed the City of late; their windows were black as pitch. Only that made sense, seeing as it was Saturday night; and even the cyber-gentry must give their fabled 24/7 cupidity a rest and recreate sometime. No, what unsettled me was that the windows in my client's house — I checked the scrap of paper to confirm the address; it was correct — were blacker still. To make matters more sinister, the nearest street light had burned out. Thus, from beyond the low wall of two-story buildings across the street, the colossal steel skeleton of a dozen live-work lofts yet to be built — its empty metal innards hung with strings of encaged, glowing bulbs — cast monstrous shadows that darkened every inch of this little side street and its littler house.

If I were a superstitious soul and, perhaps, not so keen on the $500, I would have taken my now-compiled catalogue of eerie impressions as an abundance of omens presaging some dire and dreadful fate that lay in wait for me within that bleak house and fled. But I've been in far worse spots by accident and, more likely, by intention, so I stood my shadowy ground and bided my time — a rather boring chore, I must add.

After five eternal minutes, I unbound the leather straps of my timepiece — a courtesy I observe of myself and demand of others ever since the hairs of my own balls were ensnared by the watchband of a certain prominent gentleman's Rolex — and pocketed the clock within my jacket; the hour had arrived.

I pressed the bell. It rang, but there was no answer. I pushed again; and again, there was no answer. There was no stirring of any life at all in this ramshackle cabin, one of the hundreds built as temporary housing after the Great Quake and still used as such. I thrust my finger at the bell vigorously now. Nothing. I intended to rap my fist against the door until someone appeared, but, when my flesh met wood, the door gave way.

"Hello?" I queried the dark. I knocked against the open door. "Brad?" Warily, I entered the hall. As my eyes adjusted to the enveloping dimness, I noticed, to my left, the bluish flickerings of an awake television. I moved closer, but still cautiously, towards the source of the sickly light. Within a few footsteps, I found myself at another doorway. I sighed with mild relief when I observed a too-familiar tableau from my own household of four men: a man, messily dressed in a long-sleeved T-shirt, rumpled sweatpants, and mismatched socks, slouched on a couch with a bottle of beer in one hand and a remote in the other, entranced by the babblings of that ever-flowing electronic brook.

"Brad?" I asked the man, who remained unmoving, even unblinking, as he glowed with the reflected phosphorescence of the small box.

Miss Catatonia, I decided right then and there, had all the social graces of the undead. And it was this very deficiency that reminded me of a man I had endured the experience of meeting months before. I recoiled, shuddering imperceptibly, when I'd recollected fully that it had been *this very man*! Yes, it was *he*, the bartender who'd admonished me so at the Manhole or, as I'm caustically inclined to call it, The Callused Nether Eye. My singular offense: I'd ordered a cosmo. What, my dear companion? I'm a fierce nelly faggot and I like my drinks the same: sweet, tart, and pink.

"That's a girl's drink," he'd said, in a thunderous *basso profundo*.

I replied, natch. I'm nearly certain that enough intimacies have been shared between us that you knew, instinctively, I would. My exact words were, I believe: "Then why don't you piss in it and butch it up."

Jan Philips

To the hoots and woofs of the many and crapulent animals in his menagerie, he did. Whereupon I took a sip and winced. (Talk about your potent potables; vodka and coffee so don't mix!) I plunked the drink down on the counter and then beckoned him to lean in with my crooked finger and more crookèd smile; he did. I then proceeded to hose his face down thoroughly as I forced the sullied drink back out through the modest breach between my front teeth and left, never once looking back until this unanticipated, it's-a-too-too-small-world-after-all reunion.

And so, reader, I found myself standing, alone, before him, awaiting, with some apprehension, for memory's shadows to cloud his face; I braced for the thunderclap of recognition, the downpour of recriminations, the tempest of rude handlings to come as I was to be tossed into the latening night. I shouldn't have bothered, however, to fret those unpaid seconds away; my low-rent Mr. Rochester never even attempted an examination of me.

"Brad?" I asked one last time.

"No." The creature lived! It spoke! "Down the hall, last door on the left."

With outstretched hands, I groped my way through the tenebrous gloom. I jerked when my left hand grazed an object fashioned from icy metal. Regaining my shaken, but not stirred, composure, I knocked lightly as I twisted the cold brass knob and pushed the door open. "Brad?"

As suddenly as a misfired volley of bitter and pungent cum seals the searing eye, I was blinded by the refulgent illumination therein. To bedim the awful glare of what I was later to recognize as three torchieres and a cluster of overhead lights, I shaded my recovering eyes and discerned that a figure was hovering before an immense black hutch that held three computers and all their attending cords and plastic-covered sources of life support.

"Excuse me. Could you tell me where in the hell I might find Brad?"

A man, no more than ten years my senior and two inches my junior, turned to face me and say, "Hey. I'm

Brad." He was the embodiment of minimalist Folsom Street chic, attired as he was for the classic late '90s leather scene. In short, he wore little: a black leather armband wrapped tightly around his left bicep; a swollen black leather jock made clownish by the sideways grin of its zipper; and a pair of well-polished black leather engineer boots. What would Mr. Benson have thought? The chilling horror! Tops today were dressing as scantily as his rambunctious runaway boy had on the auction block.

Nonetheless, the general absence of dyed cowhide did afford me a certain pleasure. For I was able to survey Brad's compact and finely muscled body with a distinct ease. He'd obviously spent many years working out and a number of hours trimming the thick hairs about his torso and square-jawed visage. This combination of efforts had, in my humble estimation, paid off; the latter vastly enhanced the former.

Now, the fact that I found my client ruttishly handsome — and at first sight — might alarm you, earnest reader, that this heretofore verisimilar story is teetering towards the hackneyed. Let me assure you: it so won't go there.

As a token of my sincerity and as a bit of kindling to keep those sacred fires of TMI burning bright, permit me to go even so far as to divulge a trade secret: It's rare that I find my clients physically alluring. I'm not saddened by this since I never expect it. Hence, I content myself to polish vigorously some sterling quality in their character with the hope it will arouse my ardor sufficiently to make or take the plunge.

Then again, when I'm about to perform two hours of grueling sexual gymnastics — Brad had asked for a Daddy/boy scene that included the standard kinky alphabet soup of BD, light SM, WS, CBT, and FF — raw lust doesn't hurt in making the time fly.

Furthermore, I'll confess that, as roguishly good-looking as I fancied Brad to be, he wasn't my "type." Now, like many of you, I find the concept of "type" suspect when

Ian Philips

it's introduced into conversation. It implies a fated, "nothing personal" predisposition that, once aroused from its slumber, so afflicts the opiner that he can no longer allow there to be further intercourse of any kind between the two of you, on pain of his own — most likely, social — death. But, if you listen closely, as I have, you can always hear them, under their polished mask of impartiality, whispering hatefully, "Cow."

That is not what I meant.

I found Brad to be "hot" as would say, perhaps, thirty percent of my "rainbow-hued" queer brethren and seventy-five percent of the *soi-disant* "cream of the queer crop," the Great Gay Whites. But, to have had a hundred percent of my undiminished erection, Brad would have had to have been a true Ursa Major, a big ol' Daddy Bear. (Yes, that's right; B. J. and the Bear. Go ahead; your patient perusal has earned you a laugh at my expense.) And by "Bear," mind you, I mean only to evoke the ursine aesthetic of the hulking and hirsute rather than to conjure up an actual flannel-clad and cuddle-mad member of the Bear Movement. To twit the latter further, these well-meaning boys I prefer to call "Dogs" — not because they're more randy than the next guy, for they are not, but for the facts that they always seem to hunt in packs and love to say "woof" while they slobber over your face and sniff at your crotch.

You may laugh off these niggling distinctions as the cavils of a cockhound — but let me caution you that you snigger at your own peril; for fun and games end promptly when gay men sit down to rank the object of their desires. Ask a Black man with an average dick — Sweet Jesus! — or an Asian top — Away ancient Chinese secret! — or a forty-year-old who won't play daddy — Merciful Father, no! — or a Latino who's cut — ¡ay, Dios mío! — or a fat man who prefers to be clean-shaven and has nary a hair on his back — O most cruel twist of the genetic code! Better yet, ask this very moment in time's King Hotty, a thirty-year-old circuit queen with two percent body fat who's selling some stock options to get a face lift with a side order of lipo.

Ah! unfairly harangued reader, fie! on me. I've wandered further afield than even the most peripatetic of my favorite authors; forgive me for my polemical rantings! What I intended to convey concisely was simply this: I could get it up for Brad, but he'd have to work to keep it up. Little did I realize just how prophetic that off-the-cuff prejudgment would come to be.

"I'm B. J.," I said.

"Oh, cool, you're here."

"Yes, and you are there." I gave a sly grin to which Brad responded in kind; as frustrated as I had been by the first room's glacial and the second's tepid welcome, I was, as of this interchange, on the clock and prepared to be every inch the professional that I am.

Brad and I therefore exchanged several rounds of pleasantries: compliments were offered on my outfit and his and on the Ikea-inspired decor of the room and the enormousness of his *computer* equipment; inquiries were made into the ease of my discovering the house and the level of my thirst and the state of my readiness; directions were given on where in the closet to hang my jacket and where, oddly, to stand beside the large hutch.

As soon as I'd hit my mark, Brad enclasped me by shoulders and pulled the gold flesh of my neck up to his mouth. Mistakenly, I believed that he intended to kiss or bite me, but instead he murmured, "I'm going to rip your shirt." "Okay," I said as soft in return. I found this whispering of confidences to be a little unusual; but maybe, I reflected, he was being chivalrous and letting me know the games were about to begin.

Never releasing his grip, he pushed me away from him. "You fucking punk," he said rather loudly — I'm sure his glum roommate, or lover, down the hall relished that. "You've been fucking around on me."

I suppressed my laughter. Ah, I concluded to myself, we're going to play out the *opéra bouffe* that I've always assumed happened when their travel-weary boyfriends arrived home in the hours and days *after* I'd left.

"So?" I spat back in character; I take my work very seriously.

"Shut up, you lousy punk." He shook me half-heartedly to emphasize for some unseen onlooker the sincerity of his modest severity. "I'll tell you when to talk, punk."

Oh, I muttered within. "Punk" three times in a row. So much for comic opera. Even less for one of those drawing-room comedies *à la* Wilde that are as replete with coruscating badinage and farcical contretemps as a Victorian parlor is with bric-a-brac and ferns. No, I regretted, this was going to be a standard issue pizza-boy-gets-pulled-over-by-a-cop porno with a Z-grade script. I'd be lucky to get in much more than a "Yes, Sir" and, perhaps, a "Thank you, Sir."

As I dropped my head into the required penitent-badass pose, I swear I saw Brad wink at me. At that moment, I felt a singularly bitter drop of discomfiture fall into the until-then tranquil vat of acids that is my stomach. But before my cauldron could truly begin to boil and trouble, my accuser was screaming at me anew.

"You've got cum stains on your shirt, you shit."

He threw his hand down flat against my stomach, pulled his fingers into a fist, clutching up the shirt with it, and yanked it up out of my pants. The swift-retreating fabric roughly jostled my genitalia—this was a visit to a client so I was going commando—and left them and me a tad more excited. With his precious punk appropriately disheveled, Brad now took his other hand off my shoulders and ripped my shirt, from hemline to neck, in half.

I jerked back, catching my breath so that my pecs had opportunity to heave and fall before Brad's eyes a few times. And not all the surprise was feigned. The air that November night had that insidious rainy-eve chill that burrows far below the flesh and the open door to the hallway provided a continuous supply of it. My skin pimpled; my high beams were easily flipped on despite the cold steel rings holding them down; and Brad noticed. He pinched and twisted a nipple. While I danced from the pain, he undid my belt in a series of tugs and jerks with his free hand.

"Strip, boy." He punctuated his command with an even sharper yank of my tit.

"Yes, Sir!" I yelped in gleeful agony. Perhaps Brad knew how to manhandle a boy properly after all.

To the grunts of his approval, I squirmed out of my loosely tied shoes and used one foot and then the other to shuck each sock. I popped the buttons in my fly and pushed my jeans down off my hips, leaving heavy-handed gravity to do the remainder of my work.

When the laws of physics had triumphed once more, Brad unconsciously unclenched his hand from my tit and let out the sweetest grunt of all. Now, I don't know whether you'd call it moby or not, but I want to assure you, patient reader, that my not-so-white dick has indeed — finally — surfaced, been sighted, and was, so it seemed, about to be snared by Captain Brad.

I braced for the shock of his hand. Instead, he turned me awkwardly — in my hopeful excitement, I'd forgotten to step out my 501s — away from him and towards the bed.

Subtle, I thought.

My half-hard-on began to give up the ghost as it realized we had an hour and a half more of this left. I let it go back to sleep and I took what comfort I could in the fact that I'd remembered to pocket some Viagra if the need arose. And it might. Brad was speedily tutoring me in a lesson I'd thought I'd already learned well by dating in my off-hours: what you seem to see is rarely what you actually do get.

I toddled towards my ultimate destination when I was stopped by the mechanical lament of a cell phone. Shit, I cursed to myself. I could have sworn I'd turned my nagging scrap of plastic off. The ringing continued. It annoyed me but remanned Brad. He stepped in front of me and seized my shoulders. With one bold stroke, he pulled my torn shirt off my back. The ringing ceased. I was naked except for the jeans about my ankles.

We stood there in silence for a few minutes. He lazily kneaded my ass and gave it several distracted swats; I pressed myself hard against his body to detect any sign whatsoever of concupiscence. I made further attempts with my empty hands to arouse him but nothing prevailed. Instead, I was left to contemplate how cold I was growing, save where he'd patted me on my cheeks, and to ponder the veracity of my inchoate yet troubling suspicion that Brad was occupied not with the tantalizing body before him but with someone or something behind it.

"Umm, boy," he said and I jerked at the sudden noise. "Scared, huh? Well don't be. Daddy's gonna throw you down on the bed and whoop your ass. If you're a good boy, maybe he'll fuck you real sweet."

I was now officially flummoxed. First, the whispering, then the shouting, then the stripping, then the swatting, now the long bout of hugging followed by kind words and kinder promises. How and when we would come to the evening's pre-arranged games was to remain a mystery. For it was now obvious, to at least one of us, that Brad had chosen to direct our two-hour scene from several cliché scripts at once.

Without warning, he let go of me and stood back — less to appraise me I now believe and more to get out of my way. He gripped one of my wrists and pulled me, clownishly stumbling, to the edge of his bed. I was struggling to extract myself from my pants when he gave my butt so sharp a whack that it felled me onto the mattress. I kicked my way out of the jeans as I rolled over, nearly dashing my feet against the curved metal end of the bed frame.

Finally, as I lay utterly naked and supine amidst the tousled sheets, I let myself fume; for I knew that, despite his diminished stature, Brad could have effortlessly lifted me out of my jeans and raised me up until I was cradled in his thick arms and then, and only then, heaved me onto the bed *if he'd cared*. What the fuck was wrong with him?! After all, *he* had called *me*. When was he going to get down to business and ravish me? Why wasn't he hard? Was there some other sex worker he'd wanted instead? Was I to be his sorry seconds?! I bet it's that other whore-cum-writer, the vulpine gay deceiver Marcus Scorn or that too-sexy rat-dastard David Rhys-Matthews!

Mercifully, before paranoia's fell and silent fulminations could goad me into ripping Brad's heads from their respective trunks, I took hold of my wandering wits and squeezed them until they and I concluded that we were fast succumbing to the dire curse that betrays any naïve sex worker who is ardently desirous of his own client.

It is the curse of love-conquers-all and love-at-first-sight and happily-ever-after. It is the curse of false hopes. It is that most pernicious phantasm which casts a glamour of true and instant intimacy about a boy and his john or, in my sorry situation, his Brad. It snares with that longed-for impossibility of a reversal of fortune, a reversal of roles. That is to say, a client who, unbidden, can delight you with the performances of your innermost fantasies as thoroughly as you had intended in the hour ahead, through a series of intricate elaborations of his heretofore mute wishes and their painstaking enactments, to pleasure him. And if this spell remains undetected and unbroken, it will continue to enfeeble both the mind and body of our belovèd hustler boy until all that is left alert is that one dumb limb, and even it will come to be pulverized against the craggy edges of reality's unyielding granite unless he were to surrender completely to the malediction and outstrip his client's confession of his wants and bare all of his wanton hooker soul to the unknown man before him.

And thus our dear lad would exchange his heart, freshly ripped from its broken cage of bones, oozing life with each weaker pulsation, for a wad of pressed and dried wood pulp stained with viridian ink. A wager that the simplest of unwashed bumpkins would be sage enough to reject — even if it were to be advanced by the Devil himself!

Ian Philips

How arrogant the errant numskull I'd been to pride myself on being a professional! For here I was, stripped bare before an utter stranger, and only moments away from being emotionally undone by him and thus forfeiting not only money but my own fierce reputation. I vowed that very awkward instant that I would nevermore make such a man-child's mistake; and, once my oath of such heartfelt and goodwilled intentions had been given, I laid the final flagstone in my off-ramp to Hell.

Possessing, at last, a clearer head and a newly recaged heart, I gazed placidly at Brad as he sprinted, with unrequired haste, around the end of the bed to the opposite side. He bent over me and tussled with my forearms before he pulled them above my head. He leaned in less than an inch from my face; and, where before in my brief bout of deluding desires I would have hoped him to kiss me or, at least, embosom my face, I expected no such things now. I was well-rewarded for my clarity.

For Brad was asking, in a string of breathily whispered gusts, if he could place a blindfold upon me or, as he now volunteered excitedly, a hood. Why the hushed voice? was all I could wonder; simply close the door. He posed his question once more. I declined both; despite my earlier lapse in judgment, I can assure you, gentle reader, that this whore believed himself to be no man's idiot.

"Gag me, Sir," I ejaculated with boyish brio, startling *him* this time.

Whispering to me all the while, he scavenged about and beneath his bed for a leather strap. "I can't find it," he confessed before he shouted out loud, "You're too good for my leather, boy."

"I'm not even worth your filthiest jock, Sir!" I countered, hoping he'd take the hint. "It's downstairs in the washing machine," he murmured. He appeared embarrassed; he should, I thought. "How about some underwear, then," I sighed. "Or a tie. You've got a big closet, Brad. What's in there?"

"Right, right. Thank you," he replied demurely. "Since

you like fucking around with the suits you deliver messages to downtown," he bellowed, "I'm gonna cram a tie down your throat."

Let it be silk, I prayed. I'm allergic to wool and bored by cotton unless it's soiled — oh! I fear I can keep no confidences from you, friend.

Brad got up off his knees and threw open the door to his closet. It took all the decorum I possess to suppress a shriek of combined wonderment and envy; he'd set up The Compleat Haberdashery within those walls. Never had I seen so many costly suits and shoes outside my recent trip to Barney's in New York with my Sugar-Daddy-Numero-Uno — yes, the one with snaggletoothed Rolex.

What, pray tell, could a man possibly do who lived in such an overpriced hovel — besides run arms, drugs, or Internet entertainment! — to acquire the wherewithal to afford such luxuries? I jokingly asked myself, unaware still of how deadly keen was my foresight.

From the mahogany-and-brass tie rack, he let slither into his hands a simple yet silken black tie; Brad was five paces from me so I could only fathom a guess that it was an Armani. He twisted it into a large, awkward knot and emerged from his walk-in wardrobe. "Yeah," he shouted to me and the walls, "leather's too good for you. Here's a silk tie for you instead, you fuckin' queen." Yay, I retorted *sotto voce*.

He clambered onto the bed and sat upon my crotch. My dick continued to play dead despite the pleasant sensation of the full weight of his well-built ass pressing upon it; it would take more, however, than this to rouse it from its last rejection. With much show, he waved the tie above my face before, daintily, tucking it between my waiting lips and under my head. Then, with not so much as a by your leave or a bump-and-grind, he dismounted from his ready-to-be-ridden steed.

What is wrong with this man? I asked the heavens. As usual, no one was home. And it appeared to be the same within Brad's pretty head.

Ian Philips

"That's more like it, boy. You ready to behave?" I nodded, dislodging one end of the tie. "You gonna lie there and take your punishment like a man?" I shook my head, unloosening the other. "Then I guess I'm gonna have to restrain you, you fuckin' shit."

Ah! the dreaded bed of Procrustes, you gasp, excitedly clutching whatever it might be that you clasp when so aroused. Lest you let your hands run away with you too soon, I should inform you now that the sinister will literally slip into the comical straightaway. For each shackle affixed to the four corners of the bed, when fastened tight, was as wide around as my thigh. So, once enfettered, the restraints around my ankles slouched sideways under their own heft while the ones around my wrists fell down about my elbows, leaving me no option but to cling to the chains and ponder just whom he'd been tying up of late—Paul Bunyan?

Brad seemed as unconcerned as he appeared to be unaroused with this spectacle. He glanced about the room and retrieved a pillow from the floor that he pushed beneath the one already under my now bouncing head.

In an even greater act of indignity, he made not even one lone attempt to bend down and give succor to my ailing cock, which, by now, had all but withered away in digust at his limp disregard for the beautiful catamite who lay captive beneath him. Instead, he tried to resuscitate it manually. And while the robust vigor with which the sailors of the Pequod had milked the spermaceti from the quivering chunks of blubber had incited Melville to devote a whole chapter to their expert ministrations, Brad's lackluster handjob—gently tossing Prince Albert from side-to-side until His Royal Highness and I were nearly seasick—inspired only a paragraph, this one in fact.

"You'd better brace for impact, sport."

Sport? How droll.

"I'm going to unleash the beast...now." Well, finally, I was to meet the ten-inch manrammer he'd bragged about so in our initial phone conversation. He unzipped his codpiece and I looked into the laughing mouth.

What did I behold? you ask. No less than this: with a nail that short, Brad deserved his name.

Gracious reader, I'm sure that with such a trenchant assessment asserted now so mordantly I have further damned myself in your eyes as a "vicious size queen." This, however, would be a sad misreading of my *belles lettres* since I am anything but. What I *am* is an observer of the human condition. And, usually, I couldn't be bothered one whit about the size of the condition I'm about be thrust upon.

Care for another spot of TMI? I'm actually disquieted by my own worries that *I* do not measure up to the porntastical standards of my trade. In fact, I myself have lied to assuage this particular fear. My own cock — finally, o prurient ones (if only you still remained here reading), my vital statistics are invoked — swells from its flaccid five inches up to seven and seven-eighths inches, which I, most pusillanimously, have rounded up to an even eight in my ad.

Now, I can forgive a fraction of an oversight like this because I myself am guilty of it. But my free time spent tricking in San Francisco — a city where dick size is often as wildly inflated as the rent — has left me less sanguinely inclined to excuse such gross exaggerations from a man — any man. For I have found, in that moment when your trick's cover is blown and you discern just how obscenely this mountebank has lied about the measurement of his manhood, that the first trumpet, of many, has sounded, heralding the sad fact that you are, virile-member-to-a-scintilla-of-a-virile-member, with a man of little-to-no moral fiber in his diet.

Oh! if only I had heeded that first trumpet's bleating, no louder nor more impressive than a tin whistle's — well, we'd have now reached journey's end with a hastily shorn narrative thread and a very disgruntled reader, wouldn't we? Fret not, my faithful friend! For I would, as you soon shall learn, push all presentiments aside and continue on that fateful night, pursuing with the near-fatal curiosity of the proverbial cat this particular evening's peculiar strand into depravity's most labyrinthine depths, until only the deafening wail from the walls themselves drove me out at last.

"I'm gonna have to loosen up that hole of yours first, boy, before you can take me. For such a slut, you got a real tight pussy." How kind, I chortled to myself. "But I've got something that'll take care of that." Perhaps, I prayed silently, by telling such a wicked lie some part of him might finally grow. And so I waited for an act of magic only to be accosted with something completely unexpected and far ranker than an amateur conjurer's flowering wand.

He waved a small bottle beneath my nose. It gave off such an acrid chemical stench that it could have easily stripped and melted the video heads while it purportedly "cleaned" them. Yes, my worried friend, it was none other than...a vial of poppers!!!

Now, before I consent to advance the plot a single letter more, I feel compelled to introduce to you the prime mover behind the building outrage you must hear in my authorial voice. For you are correct to assume I was incensed. What you must *not* conclude, however, is that my ire was sparked from that pile of wet lace doilies known as offended Victorian sensibilities. Please, I have my reputation as a reprobate to consider. I urge you instead to remember that it is the mores around machines, not bodies, that get my bloomers in a wad. Why, just because a boy delights in declaiming to passing strangers that he's old-fashioned, it doesn't mean he's some abstemious prig or its sphincter-tight cousin, the teetotaling prude. As if!

On the contrary, I'm as deliciously peccant and prone to bacchic abandon as the next bawdy peckerphile. And like so many others of my tender age who chafe under the dolorously uttered reminder that we were "born too late," I often seek out hours of reckless bedroom and backroom time travel to that second-coming of Fifth Century Athens' heyday for homosexuals that historians innocuously refer to as The Seventies and faggots hymn as The Golden Age of Dick. Moreover, this Yankee Alcibiades has several Socrates on speed dial with whom he can skip the dialogues and go right to living out his fantasy of "Little Mary Fairy Gets Done in the Mineshaft" — down to the Crisco and disco and, yes, poppers.

No, what had vexed me so was that Brad, without a care and without asking, had shoved the paint-peeling concoction beneath my nose. Worse, he'd left me gagged and I could have choked to a tawdry death. In today's plainer prose: the clueless asshole was treating me no better than a two-bit whore. Granted, I am mindful that I succeed at my profession only if I market myself as a handsome cock and a divine ass with a price tag. But you purchase only my time, not my liberty. I couldn't give a flying jot or tittle over how important you are; you still must ask my permission before you proceed to cudgel, slap, whip, strap, cane, or fuck the living crap out of me. And that goes for even the most strung-out streetwalker on Capp Street.

Johns of the World, heed me well; we whores are worth far more than the sum of our bits!

That said, I trust we are now on the same page in spirit as well as in letter with regards to the source of my overwhelming shock. And it was, no doubt, this very blow to the dignity of my person which thereby redoubled the punch to my body of that base alchemical stew.

For, in but an instant, my nostrils dissolved; my eyes stung; my head shook; my heart reeled; and my lungs exploded as I had a cravat crammed in my mouth and could not breathe. With strength summoned from I know not where, I vomited up the silk tie and gasped frantically for whatever air I could swallow. Then Brad, convinced my performance of a near-death experience was just that, wafted the malodorous solvent once more beneath the two gaping holes in my head that before had been my nose.

My heart, no more than a battered wineskin, was flooded rapidly by torrents of coursing blood; it throbbed until I thought my very bones would shatter. My bowels convulsed and my asshole flared wide. I was not open; I was unbounded. And Brad took this unwilled accessibility, along with the encouraging ring of what must have been several more cell phones beneath the bed, which in my derangement sounded like the faraway warblings of electronic birds, as his invitation to wedge a long, unforgiving (despite the thick slatherings of lube) dildo between my ass and up to its hilt in one! two! three! forceful thrusts.

I wish in those moments' rush of blood, of adrenaline, of shock, of fear, of pain that I had been as camp as Christmas and burst into a showtune. *Clang, clang, clang went the cell phones; thud, thud, thud went my tell-tale heart.* I didn't; I couldn't. The drug had melted my customary sang-froid away. Thus, I found myself so unnaturally terror-stricken by my present dilemma that abysmal images of panic and flight and murderous mayhem bombarded the now weakened fortifications of my mind.

As I still dread to relive that moment, even here within the safe confines of the printed page, I will elaborate only one ghastly apparition; for it haunted me most. The chilling image, which the despicable vial induced, was that of the last helicopter, filled to capacity with those fleeing certain death, as it lifted off from the roof of the US Embassy in Saigon while, all around it, the city fell on that thirtieth day of April, 1975 — which, lest you think I pad this story with odd flourishes of erudition concerning all manner of things recondite whenever I must wait for my halt fingers to catch up with my nimbler mind, is two years, to the very day, before I passed my way through Life's fleshy curtains to take my place upon Her stage.

But, unlike the historical event, my chopper was ascending from within my skull. And as the blades spun round and round they hacked at my brain and tore off the top of my head. Then the end of one propeller broke off, still whirling, and fell back within, slicing its way through my tender insides. It made short work of me and slipped out through the yawning gash in my stomach and into my waiting, bloodied hands. Seconds from death, I was determined to coat my fingers with even greater quantities of gore as I lunged, impromptu machete within my stiffening grip, towards that unseemly underbrush from the forest of manhood known to me solely as Brad, hell-bent on cutting every last little inch of it down.

Do not despair, gentle reader. Though I am, as you must have surmised by now, quite fond of the "Grand," I am much less enamored of the "Guignol." Thus I did not attempt to make good on my vision, though it begged me, with each strident ache of my recovering head, to lance this overgrown boil. Get up and get out! I hear you warn me. And I agree; it is a wise tonic that I am usually swift to administer to friend or foe. But I could not go. It wasn't the flimsy chains or the super-sized dildo jammed up my butt that retarded my flight. No, it was some unseen force that had taken hold of me. Simple curiosity? Lust for gold? Madness? Bad boundaries?! No!!! Far nobler; far more perverse. It was my deleterious obsession with the besotted bard buried in Baltimore. The book I had coveted in the window of M—'s would be mine; this 'ho would have his Poe!

But first, I had to stop Brad from blithely and literally tearing me a new one. With my temples throbbing only slightly less than my impaled ass, I excoriated my ream-happy tormentor with a string of stinging ejaculations and scalding epithets: "Jesus Christ!"; "Shit!"; "Ouch!"; "What the fuck are you doing?"; "Stop"; "You're hurting me"; "Did you hear me?"; "I said 'Stop', you dimwitted dildo-wielding dolt!" Brad merrily ignored me and said under his breath, "That's great. Keep it up." At that instant, all I wished to see kept up was Brad's head on a bloody pike. Then, without warning, I found myself beseiged by a fit of petit mal epiphany. And as I shook, electrified by the thousand imperceptible tremors, I was made to understand that if I wanted to drive my point home, I would either have to slip my hands out of the restraints and throttle Brad or whisper back the riot act.

"Brad, you either pull the dildo out NOW and fuck me with what the Good Lord gave you" — shafted you is more like it, I thought — "or I'm so out of here."

He dropped his plastic dick, just as he was about thrust anew, leaving all but the stiff silicone head dangling from my ass. With a few Kegel-inspired convulsions, I spat the dildo out. Now, both my asshole and Brad were openmouthed with shock.

"Well?" I snarled.

"Jeez, okay. I'm sorry," he muttered.

I wasn't placated; the searing throbs within goaded me on.

"It takes more than a dab of lube and two hits of poppers, Brad, to take a twelve-inch dick."

"Okay," he said with a more heartfelt attempt at shamefacedness.

"Now, if you want to fuck me, fine. Go get a condom and fuck me. But no more of this zero-to-sixty crap or I am so outta here and every hooker in this city'll have the shit on you by sunup."

To my utter surprise, that last threat seemed to terrify him and he hurried about the room to comply.

As I steeled myself for his return, I was grateful, for a moment, the only moment of that harrowing night, that Brad had not been, as he'd so vaingloriously boasted earlier that day, fashioned in the image of Priapus — that immortal troll with the foot-long schlong, the veritable John Holmes of deities.

I can only imagine the bevy of tut-tuts I've flushed from your mouths with that harmless aside. So, lest you mistake my plucky attempt at the queenly sport of archery for the crass and vinegary snipings of the mean-spirited — all right, I *am* arch, but no fiend! — permit me to undeceive you by repackaging my previous sentiments into this heartwarmingly rustic metaphor: I am perfectly able to stable the horse-hung out back; but only after the rider takes the time to open wide my doors; yet Brad, as thoughtless a rider if ever there were one, had been in such a hurry to bang them in with his long, fiery torch that he'd nearly burned down the whole barn, leaving me worried if I'd be able now to bed even his wee pony.

My would-be equestrian reappeared and scrambled onto the mattress and then me. He wore even less than when I'd first laid eyes on him as he'd stripped away the cracked leather shell of his jock so that the pink newborn chick in its slight nest of fuzz was exposed at last to all the world. But, before I squander one more of my remaining similes on a barnyard creature, I'll leave off and say that with a tug here and yank there he was snug inside a condom and then me. *E-i-e-i-o.*

Oh! reader. And I thought his handjob was dreary; he poked me as vigorously as a cartoon saw cuts wood above some sleeping geezer. At long last, one of us was stirred from slumber when a cell phone rang out from the bedside table. To my utter amazement, he dared to reach over me and pick it up. To my absolute horror, he flipped it open and spoke into the phone.

"Hey. Not much, and you?" He spoke as nonchalantly as he fucked. Someone on the other end blew a muted trombone into the receiver; it sounded like an abandoned babe weeping exhaustedly from the bottom of a deep and decrepit well.

"Oh, you're watching. Sure, we can do that." That said, Brad looked down at my baffled face with his soulless, shit-brown eyes and smiled.

At that very moment, I was sideswiped — finally! — by a big rig hauling several tons of clarity: *I*, of all people, was starring tonight on a live sex show, the Web's cross between pay-per-view and a listener's-request radio show. Mike had once tried to sweet-talk me into doing one of these with him; but I'd declined with a polite "Hell, no!"; and yet, here I *was*, recumbent and being reamed — quite poorly — while Brad took subscribers' calls. This homo might be sapient after all, I confessed; for he was certainly not as stupid as his actions had led me to fancy him. Oh no! The true ignoramus would have to have been the stooge who was undone by the subterfuge of this idiot savant. Yes, rightfully appalled reader, there was no greater red-faced fool online that hour than I — nor, mercifully, cuter.

"Okay. You going to Pleasuredome tonight?"

My thoughts raced to Kubla Khan and Xanadu and Olivia Newton-John and Coleridge. Ah! if only I had some poppy paste to smoke. Anything to whisk me away from this internationally witnessed imbroglio.

"See you around one?"

Sounds buzzed from within the phone as if it were home to a swarm of mildly perturbed insects.

"Good."

Another phone announced its presence.

"Got another call. Okay. Bye."

I would not, I swore under my rapidly increasing breath, sit — lie! — through another casual chat. Never! But the book! Oh! the stinging shame. In spite of my constant and reassuring professions of advanced maturity, I was greener than I'd believed; for here I had sagely refused to wear Brad's cowl and yet the dissembler had hoodwinked me — and through a simple gaucherie no less!

Brad blabbed away as he spoke to one who must have been a closer friend. Passion could spill forth from this man — but only by way of his lips and not his loins. Ah! the agonizing ignominy! I screamed within as I pulled my legs free of their shackles. And as that silent cry echoed round my brain, the strumming of its soundless vibrations cracked the plaster, the mortar, and the stones that made up a wall thicker than Hadrian's to keep my gentle and civilized soul safe from the most naked and brutish of desires that rampaged beyond. The more I comprehended the endless scope of my violation, the greater the fissures grew.

I was unwinding my arms quietly from the chains when a third horn sounded — a cell phone on the floor beside the bed — and with that, as at Jericho before, my more impatient ramparts tumbled down with a thunderous cloud of dust that covered all memories of my labors for the Golden Folio. Yes, that single metallic whine had achieved what a night of gross indignities had not: that most vicious of avenging spirits, the dread cockatrice, had been hatched.

Brad, forever oblivious to me, bent down and stretched his muscled and manicured frame across my torso and over to the edge of the bed; and, as he did so, I willed my legs to clasp him about the waist and brawny back in the roughest of embraces. The suddenness of my attack caught him both off guard and off balance; he toppled onto my chest with such graceless force that not only was the wind knocked out of us both but his ill-used poker was swiftly dislodged from my grateful ass. When we'd recovered our breaths, we fell, at once, into a mighty tussle.

We wrestled about the bed, slapping the metal headboard violently against the wall, until, in a moment of near Atlantean might, I flipped us both onto Brad's broad back and proceeded to thrash this weak and wheezing fucker soundly about the chest and face; and while I assailed him in this manner, I boxed him so harshly about the balls with my thigh — and, yes, knee — that he curled up rapidly round his wounded male pride. And while he made a great show of bawling out tearless, racking sobs, I dashed to the closet and back with a handful of the most precious of his silk ties. I scattered them about the bed and then shoved my hand into the knot of Brad's arms and legs and grabbed his nuts and twisted them hither and thither until he flung wide his limbs so he could let free those high-pitched screams that fluttered within his manly frame. And as he keened like a newborn banshee, I busied myself with knotting his extremities to the four corners of the bed frame.

Once Brad had been handsomely trussed, I made a more leisurely visit to his hidden haberdashery. I reappeared, after a great length in which I'd donned various and sundry of his costliest habiliments, my arms laden with a few pieces of finery, and set about to completing my splendid rack. I therefore rolled up several dapper Hugo Boss and Calvin Klein jackets within a stylishly smart Paul Smith linen suit — that ensemble alone must have cost a cool thousand — which I then wedged into place beneath his butt to cushion whatever blows might befall it later. And for my inspired and final flourish, I wrapped the Armani cravat he'd stuffed in my mouth around his cock and balls before tying it up in a big, floppy bow and I wadded a pair of black cK fitted briefs into his inveighing mouth and stood back.

I was struck by my tableau; it resembled a fashion shoot for an achingly hip magazine with a name like *flooRBoard*; a celebration of the Fall Collection served up as an abridged yet whimsical restaging of Géricault's *The Raft of the Medusa*: one survivor, no raft, and nothing under $100.

I thought, for the briefest instant, of turning away and leaving the hurly-burly of Brad's stage behind for good; but my fiery desire for complete and utter revenge and that brighter-burning pride of the fledgling artisan emboldened me to outdo myself with further acts of creative vengeance. But how?

A horribly garbled version of the first bars of Mozart's *Eine kleine Nachtmusik* — it sounded like a little girl's pink-and-cream music box, complete with a wobbling, anorexic ballerina, which had been retrieved from the sea's floor and upon being pried open, miraculously, played a very rusted rendition of its tune — accosted my addled ears. It was another cell phone; this one happened to be lodged between the two smaller computers.

I strode brusquely towards the hutch; my swelling dick pounding out a pace-quickening beat against my thigh. I was drawn to the monitor of the largest machine for upon it one white IM after another flashed as if the screen were merely a glass lid covering a pan of popping corn. As I read each new addition to these cyber-simulacras of the ribald graffiti that festoons the corroded metal partitions between toilets in a rest stop's rest room, I discovered the global extent to which I had been duped. I also chanced upon the seed from which my befouled honor's satisfaction would bloom.

"What do I descry with my eagle eye." I plucked a ball from off the top of the computer that resembled a plastic diving bell for Lilliputians embedded in an ice floe. I peered into its single portal. Another phone began to wail. "A digital camera?" Yes, dear reader, it was while I held what I hoped was the singular spyglass to Peeping Toms about the planet that I conceived of what form my rebuttal must take.

With a swift burst of savagery, I ripped the orb and its trailing nerves from their sockets, to which my handsomely restrained malefactor responded with a series of muffled cries of the severest outrage. Phones from within drawers, the walls, and down the hall added their muted screams of protest to those of their master's. They clamored with such manic tintinnabulations that I held my ears and to drown them out I shouted with all the force my young frame could contain, "You want something to cry about; I'll give you something to cry about, you voyeuristic freaks of nature!"

It shames me afresh to admit to you that these telephonic cacophonies, along with Brad's lengthening concatenation of indignities and deceits, had inflamed me so that it was no longer just my massive ire that had been piqued. And to bear witness, as I did now, to my bamboozler's speedy transformation from cocksure whelp into a namby-pamby wreck served only to harden me, body and soul, to the furthermost of extremes. With untrammeled *élan*, I shelled a condom from its pod; tucked therein my boys, Dickie and Albert; slathered on a hearty dollop of lube (Brad's precious tastes led me to expect a bottle of Clinique rather than the AstroGlide that I unearthed beneath the bed); and proceeded to push my thick, fat, ring-tipped rope—ah! what delectable caterwauls—through the tight eye of Brad's needled ass. Such was my ardent detestation for my insipid deceiver that I rammed his splayed hole and buffeted the buoyant muscle of his rump all the while hectoring him with one and only one phrase: "The screw has been turned."

And despite the all-consuming single-mindedness of my furious fucking, I was alerted, through an exceptional moment of prescience, to the sudden intrusion of an unwelcome presence who had materialized from the shadows to revel, I assumed incorrectly, in his roommate's frolicsome comeuppance. I ceased my seige of Brad's butt and turned my head towards the forever-open door. There the bartender stood as pale and pellucid as any storybook revenant. He hovered in the doorway but a moment longer, his stony face as inscrutable as a weathered gargolye's, and then underhandedly tossed a shrieking phone into the room, adding one more screaching voice to the chorus, and slammed the door shut.

Undaunted by the spectre's silent commentary, I returned to meting out Brad's richly deserved punishment. At last, I had gotten the full attention of Brad's puny prick; for it stood up and twitched back and forth as if to beckon me to return to pounding my glowing iron, like Hephaestus — go, Daddy! — at his anvil, against his resistant hole. But I intended otherwise; it was time to apportion my tormentor his share of pain.

I therefore extracted my tumid probe from the clinging embrace of Brad's ass. Once released, I used all my fingers, save thumb, to hold my place as I leaned over the bed to locate the small ampule that would vastly amplify Brad's already augmented aperture. But before I could wave the vial beneath his nose, I performed the gentlemanly act of yanking the underwear free of his mouth. Then, as the charlatan essayed to speak, I wafted the bottle to and fro like a priest swaying his censor with pagan abandon.

I returned the poppers to the cluttered nightstand and wrested the computer's sightless eye from its latest perch. Brad lay dazed below me and thus failed to notice as I placed the orb near the entrance to his underworld. Retrieving my other hand, I used both to clog his hole with so much lube it looked as if I were stuffing a turkey.

The stage was set. Let justice be done!

My half-hearted agnosticism in this goddess-cheering

town notwithstanding, I offered up my first thrust to a deity who, if I could but be personally persuaded of her existence, I would gladly follow: Nemesis, the baker of the hubris-humbling pie; she who bursts each distended bubble filled with hot, gaseous air. Her name invoked, all that was left was the reaming itself. Regardless of my brimming rage and Brad's increasingly annoying jactitations, which now mimicked perfectly the grotesque jitterbugging of the condemned at the end of the gibbet's rope, I hesitated until I felt such a chill fall about the room that I could believe it to be none other than the goddess herself inhabiting the room. Whatever doubt that remained within me was hurriedly expelled when I found myself possessed by such a spirit of righteous revenge that I was enabled — all at one fell swoop! — to retract my fingers from Brad's gape-mouthed ass and plunge the now blind eye into the deep and feculent dark. And madder than a maenad, I gave the orb's squared end three sharp twists — in the name of my father! my sister! and my ghastly host!

Never had I heard such an unearthly howl. It was as if he were attempting to sever his soul from his body by one long shout alone. And once his final reserve of bloodcurdling and earsplitting sound had been spent, Brad's frantic gesticulations also ceased and he could do no more than lay before me, inertly gasping for breath while several phones clangored on.

I exhaled a mighty sigh of relief; the swinish agent of all my slights and humiliations had been vanquished and I was of a fixed mind to gloat. I ticked my way through my mental facsimile of Brad's original wish list for our evening's merrymaking; only one thing remained to be done. And, for my final act of retribution, I vouchsafed him his request. With the lithesome skill of the naked wrestlers of old, I manoeuvred my supple and sweat-oiled body astride his panting chest until I loomed over the object of my opprobrium like a summer thunderhead above the Kansas prairies and let fly with a golden downpour of my own making that drenched his all-too-plain earth.

In an instant, I likewise was wet from the sputtering of my plume of piss as it collided with Brad's unexpectedly bedraggled and thus swiftly cursing mouth. Phones seen and unseen shrilled and squealed; the room was a nursery of newborn technologies. Soon, I could no longer distinguish their cries from his; and, far off, echoing off the walls of this small, albeit cavernous, room, like the uneven din of an approaching mob, I heard the swelling roar of my own demented laughter.

"'Tis pity I'm a whore," I crowed aloud, jubilant over both my subjugation of the embodiment of all things louche and loutish and my extemporaneous bowdlerization of the title to John Ford's play, "who's unplugged your execrable eye. What wonders it would have telegraphed to the voyeurs back home. And once doused with my youthful brine…ah, what an electrifying moment *that* would have been in the annals of streaming media!"

That said, my feats of fucking and funambulism had been finished; our time was up!

I climbed down off the drowned rat. The final drops of my piss drizzled over the carpet — it was white; imagine my good fortune — while I searched for something with which to towel off. The Paul Smith would have been perfect if it weren't already ruined. So, I grabbed up a half of my T-shirt and, as I was growing cold again, hurriedly dried myself off.

That done, it was time to collect my fee. I gazed about the room until I spotted a pair of gray twill pants draped over the back of a nearby chair, a leather and metal contraption as definitely expensive as it was supposedly ergonomic. I approached and rifled through all the pockets until I found a money clip — of course he'd have a money clip — and, lo and behold, it was monogrammed. How well does this home porno studio do? I puzzled, as I counted 20 one-hundred-dollar bills. I separated my five from their kin, refolded and re-clipped and returned them to cold dark whence I'd discovered them.

I shuddered; happy though I was to be so, I was flush

in only the most monetary of its meanings. Hence I took now to quickly dressing. Within minutes, all I lacked was a clean shirt. I threw the begrimed remnant of mine own onto Brad and then entered his closet. I emerged therefrom sporting a tasteful white number from Prada; "My tip," I mouthed to him while I tucked it into my jeans since it was useless to speak over his myriad shouted threats and groundless accusations and the concomitant squawks of the hysterical phones. I gathered up my jacket; waved a fond farewell with one finger from each hand; and, exceedingly glad to ascend out of this maelstrom, opened the door and exited.

"Brad's been a very bad boy," I announced to the lifeless blob on the couch while I threaded my arms through the heavy sleeves of my jacket. "He's taking a time out in his room. You might want to untie him after I leave; you might not. I really don't give a shit."

The face turned towards me and grinned wildly in the ghoulish blue light like a fleshless skull. The vivified cadaver arose and trod past my goose-pimpled frame. I listened to the heavy thud of his sock-bound feet as they struck repeatedly against the cold and creaking floorboards until all was silence except for Brad's mewlings and groans, which he offered up to the pitiless creature that stood alone in the entrance to his room. Without warning, the beast spoke one word in a hiss that was loud enough for even me to hear — "Yes!" — and then vanished into the white light with a single crashing clap that was followed by a flood of resounding darkness. Whereupon I found myself — once I'd regained my sight — alone — at last! — in the dancing blue and black shadows and at liberty to flee from this nightmarish pesthole of manifold perils both technological and oh-so-monstrously mortal.

Thus it happened that I ushered myself at once out the still-open door and nearly turned to wish and watch the clapboards of that cursèd house collapse upon themselves; instead I hiked, eyes dead ahead, up to the actual Folsom Street and hailed a cab; I dismissed the driver with nary a word and mounted the steep three flights of stairs to my waiting apartment; I waved to my roommates, full of life and innocent laughter, as they sat gathered round the cluttered kitchen table; I blew a kiss into Mike's room, which my ex, albeit hunched over his keyboard, heard and to which, without looking, waved absentmindedly towards the wall in return; I turned the knob to the door of my *sanctum sanctorum* and entered therein; I stripped quickly in the dark and — still ardent from the heat of battle and with my glistening rapier unsheathed and aching for a thorough burnishing before being put away — laid back on my bed and thought, for a few fevered minutes, of England before passing out into awaiting arms of Hypnos for a night of dark and dreamless sleep.

Despite the customary admonition to the contrary, I know you'll swiftly guess who called the next day. That veriest tomfool said it was *hookerboycam.com*'s best night ever. The emails were pouring in; I was an international sensation. He fulsomely begged me for an encore. With his cyber-skulduggery now roundly exposed, he even apologized for the previous night's dissimulation and promised to triple my fee. You should have seen me shouting "When sex pigs fly!" and nearly pissing my own self from laughter — my antics were so riotous they even coaxed Mike to leave the clutches of his computer and approach my open door — as I erased Brad's message and dialed Terry to tell all.

But what of the fortune and the fame?

Call me old-fashioned, my cherished and last-remaining reader, but I shunned them for a simpler, more sensuous life. And, yes, dearest friend, you are right to fear that I shall never understand that secret, and all too often fiscally rewarded, love between a boy and his computer — not even if all the sweet lads at British Telecom were, one after the other, to give me an explicit and thoroughly hands-on explanation. And soon they shall have that very tantalizing opportunity.

For I journey, in a week's time, to England where I

shall serve, happily, for a month in the employ of a certain dealer in antiquities I met here at a convention of rare books. What a page-curling weekend of carnality that was!

Yes, you have heard rightly. Rare books! England! In fact, if I perform all that my mysterious merchant asks of me, and to his utmost satisfaction (and I have yet to fail him in so doing—and oh! the things we do, one unto the other), then he promises that he will make use of his manifold powers and smuggle me into the Vatican! for a private viewing of its pornographic treasures, literary and otherwise.

Ah! the ensemble I have in mind for that night aboard the Holy Mothership. Something jaunty, carnivalesque— *a la* "The Cask of Amontillado."

But I digress. Suffice it to say that if and when I return, you, my bookish confidant, will be the very first one—after Terry, Meta, and Mike, of course—to whom I shall tell my newest little tale.

FINIS?

Stripping Towards Gomorrah

for Carol (The One, True) Queen and Robert Lawrence

I shall turn forty-four on the morrow. I was not always old. Nor was I always Queen of England, Scotland, Ireland, Wales, and France. (I shall die, however, both. An old queen, indeed. There are two of us, as the courtiers are fond of whispering loudly when my Husband the King has tottered out of earshot. Or so my faithful ears tell me. My Lord the King and I have lived apart now so many years: I with my court, planning revels, and he with his, planning wars.)

How I remember those first revels in the winter months after my James Rex had ascended his cousin Elizabeth's throne. We left London to avoid the Plague and the vast laced and ribboned and corsetted court of His Glorious Majesty King James I had followed. I was still young, still beautiful. Oh, the marvelous balles and masques that winter! A new play by our William Shakespeare. One of Inigo Jones' sumptuous spectacles that would have made the gods of old blush with envy. The fires roared like the summer sun as I and my maids of honor made our entrance as the Muses themselves, shimmering among the velvet and brocade and gold in our diaphanous gowns—nay, more transparent whiffs of silk and pearls draped over us— gauzy sirens who made even my Husband, England's Zeus, turn his attention from his various Ganymedes.

Do not mistake me. I have loved my Husband as much as any fifteen-year-old girl could when it is arranged before her birth and she is married by proxy: she in her castle and he in his. He has been good to me and our eight children. I am also his loyal subject. I have never been otherwise. But I know too that he favors the beardless boys, cheeks dusted with faint golden hairs like pollen on the petals of ripening flowers, humming with youth and vigor, like a garden filled with bees on a May morning. I do not begrudge him this. For once his boys had grown into men, he did not let them wither in exile but sent them to me. And I tended to them as they to me. None of the wine of life was wasted in my Husband the King's court. No drop spilt save upon our royal personages. Until the chalice finally fell five years ago and my beloved Henry, Prince of Wales, died barely a man of eighteen. I had already lost five of my babes before they could crawl or walk or run or ride. To lose one so full of sap is too much. All are empty entertainments now but in memory. There lies such precious heat.

And so it is tonight, a bitterly cold and long night, that I remember the first time I was ever made love to by an unabashed Sodomite, save my Husband. God save him indeed, the sweet rogue. But I have no fear that History shall remember him safely and solely for his Bible and not his love of boys. Nor for me. Do not feel sadly for me, however, for I have lived well. Befitting a queen all the days of my life. And the artists I have patronized all my years shall remember me and in their artifices and edifices I shall live on. Safe forever within some chiseled bit of stone or tattered scrap of painted canvas praising Queen Anne.

✳

As I waited for the secret series of raps at my inner chamber's door, I realized I knew nothing of my future lover except he was the most divinely beautiful and dashing lord, in both body and dress, in all the court. That and he had pleased my Husband like no other. So much so that it was only upon his twentieth summer and still no wife and son that His Majesty sent him away to marry. This time it was Antinous who lived and Hadrian who drowned in his own tears.

Now the newborn father had been summoned to court to watch over me.

I eagerly dreaded his arrival. I fanned at my burning face as I awaited the agreed-upon hour of our first meeting.

Ian Philips

I was, for once, flushed in a room that, no matter how strong the fire, had always left me chilled. For legends of his wanton deviltry had floated through the halls like invisible trails of smoke from snuffed-out candles. It could be smelt everywhere, but none knew its origin. Nor the true heat of its flame. Save I. Save my Husband.

What would such a brazen lover of men be able to do and do well with a woman's body? Certainly he had been with one once. His wife had born him his heir. But trotting around the ring without falling from the saddle does not make one a master equestrian.

I jolted and grabbed for the post of my bed — the telltale knocks! Enter, I commanded in a low whisper. He did.

Arising from his deep bow, the candles caused the porcelain of his skin to glow whiter, the rouge in his cheeks to burn redder, the black of his pointed beard and long locks to darken until they vanished into shadow. With a flourish of such honeyed poesy I have not heard since I myself performed in a masque by our Ben Johnson, he stripped myself and himself of our pearls, our ruffs, our bodices and doublets and corsets and chemises and one stood before the other bared to the waist.

My Lord, I said, you appear as a centaur standing on its head. The animal part is where the man should be. No, my Lady, the most animal part is where it has always been on a man. I feel it stirring within its cage of silks, he replied.

We laughed and he closed on me and took my breast in his warm hand. This May bud has shrunken at winter's caress, I said. Not so, said he. And he brushed it with first the longest of his delicate fingers and then his tongue. He spoke true. I blossomed under the gentle rain from his lips.

In time, between sucks of my nipples and a slow descending downpour of kisses, he stripped me of my skirts and round wheel-like farthingale and petticoats and stockings and shoes. And when I stood as naked as the newborn Venus, I reached for his shorts and hose and was well rewarded. My centaur had not lied. But he did not ravish me like an animal when he sunk his lone claw into me. Nor did he till my once-fertile earth like a farmer with his plow. But he changed with each stroke. He was, in private as in public, a dancer of the greatest skill and our lovemaking began with a reverence and slowly we walked about each other's bodies as if in a pavan before we drew closer and closer and the steps more intricate and the tempo more quick and then we were leaping to a galliard that shook the great oaken posts of our bed before dashing breathless through a furious courante and with our final flurry of steps there came a leap and then a pivot until we bowed and collapsed into the other's arms only to laugh and begin the dance once more.

His time with my Husband the King had been well spent. And in the first of many hours together soon was I. God save the King!

Perhaps the most intimate differences between Adam and Eve are more subtle than our learned men would like us to believe. For as long as Heaven allowed my Sodomite to share my bed, he was as wildly vigorous and raptly amorous whether he stormed my castle by battering wide the gates or seizing the battlements through a well-hidden back door. Nor did he revile women as is the supposed custom of his tribe. For I have never heard the word "Lady" used more often and more tenderly save in a novena. Ah, the exquisite delicacy of his words were only eclipsed by that of his frame and his kisses. And wherein he was most needful of being virile he was doubly blessed by the gods. As was I.

God save our Gracious King!

✳

Alas, my love too is dead now and I am old. Tomorrow I shall be older still. And worse, I am forever cold in this drafty overwrought barn of brick and stone and glass. It is as if the older I become the more the childhood climes of Denmark return to me. But my memories of the flaming peacocks who shared my bed and the fullest of my

Ian Philips

affections shall keep me warm until the dark earth takes my body into its sweet embrace and my soul flies heavenward into the arms of my waiting children at last.

While Visions of Plumber's Crack Danced in Their Heads

for David Christensen & Scott Knell

Roger and Randall cordially invite you and a guest to attend their annual après-Thanksgiving & pre-hibernation party.

I came prepared this time. Bearing gifts, so to speak.

I'd been to this tony Victorian before, hidden away in the warren of side streets that is Upper Market proper. Far from the madding rabble of 18th and Castro — ground zero for all things gay and for sale in San Francisco. I was the guest again of a friend who was still in rotation — as he had been on my first visit for the July 4th weekend — as the official pass-around party-cub.

And quite the party they were. The Ursa Majors of San Francisco. Or, as they were known, almost exclusively to themselves, the A-Bears. Short for Alpha Bears. An elite strike force of masculinity. I called them the Alpha-Bits. Not that I'd ever been deemed worthy to join the elect — even for a night. (Thank God for small favors.) But others had and word got around. It always does. I just helped it further along its merry way: Alpha-Bits telegraphed the most important particulars to cognoscenti and unawares alike.

It's safe to say I hate the Alpha-Bits. And it's not because they overlooked me that first visit by never asking me to join their ultraluxe den. God, no. To be honest, I'd thought they were some dumb faggy joke made up by one of the guys at the City's favorite bear den with a liquor license: Haggerty's. Honest. I truly believed all that A-list shit was for the willfully hairless someplace extra-fussy like New York City or Houston. Until last Independence Day when I tagged along to my first party because Deek, the friend I mentioned earlier, or, as he is more popularly known, Cubbyhole, had begged me to come with and cover his back.

Trust me, if you'd seen Deek's back, better yet his backside, you would have wanted to be on it, too.

And it didn't take long before I understood why Deek had requested a second. It was some den all right. A den of vipers. Now, I know — after serving nearly eighteen years as a good son at Victory Christian Cathedral in Tulsa, Oklahoma — how to handle snakes. Not literally; it wasn't that kind of church. And let me tell you, I got an earful of hissing in just those two hours. It's amazing how easy it is to overhear anybody when no one looks you in the eye.

Not once.

In two hours.

That's right. I hated them all because they simply overlooked me. And not because I'm ugly. Somehow, I could have lived with that. If I were. But I'm not. Okay, I may never win best of show but that doesn't mean I'm ugly. No, when I say I was overlooked, I'm telling the God's honest truth. They stood there and never once looked down their noses and over their beards and beyond their microbrewed macrobeerguts swathed in custom-made Pendletons with a thread count of 500.

They literally looked over me.

All 5'3" of me.

Mind you, I'm taller than either Napoleon or Alexander the Great. You could get away with a lot more in the old days if you were short. Especially short with a very large army. But these are strange times, my friend. Fantastic times even. Especially when it comes to masculinity. No one's quite sure how it's supposed to behave in today's captivity. Even what it's supposed to look like. Except when there's too little or too much of it. And right now, especially among us faggots, it's hotter to err on the side of excess.

Fine by me. That's why I was attracted to bears in the beginning. But I don't know how height got thrown into the deal. Hell, I can growl and rut with the best of them. I'm even grizzled. But nowadays every hairy cocksucker's

dreaming of getting thwacked by King Kodiac and I'm 5'3".
It doesn't matter how much I love to fuck or how good I
am at it. I've got to bend over, "boy," or get passed over.

I'm forever cub.

Well, that's if I'm seen at all.

Which I wasn't—once again—as I squeezed my way
that December night through the gauntlet of guts that ran
the length of Roger and Randall's narrow entrance hall.
Nor when I popped, red-faced, sweaty, and huffing, into
the living room. Except by an otter of a cater-waiter who
promptly handed me the single champagne flute on his
tray before returning to the kitchen. I took a sip. Beer. And
I thought after all those years in the church and in the closet
I knew surreal. I took a second sip and a slow second glance
around.

The real heavyweights, along with the hosts, were in
this large room. Actually two rooms that opened onto the
other when the sliding doors were pushed into the safe
dark of the cherry-stained wood walls. I kept peering
around this Alpha Bulk and that, wondering, "Where the
hell are you, Deek?" Nowhere nearby, I later learned. He'd
taken a cab from Haggerty's to the party and then taken
the cab driver — "wide, dark, and handsome" — back to his
place. So I stood alone in the middle of the room, a mere
mouse in the foreground of one of those museum dioramas
where the lumbering thunder lizards hugged and cruised
each other, craning my neck back toward the hall and then
out toward the kitchen. Should I search the bedrooms,
feigning to have forgotten something in my coat? That
might have worked if I'd taken it off beforehand. I was
getting frantic. Muttering, "Deek, Deek, Deek, you dick!"
almost loud enough to be overheard. I needed him to
provide a diversion while I set my "gift" in motion. Then
who before my wandering eyes should appear but just the
man to make me forget all about Deek.

He lay naked on a bearskin rug in front of the fireplace
at the end of the furthest room. I kid you not. And it wasn't
just any man. It was Daniel Bone. The linebacker with the

blond-bearded face of a cherub and the star of some of my favorite Hirsute Videos like *Prick 'N Tongue Bear* or *Blue Balls for Sal*. And spread across the pelt that covered his wide and muscled back were all the fixings for s'mores. Except for the marshmallows. They were in a big silver bowl — from Tiffany's I overheard later — pushed down between his legs and not far from the high, wide mounds of his asscheeks.

For an instant, a long, dick-hardening instant, I thought of nixing my plan. I love s'mores. I love Daniel Bone and his round, fuzzy butt. No one would notice if I sat down and ate. But the conversation behind me returned me to my purpose and my plan.

"This music is dreadful," intoned a baritone voice lazily.

"You don't care for the Vienna Boys Choir," replied a froglike basso.

"I don't care for boys Viennese or otherwise. Call me perverse, but I like my men with secondary sex characteristics."

"I can think of many better reasons for calling you perverse, Armand. In fact, I can count them with two fists."

Both voices began to cackle until they sputtered out in a string of coughs. I turned and found I was the unseen audience for a conversation between the two Alpha-Bits I'd been warned away from before I even knew there were Alpha-Bits: their Eminences, the Red and the Gray.

Now, in case you don't know, there are schools in Tulsa, Oklahoma. Some of them are even good. My mama worked two jobs to send me to one of them on a scholarship. And there, I took French. I never took to it, but I did take it. So I'd caught the initial references in the nicknames to Cardinal Richelieu, who'd loved to throw his red-skirted weight around the court of Louis XIII in life and Dumas' *The Three Musketeers*, and to his good friend, the Franciscan friar with a fondness for the gray frocks and the shadows, Father Joseph. What had to be explained to me my first week at Haggerty's was that our Red Eminence, Armand, was the chief conductor on the handball express and that our Gray Eminence, Francis, was quite the artist with a lot of rope and a roll of duct tape. That, and to never turn my back on them. Ever.

Legend — at Haggerty's, at least — has it that they share a mutual passion for unsafe wax-play. Not with candles, mind you. But the kind that rips the hair right off the innocent. There are harrowing tales of drugged tricks from the '70s onward dragged back to the basement lair in one or the other's Painted Lady — in that row of Victorians you see on every postcard picture — where enough hair was torn from backs and chests to require a skin graft. And finally there is the one horror story that always makes everyone at the bar shudder: a fisting scene that turned into the bikini wax from hell and left a brother bear hobbling bowlegged and on two canes for the rest of his mercifully short life.

"In fact, my dear, you and your fists are welcome to accompany me to Haggerty's after this wake finishes," said Francis, the Gray Eminence, as he stroked the well-trimmed point of salt-and-pepper hairs on his chin. His trademark pop eyes grew even wider as the bushy waves of his eyebrows rolled and crested and subsided.

"Ah, Haggerty's." Armand, the Red Eminence, narrowed his blue eyes to a squint as he peered over the edges of his glasses. "Our little slice of the workingman's heaven." He paused to sip from his beer. The flute rested on his blond beard, trimmed and shellacked so it resembled the spade of a gilded shovel. His thick neck flushed deeper and deeper shades of red with each swallow.

"That charmingly rustic replica of every dilapidated garage to be found alongside the highways running between my old Kentucky home and sweet home Alabama. Down to its very sawdust-and-peanut-shell-strewn floor. Yes, dear sweet Haggerty's. Watering hole for the likes of Rocco Genovesee. And from what I hear you like Rocco very much."

I flinched and then panicked that they'd seen me reveal not only that I was eavesdropping but that I knew just who this Rocco was. Biblically so. We'd begat many a good time and planned to keep on doing so. But they continued to pitch their conversation and their gaze far above my head.

"Jealous, love," said the Gray Eminence.

"Oh, yawn," replied the Red. "Go ahead if you must, Francis, and get fucked by the wee beastie. Personally, I'd like to think of my asshole as something more than a glorified pencil sharpener."

I almost snorted my beer out through my nose at that lie. Rocco's dick nearly bested mine.

"A voracious maw, perhaps."

"Fuck you, dear heart."

"Armand, if we ever get that drunk again, we'll shit our livers."

I closed my eyes till the image had passed, thankful that I'd held off from taking another swig. Well, as much of a swig as a man can take from a champagne flute.

"Ah, Francis. You are as graphic as you are succinct."

Their Eminences, The Red and The Gray, then cackled at a pitch that would have made a deaf dog howl as they clinked their glasses together. As I walked away, once again dead set on revenge, I heard Armand stage-whispering to Francis: "You'll never guess who uses Miss Clairol on his chest hair…"

In the kitchen of Roger and Randall, I found a bevy of bears admiring the cater-waiter — and the caterer who pointed to his harried assistant where to pour this and where to place that and the dishwasher and dish dryer — while they absentmindedly chatted with each other. Alpha-Bits were artfully arranged against the buffed steel of the refrigerator, the tastefully plated and panned and pictured walls, the wide marble-covered arm of the counter that swung into the center of this large room and from which platters were returned and filled and launched anew into the great hall of the well-haired.

I took a deep breath as I stood in the doorway and then strode toward the sink with an urgent purpose, my brown-guck-covered fist high in the air. I'd shoved it a bowl full of foie gras and now made excuses about my intentional mishap as I jockeyed past the dishwasher to the running water of the faucet.

"I dropped my bread in the dip and had to go after it," I offered to the faucet with a sheepish smile. I was too embarrassed to face the dishwasher in the eye because I knew what would come next.

"Oh, fuck," I shouted, staring at my hand before plunging it back into the wide hole in the center of the sink. "Oh, God, I'm so stupid," I said even louder. The dishwasher, a middle-aged Latino only slightly taller than me and with the most immaculately tended strip of a moustache I'd seen on a man other than Clark Gable or John Waters, looked genuinely concerned. His co-worker, another Latino who was taller and younger and smooth-faced except for an endearing smear of ink black peach fuzz around his lips, held the plate he was drying to his chest like a startled child he was trying to calm.

"My ring, my ring," I moaned. The rest of the room turned to the drama at the sink. Several Alpha-Bits looked as shocked as if one of the plates themselves had spoken.

"I was washing the foie gras from my hand and I lost my ring," I said as my eyes hopped from unsympathetic face to unsympathetic face until I returned to the kindly eyes of the dishwasher and dish dryer. Originally, I'd thought of saying it was gift from my grandmother or my late partner. But neither, as much as they loved me or I them, had given me a ring. In fact, I'd never owned one. And I didn't think this crowd would be moved by a sentimental gift either, imagining it a pop-top from a beer can. So I upgraded.

"It was a class ring. I know it's silly. Who knew you could get one for the Harvard School of Business? But I was young…"

Harvard+Business=Money & Power. I could almost hear various brains calculating and carrying the six figures forward.

"Get Roger quick. Now," said a older bear who looked

and sounded like Sebastian Cabot and dressed like Paul Bunyan to the caterer.

A face modeled on a vague recollection of the tragedy masks from ancient Greek drama, except it was framed all around with a mass of continuously pampered hair that had been painstakingly highlighted to outshine the few strands of gray, hurried into the midst of the kitchen, looked around and then down into my face.

It was Roger. Or it was Randall.

(Lesbian couples no longer have exclusive dibs on that adaptive property of mirroring their partner, down to the DNA, the longer they stay together.)

I explained to him what had happened. He looked concerned, but I couldn't tell if it was because I'd lost my ring, been admitted to Harvard, or was preventing the washing of the large grove of champagne flutes on the counter.

"Did you try to get it out with your hands?" he asked.

"Yes."

"Well, maybe someone with longer arms should try."

Obviously my Harvard MBA did little to increase my standing in his eyes.

"It won't help," I said. "I can't feel anything hard in there. It has to be in the pipe."

"In the pipe," he repeated in disbelief. "Where am I going to get a plumber on a Saturday afternoon?"

We furrowed our brows at the exact same moment.

"I know just who to call," I said.

I pulled my cell phone from the pouch hanging on my belt and dialed a number, explained my situation, begged the voice on the other end if he could make an emergency house call for which I'd pay him any fee he asked, smiled for the eavesdroppers, asked how long, sighed and repeated after him, "Right away," and thanked him several times before remembering to give him the address (which he already knew), thanked him some more, and hung up.

"He'll be here in about twenty minutes," I said to our host.

"Good, good," he nodded brusquely. He then returned to the more interesting guests and missed gossip in the main room and left me and the help and the Alpha-Minus bears to await the arrival of my gift to Roger and Randall and every other Alpha-Bit here: TruBlu. Or as he was known to any who'd bothered to ask his name after their initial Internet hookup that had brought them man-to-man or who'd stopped to read the side of his truck: Rocco Genovesee.

✳

Of course, I didn't know about the Internet handle nor had I seen the truck until after we fucked. Several times. Our first night. And it was and is all gravy as far as I'm concerned. Not only is Rocco Genovesee the truest of blue, he's the real deal. A real man with a true-blue heart and a dick of gold and an asshole that could milk cum from a dead man's dick. If Rocco and I were the marrying kind — and our kind could marry — we just might. As long as we could still fuck around with our best men.

But that first night I almost kept on walking past Rocco.

I was heading down from the Castro along Market Street toward that crisscross of streets with warehouses, lofts, and Internet start-ups still sputtering along known as South of Market and home of good ol' Haggerty's. Thursday is Rock & Roll Night there. And that Thursday night it was live music from City Bear Jamboree. Deek was getting fucked and good by the drummer and begged me to show up and keep him company till the drummer could solo on him.

The band went on at 7 and it was about 6 or 6:30. I was making a leisurely stroll of it. I was coming up to the Plumbers and Steamfitters U.A. Local 38, only a few blocks from where Market crosses Van Ness and fifteen minutes from Haggerty's. A crowd of smokers was dwindling inside for a meeting. And there was Rocco with his back and one foot propping him against the wall, forcing his crotch out front and center and, in my lucky case, eye level.

He was definitely a foot taller than me. Long and solid with a small belly that swelled above his belt in imitation of his basket below. The silver-and-gray shadow stubbling his shaved head only made the russet brown bush of his beard all the more pronounced. It was a well-tended and thickly woven bramble that had blown its way up his body and under his chin. And above that thicket of hair was the flirtiest pair of deep-set brown eyes. They didn't twinkle. They outright smirked and leered and whistled and catcalled like a whole chorus line of stereotypical construction workers — no matter what the little bit of his full lips not hidden by the small push broom of a moustache were up to and currently that was sucking on an ever-shrinking cigarette.

With one unbroken, nearly unblinking glance, our hothouse wallflower had me ready to take out my dick and wag it for all of Market Street to see.

Then he fucked it up by talking.

"Grrr," said the now-solitary smoker.

I ignored it. You learn to ignore most of the insane (and I do mean insane) chatter you overhear on the streets of San Francisco.

"Grrr, stud."

I stopped. This sounded not so insane. Odd but perhaps promising. It was still daylight.

"Excuse me."

"Grrr," he said through his smiling lips that were now wrapped around the burning butt of a cigarette.

"Grrr? Why, Catwoman, what a lovely beard you have."

His smile broadened and he took the cigarette and flicked it into the street.

"Thanks. So 'Grrr' isn't the way to tell a bear he's hot, huh?"

"You've heard wrong, my friend. It's woof."

"But that's what a dog says."

"Son, you're no dog. And you can woof at me any

day...or night."

*

Every Alpha-Bit had wedged his way into the kitchen since Armand had silenced all conversation in the main room by trumpeting to Francis, "Francis, love, your pencil pusher's here," and all the heads had turned to see Rocco Genovesee pass in the hall and turned back to watch Armand sneer and Francis blush. And now every one of them—except perhaps the Red Eminence—had a "Woof" caught in his throat as Rocco squatted in front of the doors to the cupboard beneath the sink. He waddled like a butch duck back a step or two and opened them and waddled the step or two forward. And each thrust of his thigh muscles forced the rim of his jeans farther down his backside. Till the hottest crack in the history of indoor plumbing—and the men who master it without the help of nary an undergarment—had appeared. A vision framed in faded blue denim. Then Rocco got on his knees and the view only got better. His ass was now pushed up like a corseted bosom in a costume drama set in pre-Revolutionary France and there were dicks as stiff and ready to fire as any musket concealed throughout the crowd of hairy and horny men.

"Yo, I need some help here," their proletarian wet dream said, turning around and startling me by delivering our well-rehearsed lines with an accent that sounded like a cross between Sylvester Stallone's Rocky Balboa and Big Pussy on *The Sopranos*. Rocco the improvisational artiste had been born. Born to play to every prejudice of the well-off peanut gallery. "Hey, you there," he pointed to me. "Can you help me or what?"

"Sure," I answered slowly as I remembered my lines. "What do you need?"

"The spud wrench." There was a snort or two in the crowd. Rocco ignored it. "It's the silver wrench that looks kinda like the jaws of a beetle."

He got down all fours and reached a hand back to me. I knelt beside him and pushed the wrench into his palm. As soon as he took it, I leaned even farther forward and grabbed his own tool through the bunched-up denim. I could hear those closest to us either titter or gasp at my bold move. Look what the little grief-stricken drunk is doing, I imagined them silently captioning our tableau. Can you say "overreach," dear heart?

"Whoa there!" Rocco bellowed from under the sink. There was a dramatic clunk as he dropped the wrench and gripped the bottom of the cupboard with his hands in an attempt to push himself out.

"Relax, guy," I said as I unbuttoned his jeans. "I figured while you check out the pipes, I'd check out yours."

"What the fuck are you talking about, faggot?"

Nice touch, Rocco, I thought. Work the straight-acting self-hating angle. Nothing says blue-collar to these educated minds. Of course, by now he could have barked or shat gold because every brain was ignoring what every ear was hearing in order to process what every eye was seeing: the unveiling of Rocco's ass.

I had his pants pulled down and myself in position. "And since you're looking for my ring, I thought I'd give yours a thorough search."

"Oh, yeah?" Rocco said with a newfound softness. The audience was breathless. No one seemed to mind the quick shift to theater of the absurd.

"Yeah, stud." And I slapped his ass hard. And as in each of the four or five scenarios of classic porn, the protester was magically transformed — with the use of the word "stud" or perhaps the "slap" or the presence of a crowd or a hard dick — into the pussy-whipped. Rocco's hands unclenched and he slid forward, his head returning under the sink, his ass rising toward my mouth, which was closer to it than those of you keeping track of the laws of physics in your cramped mathematical notation would allow because I'd been behind Rocco and on my knees since the single slap that had made him a slut. .

"Oh yeah," Rocco sighed.

Now for my turn to improvise. I parted the cheeky curtain and sighed. Coarse black hair radiating out from a hot sun pulsing from dark pink to pale lavender. Hair and a tight little hole. My two hottest turn-ons. That's right, hair and a hole together. The asscrack is the one place I demand a man be a real bear. If it's naturally smooth, I'm suspicious but tolerant. But no shaving. Ever.

It's a great and offensive mystery to me why men who wear their animal natures on their sleeves—okay, backs and bellies and necks and upper arms, even going so far to have those tattooed with paw prints—feel compelled to trim or shave around their hole. Where are we more animal than our hairy buttholes? I ask you, my brothers. Where are we more vulnerable? More delectable?!

Why the sermon, now of all places, as it's obvious I'm about to rim our studly Rocco? Simple. I'm a master asseater. (Oh, if only Nature had gifted us with a tongue worthy of our appetites. As long and wily as an anteater's and as muscular and thick as a giraffe's.) To compensate for my tongue's natural deficits and to extend my pleasure, I take my time. Never less than fifteen minutes. Even now. Let them watch. Let them wait. And all the constant lapping and lunging leaves my tongue happily rasped—but I don't want it torn to shreds on stubble in the first seconds. And one of the greatest delights to a master asseater is the contrast between hair and hole. I want to savor my way over the thinning pelt to skin as soft as the silklike mouth of the finest cocksucker. There is no fabric, man- or Nature-made, as slick as the skin inside the wet hole of a man's ass.

And what drives me ever deeper: that intoxicating scent found on the cusp of a man's inner world, no matter how obsessively he washes. A scent for which I have never learned a better word to describe it than "funk." It makes my nose wrinkle and my soul dance. It is fermented man. And as if my nostrils were greedy little mouths, I drink it up like now—all the while giving long toast after toast with my tongue. My ears grow drunk on the moans that hum down to me through the skin and are as hair-raising as a standing ovation from an arena. I grip tighter with my hands to hold back the smooth muscle and fat so I can push my nose between the cheeks almost as far as my tongue. All the senses are besotted with ecstasy, even my eyes. For their reward, I open them and look up through the crack and along the back of the man shouting into the echo chamber created by the open doors beneath the sink.

Some moments of pure beauty cannot be described. No matter how many words even a man from Tulsa, Oklahoma like me knows or how many words there are. This was one of those moments.

Of true-blue indescribable beauty.

And it ended when I had to remember finally that I am mortal and must pull my nose out of Rocco's asscrack and breathe.

We both panted.

"Jesus…Christ…I hope to God…you got something to plug the hole you just opened," Rocco said.

"Maybe…not…as limber…versatile…or agile…but definitely bigger."

"Oh, yeah," he said bitterly as he rolled over onto his butt. He was back now from ecstasy's brink, too. "Right. I know all about men in San Francisco and their shitty dick-sizing abilities. A bunch of stupid fucks calling their needle-nose pliers a pipe wrench."

Armand, who had been uncharacteristically silent throughout the first act, now coughed out something that sounded like "You should know." Francis even more loudly shushed him.

"Personally," I said as I stood and took a deep breath and unbuttoned and dropped my pants, "I like to think of this as a caulking gun."

Can I tell you something? A seven-inch dick really takes on mythic proportions when you're 5'3". Even if you're 5'3" and weigh around 200 pounds, give or take a good steak dinner.

You're probably thinking a room this full of cockhounds would have noticed a seven-inch dick on a 5'3" man. They sure did in high school and it was pure hell. *Hey, look at the miniature pony with the horsedick! Nice hose, Rumpelstiltskin.* But put on a hundred pounds, let ol' Rumpleforeskin lie in the shade beneath your gut, wear loose-fitting jeans, and you really have to want to look down there to see it swimming below the denim's surface.

But now it had surfaced. A fat cock with a fatter head that looked, if I might bearishly brag for a moment, like a wild animal with a mane of its own as black hairs intertwined with blue veins up almost half the shaft.

This got the crowd to stirring. A chorus of stage-whispers and loudly caught breaths. And had their Eminences carried the ladies' fans their constant cattiness demanded — and they not so secretly craved — they would have had them out, whipped open, and fluttering furiously in front of their very red faces.

"Whoa, where'd that come from?" Rocco sputtered a little too perfectly.

"With the body," I smirked.

"I need a better look."

With that, Rocco got up from the floor, lifting me and my growing dick aloft before the appreciative crowd like a proud father showing off his son. For a perverse instant, I felt like shouting or singing out, "Today I am a man." Then Rocco put me down on the edge of the sink.

"Looks even better up close. But how's it taste?"

"You'll never know if you don't put it in your mouth," I said. And I swear, for my benefit alone (well, this and then almost making me faint from the blow job he's about to give me), he said "Grrr" as he swallowed my dick.

Grrr, indeed.

The neighbors must be loving this, I thought as Rocco sucked me off, my legs buckling on the kitchen sink, my butt bobbing a foot from the large window above it. Deek had told me they were a concert pianist and his lover. How he knew, I never asked. But I noticed, with the part of my brain not lodged in my other head in Rocco's mouth, that the pianist, who'd been rehearsing some complicated piece that ran up and down the keyboard throughout my time in the kitchen, had stopped. I imagined he and his lover were getting an eyeful of Rocco and an assful of little ol' me.

Rocco gripped my dick at the base and pulled his mouth away. He let his hand drop from his own cock and panted in time to the rhythm of strokes he kept beating out on his dick. "Oh, God, this is fucking hot, man. Your dick gets even wider as it gets harder." He put his lips around my head and slid up and down a few more times before he stopped. I watched my dick twitch from the cold as his warm spit dried. "Something's not right," he said. "Something's missing."

There was a gasp of expectancy from every mouth in the packed kitchen, save mine and Rocco's and Armand's, as every pair of ears hardwired via an overexcited bundle of chemicals and nerves to those gasping mouths heard: Someone is missing and that someone is you, daddy bear.

"I've gotta have you fucking my ass…"

"No problem there," I agreed.

"But that's gonna make me howl. So I gotta be stuffing my mouth with some other hot guy's dick."

"Fine. Who'd you have in mind?"

Not since that fateful beauty pageant of goddesses judged by a very impolitic shepherd boy had there been so much posing by the powerful in hopes of winning the affection of the help. Paunches and packages rearranged. Beards and guts thrust out and asses thrust up. But the Judgment of Rocco would find all wanting except for me and one other.

"If I could, I'd just suck my own." It was a rejection that still managed to excite nearly the entire den. "Ah, hell, let's go to Haggerty's. It's getting too stuffy in here."

"Sure. We can pick up a side of all-American beef sandwiched between two buns there and go back to my place."

"Mister, you've got my mouth and my ass watering."

I tried to keep from laughing at Rocco's improvised rewriting of our script.

"Let's pack up your tools and go," I said through tightly pressed lips. It was a line-reading worthy of a robot doing an infomercial. It didn't matter. These hopeful suckers (or should I say, suckees) only had eyes and ears for Rocco.

"L-l-leaving so soon. But what about your ring?" stammered Roger or Randall—like I said before, I never could honestly tell them apart, a hairy Tweedle Dee and Tweedle Dum in flannel shirts and chinos.

"Yes, can't your 'buddy'"—and as the other one who was either Randall or Roger said "buddy" he almost whelped with longing—"stay longer and search the pipes harder."

"Yes," piped up some of the others.

"Longer."

"Harder."

"Fellas, I looked as long and hard as I'm gonna for something that ain't there," said Rocco as he hoisted his pants in three tugs, each tug causing his dick and balls to flop, each flop causing various guests to grunt and sigh.

"Ain't there?" the hosts said tilting their heads in the hopes it would right the confusion in their heads.

"Isn't there," muttered Armand to Francis. "The King's English isn't completely dead yet."

"Ain't there. Not now. Gone. Washed away."

"Oh, my," Roger or Randall said.

"Heavens," Randall or Roger added. "I'm so sorry," he said as he turned and looked down at me. "What can we do?"

I knew it was a rhetorical question and smirked. Always an Alpha-Bit, always an asshole.

"Accept my thanks," I said.

He looked puzzled. Like he'd discovered the cater-waiter had a Ph.D. or the dark-skinned dishwashers spoke not only their own language fluently but English as well. (All true, by the way. I was in the kitchen over thirty minutes waiting for Rocco to arrive.)

"Yes, thank you for a wonderful party. And thank you most of all for this wonderful party favor. C'mon, Rocco."

"Lovely party," Rocco said before kissing the startled hosts goodbye. "But I really wished I could've had some s'mores."

"Why then you must. Please, stay and have some before you go."

"You know, I think I'll take mine to go." He winked at Daniel. "I've never had a walking-talking doggy bag before. Now that's class. C'mon, pup."

Daniel jogged ahead of us toward the door. Naked. A vision of dancing buttcheeks. It would be a brisk, but brief, climb for him down the stairs to Rocco's truck in the driveway. Blue balls for Sal, indeed.

And as I walked out of the kitchen, I felt something I'd never felt before: all the eyes in the room were on me. My whole body burned. But the smoke in the room wasn't coming from me.

No, not at all.

Ah, how I love the smell of hairy nuts roasting on envy's open fire.

Makes me proud to be a man. A short man. A short and very smart man going home to fuck two very hot men for a long winter's night.

So proud that I suddenly found myself filled with the spirit of the season. And with all the charity I had learned in Tulsa's Victory Christian Cathedral, I turned to that kitchen full of sugar-plump fairies and, laying a well-chosen finger aside of my nose, silently wished each and every one a beary merry Christmas and a happy new year.

Then I roared before disappearing out of sight: "And to all you motherfuckers a good night!"

But to you I give this priceless gift of advice: If you ever find yourself in the presence of a self-styled A-Bear, tell him to go drown in a bottle of Nair and move on. No looking back. No regrets. You'll thank me, my brother. And I'll keep a warm seat waiting for you at Haggerty's—

right between Rocco and me.

7 Just 7 Tales of Lust on a Bed

for Kevin Killian

$\mathcal{I}$was not born speaking your kind's language or knowing your ways. But when I was torn from my family and the rest of my kind and forced to live in captivity in one of your zoos, I learned all about you.

You are a furtive creature. You want, but you are ashamed of your wanting. Of your myriad wants, you get many of them openly but savor them most in private. You like to lie about on my kind and dream of those wants you have yet to possess. You then like to lie on or bounce on or roll on or kick on one of your kind as you do day and night on one of my kind and often at the same time. This is a favorite want of yours of which you never tire. Perhaps, if I tell your secrets, you will realize that there are many silent creatures watching you and your loud antics. Perhaps then you will release me and my many kin in captivity. I have thousands of stories about you that I know you would rather I kept secret.

Here are just seven.

I hope they haunt you as they do me. You have been warned.

Let us go:

One

Adam and Eve check into Room 18 of the Argent Motel, a mini-mall unto itself of brick and glass and crumbling stucco somewhere urgently forgettable between Los Angeles and the Grapevine. They check in under assumed names (who would believe Adam and Eve, just Adam and Eve, are real names unlike Viggo Mortensen and Exene Cervenka? who would believe they are *the* Adam and *the* Eve? — though they are and they look good for their age, something in that apple bite — the rest of you humans sag faster than my kind yet everything gathers in your middle, too). Adam has promised her something different, at last. Eve knows better. She lies back as he sucks on her nipples, hoping in time he'll enter the gates to her garden with his blazing tongue. But once again, he plays "You want another of my ribs?" and pokes her till the "rib" breaks, spilling its marrow, and grows soft. Eve doesn't make a sound. She's given up faking it several millennia ago. She grimaces as Adam snores and fingers the stem of her own hidden fruit from the tree of the knowledge of good and evil until she comes.

Two

Twelve hours after Adam checks out, he returns with Steve. But again, they do not want to draw undue attention to themselves and check in under false names. Kevin Killian, who is the night manager of the Argent Motel, always plays along with Adam because he is more entertaining than the sunburned families with mewling offspring coming to and from Magic Mountain and he pays in cash. And Steve is hot. He is a dead-ringer for River Phoenix. But River is dead and Steve is not. Kevin, who is also a writer, nearly laughs in Adam's face when he checks the register to write him a receipt. Adam and Steve are now Mr. Edmund Picano and Mr. Felice White. For two ancient fuck buddies, they are still new to the gay scene. And mightily buzzed on coke.

How's Blanche? Adam asks Kevin while he waits for Kevin to hand him his receipt and the key to room 18.
She's fine, Kevin answers. She gave us a scare the other day. Dodie and I thought she'd run away but we found

her curled up in the back of the closet.

Your wife sleeps in the closet?

No, the cat.

Adam always confuses Kevin's wife, Dodie, with their cat, Blanche.

What crazy lives you writers live. C'mon, Felice.

I'm Edmund, laughs Steve.

And I'm lucky, howls Adam, too high to give a fuck for the rolling of Kevin's eyes.

Once he's closed the door to Room 18, Adam orders Steve to strip and they fumble with their respective clothes. Then Adam pushes Steve onto the bed and licks his face and across half of one of his pecs before rolling him over. Adam is tugging at his dick as he hunches over Steve's ass. Steve is rubbing his dick against the Vellux blanket. The material feels like spun plastic and it is easy to spark a pleasant, warming heat out of it. Meanwhile, Adam spits into the crack of Steve's ass. He pushes the spittle down between his cheeks. He mounts Steve and presses his limp dick as deeply into his buttcrack as he can. He passes out thinking he has come. The extra weight on Steve's back makes the burn all the more intense. He does come. He rolls out from under Adam to leave him to wake up alone, the cold of the wet spot stuck against the small of his back.

Three

Kevin watches as a Corvette the color of a Red Delicious apple drives out of the lyrics of the Prince song and then past the front of the lobby's automatic sliding doors. It has missed the mark and reverses. A car's equivalent of a double take. Out of the driver's door come the heels, the legs, the thighs, the torso and laughing head of a woman known two days ago as Exene Cervenka. The also-laughing head of Steve rises over the roof of the car from the passenger's side door. A waving hand and arm join the head. Tonight, she signs them in as Mr. And Mrs. John

Doe. Newlyweds. And, it looks like, if Kevin squints his eyes just right, that the third head in the car belongs to the maid of honor, a sister (?) of the bride (?) or groom (?).

Eve & Steve & Lornette.

You thought I'd say Lilith. She ditched this crowd when my ancestors were wool bags filled with straw and an exoskeleton of ropes and kindling. Lornette is a word of its creator's own making just as she is a woman of her own making, with a little help from some hormones and perhaps someday a surgeon's costly knife. Once she was Loren and once she discovered the word "lorgnette" and fell asleep dreaming she had fallen, like another very special girl, through those two bits of two-bit glass into a world of red-velvet curtains and bright lights and wildly elaborate makeup and dresses and songs played by full orchestras. Each night she falls farther and dreams less.

Tonight Steve, one of Lornette's favorite clients — always cash up front and more than she dreams to charge for an hour, a night, a week even (he claims that unlike Al Gore he really did invent the Internet or some pricey part of it) — has brought her to Room 18 of the Argent Motel. Up for a threeway with the Mother of All Women? Steve asked her several hours earlier from his cell phone. Eve wants to play like the boys tonight, he continued, and strap one on and fuck me till I scream like a girl and I'd like to share the wealth and pass on the pleasure to you. Lornette said yes and sighed with relief when Steve had hung up. She was out of Viagra — Estrogen giveth and Estrogen taketh away — and didn't feel like fucking anyone else today anyway. Never a problem with Steve since he only topped with her — something he never could do with his boyfriend or so he said. But straight men only wanted to bottom to her. And they always have to be gripping something that hollers HONEST-TO-GOD-WOMAN when they're sucking my dick or getting fucked up the ass, Lornette had thought as she stared at the newly mute cell phone clutched in her hands, her French-manicured nails clacking against the LED display as if waiting for it to spell out to her why straight men are so odd. Perhaps Steve is going straight-for-pay tonight? He's rich enough to find that perverse. Whatever, she concluded. A postmodern daisy-chain she could handle.

And so tonight our thoroughly pomo pre-op Alice finds herself falling once more. Tonight she lies face-first on me. And on her lies Steve, harder than he's been in years thanks to the miracle that is a rare moment of genuine novelty converging with a Walgreen's worth of modern pharmaceuticals, pushing farther and farther into Lornette's expertly accommodating asshole. And on Steve lies Eve, her eyes only on her dick as she watches it slide in and out. She pulls all the way out and pushes all the way back in over and over. All she can do is watch. Watch Steve's huffing and puffing hole suck her newfound nine-inch dick down to the harness and spit it back out. Whole. Unbitten. So unlike the apple. She has never laughed harder. It spreads from her to him to her to me. But I do not give in. I hold my coils firm. For I know: Eve into Steve into Lornette equals one sticky tangle of sheets and puddles here and there that will never wash out even if some human ever bothered to bathe me.

They leave me a reeking mess in the morning.

Eve & Steve & Lornette.

Four

The door to Room 18 opens and Lornette returns almost thirteen hours later with her two johns, Cain and Abel.

You: Hold the phone! You're telling me that all those names intoned in that endless hour or two of Sunday School each

blanket nubby with age tucked under its master's wizened head, from the fact that you each look so much alike. Then you panic when someone refuses to play along and reminds you that you are alike but you are not the same, when someone reminds you that Flux is the Mother of us all. Even a newborn cradle knows this. That is why your kind have always linked our children with the grave.

I have many hours to think about this as Cain's hot-as-a-lion's-breath blood gets chummy with my fluffy-as-a-lamb's-ass stuffing, soaking its way through to my springs. Until the night and Cain and his blood and finally I grow as cold as the first star of the morning after the longest night of the year.

Five

Maria Montez, the head of housekeeping, calls the head of security, Vin Diesel, in to help her turn the blood-stained mattress. Head is such an odd choice of words when they are as much the whole body without another person in either housekeeping or security to call a neck or torso or even a limb. And as for me, I too lack better words since all I know are my captors'. I am nauseous because my "stomach" somersaults to where my "back" once was. Nauseous for a good hour. An hour in which Vin lies with his feet at my headboard and his head at the other end where Maria squats until she straddles him. You look like one giant dildo, she hisses as she pushes her lips against his freshly shaved head. She'd waited, naked, on the bed while he spent thirty minutes shaving and reshaving and anointing the dome of the rock that is his body. His skin, the color of the meat of olives or nuts but pale from years on the night shift, is warm and smooth. There is only the occasional and briefest prick of stubble against her tender and enflamed flesh. It drives her wild. That and watching his scalp grow slick. She barely notices him jacking his dick. Vin doesn't care. He's aware for the both of them. In time,

Maria will be swollen and slobbering enough to climb onto the bed and rest her ass on the hard pillows of his pecs before pushing her cunt into his face, the tendons in his neck bulging like underground fiber-optic cables as he lifts himself from the bed's edge into her bush. Though they touch, they only feel themselves. Even when she slides backward along the ungiving ridges of his chest and stomach and onto his fat cock that is all bulk like his body, ending in a small smooth sometimes (like now) red head. She bounces and he bounces and I bounce. She hisses and he cries and I scream but no one expects my kind to speak so they do no listen. I am reduced to background noise, a series of squeaks that makes them think they are really fucking the shit out of the other. They bounce even harder. Maria comes and comes and comes but my torture only ends when Vin, first stiffening like he's in an early stage of rigor mortis and then growing limp like he's in a coma, shouts, Go, go go!

If only I could.

Six

Ian Philips is sunburned and foul-tempered as he wheels his luggage into the room. He fell asleep in the sun reading *The Life and Opinions of Tristram Shandy, Gentleman* on one of the manicured lawns of Magic Mountain, too afraid to ride any of the roller coasters that his partner in all crimes, Greg Wharton, so adores. He is bold only in print. Greg enters after him, flushed and red-faced. He glows from the sun and wind that blew past him again and again.

Ian begs off sex tonight. He is too burned to enjoy even one of Greg's virtuoso blow jobs. And he is ashamed his red head looks a cherry on an obscenely uncreamed, unfudged, unnutted scoop of vanilla ice cream. Greg would scowl if he knew Ian was thinking this so Ian doesn't tell him. Instead, he offers Greg an ample pacifier. Which dildo am I tucking you into bed with, Monkey? Ian coos. Matthew Rush or Aiden Shaw? Matthew's life-size replica reminds Greg of a small traffic cone used only in driver's ed. He chooses Aiden's. Though he has not read any of Aiden's novels or poems, Greg imagines Aiden's dick is filled with literary possibilities.

Ian is anal. Greg knows this intimately. So he is not surprised at all to watch Ian remove the bed cover and fold it and then pull back the blanket and the sheet and spread towels across the fitted sheet like they are spending a day at the beach. Greg is naked and halfway down Aiden's stunt cock before Ian is finished folding his shirt and shorts atop his shoes and placing the rolled-up pair of socks on top of the pile. Ian crouches into place beside Greg to assist with the final thrust of the silicone monument only slightly shorter than Nelson's Column and the good-night kiss. Greg moans himself to sleep while Ian methodically lubes himself from toe to crown with aloe vera. He lies back, places his hands in the air above his chest, and claps out in code to the room's magic lamp: *Fiat nox.*

All is dark.

Seven

On the seventh day, Adam returns to the Argent Motel alone. He is drunk and signs in under his God-given name. Kevin, ever civil, smiles as Adam calls him a fucking pervert. It seems Adam does not like Kevin's reply (Dodie's fine.) to Adam's question (How's your wife?). Jesus Christ, you killed your wife and married your cat, Adam continues. I thought my family was sick. Oh, hey wait, Adam says as he staggers to turn around in the archway created by the open automatic sliding door, you are my family. Fuckinfigures, he slurs as he stumbles into the parking lot where Night and many rented or stolen vehicles sit cooling. Kevin rolls his eyes and returns to tucking in the newest twenties and tens and fives and ones. Sleep tight, he whispers as he slides the register shut.

Adam falls back onto the bed of Room 18 as if it were a mound of new-fallen snow and he a boy one-thousandth his age, giddy with cold and ready to fly on his back, an angel made of water crystals. He spreads his wings and undoes a few buttons on his shirt and his belt and the zipper of his pants. He pulls his clothes as far off as he can without getting up. He clicks on the TV and it is an episode of a show he has seen. In his life, he has witnessed every possible twist of every possible tale that one of his children can beget. "Beget." That word reminds him of the man he used to be. An oozing floodplain of fertility. A river delta of sperm. He mutes the TV and rifles through the drawer of the side table for the Bible. The Gideons do not disappoint. He opens to Genesis 5:3 and strokes his dick for every "begat" that follows. He may have begun with the breath of God and Eve with Adam's own rib but every other poor fuck after them came from his seed. Or so he consoles, convinces himself with each flick of his wrist. He is pumping like a cartoon engine by Chapter 10 and the cataloguing of the generations of the sons of Noah, Shem, Ham, and Japheth. He catches his breath for a moment as his children build the Tower of Babel. His dick convulses in his palm, ready to free itself of the hot liquid breath within, be free of his fever for the rest of the night. The "begat"s begin anew and the dick of Man gets its wish. Adam, with enough trumpeting to topple the walls of Jericho once more, begats handful after handful of seed. And then he weeps. Adam weeps, not because he is drunk or despised, secretly, by all his children and their children unto the ends of the world. Adam weeps for his son Onan, struck dead so long ago. So long ago the Lord no longer remembers why He killed him. The Lord no longer cares who spills His seed — every single one on loan from Him the Almighty. There is too much seed and so much of what has been planted has come to naught because men have been made in His image and likeness and thus they all have a jealous streak a galaxy wide and let it goad them to smiting each other down and down and down. No, the Lord no longer cares. But Adam, too old for nostalgia except on a night like tonight when he is drunker than Noah, does and he weeps for his smitten son Onan, so long dead.

In time, he forgets to weep and passes out.

As his tears and drool soak my back, I feel my coils soften, for a moment, against him and his kind. It lasts until Adam awakes, rolls over, and throws up against my side.

Burn me now, spawn of Man, or let me go.

I will choke the next of you in your sleep.

You have been warned.

Let us go.

Just Another Lesbian Potluck

for Gina Gatta, Dyke Daddy of AltaGirl Press

"Quid? vos, inquit, nescitis, hodie apud quem fiat? Trimalchio, lautissimus homo,..."
—Petronius Arbiter, *Satyricon*

Sssssssss.

I'll admit this is an odd way to begin a story, but then, this is an odd story. It's not a snake — this *sssssssss*. No, it's not even the audience during nearly every preview at San Francisco's Castro Theater, giving a rousing "lesbian hiss" to any and all manifestations of The Oppressor.

It's steam.

*

Sssssssss.

A hot hissing mist. Clark felt it. He heard it. But he kept his eyes closed. This was, after all, the steam room in a sex club. What little that might be going on he'd seen before. Besides, Clark enjoyed it — actually, everything — with his eyes closed.

He sat still while pore after pore flung itself open to allow its overheated, drowning occupants to pitch out pail after tiny pail of hot salt water. His back meanwhile was caught up in a sloppy wet kiss with the wall behind him. The towel that spread across his lap – you might as well know that he believed he had good reason to be so modest – the towel lay heavy against his long, lean thighs as it sponged up the air.

If he strained his ears, imagining them to be bionic, he was almost certain he could hear, behind the *sssssssss* of the steam, sounds of shifting, sighing, slurping. Yes, there it was — that *smackgurgleplop* of a man taking a dick too big for his mouth too fast. How did he know? He knew. He'd heard this sound before, and he would hear it again.

For Clark, you see, had been, like one of the Big Ten colleges, very generously endowed. But there was a price for such gifts: the public will always expect an equally exceptional level of performance. Alas, gravity, genetics, and several other anonymous natural laws had thought otherwise. They had conspired to keep his dick — hard or soft — at a permanent 225° angle. Steadily and cruelly, he'd learned what a difference a degree makes. 180° was the golden mean, 135° was standard, 90° awkward, but 225° — it just lay there. Or so many men had said silently and not so silently as they'd walked away or gotten up from bed. Each took it as a personal insult, leaving Clark behind with his dick hard and his soul harder. In time, he'd become increasingly protective of his dick — thus the aforementioned towel. Just tonight even, he'd let men *smackgurgleplop* for a while. Then, he'd weaned them and got himself off, alone.

So there sat our prince, spent, yet still dreaming of the mouth that would someday fit his cock and failing to notice that a little black bear had sat down beside him. He was a small, solid block of dark brown sugar — solid except for his soft breasts with wide nipples the color of lightly roasted coffee beans. These two trophies, prized by chubby chasers and bear hunters alike, rested comfortably on the ledge that was his stomach. Not far below this dozing pair began his towel, a white beach towel that almost reached, now that he was sitting, to his round knees. It seemed Clark had met his match in modesty.

The bear flared his already wide nostrils and then let out a snort to tell Clark he was here and horny. Clark didn't budge. The bear didn't give up. He placed his wide hand over the ridge in the middle of the steam-soaked towel. He squeezed. Clark didn't even flinch. So the bear continued to squeeze his way slowly toward where he imagined he'd find the end of the dick. But it wasn't there. His eyes widened and he kept on squeezing.

"Hey, Jody," Clark said casually, his eyes still closed.

"Hey, stud. How'd you know it was me?"

"You still grope like a girl." He opened his eyes to watch Jody's response: Puzzled? Pissed?

"Fuck you too, bitch." Another hiss beneath the sounds of steam.

"Ah, Jody. C'mon. It's just a little constructive criticism. I just meant you still squeeze too delicately. Like you think it'll break. You've got to grope my dick and balls as if you were mashing the last lump out a boiled potato."

"Thanks, I'll remember the cooking tip."

"I didn't say I enjoyed that. I just know you're still nervous about passing. You know."

Jody's goatee caught Clark's eye. He followed the thin moustache growing at the edge of his upper lip down through the sparse patches along the sides of his mouth to the wiry, black thickets covering his broad chin. He noted a wet clump with a waxy sheen.

"How's cocksucking?" Clark smiled.

"I did all right."

"I can tell." His lips and his eyes widened simultaneously.

"What?"

"You've got something in your beard."

"Huh?" The steam continued to silence their stage whispers.

"I said you've got some guy's sperm in your beard."

"Oh. Now don't worry, mom. He came in my hands, not in my mouth."

Clark turned his head back against the wall. He closed his eyes while he laughed.

"Can I borrow your towel?"

"You've got your own."

"Okay, you're right. But I'm still a little pee shy. You know what I'm saying? I'm not sure if the guys here believe a man is a dick is a man. Even if this is San Francisco. And I really don't want to find out tonight."

Clark sighed. "Okay."

Jody lifted the heavy towel toward his face. He swiftly wiped around his mouth, then began to return it. "Shit, Clark. Doesn't that thing ever crawl back into its cave?"

"No. It's too limp to move. Ever."

"Sorry." Jody paused to cuss himself out in his head. "Were the boys mean to you again?"

"Nope, tonight I only let them suck it. When it's just sucking, they could care less."

Jody sensed Clark's mood growing as glum as his dick. And since he'd already had to beg hard to get Clark to come out and play tonight, he quickly changed the topic to something more upbeat.

"Lezzie's having a potluck, wanna go?"

"Huh?" Clark had drifted — his neck and shoulders were caught up in another slow, sucking kiss with the wall.

"Lezzie's having a potluck. I'm going. Wanna come?"

"No, Jody, thanks. Once I come it takes days before I can think about sex again. I'm weird that way..."

"No, you're just deaf. I asked if you wanna *go* with me to Lezzie's potluck."

"Lezzie?"

"Lezzie Beddeath."

Ah, Lezzie Beddeath, Clark lazily thought. "No, I can't," he answered after a long minute.

"C'mon, Clark. She's heard all about you from Bibi. And I've told her you're one of her biggest fans." Clark had closed his eyes again while his back and the wall slobbered over each other. "It's tomorrow night, and I know you don't have anything going on. Ah, c'mon! It's just another lesbian potluck — you don't even have to bring anything except yourself."

Clark had shut Jody out again. This was too much. First, he'd said he groped like a girl and now he'd gone stone silent. Jody realized he was still holding Clark's towel. The *sssssssss* of the steam whispered something in his ears. Yes, he'd give him back his towel, all in good time. But first he had a lesson to teach his new best friend.

This time, his hand grasped Clark's nuts — *Where did*

they get that name? Perhaps if nuts didn't have shells. They were more like fruit. Large grapes. Jody stopped his mind from trying to discourage him. He'd already grabbed Clark's balls. He tightened his grip so they rubbed together making what he hoped were sweet sparks of pain. With a series of deft tugs and twists, he soon had most of the large ball sack in his fist. His thumb remained free, and he put it to good use. Jody dragged it up and down the fleshy hem that held the tightening skin and all its contents together. *These grapes are shrinking, but they still ain't no nut.* Jody concentrated by increasing his grip. Clark shifted. Jody glanced up to see that Clark's eyes were still closed. Listening for any sound Clark might make, Jody instead heard only the snort of his own breath and the sigh of the room. *Fine.*

Jody took his free hand and wrapped it around the shaft under the head of Clark's dick. He squeezed. Hard. His thumb and index finger were a tight collar around this neck and head. Silently, it began to choke, swelling, growing more purple than an almost-ripe plum. Jody loosened his grip and watched to see if this mouth would gasp for air. Nothing. So, his hand dug in deeper. He dragged his index finger up over the head and through the slit to the top of the now bruise-purple cock. The finger began to trace and retrace its slow steps. Even though Clark's dick looked limp to the naked eye, Jody's hand felt the difference.

The finger stopped and rubbed beneath what must be the chin of this dick's head. Jody continued until the whole of Clark's cock pulsed in his palm. Before it became too much too soon, he let go. Once again he dragged his finger through the piss slit now bubbling with pre-cum. He pushed its pad into the wet skin and then used it to polish the pate of Clark's dickhead until it shone.

All the while, Jody's other hand was still trying to make fire in the dick's belly by rubbing the balls together again and again. At last, with a shudder he could feel shake Clark's whole body, they pushed away from each other and pulled themselves as far out of the reach of his relentless fingers as they could.

Feeling this retreat and seeing that the mouth of Clark's dick had begun to drool like an idiot, Jody was finally convinced he had Clark by the balls. So he stopped. He took his finger away from the screaming head and pushed several others against what felt like a huge vein running from Clark's balls to his asshole. As he stemmed the tide, Jody spoke.

"Still think I grope like a girl?"

Clark broke his silence. His lips were quivering so hard Jody could barely hear him say, "No."

"Well, since no one likes a cocktease, even if it's his best friend...."

"Please," Clark hissed, "let me come."

"What? You really want to come to Lezzie's potluck? Good. And since you've changed your assessment of my skills in elementary cock-and-ball torture, I'll even let you get off."

"Yes, please, now."

"If — if you promise not only to come to the potluck tomorrow night *but* you also promise to do whatever, *whatever*, Lezzie asks you to do. Promise?" Jody gave a firm tug to Clark's grapes.

"Yes, yes...." Clark shook as if he were freezing in this very warm, very wet room.

Jody let up his fingers and replaced them tightly around Clark's dick head — a final throttle. The head turned deeper and deeper shades of purple until it began to choke violently. Suddenly, gasping and gagging, it coughed up a hot, pearl gray phlegm that poured out over the edges of Jody's fingers — cooling as it fell into puddles on the bench below.

When Clark could shake no more, Jody gently released his genitals, wiped his own hands, and handed Clark back his towel.

✳

Clark looked at himself in the window — a fluorescent shadow hovering at the corner of Church and 24th Streets. The doors of the light rail train lurched open. He stepped down and left the luminous beige world behind. Outside, the early winter sky was rapidly darkening — a solid stroke of deep blue that hinted of light only at the edges of Twin Peaks. There the Sutro Tower, that enormous strand of mutant DNA, stood defiantly over San Francisco, its city. All its red eyes blinked and blinked and blinked. On a hill behind it came several of its children, each a single tower with one winking red eye. Beneath this family there were the flashing white lights from the cameras of oblivious tourists.

Below, in Noe Valley, mercury street lamps gave off the odd amber light of night. Clark had arrived at the new isle of Lesbos circa 1996 — well, what was left of this year. For it was here, long after Sappho had leapt into the sea, that many of her transhistorical daughters had washed ashore. And after them had floated in the flotsam and jetsam of coffeehouse franchises, ATMs, stores of authentic Third World jewelry and clothes, shops with cards or candles or curios, and wave after wave of strollers.

Clark stood frozen at the corner of Church and 24th Streets. He was surrounded on all sides. Women with women with strollers came at him from the east, south, west, and north. Occasionally a goatee and a gay man would pass or a gaggle of urban grunge dandies and their ladies. He scanned the crowd for that little black bear. In this neighborhood, he thought, it should have been easier to spot him. Somewhere out there was Jody.

Jody, however, easily spotted Clark. At six feet and three inches, he stood out like a signpost. His brown hair, buzzed close to his head, looked like a cap and his sideburns — though Jody'd never dare tell him this — earflaps. For a final flourish at the manly art of sprouting hair, Clark had even cultivated a cluster at the tip of his chin. But it was his wide nose, which his two blue eyes constantly hugged, that always caught Jody's attention. It was the one adult feature on Clark's boyish face.

Well, actually, his most adult feature—which you, hopefully, haven't forgotten and Jody, certainly, hadn't—remained swathed in a pair of blue polyester pants. But don't worry. I promise it'll peep through those curtains sooner or later.

Jody surfed the latest wave of strollers toward Clark. And he would hear their plastic wheels clattering away into the concrete distance long after he'd stopped in front of the tall, tall boy.

"Hey, stud," the little black bear said.

"Hey, Jody."

"You live nearby."

"No. I was hoping you'd suck my dick here."

A passerby tried to remain oh-so–San Franciscan and not stare after hearing that remark. Her face, well-tended through her fifty-odd years, remained as tranquil as a Zen garden. Except for her widening eyes. They must make her look, she regretted, like some Tibetan demon. She clutched her one sack of groceries closer to her tasteful black business suit while her unscuffed cross-trainers took her quickly away from this very odd couple.

Jody turned to watch her until she disappeared in a crowd. To keep from laughing out loud, he locked eyes again with Clark. "How about after dinner?"

"Nope. It's a meal in itself."

Jody grinned. "Now don't go and use up all your clever retorts before we get there. Lezzie shows no mercy to the slow-witted." They started to walk toward Twin Peaks.

"Okay, Daddy. I'll be a good little boy. Speak only when spoken to."

"That's definitely my kind of man."

They'd come to a new intersection. They stood and laughed while they waited for one of the four hesitating cars to turn left. Jody grew tired—the gray Volvo station wagon in front of them seem paralyzed—so he walked in front of it. Clark loped across the road to catch up.

"Daddy Bear, wait up," Clark whined loud enough to

get a few stares from both sides of the road.

"Very cute. Just don't call Lezzie Daddy. Mommy-play is all the rage this year or so she says."

"Does Mommy Sir live on Sanchez or Noe?"

"Um, I think it's up Noe and off Elizabeth. Actually, I forget the cross streets. I just remember what the house looks like."

"Great. All the houses around here look alike."

"Yes, all houses *do* look like houses. But I think I can find this one. I've been there several times before."

And, after ten minutes of turning up one street then down another and turning back and then turning up yet another street, Jody finally decided which house it must be. They clomped up the stone steps toward the door on the far left. Jody pushed the buzzer impatiently. Then twice again. From above and beyond the other side of the door came a yell. Then a rapid succession of thuds. Someone very big and very angry was almost at the other side. Clark braced himself. The door lurched from its frame and shot inward.

"What the fuck — oh, hey, Jody."

It's Lezzie Beddeath herself, Clark shouted to the other onlookers in his head. The legend. The king of lesbian performance art who'd launched herself into San Francisco dyke superstardom with her dramatic readings of classic '70s gay porn. Then, fresh on the heels of that triumph, she opened and hosted Wilkommen, a weekly '30s-style cabaret at the hip Café dos Maggots. And now, she was here — here before him, in the very pinkish flesh and an even pinker terry cloth robe.

Even looking down on her, Clark could tell she filled the door's frame. From the bulges in the robe, he knew she was broad-shouldered and barrel-chested with large biceps and forearms that tapered before his eyes into small, strong hands. Her head sat squarely on a neck that was thicker than his thigh. Glancing down toward her feet, he imagined her thighs must have been thicker than both his legs and neck together. She could have easily snapped Clark over her knee. Quickly looking into her eyes, he also realized she'd probably enjoy doing that very much. When he should have looked away, he didn't. He just stared into her eyes. For her glasses — thick black plastic frames worn by the heads of university science departments throughout the '50s — magnified her blue eyes, giving her the appearance of a very, very intelligent cartoon racoon.

She smiled and slicked back a lock of her brick red hair.

"So, Jody," she said, "I must say, son, you're looking more like Mr. French every day."

"Hey, Lez. Still watching those *Family Affair* reruns for your dissertation?"

"It's Ahenobarbie, tonight."

"And a hyena to you, too."

"Cute, Boo-Boo, my boy. It's A-he-no-barbie. I know, I know. It sounds odd, but it's short for *ahenobarbus*. It was the family name of Nero's daddy. Seems the flaming emperor had red hairs on his chinny-chin-chin, too." She wagged her broad jaw which did end with some impressive hairs.

"Okay, barbie. I'd like you to meet Bibi's friend, Clark."

"You brought him. Good." She smiled. Clark, speechless and starstruck, smiled back.

"So why the Roman name?" asked Jody as he came through the doorway, pulling Clark with him.

"Boredom." She let them pass and then closed the door. "I'm so over the whole Weimar cabaret thing. Three years of hosting drag queens doing Liza Minnelli and drag kings doing Marlene Dietrich. It was tired from the *first* show. But the suits, the cigars, the scotch always got me laid." She gestured with her hand for them to go up the stairs. Instead, they stood waiting for her to continue. Eager to get back to her guests, she pushed her way through and began the climb.

"I'm thinking about starting up a new club. Something like the casinos of Havana in the '50s. I hear lesbian tango halls are all the rage now in Berlin. So why not have one here with a big all-dyke band playing mambos, rumbas, congas, tangos? I could break out my white tux jacket and black tie, slick back the hair, light up a cigar, and limbo beneath the cutest femmes in town." A self-contented leer spread across her face.

At the first landing, Clark discovered he had the courage to speak. "I like the casino idea. So will tonight be something like Caesars Palace in Vegas?"

Lezzie's leer shriveled fast. She turned on the creaking wooden step. "Uh, no. But kind of you to join our little conversation. Why can't all the cute boys be as quiet as you?"

Clark blushed. Jody caught his eye and smiled. Telepathically he tried to warn Clark to do the conversational equivalent of playing dead.

"No, my boys," she said as she returned to climbing, "I went Roman tonight simply because I believe they knew how to throw a dinner party. Lots of food, lots of drink, a little gossip with some elitist philosophical chitchat thrown in. You even get to recline through the whole thing. But the best comes with dessert — all the slave pussy you can eat."

"Slave pussy?" Jody stopped.

"Ah, yes, a little circus to go with the bread." Lezzie was a few more steps ahead.

"I hope to God I never hear that you've called me that behind my back."

Lez jolted a bit when she realized the conversation had rolled over a rather large speed bump. Now quite alone on the next flight of stairs, she stopped and turned again.

"Jody, Jody, my fine, fine, *fine* African-American man. Don't get your panties all in a wad — the metaphorical ones."

"Fuck you too, Lez."

"Jody, how long have we known each other?" She went down two steps.

"Six years."

"Six years, right?" Lez took another three steps and

they were beside each other. "Right?! And it may sound like I just shoved my foot in my mouth and then my whole head up my ass. Maybe I did. If so, I'm sorry. But, c'mon, how stupid do you think I am? Safe, sane, and consensual slavery. Sex slavery. Role play. Do I have to go find that copy of *Miss Abernathy's Concise Slave Training Manual*? Show *you* the difference? How big a white fool do you want me to make of myself?"

"You're doing a fine, fine, *fine* job."

They all laughed—each, however, for a different reason.

Once the air had cleared enough, they took the last few stairs toward the source of the faint light above them. At the top, to the left, an old sheet flickered from what must have been several dozen candles on the other side. Just as Lez moved to push it aside, Clark smiled. The pattern on the sheet. It was her. Wonder Woman. In and out of her invisible jet. Though it had faded from many years and many washings, he could make out the latticework of golden lassos binding each vignette to the other. The flickering grew brighter and the curtain dropped behind Lez. Clark, feeling courageous in the presence of one of his childhood heroes, put his hand against Jody's forearm, turned, and, with his eyes only, asked him to stop.

"Is she always like this?"

"If I know Lez, she's going to say much worse before the night's over."

"And she's your friend?"

"Yeah. And my ex."

"Oh, great. Before or after."

"Both."

"Jeez, Jody."

"Welcome to San Francisco."

✳

Clark pulled the sheet aside. Jody darted in under his arm. Then Clark passed through. Lights and shadows fluttered up into his face. Just as quickly, they retreated to their fixed niches. His eyes adjusted to the room's dim brilliance.

A few feet in front of Clark, an avocado green recliner held Ahenobarbie in its rigid embrace while a shimmering patchwork of gray duct tape held it together. Not all the chair's wounds, however, had healed, and, in a few spots, its foam innards had poured out and hardened. Once again, he stopped, stood, and stared at Aheno. She'd begun to busy her hands in her crotch by gathering up the folds of her robe into her lap. The longer he looked at the green chair and its many-shades-of-pink occupant, the more he thought that this couple reminded him of a monstrous watermelon wedge. Aheno stretched back. The footrest popped out and pointed Clark's eyes toward the rest of the room. Two battered coffee tables, pushed end to end, ran across it. On either side, Clark made out the shape of a futon couch turned sideways and opened its whole length. On top of each, an odd assortment of women was sprawled with even less care than the half-full and half-empty plates and cups that littered the tables and floor.

There in the center of the futon opposite him sat a Buddha with the largest breasts he'd ever seen. On a Buddha at least. And usually a Buddha this big had a smile as wide as Santa Claus'. This one only scowled. He tried not to stare at The Buddha's breasts. But, in her silver lamé wife-beater T-shirt, they really did look like honeydew melons or cantaloupes bulging from the bottom of a glitzy plastic grocery bag. Then an even brighter shimmering caught his eyes. He stood transfixed by the near-miracle of her bald head. Somehow, with a serendipitous tilt, she'd angled it to reflect the glint of every candle that watched from the ledges of molding that perched halfway up along all the room's walls and the twinkling of every little white bulb in the strands of fairy lights that hung above all the room's windows and doors. The scowling Buddha had been transfigured into Our Lady of the Beatific Disco Ball Head and Silver Lamé Breasts.

He blinked. His vision had disappeared. An unexpected movement had made The Buddha shift her head out of the light. The mop of black hair piled up next to the Buddha's nearest knee twitched again. Clark followed the hair as it trailed out through more shadowy piles into a pair of pale legs. Once he understood that this would be the extent of its stirring, he looked to the right of the Buddha. There, stretched out as far as she could, was a very short dyke — a dykette, actually, for she was as young as she was small. With a flick, just one, of his eyes, he'd surveyed her from head to toe and back. Over her toes, she wore the daintiest, yet still somehow butch, combat boots. Over her head, she wore the requisite baseball cap with its bill turned backwards. And across the small gap between each extreme, she'd covered herself in an enormous pair of vintage coveralls with some man's name sewn into a patch. He tried to read it sideways without turning his head. It looked like "Joe."

Joe had propped her chin up with her left arm and hand. And this allowed her sleeve, which she must have had to roll up six or seven times just to see the tips of her fingers, little choice but to collapse under its own weight in a heap around her elbow. The dykette spoke in rapid monosyllables to Jody, who'd wasted no time getting comfortable on the futon across from her.

Looking over Jody's broad back, Clark also noticed that both Joe and Jody were talking to another lesbian. She looked — he couldn't quite tell with all the shadows — like she'd dressed only in black and leather. A black leather shirt, black leather pants, black leather motorcycle boots, even a black leather vest. She was all black except for her pale skin and her platinum blonde hair. *Why'd she do that?* he wondered. *Draw everyone's focus to her hair.* For her hair had been cut short on top and billowed from the back in none other than honest-to-goddess tresses. *She must be the last lesbian in San Francisco with a mud-flap hairdo. Maybe she's making the transition from the East Bay to the City? Or maybe* — he cautioned himself before the cosmos once again demanded a payment for unearned attitude — *maybe she's the first to ride another retro wave? Look at her ear.* It hung with silver hoops from tip to lobe. *And her nose.* Pierced twice on the one side he could see. *And her lip.* Pierced again. *Yes, it must be an intentionally reclaimed hairdo.* He smiled. That must be it. For he had never yet met someone from the stylish tats and piercings scene who wasn't the late-twentieth century's equivalent of the fop.

Of course, he didn't really know why it was so important for him to run a fashion check on this particular woman, but, somehow, it made him feel like he'd lived in the City longer than the ten months he had. Like he belonged in this room as much as anyone else tonight.

"Okay, boys and dykes, here go the introductions," said Aheno, now comfortable enough in her chair to play hostess. "Get ready to make your mental name tags because I'm only doing this once.

"To my left, our designated drinker for the evening is Alice. To her left, Clyde. To her left, Billy Joe. And in this corner is our designated delusional, Mal. She thinks she's Pat Califia circa *Macho Sluts*. But, Mal, I've seen you cane, and, honey, you sure as shit ain't no Pat Califia. *That* woman knows how to draw blood." Toward some invisible image, Clark watched the Buddha — Clyde — smile.

"You freakin' cunt," Mal laughed. She turned to her sisters for help with a collective retort. But all her sisters offered were smirks. "Fine, I was going to take this off anyway." Her sisters laughed. Clark was stunned when the "this" that came off was her hair. Between all those years spent back home in church and then in several gay bars, he'd become convinced he could spot a bad rug at a hundred paces. He was even more surprised, however, to notice what had been under the hair. Her head was shaved as smooth as Clyde's. But following the hairline as a pattern, it had been tattooed a solid blue. He'd never seen anything like this, and after being Jody's pal all these months, he was sure he must have seen everything — once.

Aheno, unfazed, moved right along the futon. "And I

think you all know Jody." Her call was met with a response of "Hey, Jody"s.

Another glint tugged at Clark's eyes. A pair of earrings, eyes, breasts and one plate rose up beside the far arm of the recliner. The Naugahyde smacked as Aheno pulled herself up and turned toward them. Then the entire chair sighed as she lifted herself onto her hip and let her hand hover over the plate. "Hold on. Hold on," Aheno said, as dolma after dolma slipped through her fingers. Everyone did until she held one firmly around its dark green middle. "Jody," the chair coughed while Aheno rolled back, "you haven't met my slave pussies for this evening." Jody smiled coolly. A few others chuckled.

Aheno made the recliner creak all over again as she reached back out with her free hand and held, with surprising tenderness, the chin of the naked woman. Actually, Clark wasn't too sure she was completely naked. Yet he could clearly see, as he traced the pattern of freckles across her small, upturned breasts, that she was topless. But the rest of her body, except her red and ringletted hair, hid behind the chair's bulky arm or receded into the shadows.

Without letting go, Ahenobarbie managed to turn just her own head back toward the boys. "Jody, Clark, this is the plate that tonight only I may eat from. Call her Beth."

"Yes, O mighty Isis," said Jody. *Fuck you*, Aheno mouthed back to him. He laughed and the three butches felt free to join in. Even Beth couldn't help a very little, very coy smile. Clark stared at her and her eyes; the odd alien glow of her colored contacts had hypnotized him.

Jody, seeing only her smile, winked at her. *Where does that dog find them?*

A squawk from the chair and Aheno had propped herself on its other arm. She extended her hand into even deeper shadows. Clark followed it until he realized there'd been another woman—definitely a naked one—kneeling there on a large pillow the whole time. Aheno's wide hand encouraged the slave to look toward them.

Her face sparkled. Braced across her nose were silver glasses and hanging up and down her ears were silver hoops and studs. Her deep-set eyes were almost a dark as her mane of long black hairs — this was the best description Clark could think of since the sides had been buzzed to the scalp and the remaining strands pulled back tightly behind her head. She too smiled. Her already broad nose widened and her cheeks pushed up the rims of her glasses and lifted up her thin upper lip like the hem of a skirt.

She bowed her head in further greeting and the boys followed the downward tilt past a silver pendant to the blue glass chalice nested in the crevice between her very impressive breasts. Jody told himself that before this night was over he'd have to touch those airbrushed-smooth, milk white tits to his lips. Maybe even let a cotton-candy-pink nipple melt in his mouth.

She raised her head up and turned her attention toward her master. As she moved, her many pieces of silver again caught the candlelight. She sparkled. Except this time Clark noticed one dull glint below her stomach. *There's something plastic between her legs?* His eyes trailed a thin strip of material out from her crotch and around her waist and down beneath the cheeks of her equally white ass. *A jockstrap? Hello, stupid. You're in the land of the lesbians.* He paused. *A dildo harness!*

"And this, my jealous old flame," Aheno had to raise her voice now to be heard over Jody's deep belly laugh, "this is the cup that tonight only I may drink from. Call her Keri." Jody opened his mouth and the three slaveless butches did the same. "Yes, O mighty Isis," the chorus droned.

"Fuck you all, my dears. And just when I was having second thoughts about sharing."

"Yeah, right," said Clyde. "I've heard that before."

"Safeword," squeaked Joe, looking nervous.

"Joe," Aheno said, "don't wet your diaper, girl. You've been up north too long. Clyde and I settled that old score. Didn't we?"

"Yup. The she became a he. Didn't you, Jody?"

Clark snapped his head to his right in time to see Jody, just barely, stiffen.

"Clyde," barked the hostess, "this is supposed to be a fun little holiday potluck. Don't you fucking dare turn it into another process session." Clyde grumbled and picked up a cup. "Besides, I'm not done with my introductions." Aheno looked up at Clark. "Everyone, this is Jody's covered dish, Clark. Clark's a friend of Bibi's." Various heads bobbed in time with the sputtering candlelight.

Emboldened by his recent vision of Wonder Woman, Clark decided to invoke his true patron saint — the Bionic Woman, Jamie Sommers. He summoned every ounce of her wholesome California casualness and tried once again to make polite conversation with his daunting hostess. "Will Bibi be coming?"

"Most likely. But not here, and not under us."

Clark blushed. Ahenobarbie scrunched up her nose as if she were about to sneeze and snorted out a loud laugh. "Bibi Czar, superstar," she sang. "Who in the dyke S/M community do you think you are?" Laughter and polite applause rose from both futon couches.

"No, Clark, this particular potluck is too tame for her. No needles. Little blood. But she did offer to compromise and come as a Roman augur — read my fortune in entrails. I just wasn't too sure the entrails wouldn't be my own." She picked a piece of pita bread from Beth's tray and daubed it with hummus.

"Besides, could you imagine any Roman other than that old drag queen Nero in a pink feather boa with matching pink jelly clogs? Not that she wouldn't have made a wonderful Nero. Okay, okay," she said between chews, "I'll admit I was tempted to play Nero's mean old mama, Agrippina, if she did grace us with her presence. But then I remembered, as several others in this room might too, what happened the last time the two of us played together. And that was too much even for a perverted old classicist like me."

Aheno used the moment of silence to dab about with another slice of bread. Once she'd swallowed, she continued. "So Ms. Czar and I decided to plan a different theme party for later. Something more in line with her newfound Gothic sensibilities like, um," and here Aheno waved her third piece of pita before her audience, "a shooting gallery for the undead."

She looked around for encouraging smiles. When she'd tallied up enough, she continued. "Well, ladies, you and I both know this wouldn't be much of a potluck if we didn't trash our absent sisters. As hostess, I've started. So, who'll help me malign Bibi, our fair city's brattiest bottom? The latest coming of the Great Media Whore of Babble-On."

"Sssssss," the three others butches hissed, mimicking the sound of Lezzie's sharp tongue deflating Bibi's rising reputation in this Dykedom by the Sea.

The sound struck Clark's mind as well and he realized he was still standing, alone, in front of the whole room. He blushed and smiled simultaneously at his hostess. She returned this with a genteel grimace. A few seconds later he had spread out beside Jody on the couch.

"Hey," Jody said in a whisper. While the women grew bolder and louder with their insults of Bibi, Jody quietly reached his hands under the table. There he fumbled for a clean plastic cup and then pushed several bottles of spring water aside for a large green jug of wine. He pulled it out by its neck, braced its wide bottom with his other hand, and poured until the cup was nearly three-quarters full. He put down the jug; he picked up the cup; and he stretched to place it between Clark's arms, which dangled almost as far off the couch as his legs. "Here, stud. Drink up." Jody nudged Clark affectionately with his elbow. "Don't worry. She likes you. Believe me. I guess Bibi never told you about them."

"I guess not," Clark looked down and shook his head. He took a big, stinging gulp of wine.

He coughed. His eyes watered. He looked up. A shining blur danced in the corner of his left eye. He turned and focused. The candles had found ten or more dull silver mirrors on Keri's fingers. The flickerings bounced from the dark window panes to the wall's glaze of varnish to the glassy sides of the cup in her hands. She raised herself up on her knees and leaned in toward her master.

Aheno grabbed the mug mid-sentence and punctuated the rest of her tale with gulps and burps. Clark had actually heard Bibi tell this one. It was the story about her infamous late-night trip to the supermarket. The one where she'd been caught *in flagrante delicto* with a fish in the frozen food section. Of course in Aheno's version, and she claimed it was the naked truth, he learned that Bibi had failed to tell him what she'd really been wearing beneath her red faux fur coat.

A final belch and Aheno was done with her drink. She handed it back. But before she finished Bibi's dressing down, she held up her hand. *Odd but dramatic*, thought Clark. Aheno turned her head and looked only at Keri's breasts. Despite their size and gravity's heavy grip here at sea level, Keri easily lifted the soft bulk of her right tit. She then dragged the nipple around the rim of the cup with such firm and deliberate slowness that Clark wondered if she honestly believed it was a sponge, able to absorb the last drops Ahenobarbie had failed to suck down. *Why doesn't she just use her mouth?*

Keri then set the cup on the floor, raised herself even higher on her knees and leaned in even closer to her master. The chair rocked and Aheno rolled over its arm. Keri's breast leapt from her hand into both of Aheno's and then again into her master's mouth. Between sucks, Ahenobarbie tongued in wider and wider rings out from whatever skin might have touched the cup. As Clark watched, he learned just how big a mouth Aheno had. It could hold so much more of that breast than Keri's hand ever had. Clark was spellbound. He secretly wished she'd try to slurp the whole tit down. But she didn't. The breast leapt back to Keri and flopped against her chest.

Another buck of the chair and Aheno had lurched back

toward her guests and launched back into her tale.

During all this, Clark had ignored the entrance of three more people. He'd heard the rise and fall of the other curtain along the far right wall. He'd felt the room cool and the candles sputter. But only when several glints jumped up and down in the corner of his right eye did he turn and see three pairs of glasses reflecting a room full of little white lights.

They must have been wearing only black in that shadowy corner for all he really made out were their three pale heads and not that well. Oh, sure, he could spot the obvious. Here a nose, there a mouth. But other than that, all he could do was guess that they were older, shorter, and fatter than he. And that they were musicians. Actually, that was an easy guess since two of the six hands held a recorder, two more a mandolin, and the last two a little drum.

Slave pussies, musicians, a recliner. Clark didn't really know if these things made this potluck Roman, other than the fact that Aheno had said they did. But he was certain that they were all weird enough to make this evening thoroughly San Franciscan.

Burop.

The thunderclap of a belch came from Clyde. That sound — Clark had heard it before. It was *her*. Of course he hadn't recognized her sooner. He'd never seen her before with her head bare and her breasts covered. In fact, the last sighting had been a Saturday night in October. She was the headliner at Mirken-A-Go-Go. That night, San Francisco's only sumo drag king had stood center stage and ankle-deep in a wading pool of instant chocolate pudding. Crowned with wig-perfect topknot and girded in a white-leather recreation of the *mawashi*, she'd let the rest of her mighty, mighty olive breasts, belly, and butt all hang out. Her opponent, here to raise money for charity and promote her new CD, was the equally beloved drag queen Cristal Lite. And, once again, Cristal had captured the essence of Linda Evans during her *Dynasty* years right down to the shoe-box shoulder pads and the vacant stare. But she would be no match for Clyde Akutagawa. A few sumo body slams and victory was hers. To the cheers of the crowd, she pushed Cristal's face down in the muck and let out her trademark belch.

Burop.

Clark nudged Jody's arm. "Clyde's Clyde Akutagawa, right?"

"Uh huh. You really know your local dyke performance artists. Maybe next time you're out back at Red Dora's they'll even let you sit at their table. You know the other two are also stars in their own minds?"

Clark answered Jody with a blank look.

"Billy Joe is Billy Joe Bumbershoot of Seattle. And Mal. C'mon, you've heard of Mal Toupé?"

Clark shook his head.

"*The* recently published authoress of that definitive collection of her spoken-word performances entitled *Pud*?" Clark shook his head again. "*The* recently crowned drag king of all New York?"

"Nu Yourk Citee!" Clark tried to cover up his provincialism by making Jody laugh.

"Cute." Jody smiled, pleased that Mal had yet to become as infamous as she'd bragged and that Clark's face had begun to shine again. "My best guess is that they're in town for the holidays. Trawling for new material and new women."

"And who's Alice?"

"None of the above."

"Fine, but who *is* she?"

"I doubt you've ever seen her before. And that's because she performs everywhere except on a stage."

"Jealous?"

"Like hell. Lez and I broke up long before she joined the femme-of-the-month club. In fact, let's just think of Alice as Miss December."

"You *are* jealous."

"No, I'm disappointed. Lez could do a lot better."

Clark frowned. He felt sorry for Jody, but he also felt hurt that there was something else about Jody's past he hadn't told him. Didn't he trust him yet?

Clark's concentration jumped its tracks with the speed of a late-night Amtrak when the mop of hair moved again. It twitched a few times, and, suddenly, it was levitating. It continued its rise until it began to tilt backwards, letting the hair fall away. Clark saw that there had been a face beneath it all the time. A face that he found to be rather pretty in spite of being so heavily dyed and painted. Since her skin was as white as a bleached bone, he could easily tell that her hair had been colored several shades beyond black and that her greenish eyes were fluttering under the weight of a few layers of black mascara and blue eye shadow. *Very Elizabeth Taylor in* Cleopatra, he thought. *Well, except for the kelly green nightie. And the nose.* It ran ahead of the rest of her face. *And the lips.* They fell on the spectrum somewhere between bee-stung and punch-swollen.

The face, the hair, and the rest of the body all turned over until they were stuck, mid-roll, against Clyde's log of a thigh. "I want to sing of many things, of shoes and slips and ceiling wax, of cabbage-patch kings," slurred Alice. She rolled back onto her stomach. "Who'll join me?" she asked as she got up onto her knees. She leaned forward to pick up the plastic equivalent of a tankard, some "Super-Duper-Suck-Me-Down" cup from a convenience store. As it rose shaking, it dribbled deep purple streaks down its once-white sides. She pointed it and her arm toward Aheno. Now it was Alice herself who shook, with a tiny child's giggle, and words spilled over the rim of her mouth. "My friend, the Walrus, you'll sing along."

"Watch it, little girl," said Aheno, startled by Alice's use of a pet name in public, "or I see an oyster who'll be left uneaten if she keeps that up." Alice tittered and lowered her eyes and then her mouth into her cup. Aheno stage-whispered to all, "I'm afraid she's fallen through the looking glass and can't get up." There was laughter, except from Clark. Aheno noticed this and spoke directly to him.

"I know, I know. It's obvious women are my weakness—especially when her muff can warm *both* my hands."

Again everyone laughed—even Alice from inside her mug—while Clark sat puzzled. *Two strikes*, concluded Aheno. *Oh, well, Bibi never made any promises about his personality.* Trying not to appear disappointed, she graciously observed, "I see you know little about femmes or fists."

With that said, she let her eyes peer over the top of her glasses like welcoming neighbors come to the shared black-plastic fence. But Clark's eyes said nothing back, not really to be rude—they just had nothing to say. He blinked. Neighbors, fence and all disappeared as Aheno pushed her glasses back up her nose. This must have also been a pre-arranged signal for now everyone was aware of the musicians and their instruments. The room filled with eager tooting and pounding.

"Like the music?" She spoke directly to Jody. "I know, I know, it's too Ren Faire. Actually, that's where I met Beth and Keri and these Bremen Town Musicians." The drummer, as best he could on his tabor, tried to pat out a rim shot. Aheno accepted his gift with a grin and a queenly flourish of her wrist. "You remember that summer, Jody? The one where I did guerilla performance art at the fair. I was," and her fingers rapidly bowed, pantomiming quotes, "The Hooded Pearl, Lesbian Highwaymyn. Seducing bawds, cuckolding gentlemen." Jody grinned and nodded.

"Actually, tonight I'd hoped for music a little more ancient, a little more Greek. Something that sounds a lot like someone playing a Japanese *kitaro* with a little *shakuhachi* thrown in."

"Don't forget the *wasabe*," said Joe.

"Mal, honey, you look lost. Is this conversation to West Coast for you?"

"Fuck you, Lez."

"You probably were thinking hibachi when I was saying *shakuhachi*. It's a bamboo flute. I know you've heard one. I'm sure you'll recognize it next time Gloria makes you rent *Karate Kid*."

"We broke up."

"Oh. Sorry." Aheno bit her tongue to keep from saying out loud: "Wax on. Wax off." "Anyway I even asked Clyde if she had an extra shoot of bamboo she could spare me..."

"Cunt," Clyde burped into her mug. The word hovered over the conversation. In a few long, long seconds, the room had grown still enough to hear the mandolin player's fingers sliding along the strings and the notes falling to the floor.

"Why that's just what she said the first time." Aheno was determined to take back her guests' attention.

Clyde perked up — she smelt blood. "Listen, Lezzie Badinbed, I'll be happy to discuss with you any and all possible cross-cultural similarities in the tonality of ancient Greek and Japanese religious music just as soon as you discover your own roots."

"But I have. They're mostly dark red with a few streaks of gray."

"Ironic, isn't it?" Clyde looked directly at Jody while she spoke. "Big girl. Small wit."

Joe and Mal laughed. Jody shook his head. *Ah, shit. Here we go again.* Alice turned her wide-eyed gaze from Aheno to Clyde and back.

"Hey! I'm a Euromutt. A little bit of everything with no idea how much of what. We deal with our lack of awareness by being insensitive to all other cultures — what remains of them." Aheno took the chalice out of Keri's hands and gulped from it.

"What a bullshit excuse." Clyde felt confident enough to shift her gaze to the guests' platter of pita bread and hummus.

"Fuck you, too." Aheno paused for a belch that sounded more like a croak. "It's the best I could do. This wine's cheap, but strong." She handed the cup back to Keri. Clyde smiled when she saw that Aheno didn't even wait to watch Keri wipe the rim again with her breast.

Clyde was certain she'd won this round. She took

another bite of the bread. "Yes sir, Commodore Perry, sir," she said between chews. "Whatever you say, sir. But you're going to have to strap on some big fucking guns if you ever hope to open *this* country to imperialist western devils like yourself." She leered at Aheno.

"Guns for big fucking." She rolled the images over in her mulled mind. "Someday, Clyde, someday." Aheno smiled. Her prodigal guest had returned. "Well, now that we've picked out Mama's new year's resolution, who's next?"

Alice began to twitter, but Clark wasn't listening. He turned to Jody. "Who's Commodore Perry?"

"I have no idea. Don't worry, it wasn't meant for us. They were just feeling each other up again. They do it all the time."

"Oh," sighed Clark. *Who knew lesbians had so many secret customs?*

Jody could see now that Bibi was one of those rare subjects of constant gossip who didn't gossip herself. He would have to fill in Clark's blanks.

"It's a butch thang, girl." He tried to get Clark to laugh, smile — hell, even blink. He put his mouth close to Clark's ear and whispered. "It's like arm wrestling, only these two do it with their mouths. You know. They're both perfomers working the same circuit in the same city. They're both in graduate school. They've both chased the same women." Jody marveled at how much herstory he could condense, and, like Bibi, how many secrets he could keep.

"Anyway, it's gotten nastier lately since Clyde got into UC Santa Cruz's History of Consciousness program and Lez — Aheno — whatever — didn't."

"Oh," was all Clark knew to say.

Jody surprisingly misread it as a signal of comprehension. The cheap wine *was* strong. "Yeah, they felt her thesis dabbled too much in 'low theory.' None of us are sure what they meant by that — except that now the fight is really on to be the king of queercore."

Aheno had been watching Jody's head bobbing at

Clark's ear. When neither had closed his eyes, she knew Jody wasn't tonguing him the way she'd hoped. Here she had just brought one guest back and two more had wandered away from the fold. What was it Phillipa Marswell had told her? Good old Phillipa, the City's one-stop-shop for all dyke gossip in those days before the Internet. It was something that Aheno's most recent ex-girlfriend had been saying about her. A top is a bottom's bottom. She took in a deep breath. That was it. *May that foul-smelling swamp between her legs dry up into a desert.* She started sipping the air in through her nose and spitting it back out through her mouth. *That bitch wouldn't know a top if she fell on her. And lord knows — hell, everyone in the building knows — we tried that too.* Before she could hyperventilate, she stopped breathing altogether. *And what is a hostess but a bottomless top — putting out so much and getting back so little.* She stopped her mind mid-monologue and began to breathe. Jody was now staring at her.

"What's going on over there?" Aheno asked him as soon as she could remember why she'd first looked in their direction. She arched her eyebrow. "Perhaps you boys would like to share with the rest of the class what is so important that it must be whispered?"

"I was just asking Clark if he was as hungry as I am?"

"Right. I'm sure you were. So you boys are hungry, eh? Well, good. Mama Roma has something she knows you'll both enjoy eating."

✳

A small bell suddenly dangled from the tips of Ahenobarbie's left thumb and index finger. As daintily as she held it, it chimed. Then came an echo. Fainter. *No,* Clark realized. *It's another even smaller bell.* He'd guessed right. But what he didn't know was that it was the sound of two bells. Two tiny jingles coming to the other curtained door.

The flickering room filled with more light. Two shapes entered. As everyone's eyes adjusted, Clark doubted his really had. The shapes were as amazed to see him as he was to see them. For neither he nor they had expected there to be other boys at this lesbian potluck. But there they were. Two boys. Two naked boys.

Well, as you'll soon hear, they weren't really boys. No more than Clark was. But they were very much naked.

As for Clark, stunned as he was, he was still able to do a brief-yet-detailed inventory scan. Certainly they were more alike than different. Both about the same height. Both white. Both cut. And both even had the telltale shaved calves of bike messengers. But there were a few obvious differences. One had also shaved all his head and most of his face, except for a clump of reddish hairs fanning out from his lower lip over his chin — the hipster version of an Amish goatee — and his dick and balls huddled together in a tight little cluster — a lone wild mushroom in a patch of dark red moss. The other was crowned with bleach-white dreads tied in one enormous, awkard knot on the top of his head, and his cock dangled down a good six inches.

It wasn't that the bald one was ugly. He wasn't. He had a nice face, a sweet face. Perhaps that was why Clark barely noticed him. No, all he saw was that the dreadhead, though naked, was still clothed in so much attitude. As if he were the queen of all the City's street-clattering skate-punks. Clark would have laughed out loud if this boy hadn't made his dick burn.

And being naked wasn't the only indignity that this warrior princess had to endure. He and his friend were staggering under the weight of a broad platter of skewers strung with reds, yellows, greens, browns, and purples. And each was followed by what looked like a long string with a little silver bell sewn onto the end of it. Clark wasn't quite sure where the other end began. But he had a hunch that made his own balls tingle.

"Pauls," said Ahenobarbie, clearly amused by the reaction of each pair of boys. "Pauls, I'd like you to meet Jody and Clark." Jody shot her a questioning glance. Aheno beamed. She'd surprised even him. She paused for dramatic effect. Then, when she knew she had everyone's attention, she answered Jody's silent question. "Goddess bless bi-curious women and the men who love them."

Jody rolled his eyes. Clark quickly turned his gaze toward Beth and Keri. Both tried to remain in character. Keri kept her glasses on her master for this dinner while Beth turned her head and spoke a wordless message to one or both the Pauls.

"Jody, Clark, these are the Pauls. They really are both named Paul. Coincidence or merely bi-popular? I don't know. But to keep them straight, I've color-coded them. You'll notice one has a white silken string and the other a red one. So we have Paul the White and Paul the Red. I know, I know — Jody, don't even give me that look. I know they're whiter than Wonder Bread. But I was tired. You missed all the fun of getting their butt plugs in. Why, with all their thrashing about, you'd have thought we were branding them. And, Jody, get this. We only used those little black vinyl ones." She left a space between her outstretched index finger and thumb for an object no longer than the average steel-tipped bullet. "No ridges. Nothing."

"They don't say much," Jody finally spoke.

"No. Not anymore."

Clark looked nervously at the Pauls, then at Ahenobarbie.

"Oh, Clark, please. You boys and your fears of angry dykes with knives. Clyde and I just gave the Pauls a little etiquette lesson before you got here."

"I'm hungry," blurted Alice. She slid out her chin and lower lip till they assumed the position of a pout.

"Ah, the squawk of my little bird."

Ahenobarbie raised her hands and tapped her right fingers against her left palm in imitation of the staccato beat of castanets.

For the next half hour, Aheno ceded center stage to the food. The platters were even larger than they'd first seemed. For as Paul the Red went up one side of the table and Paul the White went up the other, they were able, working from their platters alone, to give each guest, even the musicians, a clean plate with five, six, sometimes seven skewers of grilled vegetables and curried tofu and a generous dollop of peanut sauce.

"You must have been cutting all day," said Clark as he used his fork to pull everything strung along the stick onto his plate. For a man his size, Aheno noted, he was oddly delicate.

"They were," she answered. "And grilling too."

"Where?" asked Jody. He smiled at her as he licked the peanut sauce off his bare skewer.

"Out back," she said at the same time she chewed and laughed. "On the little hibachi you gave me."

"Outside? Naked? In December? Lez, I'm going to start telling everyone you're an unsafe top." Jody smiled again.

Now she smiled back. While their wordless dialogue continued, Aheno said out loud, mainly to calm Clark, "Not outdoors. On the back porch. It got hot enough in there to roast wienies — Mother of all gods, Clark! Put that back in your mouth. Now! It's just tofu."

Shaking her head, Ahenobarbie paused to push her third satay stick through whatever peanut sauce clung to the rim of her plate. She then sucked off a mushroom and a rectangle of grilled red pepper. As she chewed, what to her wicked eyes should appear but the two white bubbles of Paul the Red's rear. "More sauce," she said to them. Ignored, she pricked one with her now-bare stick. Both jumped and Paul almost dropped his platter of plates. "Hey, bell boy." He turned quickly before she could poke him again. "Take those dirty dishes to the kitchen and come back with a fresh bowl of sauce. In fact, take Tweedledum with you too. Just make sure he comes back bearing a bowl of his own."

With a fluttering of fabric and many little candle flames, they left and returned.

"Now, boys," Aheno said to Jody and Clark, "I have the perfect treat for you. Pauls, serve the boys their penis sauce." Paul looked at Paul who looked at Ahenobarbie.

"Eeeuwh," said Alice. Jody laughed, guessing what was to come.

"Well, go ahead. God gave you your dipsticks. Now put them to some good use." Jody held out his satay stick until it was not far from Paul the Red's hanging moss. He nudged Clark to do the same. "Pauls, we're waiting. Dip your dicks in the peanut sauce."

"Eeeuwh," said Alice even louder.

Paul the Red gingerly positioned his bowl of peanut sauce with his right hand and took his cock in his left, pushing it into the warm goo. Except for the head of his dick, he felt very cold. He pulled it out, a large blob of browns, some of which fell lazily back into the bowl as the stem of his mushroom grew and grew. Jody thrust the tip of his satay stick at Paul. He brushed the first cube of tofu against the quivering base of Paul's dickhead. Paul and his prick lurched. Slowly, Jody rubbed it up and over the head until cube and stick were smeared in sauce. He pulled it back toward his mouth. He looked only at Paul, smiled, then opened his mouth. The shades of darkest browns that were his moustache, lips, and beard hovered like twilight around the cube. And then night fell. He slid the skewer free while Ahenobarbie politely applauded.

Jody now looked only at Clark. Clark was blushing — a hot, excited blush. But Paul the White stood still, his hands holding his bowl of sauce close to his chest. His dick remained undipped.

Aheno grunted. "Clark, have you ever heard of the ancient Roman equivalent of chips and salsa? They called it stuffed doormouse. Gross, huh? Now don't get that look. I'm not going to make you eat a dead mouse. Well, then again, it *is* pretty lifeless," and she gestured toward Paul's dangling dick. "Go ahead. Try it. I bet it tastes delicious with the peanut sauce. Slave dude, offer our guest your appetizer!"

But Paul the White didn't budge, not even his dick. "Clyde, Joe, Mal," the hostess called out. After the clattering of all her earrings against one another and the *clomp*, *clomp* of her boots, Mal was up and holding Paul's left bicep. Joe scooted up and off while Clyde took her sweet time rolling over a giggling Alice. Joe then grabbed hold of Paul's right forearm and gave a very surprised Clark the bowl of sauce.

Clyde finally stood and from somewhere behind or beneath the couch she'd retrieved a whip that looked to Clark like a black leather replica of the handle bar and tassels on one of his childhood Huffy bikes. *Clthack*. She hit it once lightly against her left hand and grabbed the tassels taut. Then, for a woman a little over five and a half feet tall and a little under three hundred pounds, she gracefully lifted her right leg up behind her and pushed the sole of her foot off the closest coffee table, which lurched toward the wall, pushing the other along. Cups, dishes, bottles and glasses rolled around the floor. Yet, for all the noise, none had broken. Now she and her whip stood where the tables had been, right behind Paul's vulnerable backside.

The room grew still waiting. *Ffffthwack*. The many lashes leapt off his back and made their way home. Mal and Joe let go. Paul loudly exhaled through his nose but didn't move, as if he honestly imagined he were a proud stallion snorting his disdain for the surrounding horseflies rather than swatting them away.

Clark felt his flesh prickle and lift all his hairs up on end. *What a stupid sonofabitch!* He couldn't have weighed more than Clyde's right arm with the whip thrown in. But he was going to stand there until she gave him no choice but to come to Clark. Now he'd seen absurd displays of male bravado all his life, but this was the oddest. And what was weirdest to Clark was that it made him find Paul the White all the hotter.

Joe and Mal wound their hands around his arms again. Paul turned his head slightly and locked eyes with Beth, her hair bouncing just barely because she was getting very cold or very hot in the drafty room. Clark took advantage of the fact that Paul was no longer staring above his head to soak up all the details of the slave's face.

He watched Paul's small, black birdlike eyes glare past his impressive beak of nose toward Beth. His chin and cheek bones ran out from it in straight lines like an ancient statue. In fact, as Clark observed him, he realized that Paul's hair had been pulled back and up to show off all the chiseled angles of his profile. Then, there below his two thin lips, he saw a grunge beauty mark that told him the boy was even vainer than he'd imagined — a thick patch of hairs at the base of the lower lip, a soul patch, dyed an electric shade of blue.

Ffffthwack. Clark snapped out of his reverie. Beth winced. Even Aheno could feel her little slave's heat rippling out through the girl's artificially reddened and ringletted hair. Warmed, she reached out her hands to both sides of the recliner to let her pussies know they had nothing to fear. "Ladies, please," she cooed, "the only creature ever made to suffer because of *that* flogger was the velveteen rabbit that was skinned for it."

Before any guest could get in a laugh, Alice had screamed, "Nooo!!! Not my Velveteena!"

"Girl, what the fuck is wrong with you?" Aheno yelled back. Alice just stared at her, her eyes wet. "Have you finished your wine?" Her little girl shook her head. "Well, you'd better be done by the time I send the Pauls back to the kitchen or no dessert for you." Alice bowed her head into her mug and was silent.

Clyde was growing impatient. She took aim for his already-tender ass. A strong solid stroke. He jerked now. Then another, harder, for good measure. The boy's jaw muscles bulged like croaking frogs. Gritting his teeth, he pulled free of the butches.

Clark quickly understood this was his cue. Bowl in hand, he sat up on the edge of the couch. His dick, relieved to have Clark no longer mashing it against the mattress while he stared at the slave, rolled up too. The polyester pant leg would have wrapped snugly about the thigh, but with his swollen cock thrust in along with it, the fabric was beginning to strain. Of course, to the untrained eye, it would seem Clark was bored beyond belief. For that eye, basing what should be the appropriate response merely on the lore around a dick of such size and the common trajectory of a true boner, would have settled for no less than seeing Clark's prick rip through the fabric and, as it sprung toward his stomach, knock the bowl of sauce right out of his hands. But Clark, and Clark alone, knew he hadn't been this hard in years, and the dark stain mid-thigh was his proof.

He even had a hunch as to why he was wetting his pants so. It was his first time. You see, all his life he'd had hundreds of pricks pointed in his face, but he'd never had one whipped toward him. And he'd never before seen a man act as if Clark were so unworthy to receive it all the while he was inching closer. In fact, Clark had never had a man refuse him his dick before. Of course, they'd always seen King Cock first and then offered up their humble wee-wees — and humble they always were by comparison — for the chance to choke on his.

Paul the White had moved forward another inch and was now close enough for Clark to count the hairs circling his dime-sized nipples. Clark followed single hairs and freckles along his flat chest and over the low muscular ridges of his abdomen. An arm swung in the way of his view. He noted the forearm was threaded with ropy veins that would have inspired lust in the coldest of hypodermic needles. Then his eyes picked up an intricate blue pattern around the bones of his wrist. It was a tattoo that by its design and its location looked like a Celtic charm bracelet. The arm moved out of view. Clark was face-to-face with the taut slope of skin stretching from his pucker of a belly button down to the border of his overgrown bush. He smelt the tang of unwashed boy. He took a deep, contented breath. His eyes followed a new vein out of the brush and along the pale shaft to the head of his dick. *Not too big, not too little.* It would be just right. It was time for the porridge.

Never looking up once — he didn't dare lose his nerve — he gripped the bowl with his left hand and took Paul's cock between his thumb and forefinger. He pulled it away from the thicket it had tried to hide in. The dick didn't shrink away. Clark was relieved. Nor did it rise to the occasion. *Oh, well. It's now or never.* Clark decided to make the most of this now.

He dunked the thumb, forefinger, and the slave boy's prick in the thick sauce. He swirled them all slowly around the bowl. For a second, he'd have sworn he'd felt a fluttering below the surface of Paul's skin.

He lifted all three up and out. The sauce congealed around the tip of each. Nervous or not, Clark decided that in a room with so many performers he'd give Paul, who he knew, somehow, was no longer looking straight ahead, and Jody, who hovered just beyond his right shoulder, a taste of his showmanship. He let his third finger take the place of the forefinger. As it jutted up, he lowered his lips and in one slow suck cleaned the sauce from it. Then, he lowered the now-wet finger below the boy's dickhead, leaving his thumb popping out. He sucked it clean and returned it. Now, there was only Paul's prick left. Thumb and forefinger slid back along the shaft away from Clark's approaching mouth. He wrapped his lips midway down the dick. He let it flop on his tongue. He could only taste the sauce, but he felt the tube beneath the neither-hard-nor-soft flesh — an odd state for a cock, yet perfection in a piece of cooked calamari. *I'm such a freak! Putting Thai peanut sauce with calamari.* He salivated a little longer. *Maybe not.*

He tightened the wet grip of his lips and pulled his head back. But before the dick plopped free, he tongued the tip. This time he knew he'd felt the tentacle wriggle.

Clark sat up and smiled at Aheno. By the arc in her eyebrows and the nodding of her head, he could tell even she was impressed. Jody patted him on the back. He looked up and found Paul's eyes boring into him. What they were saying, what Paul was feeling, Clark couldn't tell. But he kept his eyes locked on Clark as he backed up into Mal and Joe's waiting arms.

"How's it taste, dear?" the hostess finally asked. "I

made the sauce myself. I hope Paul didn't spoil it with too much salt of his own?" She smiled at her cleverness. "That was fun, wasn't it?" she said to all her other guests. "How about some more games?" She was answered with eager clapping, tooting, and pounding.

"I know, I know—I have an idea. One I got from reading 'Savage Love.' Imagine that!" The other devotees of the column snickered that smug snicker of the initiated. "Some twat wrote in about how she called her vulva," and Ahenobarbie let this word slip from her mouth like a second tongue, "she called it something like 'Yoni's pleasure playhouse' or 'Temple Mound of Venus.'" She waited for her guests to finish chuckling. "Okay, okay, I don't really remember, but it was something embarrassingly woo-woo. Anyway, I have an idea. Before I send the boys back to the kitchen, why don't I have each one come on up to the door of the playhouse. The one who renames it best gets to come inside and — play." She continued to shout over the louder laughter of her guests and the silent screams of all her slaves.

"Now there will be some rules. The name must be either wicked or witty or both. There will be demerits for anything attempting to soar to artistic heights as well as for anything that even slightly smells with the euphemism of, say, a summer's eve. A swift lashing if he even mentions a shellfish or any other creature of the sea. And the boy will be painfully disqualified if he uses any of the following old favorites," and she raised her fists even with her breasts and they began to sprout fingers, "like 'vagina,' 'pussy,' 'cunt,' 'some,' 'her sex,' or everyone's playground favorite, 'down there.'

For the next few moments of hooting and howling, Disorientation and his even shier twin, Dissociation, were able to grab and hold onto Paul the Red.

He'd been able to lose them in the crowded kitchen and dining room all day. But his excitement and curiosity had flagged after the peanut sauce hardened. Now, with all the laughter and music and this contest, he couldn't help but be aware of how exposed he was. He didn't feel totally foolish, despite the butt plug and bell. He was a good sport. Besides it had been kind of fun, sort of, and scary, but he kept getting hard, and Keri just looked so hot. But now, with more people, all this new stuff, he just wasn't so sure. And that had been Disorientation's chance to wrap his fingers lightly around Paul's brain and pull him toward the kitchen. Dissociation, meanwhile, used tiny tugs on the butt plug's string to help his brother.

Then, just as mysteriously, they were gone. Two hot hands held Paul around his right bicep and his left forearm. He looked — it was Clyde and little Joe. Paul warmed as he sensed the room watching only him. He felt the pull of the strong hand on his right and its little echo on his left. They moved him in front of the recliner. Clyde let go and placed her hands against his shoulders and pressed him down onto his knees. At first, he felt only the rough fabric of the throw rug chew into his knees. As he leaned back to rest on his calves and his heels, he sensed every muscle in his ass, especially around his asshole, shift and spread. He didn't realize how hard he'd been gripping until now — now with the hole widening and the plug slip-sliding away. *Oh, shit. Not here. Not in front of everyone. Shit.* He clenched as tight as he could to fight the current's insistent push downstream. He held his breath and squeezed. He felt the recently full space hollow. It was a painful emptying, but he'd become very awake, very aware. Of the warmth inside him. Of the cool air against the crack of his cheeks.

He held tight. Then he breathed. He looked up at his mistress. She looked down, puzzled. She'd been trying all this time to figure out where inside himself he'd gone. But now with her audience back, she was ready to raise her curtain. She spread her legs out toward the arms of the chair. The pink terry cloth parted. And out came that smell he knew could only be pussy. Keri never smelled so strong. He subtly moved the focus of his breath to his mouth, trying hard not to gasp, afraid that this might pop out his plug. *And then,* he thought, *my smelly hole'll outrank hers.* He stiffened his whole body and took in a few shallow, scentless breaths.

Fffthwack. He spit out all the air in his mouth. His back stung with alternating strips of cold and gently burning skin. "Welcome back," smiled Aheno as their eyes met again. "Want to play our little game? Or should I let Clyde tickle you some more?" Paul's eyes were wide yet his face was pinched. *It can't be that hard,* she thought. *Hard. Ah.*

"Is someone's plug too small to stay put? You want a bigger one, don't you — don't we all?" He flinched. *Finally I've got his attention.*

"Rosebud," he blurted.

"You want a sled?" Aheno was sincerely confused.

"No, that's my name for your you-know-what. Rosebud."

It was now Aheno's turn to take in a breath. "A poet," she spat. "I guess it could have been worse. One of those Adrienne Rich fern fronds in a grotto — or some shit like that." She waved him away like a fart. Clyde and Joe bent down, grabbed an arm, tugged him up, and pushed him aside. He moved past Paul the White to the unoccupied corner near the curtained door. There, in the shadows, he would spend the following minutes discreetly trying to finger his butt plug deeper.

Clyde had Paul the White on his knees in one push.

"Dick-warmer," Paul said straightaway.

Aheno saw Beth, out of the corner of her eye, smile that little smile of hers, and then Paul, right before her eyes, smile back. She stopped both with a laugh.

"Listen, dinky-dong, my cunt's a little more complex than a Betty Crocker Easy-Bake Oven." His back stiffened. "See if you can't come up with a name for my genitals that leaves your own out. Okay, fishstick?"

"Fur pie."

Aheno laughed again. "You just said that because I brought up the word 'oven.' Gee, Beav, running out of ideas?"

Paul tried to stare her down.

"Oh, did I just use up your next choice? Sorry."

He glared. "Split tail," he spit out with all the ferocious dignity that a naked, kneeling boy with a string and a bell trailing out his ass could muster.

She closed her eyes to render her verdict. It fell out in one word. "Wuss."

He was quick with his motion to appeal. "Hole."

Aheno's eyes were suddenly very, very open. "The albino rastafarian has spoken. Boy, you don't even know what a hole is — yet."

Her leg swung out from the side of the chair until the sole of the pink and fuzzy slipper was aimed at Paul's bony shoulder. He was so startled that she didn't get to kick him. Instead, he fell back on his own.

Fire in the hole! His tailbone dug through the thin strip of muscle and skin and almost made its way out into the rug. He felt every other bone that rested on it teeter too. Until. Until all he could do was swallow a howl. The plug had, in one sharp thrust, burrowed deeper. He shook. The roof of this tunnel felt like it was caving in. He shook more. Next his stomach dropped into it. Then his cock, balls, even his thighs began to slip toward it. Slowly the shaking subsided, leaving everything around the stiff shaft throbbing unsteadily.

Huh? Somehow he was hovering, he thought, above his body. But when he wobbled his eyes left, then right, he saw that Clyde and Joe were lifting him up. Somehow, his legs still knew what to do without his mind. For that too had fallen down the chute of his spine into the hole. A dull burning thickened around it with each stumble and lurch toward a face. A kind face with two quite large, quite frightened blue eyes. *Paul? What are you doing here, man?*

"I need a gay man," said Ahenobarbie. "No one has a fouler mouth — except a dyke." Clyde gestured grimly with the handle of her whip for the slave boys to go back to the kitchen and for Clark to approach the chair. His heart skittered around its cell.

"Child," Aheno said to Clark alone, "you've watched

some porn, right?" Clark nodded. "Good. Come over here."

He felt everyone's eyes pressed up against the burning skin of his face. He tried to sweat, to cough. He was finally able to shudder. He didn't have a name for her playhouse and didn't really want to see IT and certainly didn't want to go inside and "play." But, and here some ancient part of him remembered to exhale and then inhale, he'd promised Jody last night. Jody, his new best friend. But Jody's ex scared Clark shitless. And what would he find down there between her legs. Teeth? A drooling, man-eating alien? *Okay, probably not.* But what if, when he had his head between her bulky thighs, she decided to press them together and suffocate him? And while he watched his future self flailing in the airless dark under her pink terry cloth robe, his present self listened sadly as the jingling of boy bells grew fainter.

"Clark? Come on down, boy." He stood. *What had they said in those films?* He was finding he'd forgotten this as easily as he had the synthesized score. He crouched at her feet, his head almost even with hers.

He spoke and his voice stumbled between the octaves just as it had when he'd been a young boy drunk on his own hormones. "Give me your big clit, Mommy Sir." He gulped down more air in hopes it could lower his voice to the appropriate *basso* for gay male pornospeak. "Yeah." No such luck. He gulped again. "Yeah, let me suck your big cunt."

She groaned while everyone else, except Clark, took turns laughing.

"I think it's time for an experiment," she said. "Give me your hand — your index finger — no, silly, the long, long one." She fumbled about the TV tray to her left side and brought back what looked, to Clark at least, like a latex thimble. She tugged it snuggly about the tip of his finger. "Safety first," she smiled dangerously. "One never knows where you boys are putting your fingers these days." A minstrel coughed. Jody groaned, worried about what his ex was planning to do to his best friend.

Ian Philips

"Now, Clark, do you even know where my clit is? Well? Go ahead, stud, touch it." She started to reach for his hand. He took a deep breath, closed his eyes, and reached out toward IT.

"That's my inner thigh." The women laughed. "Close though. Try again, honey."

He opened his eyes and swallowed. He believed he was on his own now since he was certain his patron saint, Jamie Sommers — and here he was very mistaken — could no longer bionically whisper to him what to do. So Clark just pushed his long right index finger past Lezzie's unimpressed lips as far as it would go. He stopped. He moved the finger neither up nor down. He was too surprised. Here he'd been expecting only THE VOID, and he'd found his thin bone of a finger wrapped in the soft, thick fullness of flesh.

"What is this? The Dutch boy and the dyke? You're not plugging a hole, Clark!" She calmed herself by slowly pulling his cold, dry finger out and then patting his head. "But if I ever need someone to help me hold my piss, you're my man."

Clark was bright scarlet. He'd barely heard a word she'd said.

"Jody, show us what a real man can do."

He stretched. Once Clark had collapsed back on the futon, Jody rubbed his palm reassuringly over his friend's still blushing head, and stood. While the mandolin player tuned his instrument and Joe finished laughing at Mal's latest aside, he slowly knelt before the recliner. He put a hand on each of the hostesses' thighs, then smiled, then spoke. Aheno flushed and the room grew warm with her. Clark had barely heard it over the ringing in his ears. It sounded like Jody had said something about a fuck tube, hot and wet.

"I think we have winner."

"And do I get a finger cot, ma'am?" Jody rested his head at the edge of her left knee and batted his dark amber eyes at her.

"If you want one, but, then, I know all too well where your little fingers have been." He yanked off his sweatshirt and pitched it back to Clark. The sparkles around Tinkerbell in the center of his pink wife-beater glowed in the candlelight. He flexed his biceps, then his chest, before cracking his knuckles once above his head and once below his gut.

He was ready. To properly heat and wet this fuck tube, Jody decided to start simple and use the bare bones of *Lesbian Love 101* — the fingers. One by one they came together to pull back the folds of swelling skin. From her dark opening he was greeted with a heavy gust he hadn't smelled in years. The mightiest mansmell — though he knew he could never tell any man this — was like the bitter smoke of incense compared to this musk, real musk, that straddled his nose and mouth and pressed its full weight down onto both. Keeping every finger in its place, he pulled his head up and spoke again. She laughed, and it echoed out her cunt.

He moved his fingers in on the clit. First came the innocent rubbing. Then he brushed more firmly up against it, making it buck over the finger tip, then ride up to the knotty point of the knuckle. Slowly. All very slowly. No nervous fumbling, no false moves. He was gentle, then brusque. Whenever her clit became used to his touch, he'd remove it, trace around the edges of her fattened lips, waiting for the welcome smell of her watering cunt. He'd quote to her, then, feeling the air warm, ferment, around his nose and mouth, he knew it was time for his tongue to add wetness to wetness, to slobber around the clit, to daze it, to let it harden in the soft folds of his own lips, then to give a swift stroke up the — *ohfuckityes* — sensitive underside.

Clark blushed again. Not so much for what he thought Jody might be doing. He couldn't really see that well from his place on the futon. It was for what Jody would say each time he lifted his face from the hair-hedged hole where he'd been digging like an anteater feasting on termites. And as that thought echoed around his head, Clark grew embarrassed that he'd only been able to imagine an anteater and termites. But he'd never been "down there" before tonight, he shouted over the echo. Never really thought about IT — never even feared IT. Or so he kept telling the Lesbian Review Board he suspected to be standing, arms folded and scowls in place, in the room's shadowiest corner.

And while Clark's mind chattered to itself, his wise ears waded beyond the brain's white noise until they could hear only Jody's voice. They wanted the words. Words that made that place, that hidden nerve cluster behind Clark's balls and before his asshole, twinge. The shudder rode his spine to the base of his neck, teetered on his shoulders, slid the lengths of his arms and out through the tips of his fingers.

The words. Jody seemed to blurt out whole paragraphs — filled with references to intercourse, dirt, sadism and death. Fucking, feeling the fuck, possession, the fuck, the fucked, the fuck. The ferocity, the graphicness. But Aheno was delighted. Flushed with the perverseness of it all. She was getting off royally to her tranny-boy ex reciting vintage Andrea Dworkin while eating her out. And only she and Jody, and Clyde probably, knew just how depraved this all really was. *Now this*, she thought in her random few seconds of clarity, *is performance art!*

The words? you ask. What were those exact words? I know — if it were another time, another place. But, nowadays, a poor storyteller like myself must heed the gilded advice of an attorney. Why? For a tale, even a tale as tall as this one, can often be mistaken, in Canada's courts at least, for one that is slanderously and libelously obscene.

What I can tell you is that our not-so-little prince had found himself staring up over the corona around Clyde's head to find Our Lord at His Last Supper and one or two apostles staring right back. Actually, all the apostles seemed aware of the dinner party below; their eyes looked wider; their protests had become all the more posed; it was clear they were torn between denying their betrayal of the Lord and witnessing the spectacle below. Clark believed he even caught a glance passed between the Master and His Beloved — a look that was almost envious of a certain dyke on very good terms with her ex.

"Turn the mother out," squealed Alice. Somewhere beyond the musicians' coughing drums and wheezing recorder, she had somehow been able pick out a funky bass line. Alice's head wobbled loosely on her neck. Her shoulders tried to reach up and steady it, afraid it might roll free. Aheno hissed from the depths of her pre-orgasmic trance, "It's *thisss*. Turn *thisss* mother...outtt."

The drummer took this as his cue and began to tap faster. Clark grew nervous, not that Aheno was about to come but that the others might start chanting something like "You go, girl!", drowning out Jody's words. And Clark wanted to hear many more words.

But Jody, even though his mouth was wide open, was silent. He was thinking. If only men knew just where he'd learned some of his best moves. *Here — in the wet hot dark of a cunt.* And perhaps tonight he could finally repay one of his teachers for the favor. Thank his ex with a few new tricks he'd learned. Make the most of the tight bristles of his close-cropped hair. After all, it had only taken a few good brushings against the balls of some of San Francisco's toughest daddies to make them thrash about. Now it would be mother's day.

Of course, Jody knew that he would fit his head between the lips of a woman but once in this life. This tale isn't that tall. His chin, however, was a different matter.

Slowly, very slowly, he pulled it up against one slick lip then down the other side. Tiny, shivering pricks bit into Aheno's skin like the raspy tongue of a very patient beast. Then Jody moved his lips as close to her clit without touching it. It strained to reach his mouth. Aheno felt it pull her entire body. But Jody kept a breath away. He echoed her funky exhale with his own. Until the fleshy curves that hugged his face began to trickle with a thick, sticky juice. Until her clit beaded up with a heavy dew. Aheno could only push her thighs out, deeper and deeper into the sweat-slick arms of the recliner. She could only wait, expecting the gentle tug of his lips or a teasing bite. But Jody knew all too well that he'd have to play rough if he wanted to score with Lezzie Beddeath.

So, instead, he angled his soaking chin as best he could and scraped it up along the dazed underbelly of the clit. Aheno grabbed his buzzed head and dug her fingers in. All reality dropped away from her, even the weight of her own body. She floated for a second, maybe. Then she belly flopped back into her body with a thrash that shook her, Jody, and the chair. She bucked and bucked and bucked her hips. She used the whole frame of the chair to lift her cunt, her clit, up against the searing little pin-pricks of his beard. She tried to mash them flat. She tried to embed them deeper. She tried to push, push, push into the pain. The bristling, burning, slobbering, sweet pain.

She came, twisting and sparking like a power line cut by lightning and wet with rain. Until all her juice was spent.

Eyes closed, she pushed her glasses up her slick nose. She heard the happy plucking, tooting, and pounding of her musicians and the applause of her guests. She opened her eyes and spoke.

"Thank you. Thank you. And thank *you*, Mr. Man. Does my Jody know how to eat a woman out or what?" Suddenly the musicians stopped playing and began clapping too.

Jody peeled off his sopping T-shirt and wiped it against his face. He lifted his head and noticed The Other King across from The Last Supper, looking down from His Graceland in the black-velvet sky. Inspired, Jody gave the T-shirt a few spins above his head that would have made Him proud, and threw it out over the room. It landed flat on the drummer's balding head and graying pony-tail. The room watched as he peeled it off and sniffed it, then happily shoved it down between his legs and behind his little tabor.

The tooting, pounding, and clapping began all over again. Clark tossed Jody his sweatshirt. He pulled it on while trying to stand. A few tugs and it was on and he was up. Then he was down again on the futon high-fiving it with Mal. Aheno took a long plastic water bottle from Keri and drained it. "Well," she belched. "I'm full. I don't know about the rest of you..."

"What!" squealed Alice, sobering quickly. "That's not very mommy! Mommies don't just think about themselves. They take care of everybody and make them feel all better. You're no Mommy." She began to pound her fists on the futon while her feet paddled from behind. "I want a mommy. I want a mommy. I want my mommy."

"You'd better shut up now, Alice, or I'm going to come over there and shut you up."

"Mommy! Mommy! Mommy!"

The other butches smirked. They stared like one great unblinking eye. *Can't control your own femme,* they thought collectively. *Telling us daddy-play was so passé. That being a bitch with a baby wasn't cliché. No, it's cutting edge now. Yet look how the mightiest butch has fallen before her Drunky-Wunky Betsy-Wetsy.*

Aheno felt torn. She needed to make a choice. For while Jody had been wetting her cunt faster than she could, Aheno had pressed the rest of her body into a deep embrace with the Naugahyde. She did not want this to end. *But,* she thought, *as cute as a drunken femme might be, a shrieking, drunken femme is another matter.* Aheno stayed silent a few seconds longer until she'd fully accepted that she would have to share the spotlight if she were to remain reclining happily ever after.

"Fine, girl. Come on over here and let Mama rock you to sleep."

It took a moment for Alice to realize she'd been spoken to. Her chanting and thrashing stopped. She looked around coyly, then stood up and triumphantly skipped over to Aheno and her recliner. Like a just-opened parachute catching the wind, Alice's nightie flared out as she leapt back onto her mama's lap.

Aheno let out a low growl. That had done it. It was

time to take control of her bad little girl. Aheno pulled Alice tightly to her, spun her whole body sideways and scooped her up onto her back. She cradled Alice fiercely in her arms, the muscles in her thick forearms and biceps swelling to the surface.

Aheno's right hand let go to pull at the edge of her robe. She freed her breast and cupped as much as she could in her squarish palm. "Suckle," she ordered. Alice looked confused. With those lips, that ever-wiggling tongue, no one, not even Clark, believed she'd forgotten this most ancient of instincts: to eat. Aheno had no patience now. "Suck." She grabbed Alice roughly by the largest cluster of curls at the back of her head. "Suck Mama's tit, you dumb bitch."

Instinct prevailed. Alice gobbled up all the pink nipple as well as much of the breast's surrounding white skin. Aheno flinched. *It must have tickled*, thought someone. *How many times have I told Alice about covering those teeth of hers*, thought another. Slowly, Aheno's curl-clutching right hand softened. Veins and muscles ceased to swell. Instead, they slackened below the skin where it was growing warmer and warmer.

Aheno felt her nipple toughen as the lips grew softer and wetter around it. Alice tugged slowly against the tit. Her tongue washed up against the breast's wide underbelly while her teeth — her infamous overbite actually — grated gently along the nipple's tip. Alice's mouth had become a watery pulse, steady like the tide.

Most of this, of course, went unnoticed by the guests. Joe and Clyde made some whispered asides about this odd *pietà*. The mother, eyes shut and fluttering, continued to nurse the child. One of the musicians started to pick at his mandolin. Now Clark flinched. *Please, not Greensleeves*. After a few notes, he realized it wasn't. He sighed and took advantage of what he thought would be a brief lull to finish off his curried tofu satay with vegetables. He wished he had more peanut sauce, but Paul had taken it with him and now didn't seem like the time to interrupt their hostess.

The woman musician, without her recorder, had wandered off to the kitchen or bathroom. So only the drummer joined in with the mandolin player. He tapped out a slow rhythm, hoping he was keeping time with Alice's sucking.

"Clyde." Clyde stopped her stage-whispering and looked directly at Ahenobarbie. "Glove me." Aheno let go of Alice's hair and held up her hand. "Stat." Clyde scooted to the edge of the futon, rolled herself and then her breasts up into a sitting position, and pushed herself off. She shuffled in her socks over to the beat-up metal tray beside the recliner. There, among three large black remotes, used napkins, several ceramic mugs, the bell, wads of finger cots and dental dams, she found a box of gloves. She fished her hand into it and pulled out a latex blob. She peeled one away from the others, crushing the rest into a tight wad that she shoved back into the box. Patiently, she tugged the one glove around down Aheno's hand.

"Lube me." Clyde looked over the tray — *not even trial sizes*. Aheno sensed the hesitation. She opened her eyes and looked to Clyde. "Behind the chair." Clyde reached down and groped behind the recliner. Her hand stuck to something plastic. She pulled the bottle out. She grunted. *Too cheap to buy the good stuff.* She hated how this brand always devolved into slimy little strings. She squirted a blob into the palm of her dry hand. Next, she put the bottle down, smeared both palms together and then added the gloved hand to the mixture.

The latex was cool for a moment. Then cooler and slimy. Slowly Clyde's hands warmed, then Aheno's latex one. "More." Clyde began again. Alice's sucking was no longer rhythmic. She'd been listening to Aheno's commands. As soon as Aheno had said "more," Alice had begun to bite at Aheno's breast in anticipation. Wincing happily from her baby's cue, Aheno agreed — it was show time.

She pushed Alice's nightie up with the back of her lubed fingers, tracing teasingly along her skin with her blunted nails, until she'd left four silvery snail trails along her stomach that ended at a wall of fabric just below her breasts. Then she lifted her hand, righted it, keeping it palm-upward, and drew her fingers tightly together until she could feel each one warm against the other. She lowered her hand down into the valley of Alice's upper thighs. She began to push forward, spreading Alice's legs to either side, until her fingers pressed against the lips of Alice's cunt. Aheno rubbed the tips up and down and up against them as they swelled, parting a bit on their own. It was too dim to see but she imagined them reddening as they had done so many times before.

The wine and her libido softly conspired with Aheno to get her to attempt the superhuman and lift Alice by her asscheeks alone up to her mouth. There she could chew, they promised, on the meaty folds of her little vegetarian until they were blood-raw red. *So tasty. So tempting.* But Aheno was a gourmet vagitarian. She would take her time. Besides, she had intended from the start to rock her little girl to sleep. And rock her she would.

She continued to tilt her hand downwards, tipping it so her fingertips touched at the drooling edges of Alice's smaller mouth, waiting to suck Mommy in with one swallow. Aheno gave it the tips of all four fingers. She let them rest at the rim of Alice's vagina. There she would keep her hand a while, cupped to catch any stray drops trickling down the pulsing walls or dribbling from beneath the clit. Perhaps, if she could wait longer than a while, enough would pool there for her to drink, or, at least, to cool her own flushing face. But Alice did not want anybody to wait.

Beneath the peaceful ebb and flow of her other lips, Alice's teeth began to close down on the hardened tip of Aheno's nipple. She bore down until her mommy shuddered. The bite was too slow to break the skin, but it was sharp enough for even the nerves in the flat soles of Aheno's feet to feel singed.

What a hungry little girl! Well, let's see if she can eat all that Mama has to feed her.

The muscles of Alice's vagina tensed against the sudden push of Aheno's hand. Then they deceptively softened to welcome all four fingers and finally the thumb a knuckle deeper. The slow dance had begun.

Alice shifted. She tried to spread her legs wider in the hopes it would allow her cunt to deep throat the fist to the wrist — *now*! The hand wouldn't budge. She grated her teeth back and forth over the breast and now-bruised nipple to signal her impatience, her need, her surrender, her willingness. Aheno chuckled from the pit of her stomach. Then she began to breathe into the sting and the suck. She looked down at her nursing femme. Alice's closed eyes had begun to flow with wide black tears. As she watched the mascara and sweat streak her little girl's face, Aheno became aware that her mind's eye had strayed beneath the surface of her own skin. There it followed several of her own salty beads as they stumbled drunkenly down her back before falling into the crack of her ass.

Ahenobarbie's cunt, not to be outdone by a few wine-warmed sweat glands, had to work quickly to recapture her body's whole attention. And that's just what it did once it broadcast, through its unique semaphore of scents, that it had begun to stew in its own juices. Even her brain felt the strong pull downward until it, too, lay trapped, steaming, beneath the thick pink terry cloth and Alice's full ass.

Perhaps it happened now or perhaps later, but at various moments during the slow time of fisting, Clark swore he heard Mal whispering to Jody something about her *Pud*, a reprint, a third one coming soon, did he have a copy?, did he want her to sign it?, punctuated by Jody's replies of no shit, no way, shit no, sure.

And, at some time after, maybe much longer after that, Ahenobarbie, growing very hot, curled her fingers in while pushing along the roof of Alice's vagina, kneading for the g-spot — or gush-spot in Alice's case. The lube and cunt juice coaxed the budding fist deeper in its slide. Alice gasped. Her mouth opened to let cool air hit the bruised nipple. Aheno jumped at the shock of dry, cold air. Then again, for Alice's other mouth had clamped down hard and now sucked on Aheno's wrist.

Alice was filled. So filled she feared to breathe. There was no space left to store air in her lungs. So, for a moment, she ceased to breathe. There was no space left even for her blood to push and shove its way around the circuit of her body. So, for a moment, her blood coursed round and round the faint-pulsing lump deep within. Did it burn or did she?

She pushed against the arm bracing her back. Her head rolled on its neck and peered over the ledge of her shoulders. A breath. She could take one now. But as she exhaled the air, she inhaled more of the fist, wrist, and arm. Her mouth fell open. Pushing its way through the crowd of teeth and clambering over the thick wall of her lower lip came a very insistent "Oh, God!" And after so much effort to arrive, it felt it should introduce itself several more times to all the guests.

Meanwhile, layer upon layer of muscle was wrapping itself around Aheno's hand — a pleasant crushing between the slick coils of a snake. But her tit was so cold.

Alice had begun to breathe evenly again as she grew still around the fullness. Somewhere she heard the dizzy beat of a drum. From her heart? Her cunt? Then it came — a full-body shudder. Mama was showing her pride in her little girl with a slow, slow flick of her wrist.

And though this gift had been well-earned, sadly it had been given too soon. Alice's body had grown weary and confused. Something that wriggled this much was ready to face the outside world on its own.

Once more, the expulsion from paradise began. This time it would be just as theatrical but not as epic — no pissed-off angels, flaming swords, curses — as when that bony girl, you know who, and her dirt-bag boyfriend got eighty-sixed from you know where. But that's another fairy's tale.

No, this time, the serpent just coiled tighter and tighter and tighter. All in time to the pulsing *tap-tap* of the drum and the louder *unnnhs* of the little girl. The rhythm was growing more and more urgent within and without. Aheno felt her hand slipping through the coils. They contracted and contracted again. Then all was still. She'd been squeezed out. And there, at the mouth of the underworld, Aheno's hand, wet and quaking, decided to rest.

Ahenobarbie took a few deep breaths. With Alice collapsed against her breast, she was able to move her other hand gingerly along Alice's back until she could push her glasses up from the end of her nose. *Ta Da* the musicians played on cue. She chuckled as her guests clapped.

"Dessert, anyone?"

After the slaves had cleared the empty bowls, streaked with the remains of mango sorbet and raspberries, and poured a second round of coffee, Aheno let loose a belch that rattled the old windows in their frames. She smiled. She had everyone's attention.

"Well, this is the moment our Pauls have been waiting for. They thought they'd get to see their girlfriends do each other in front of all of us — well, that's what I led them to believe. A nice idea, but so traditional. Maybe," mused Aheno, "if I blindfolded them, I'd allow it. They could hear them, smell them, but not see them. But I don't think their imaginations have been stretched enough yet to make the most of it. No, no, I think we'll do something more festive. Who wants a festive finale?"

All those who'd consented not to be slaves clapped, even the musicians.

"Good. Since I hate to see women with dildo harnesses go to waste, I think we'll have our lovely slave girls fuck our lovely slave boys." To the *ooohs* and *aaahs* of the guests, the slave pussies reddened while the slave dudes grew all the whiter.

"Chill, slave dudes. Since this is your first time at the sport of queens, I'll let you be fucked by your own girlfriend."

Paul the Red stood dumbstruck. Paul the White, equally speechless, started edging his way back to the kitchen curtain. "Clyde. Mal." He bumped up against the two dykes.

"Paul," said Aheno, her face a mask of concern, "don't you want to play anymore? You do remember the safeword I gave you? If you want to use it now, fine, otherwise you stay. But think hard. It's very cold, very late, and I've hidden your clothes." Paul, however, was as determined as a windup toy against a wall and kept trying to walk his way backward through the women.

"Oh, are you a natural man? No fake phallus for you, I bet. Hey, that's cool, man. Bibi has been very kind to provide us with an actual real-live dick of dildonic proportions. Clark, would you mind being Beth's stand-in?"

Clark blinked. He blinked again. He groggily replayed — he'd refused any coffee — the various odd things his hostess had said to or about him. A synapse flickered. He blushed when he realized why she'd invited him. His blood was beginning to tire of this constant racing from his face to his cock and back. "Clark," Ahenobarbie continued, "please show our contestant what he wins if he chooses what's behind zipper number two."

Maybe it was the spirit of the evening, the wine, the peanut sauce, the day-after-tomorrow he would ask himself again and again, but, at this moment, he stood up in his spot on the futon so he almost touched his head to the ceiling. In three deft tugs, all Clark's curtains fell away so — just as I promised earlier — once more his cock could take center stage.

"Well, well, well," said Ahenobarbie as she stroked the tuft that was her prized beard. "The legends *are* true. I don't even want to know how she knew, but Bibi was right — two Coke cans long by one wide."

"Eeeuwh," said Alice. The piper stopped piping; the drummer stopped drumming; and the three other butches smirked yet again. Then there was Paul. He stared wide-eyed. He was ashamed — in spite, despite, because — of being aroused.

"Your choice, my boy. An itty-bitty silicone corncob or the white whale. Clark, will you need the assistance of a fluffer?"

Jody flinched. So Bibi did gossip after all. But had she told Lez everything? Jody tensed, praying that tonight, and just tonight, Paul was more curious about his girlfriend's bisexuality than his own.

Jody sighed. Without a word, Paul inched his way toward the recliner.

"Oh, Clark. I *am* sorry. I'd really hoped to see you stick it to the man. Maybe later." Clark grinned and bent down to retrieve his pants. While he stood tucking himself in, Aheno made the most of the dead air. "Let's thank Clark," she said as she looked around the room, "for being such a good sport. And while we're at it, why don't we thank Mother Nature for her bounty."

Clark finally knew he was drunk when he noticed he was the only one left clapping. *Fuck, I'm wasted*, he thought while he watched a blue-headed blur run beneath him. He looked down and saw Mal and Joe scooting one of the coffee tables into the next room. Several wooden-sounding scrapes and they stopped. Clyde motioned with the stiff end of her whip. Up. Out. They did just that. She pointed the fat tip accusingly at Jody and Clark, then at the remaining table. One stumbled down from the edge and the other rolled off. The second table was lifted up and out.

"Any ideas on a position?" asked Clyde as she bowed her head low into the recliner.

"You're my guest. What do you want?"

"The bridge."

"Ah, yes, the bridge over the River Bi. Akutagawa, you're one evil fucker."

"Thanks, Commodore Perry, sir." Without another word, Clyde and her whip policed everyone into new positions. Clark and Jody found themselves sitting on the slave girls' pillows. The slave girls now stood, one on each couch, opposite the other. The Pauls were dragged by Mal and Joe into the valley of the coffee tables to stand right below their now quite-tall girlfriends and their quite-erect dicks.

Mal lifted Paul the Red's right arm and draped it over Paul the White's left shoulder. He stooped forward. She did the same for his left arm. He stooped much farther. Now Joe tried to budge Paul the White's arm. She turned her head and her eyes asked an old friend for help. *Thwap.* Clyde had flicked the ends of her flogger up against Paul's balls. He hurried himself into place. The span of the bridge had been laid. All that was left was to attach the final two girders.

"I hate to admit this," Aheno began, "but I've made an embarrassing display of discrimination — ordering only the boys to be plugged or whipped or fucked. So, in the spirit of gender parity, I've decided to award my two slave pussies some compensatory damaging. But before I decide just how much, I need you to be honest with me. Okay." Both nodded their heads eagerly.

"Good," and she took another gulp of wine to clear her throat. "Now when you answered my personal, you said — both of you — that you were bi-curious. And to go as far as you've gone — to go as far as you've let us go with your boyfriends — you're definitely very curious. Down right odd even."

"Queer," smiled Jody.

Aheno smirked and nodded. "That too. But the bi-stuff. Now I want you to tell me the truth. And don't be scared by all my bi-bashing. It's just how I work out my aggression for a certain ex."

Jody was surprised to see them quickly glance over at him.

"No," Aheno jumped in, "not that one. I'm sorry. I'm turning this into group therapy." She stopped for another gulp. "All I meant was I just need to make sure of something. Neither one of you has had sex with a woman?" They shook their heads quickly. "Not even with each other?" They shook their heads more slowly while their faces took on various shades of red. "But you'd like to have sex with me—I mean you'd like to have sex with a woman?" Now it was Aheno's turn to blush while earrings and ringlets bounced on the two fast-bobbing heads. "Good that's all I needed to know." And now she turned her attention to include the rest of her audience. "Cuz I'd hate for anyone in this room to leave here tonight thinking I condone the old claptrap that femmes don't know squat about fucking. Hell, only a femme could squat and fuck at the same time."

"In heels," added Joe.

"In heels," Aheno nodded. "Cuz, goddess knows, the last thing I want is a posse of pissed-off femmes hunting me down."

"You wish," Clyde muttered.

"I'm drunk, Akutagawa, not deaf."

"Yeah, I'm sure you'd hate for Bibi and her Vespa gang to trap you in some alley South of Market."

"Uh huh."

"And tie you against a dumpster."

"Uh huh."

"And punch you with her itty-bitty fists."

"Uh huh."

"And whip your ass with her glitter-girl backpack."

"Uh huh."

"And fuck you with one of her pinkest stiletto heels."

"Unh, I'd so hate that," she said to someone on the ceiling.

"Please, girl, it's so obvious you'd give anything to be a fish thrashing around in her net."

Aheno dropped her head and looked right at Clyde. "And why not? You sure enjoyed Bibi." Clyde grunted and glared at her feet. "And what about you, Mal?"

"Jesus Christ, Lez! I told you not to tell anyone. God, you are such a freakin' cunt!"

Joe's eyes couldn't get any wider. She burst out with a loud laugh.

Clyde looked up now. "People, we're losing focus here! Let's remember the slaves."

"Fine," said Aheno. "Back to the compensatory damaging. Each pussy will be attended by at least one butch-in-waiting. Said butch will assist said pussy to fulfill her duties. Whether that be to help her adjust her harness, aim her dildo, finger her clit, bite her tit — shit — I'm drunk. I'm rhyming." She covered her embarrassment with several belches.

The slave girls looked at her, half hoping this butch stuff had all been drunken rambling.

"Pussies," she began again, "I think it only fair that I make fucking virgins when you're virgins at fucking worth your while. After all, the only women I could imagine with clits big enough to get off just pumping against the base of a dildo — and correct me, anyone, if I'm wrong — the only ones would have to be that dykey nun — no, no this is a very particular dykey nun — you know, Clyde, you loaned me the book. Fine. They'd have to be that nameless nun, the one convicted of witchcraft in the Middle Ages because of her three-incher, and the few tranny boys I've been pleased to enjoy." Realizing her rhyme and something else, she blushed until she was several shades darker than her wine. "No offense, Jody, my love."

Funny how she always managed to mention his clit whenever they were in public together. Jody smiled stiffly. Clyde whispered in Joe's ear. They sneezed out a few guffaws.

"Everyone," Ahenobarbie bellowed. She shook the shadows but the femme in her lap remained passed out. "Okay, everyone. I think it's time we salute the slaves who are about to fuck for us with a toast. Raise your glasses, cups, water bottles, whatever." She lifted her chalice until it shone with the room's flickering light.

"Up your bum." The others echoed her. Except the slaves who said nothing and the musicians who shouted something Clark was pretty certain, though only Bibi would have been able to tell him for sure, in Klingon.

Pound. Pound. Pound. The drummer started to paddle his drum.

Hands were gloved, dildos wrapped with latex then smeared with lube. Plastic grocery sacks, "doggie-style bags" Aheno'd called them, were flapped open and held beneath the boys' asses, waiting to catch the silicone bits being pulled down to them.

Paul the White gasped when the butt plug was tugged, slowly, out. His whole body sighed, but the breath came from his asshole. *Like that* aaaah *that comes with the first shit of the day*, he thought. Yet it was also different. His hole continued to pulse. He could feel it even in his heart. The hollowness. The sweet, small ache. Next the cold latex fingers of Beth and the warming, oozing lube. His asshole ate it up. *More.* She knew. The pressure of her fingers was gone. Then it was back. Warmer. Wetter. With the cunning of the naïve, she daintily traced the ridges of his sphincter. *Fuck.* It felt so good. Maybe someday he'd get drunk enough to tell Jonah and Doug about tonight. They'd shit. *Shit.* His spine was only a pole now to which every nerve was strung. The pole shook and each strand danced. *Shit, this rocks. Hurry. C'mon, hurry. Just shove it in. Now. I'm cold.* While those words faded within his head, the butches no longer waited and did just that to the friend in front of him.

"Okay, rub it against the hole real slow." Joe's mouth closed so Keri was only aware of the hand as it brushed over her left breast. She felt it drag itself down her side to the strap along her hip.

"No, don't look for it." As Mal began her turn to coach, Joe's hand slunk toward the slick edge of the slave's crotch. "Feel the hole, Luke. That's it." Mal, still speaking, pried Joe's hand loose and flung it away. "Now drag your dick up and down his crack. Slower. Up and down. Find his asshole again. Push the tip against it. Don't push it in yet. Just tease him." Now, Mal's hand was free to slip under the harness. "Yeah, that's it, girl, make him beg."

"Push it in," said Joe. Keri did, then Mal. "No, no. Not so deep."

"Hold it, girl." Keri wasn't sure if Mal meant the finger in her cunt or the dildo in her boyfriend's ass. "Yeah, that's it. Let him squirm a bit. It's okay. He's loving it. Yeah, loving it. Trust me."

"Okay, push further. Slower." Joe let her hand climb back up Keri's side. "Slower." It cupped the same breast it had only brushed before. "As far as you can go. Until you're up against his ass. You're doing fine. Let him catch his breath. Good." Joe grabbed the nipple and listened to the row of earrings jangle. "Now pull it back out." She rolled the nipple between her fingers. "Faster. Now," her fingers bit down with a fierce pinch, "shove it back in."

"Yeah," Mal grunted, sliding another finger deep into Keri, "until you can ram your freakin' cunt up his ass."

Clyde, on the other side, overhead some of this and scowled. She hated small talk. She simply placed her left hand square against Beth's left thigh. She dug her fingers in and pulled herself up against this slave's ass, the double-thick denim of her buttoned fly chafing against the crack. Clyde then took her right hand and reached down along Beth's pulsing stomach and under her cool dick. She held it and the slave — steadied them both. Breathing hard on the back of Beth's ear, hot gusts that made her ringlets flutter, Clyde pushed herself, the girl, and the cock against the hairy slit of the boy's butt. She touched the end of their dick against the shaking rim of his hole. She plunged dickhead-deep. She paused to let everyone catch their breaths. Then she plunged on until she could push the slave girl no farther.

Pinned between the strap-ons of their girlfriends, each Paul had had no choice but to fall upon the other. Both men's shoulders nearly gave way under the weight of the other man's arms, as they desperately tried to stay standing. It was more than Paul the White thought he could bear. That first swift thrust, like a confused and angry turd trying to swim upstream. Then the long burning of her second push. Her cock had looked so small. Shoved up his ass, he swore it had tripled in size. He wanted to shout. Pop his ears. Anything to relieve the pressure building up from behind.

He tried to take a deep breath, mistakenly assuming his asshole would expand for the air just as his lungs must. He breathed again. The thick, unbending fullness inched deeper. He sighed. Somehow, it slid back. He'd managed to start pushing it out. Then a new searing, hard slam. It was back. It felt liked he'd fallen on the butt plug all over again, except this time it was more like he was bouncing around the room on his ass.

For a moment, he shifted his attention up to his other cheeks. Paul the Red, in time with the bucks of his own body, was dragging the stubble of his 3 a.m. shadow back and forth across his friend's face. And his breath each time whistled closer to Paul the White's ear. At last, Paul the Red could blow in it. Then his face scraped away. Then it brushed back.

Paul the White wanted to shout all the more. He had to find a way to vent some of the pain out of his body. He pulled his head back as far as he could without letting go of Paul's shoulders. He had a plan. He was desperate, he was desperate, he kept telling himself as he let his face fall onto Paul's. He smashed his lips against his. Paul the Red, stunned, stumbled backwards, impaling himself onto his girlfriend's quick-thrusting prick. Frenzied, he leapt the same step forward and his lower lip landed in Paul the White's open mouth, then between his pinching teeth.

Paul the White tugged at his bud's lip. He felt some of his pain slide out his mouth. He let his tongue follow. He jabbed here and there, digging at the roots of Paul's tongue or the roof of his mouth or along the smooth sides of his teeth. Paul the Red remained surprised at his friend. Who wouldn't have been? But he was growing very excited. He decided to thrust back. The two tongues wrestled in the dark of his mouth.

A few minutes more and both boys' mouths were wider than a dying fish's. They sucked on each others tongues, then lips, then tongues. Never stopping to breathe. Snorting in air through their noses all the while they were mashing one against the other. Inspired by the fires burning their insides.

Pound, pound, pound went the drum, their hearts, their girlfriends' dicks. *Pound. Pound. Pound.*

Paul the Red was growing more passionate, more daring. He pulled his mouth along the side of Paul the White's face. It slipped over the sharp edge of his jaw and attached to his neck. He tried to suck the salt and blood out from his friend's skin. The White Paul strained his neck into the Red Paul's bite.

And these two fucks might have stayed a while longer as sucker and sucked if, at that very moment, after hours of hiding his woolly thighs and brays of laughter within the mats of Paul the White's hair, our special guest star hadn't decided to up the ante. Who? you ask. Why old rough-and-randy himself. The Great God Pan.

Of course, the divine old goat is very sly. To appear in full now would have startled no one, but it would have drawn too much attention away from the outcome of the trick he planned to play. So he stayed put in the hairy roost and from there made sure that Paul the White saw just what Pan wanted him to see.

What's that? you ask again. Why Clark's cock, of course. Who else but that trickster himself could have granted Jody's earlier prayer when Clark flashed Paul his dick—only to undo it now simply because he too wanted fireworks for the finale?

Yes, it was Pan—stooping to the old deus ex matted hair shtick—who helped Paul see what he'd craved at first sight and who slipped his right arm off the other Paul's shoulder and let his head take its place. Yes, it was, Paul would later swear. Or some boozy demon. Maybe the devil himself.

So now, when Paul the White looked down past his

dangling arm, instead of a mushroom straining valiantly
on the tip of its stem, he saw the long, round branch that
could have only stuck out from Clark's trunk by magic.
Paul the White took a swipe at it. Then several more. But
just as with Tantalus and his hellish tree, the fruit dangling
at the end of this branch was never — close — enough.

Pound. Pound. Pound. Paul's hand kept swinging back
and forth. His lips stood out from the edge of his mouth, a
ridiculous pucker, blind to every other absurdity except
their belief that they could reach beyond his arm and slide
down around the distant shaft. His hand made a final
lunge. He got it. His index finger and his thumb twisted
themselves into a slipknot around the dickhead. It held
with each buck, and it wouldn't slip free. Not until that
dick was in his mouth.

Paul the Red opened his eyes. He hadn't smelled
smoke, but he'd certainly felt the burn. He tried to shove
his dick into Paul's hot, clammy fist. But Paul the White
kept yanking it. So Paul the Red forced his arm to tumble
off his friend's shoulder. Down it fell and his fingers
wrapped themselves easily around Paul the White's longer
and redder cock. His hand switched over to auto-pilot,
following the brief flight plan of all masturbations past. If
only Paul the White — if only all men — would realize that
how Paul the Red pulled Paul the White's dick was how
he wanted his own dick pulled.

White. Red. Both dicks were looking a very feverish
purple to Clark. He could no longer keep track of whose
hand was where. The arms pistoned. The bodies bucked.
The candlelight wavered. *Pound, pound, pound* went the
drum, Aheno's deep wheeze, his aching cock. The stain
was back on his pant's leg. It had first seeped through no
bigger than a dime. Next, it had spread out to the size of
quarter. Now, it was larger than any silver dollar. He
looked up. Only a few feet in front of him, two more piss
slits had begun to leak.

It would be soon. The water within was coming to a
boil, leaving behind this dripping salty residue. The fire in

their asses had snaked its way down around the base of their balls, pulling them tight, then vined and vined itself up along their poles until it flickered at the tips of their pricks. A few more gusts from the bellows in back or primings of their own pumps and their whole bodies would be ablaze.

Paul the White suddenly let go of Paul the Red's dick, leaving it shaken, pointing toward the ceiling. He batted the other's teasing hand away and squeezed his cock until the head looked like it would burst.

"Oh, God. Yeah. Fuck yeah. Fuck. Fuck. FUCK. OH, GOD, THIS IS SO FUCKIN' SWEET!!!" After all this sound came the fury. His cock spit. The spittle slammed against Paul the Red's bent knee and then slid down over the skin and stubble of his calf. Paul the White hung his head and panted. His cock followed, drizzling cum across the floor.

Paul the Red's fingers now stroked up then down his own dick. They traced the thick underbelly, bulging until it dipped at the most sensitive spot where the dick meets its head. Here his fingers alternated between caressing with their stone-smooth pads and their blunted nails. Over and over again until he began to choke on his own groans.

He fell dead still. A hot wad hit the wall of the other slave's stomach. Another splattered over his left thigh.

"Not bad, not bad at all," Aheno nearly whispered. "But boys always come too soon."

She raised her voice so no one would notice it still quivered. "Butches, help our pussies shake off whatever they've caught on the end of their sticks. Then get them out of their harness and get them off. Any volunteers from the audience?" Jody was the first to rise. "Good. Feel free to help them out." The music began to grow quieter as the recorder dropped out and then the mandolin. The drummer beat his tabor alone.

And, until that final sputter of his drunken synapses when he blacked out, Clark lay on his back watching the odd flickering shadows along the walls and across the ceiling and the wild bouncing dreads above his dick — all the while listening to the constant *pound, pound, pound* of the drum and the *clackety-clack* of hooves.

✳

Clark's head rolled off the pillow and slapped against the cold wood floor. He was awake.

The room smelled of burnt wicks and spilt wine, spent dicks and cunts in full bloom. Bleary-eyed, he strained to focus in the gray light. All around him were piles. Of clothes. Of empty lube bottles and unused latex gloves. Even a recorder sheathed in a condom. And people.

He sat up on his knees and was sure he'd hit his head on the ceiling. He could hear his own blood *thud, thud, thudding* up his neck, through his ears and around his head. He steadied himself. He tried to stand. He knew he could hear Jody, somewhere, snoring. He looked to his left and saw Aheno asleep in her recliner. A grin had cocked itself to the left of her face to counterbalance the rightward tilt of her head. Alice had left her lap sometime in the night. But Aheno was not alone. Both her hands were buried snugly beneath her robe and between her legs.

He looked toward the two fuzzy white rectangles he guessed were the windows. Beneath them he could make out the shapes of Clyde, Mal, and Joe. And, underneath them all, was the familiar mop of black hair. *But where's Jody?* Finally, Clark looked right into the middle of the room.

Sleeping naked, wrapped in a blanket of slaves and musicians, was Jody. Clark tried to smile without angering his head. When he'd gotten as far as a grimace, he decided to let the boy wonder sleep this one off and head home alone. He'd call him tomorrow or the day after — whenever he woke up next — for a play-by-play.

Clark made his way down the dark hall to the bathroom. No longer able to tug deftly, he fumbled about until he held his dick in his hand. He pissed in the general direction of the toilet — he hoped. He sighed with relief when he heard his stream hit the water with a resounding *splottt*.

Later, while he listened to the toilet gurgle, he tried to focus his eyes in the mirror so he could splash the dried morning-after drool — *well, I hope that's drool* — from his face. Done, he then searched the hall and several rooms for his coat. Several minutes later he'd found it, and, after several more, he'd wobbled his way down the stairs and out the door.

The sun had been waiting for him. It spit good afternoon into his eyes. He reeled, then righted himself. Squinting through the two holes in his aching head, he plodded down the hill toward the slow-moving stream of women with women with strollers. And with each successive step kicking him even harder in the head, he could only marvel as he watched them. Marvel and wonder: *Where do dykes find the strength to do all they do and go to so many of these potlucks?*

I told you it would be an odd tale, and now I've told all I know of it.

Now run along to rut. Go now. Shoo. You sat on that rock and you on that log for days on end. All of you, let's clear out of this clearing. The Faeries want their forest back.

As for me, my fingers are all tapped out and my dick's as hard as a horn. I'm off to find Pan and Nux and Ganesha.

Home again, home again to Arcady. Hey diddle diddle hee hee hee.

That's ancient Greek for Hate to go, but I gotta blow.

There's no place like home. There's no place like home. There's no place like ho...